EZEKIEL
SAW A
WHEEL

by

Keith Van Allen

Piney Knolls Press

This is a work of fiction. All names, characters, places,actions,
circumstances, characterizations and incidents either are
the product of the author's imagination, or are used
fictitiously. Any resemblance to actual events, locales, organizations, or persons, living or dead, is entirely coincidental and
beyond the intent of either the author or the publisher.

EZEKIEL SAW A WHEEL
Copyright 2016 by Keith A.Van Allen
First Edition
ISBN: 0-933862-32-6

Cover art and book design by Keith Van Allen
Published in the United States of America

God bless Mommy Daddy n' Russ, Hugh and Willie,
Aunt Nealy and Uncle Dudley...

Also his nibs,
Mr. Ray Bradbury.

CHAPTERS

"The appearance of the wheels and their work was like unto the color of a beryl: and they four had one likeness:and their appearance and their work was as it were a wheel in the middle of a wheel."

Book of Ezekiel; 1.16

"A ball of confusion. That's what the World is today."

The Temptations

EZEKIEL
SAW A
WHEEL

The following narrative I was compelled to write, I...had no choice...

The Author

CHAPTER 1
A Road Twice Taken

The red tail lights of an unknown car bobbed far in the distance, in and out of curves, below and above rises in a long low and lonely stretch of Route 6, with it's two black lanes divided by double yellow lines. A hypnotic quiet had settled over the family of four within the car, all passively concentrating on the far distant automotive mandala. Follow those lights and you can't go wrong. Maybe.

It was the 60s. In the back seat of the old blue 51 Dodge,five year old Zeke,(short for Ezekiel) and his older brother Buzz (a name he preferred to Clarence) periodically tried to guess the make of the distant car, with Dad joining in now and then. Mom rode contentedly, not overly knowledgeable about automotive design.

"Mercury!" said Zeke with enthusiasm.

"Either a 58 DeSoto Fireflite or a 56 Dodge Coronet!" shot back Buzz. Mom made an attempt at joining the boyish banter.

"I rather liked that pretty aquamarine Buick we sat next to at Kelly's this afternoon."

"Chrysler Mama,"corrected Zeke in a serious tone.

"Those hamburgers *were* good were'nt they?" said
Dad.

"And that jet fast service!" Mom agreed.

Zeke shouted defensively, "Could be a
Studebaker!"

"Studebaker!!? That ain't no Studebaker!!"
shouted Buzz.

"Don't say ain't" said Mom.

"Are'nt...isn't....tell 'em Dad!"

"Well, it could be a Studebaker Lark..." he answered. Ever the peacemaker, Dad had returned the
car's interior to the gently rolling and rocking sanc-
tum it had been. The ca-plack ca-plack of the seams of
road tar gradually lulled Zeke's eyelids heavily downward.

"See..told ya.." he murmured. Finally Buzz let
loose one last retort.

"58 Dodge Coronet..." But now sleepiness reigned
supreme over the two boys, and only the constant
stars in the rear windshield above them remained to
watch.

An exalted feeling of peace and perfect painless energy was somehow connected to this event in Zeke's
mind ever after. This and a few other misty memories
connected with it stuck there permanently in his adult
brain. The strangeness and weird energy were very
much part of the attraction too, the long long road of
darkness, the deep red railroad signal lights running
along periodically nearby. There was fear, but also a
love of being afraid, of being on the run, and also the
coziness in the car inside with his family,them against
the wide expansive unknown. Outside, the great

amazing world with all it's dangers but also fascinations. These were all somehow little pockets of spiritual or vibrational comfort against later slings and arrows of sometimes disappointing adulthood. Need some sleep? Think of those mysterious bobbing far off tail lights.

Also, it seemed another memory came close on the heels of the other, as if it followed on that same night. It was him being bundled up and carried in a torrential rainstorm after pulling up the deep rutted gravel and red clay driveway to his grandmother's farm house under the great oak trees. It was an uneven climb up the water washed tracks of shale and quartzy rocks over protruding tree roots, because the car got stuck a hundred feet from the house. He seemed to be coughing or catching cold, and was put to bed all by himself in his grandmother's large bed upstairs for the best sleep in his life bar none.

That sleep was so deep, so slab solid comfortable, the cold freshness of the old farmhouse, the snugness of the comforters on top of him, the adults fussing over him. But why had he suddenly gotten sick? It felt somehow profound, such a strong memory to last a lifetime. But that was all Zeke could remember, except the feeling there was something more, a missing piece, a gap. His mind would then automatically roam back to nebulous shrouded images and shapes back on the road. Headlights staring into misty layers of river fog across the low grounds. The rounded shape of the 51 Dodge stranded in the ditch. Bobbing shadows about 4 feet high. Little big headed people? Reaching and grasping, carrying away his father, his brother,his mother, and he himself far away from the car into a field of deep night. An indistinct and throbbing white glow in the distance...whirling, silent lights.

Naw!..he was making that up. But the fear--(or was it an all incasing energy?) Or was this a later supplanted idea from his adult life, added subconsciously by too many comics and TV shows? He did like to draw little doodles of spinning space craft, often without thinking in the margins of his school notebooks. Also various big-eyed goofy characters. This had made him a cartoonist. They seemed to speak out to him from the paper. But the power associated with the experience was also like a transcendental or religious ecstacy obscured in detail and blurred by time, full of energy, ever drawing him backward when his brain was disengaged and thoughts were adrift. It was like a little secret but powerful battery had been installed in his mind as a root he could tap into when he needed strength over some obstacle in his life.

Childhood can be like that. But was that all there was to it? Vague images and feelings mixed with other warm and welcome ones of good times at Grandma Gunderson's ? The family reunions with seven types of fried chicken, Uncle Ralph's constant jokes and one liners, Uncle Charlie telling Zeke, "Boy, you're in the country now, we gonna make you pick peas!" His grandmother's sweet face, the roaming and playing over the rich friendly grounds under the oaks with cousins, down through the woods and hills, over the bluffs, down to the refreshing and fondly loved spring house and the river beyond, splashing fun and adventure in the swimming hole and in the fields of old family remembrance.

A blinking of heavy eyelids. Zeke shook his head. Flash forward 30 years. An artist's studio in a cluttered apartment full of odd artifacts. A "Galloping Gunther" pencil holder with wide staring eyes clamped to the edge of his desk watched his hands as they drew. An autographed picture of "Sailor Bob", a poster of "The Bowman Body",(both favorite local TV personalities in Richmond and Central Virginia). A magic marker poster drawn by Zeke,of William Shakespeare standing on a tired and panting Earth with the caption, "If all the World is a Stage, Why Burn Down the Theatre?" Mugs and jugs of cartoon character faces staring outward, all in a turn-of-the-century town house in the historic section of Richmond known as "The Fan". Little birds flitted near the window for the occasional peanut they knew would be thrown to them.

Zeke stared over his drawing board, on which were piled drawings and sketches for his comic strip, "Melvin the Gunk", about a wayward little blob-like alien making his way across the back roads of America, with his pal, an out-of-work 50's animated cartoon character, "Stupid the Cat". They explored the countryside, meeting a wide variety of characters while driving a red 39 Ford convertible coupe—(what else would they drive?)

Zeke got back to work, forgetting the old memories which cost him so much time. But drawing the old car caused him once more to recede into that old far away world, which indeed fed his creativity, but didn't necessarily help productivity.

"An artist is a professional day dreamer," he remembered his Dad as saying when he was a boy. Zeke had watched him paint a deer running through a forest, the kind of thing you'd see in magazines like 'Field and Stream'. "Without that, the drawing is nothing..." he had said with affirmation.

Once again that mental bookshelf of disjointed but connected memories flipped before him. The tail lights on the road, Grandma's bed, the spring house, and "The Golden Afternoon". Oh yes, *that* one, which possessed it's own "title" in his mind. Recently he had made a painting of it just to get it out of his head. There was Zeke, standing in the backyard of his parent's house, about age 5, soaking up the brilliance of a late August afternoon, the grass a green that was almost yellow, enormous butterflies and bugs buzzing by, and his favorite toy red pedal tractor. The red clay of the old driveway ruts was heading straight to the white washed garage. The sky was a deep amazing blue. On Zeke's face was a sense of wonder but also a look of fearful awe, for behind him in the sky, were two floating giants. The planet Saturn with far flung blueish rings, as well as a great angry red Moon of primordial age, hung there, still red with lava, both as large as if two blimps were about to crash just beyond the pine trees.

But somehow it all seemed natural,like so many secret invisible friends known to so many children. He could never shake the positive feeling that it had *actually* happened.

Crash! BOOM! Rumble...the lightening and rain of that ink dark night at his grandma's came back as Zeke struggled to focus on his art. Where had it come from? All that lightning and rain had seemed to come from nowhere. Now the 51 Dodge was rushing up Route 6 with a great urgency, with no memory of anything having happened except a sudden storm. Melvin and Stupid stopped in their tracks on the drawing paper and looked at their creator as if to ask, "Is this in the script? We thought it was fair and warmer!" Nebulous waves of light and dark intruded into Zeke's train of thought. Indeed, so did a train whistle, shattering the night. There *were* train tracks near the road where it all happened. *What* happened? Why? He shook his head and returned to his drawing board. He had a deadline after all.

But soon however the childhood scene with the planets in the backyard intruded again. He was now leaving his beloved toy tractor and following his family indoors to eat delicious fried chicken and mashed potatoes. Yuuum! Sitting down at the table, among the steaming pots and plates, and the ol' blue spotted roaster which encased the magic bird, the hated butter beans,(they always seemed like little brains somehow),the happy pre-food talk, and the dog hanging nearby below hoping for a hand out.

"Aunt Nanna, you want some delicious mashed potatoes?" said Mom.

"No thank you dear, I'm watching my weight.."

"Nanna you've been the same weight for 40 years and you know it!" said Dad, wolfing down a goodly spud lump on the sly.

Buzz piped up. "Is that why you put grape juice on your cereal Aunt Nanna? For your figure?"

"Buzz!" said Mom with tension, "Mind your manners!" They all questioned this eccentricity of

Aunt Nanna's, but it was quite verboten to talk about it to her face. Nanna simply smiled and adjusted her napkin.

Adult Zeke then raised his head in a clearly awake mode at his studio desk. But in his mind's eye was another family dinner at the same table many years later, in fact a few Thanksgivings ago.

In another table discussion, in that relaxed mood after most of the food was eaten, when wishbones were exposed and thoughts were on second helpings of pie, family memories were popping up in conversation, and Zeke brought up the early trips to Grandma Gunderson's in the 51 Dodge. On mention of the car, and the bobbing tail lights in the distance, brother Buzz, an engineer and normally an extremely practical guy, was staring blankly. But he suddenly spoke up.

"Yeah, and remember that really dark stretch...where we stopped, because there was an owl in the middle of the road?" Zeke stopped still. He'd been reading a month or so before in Whitley Strieber's famous book on alien abductions, of how abductee's sometimes remember seeing an owl or a deer, as a "cover memory" to protect them from the awful truth of a night time invasion. This was not like Buzz at all. Numbers, equations and spreadsheets was his racket, not goofy lights in the night, not *seriously*. Zeke hardly knew what to say. This was real, not a chilly chapter from a cool paperback in bed at night.

"W..What?" said Zeke finally. "An *owl??*"

Buzz still stared blankly. "Yeah..it was..staggering around...in the road.." Then Buzz shook his head as if he didn't know what he was saying. His normal engineer mind and practical veneer had once more slammed shut. Zeke tried again to get him to talk, but Buzz's confused look told him it was best to drop the subject.

CHAPTER 2
Drawn Away from the Drawing Board

No matter how hard he worked on his comic strip, the places and events of those early days still preyed on Zeke's mind. Why, he owed the very existence of the artwork before him to it. It was about that same time, when he was 5 that Dad had spontaneously drawn for him a frightened blobby being about 4 feet tall with big eyes and no mouth, leaning backward in a cartoony "screeching to a stop" position, frightened in the middle of the road. "This is a 'Gunk' ", he had said, and soon Zeke was dutifully drawing it as well. His first childhood cartoons were based on it. But now the connection had finally jived in grown-up Zeke's mind, a 4 foot being, light colored, big eyes, no perceptible mouth, (but Zeke had added a big happy grin). Those alien descriptions he'd read about. It had always been there, even as a kid when Dad got into a UFO kick, buying all those books.

There had been strange sightings by friends and relatives, especially cousin Tommy. Then there was Rod Serling was on TV, "The Outer Limits" etc. Dad's brother even worked for the space program as an electrical engineer. On a tour they had shown him an early rubbery piece of fiber optics which projected a newspaper clipping several feet to your hand. Grandma Landover talked about it for months. It was a heady time to be a kid, soaking it all up and dreaming strange dreams. It was so much fun, at least half the time.

But then things started to happen to him around age 6. Things that kept his life from being normal. And when you're a kid that's the main thing you want to be. Things started slapping him down in life. Early on, not long after the strange "occurrence" on the road, Mom opened the front storm door one day and the reflected sun light blasted his face. He started sneezing like no tomorrow and it went on for an hour. He suddenly gained weight, became addicted to eating white bread, and for years had to struggle through the life of being the fat kid with the weird body, and the sometime pugnacious kids who "slapped down" his naturally extrovert personality. It made him highly sensitive and sometimes reactionary. At times he'd nearly jump out of his skin at the least prod of teasing. Why were people like that? All he wanted to do was laugh and have fun and adventure. A great out-goingness coupled with a fear of the crowd made for a somewhat schizophrenic lifestyle. Because of his body he was daily humiliated, but in art he could shine and be the envy of the class, even the whole school. In art he had been a prodigy, in social skills he was a very late bloomer, despite all his talent.

This was mostly in public, for his family was always a refuge of warmth and good feeling, even if it was a somewhat sheltered existence. He was the kid old people loved to talk to and he to them. Meanwhile inside his head he was having blissfully fantastic visions of nature, cartoons,comedy, adventure, fairy tales and sci fi, as well as Barbara Eden and other lovelies from 60s TV. But as excited as he became on

his imagined "ecstasies", he also drew inward, devel-
oping a shell, while soaking up show biz like a
vacuum cleaner.

In later years he learned that such "after effects"
were often con-current with alien abductions. But that
made him a good artist too he felt, forever doodling
instead of playing baseball with kids who didn't want
him. Those doodles also had a mysterious inner language for Zeke, which he felt intimately but still
didn't understand, like dream symbols they were, or
so he thought in college after studying Carl Jung. One
constant motif in his notebook margins were images
of 2 lane roads, with lines down the middle. The road
always beckoned. All the frustration and dreaming
developed within him worlds upon worlds of imagination. Even though he was known as a goofy kid with
lots of talent, energy and humor,sometimes he cried
long and deep when he was alone. Emotions of all
kinds became strong within him.

Growing older, he took religion too seriously,
becoming something of a mystic, all the time keeping
to himself mountains of sexual energy. He had an
extreme love of Nature and animals of all kinds. He
just kept going on, trying to be normal, bursting out
with humour, sometimes terribly depressed, sometimes confused, but just as often proud to be his own
strange and special self. At least he had his imagination to keep him warm.

It was not long after such museings at his drawing
desk, when Zeke had all but finished his latest comic
pages and had some free time,that he decided to take a
trip. Not a long trip, a ramble really, a drive in the
country, a following of one's nose which he always

found relaxing as well as artistically stimulating.

Places. A certain bend of a road, a placement of a building in relation to a line of trees, a hollowed out area where some funny ol' people dwelled, unique antique architecture, particularly if it was odd enough along with a rustic beauty. "Oddchitecture" he called it. Scenes as if from dreams. One such farm on Rt. 6 always reminded him of a St. Bernard dog. Why? Because, he'd dreamed as a kid of being with such a dog in that field. Such were the inner workings of the mind of Zeke Landover.

The undulating hills of Goochland County, moving toward those of Fluvanna along Rt.6 wound before him in aimless pleasantry on a fine day. Hills of life-giving trees unfolded along the roadside. There was the slope full of cedar trees that Dad had said were 'marching' uphill. Indeed they looked like just that. But suddenly he flew off the handle, shouting out the window- "GOD DAMN IT! GOD FUCKING DAMN IT!" Zeke was both ashamed at his language but also pleased by it. God *should* damn what he saw--another scarred chunk of landscape with a huge new metal box storage facility for run away consumer growth, as well as a subdivision of "McMansions", thrown up over night so people could have their pre-packaged American dream while simultaneously destroying it. But this scene passed, and he was soon restored to his normal dreamy self, forgetting for now his past in-volvements in environmental causes and legal battles which could be frustrating.

Mindless creative wandering he may have called it, but he soon knew where he was going.

To the place. *The* place where *it* happened, what-

ever *it* was. Soon came the long stretch that followed
the railroad tracks and the remnants of the old
Kanawha Canal,(dating from when Washington commissioned it), that stretched onward and straight, with
the river far across the bottom land to the left. He
passed a low slung house by the embankment, which
he now knew from his historic research to be originally an old canal boat or lock keeper's house, and not
just part of the eccentricity and style of the Virginia
landscape he knew and loved.

There were the railroad signal lights which had
shown red on that night, and the reflective crossing
signs within the faint headlight glow from his Dad's
old Dodge on the black road. But that was just a
thought-glance now. He somehow "knew" he was
approaching the place, somewhere this side of Colombia. A spot which for no particular reason had always
stuck in his mind, much like the field with the
St.Bernard, but with much less to hang your mind on.

He slowed down, checking the landscape for the
right feel. It was near one of these old tractor roads
leading into the low grounds beyond the tracks on the
left, but just before the rocky outcropping on the right.
Beyond this the hill rose up sharply and there was that
funny steep driveway with a sort of "johnny house" at
the end of it, (built for waiting on school buses in the
rain). "I guess that's what they are", thought Zeke.
"Mom always said some of Uncle Ralph's people
lived up there." He looked back toward the river.

"Yes, I think this is it. It feels and looks right."
Zeke parked and got out, walking along the road side.
Crunch, crunch, the small dark grey gravel under his
feet made him self conscious. As a car whooshed past,

he pretended to be looking for a aluminum beer cans for recycling. Here was the right tractor road, heading down and across the tracks into the broomstraw. It had a sinister feel to it, like that Van Gogh painting he did before he shot himself. But why? It was just a tractor road. Zeke could, however easily imagine the owl right there in the highway, staggering around with it's white face and empty dark eyes. Then—a quick shift to large headed aliens spiriting his family away. No— *he had just made that up!* Everyone said he had a wild imagination. That's why he was a cartoonist right?

Characters, always characters, with big cartoony eyes like the Bob Clampett cartoons he grew up on, like all those puppets he used to sleep with for a while. They argued, they jabbered (as *he* did their voices of course), so much so he couldn't even sleep, and his body was crowded way over on the edge of the bed! It was like he'd been one of those mad horror movie ventriloquists, but as a kid. Just him and his imagination again. But the images came back—his dad, his brother, his mother, oh God the possibilities, he couldn't think of it. And what about himself? Down the tractor road into the darkness it happened. Maybe...and with a faint throbbing light in the distance...

What was he doing? "This is stupid." he thought. Funny how strange one can feel when one puts into action some plan one's long been planning. Anyway, this seemed about it. He walked over the tracks and into the field beyond. Again, just a field.

It was fun but now it was over. He took some pictures, after all it was one of Zeke's favorite landscape motifs and it would be good reference for maybe a painting or two.

Various bits of aged farmyard fence and roadside junk, the tracks, a distant signal light. Fun stuff, especially as a kid. He would've been in ecstacy over them then, and still a bit now. The smell of hot iron rails and creosote soaked ties, bits of scattered coal from the endless rail shipments from the Alleghenies, tearing those poor mountains down. Well, it was time to get going.

He stepped back across the tracks to his car. And then he saw something. Something also kind of stupid but so coincidental he could'nt ignore it. Across the road on the hillside, partially obscured by vines and leaves was an old yellow advertisement sign, part rusted, but still showing through from years past.

ALL BELIEVERS NOW
Inter-Faith Tabernacle

He'd seen them before in this area. But now with the thick growth of leaves it read-

AL   IE   N
ter a   T er a

Zeke just stared, then turned away, then stared again.Alien plus Tera? Terra means Earth, or maybe Terror? It also means a trillion. The usual "believe it or not" process went through his head, but having had experiences with synchronicity in the past, as well as a fair amount of dabbling in the paranormal, he took it as an important sign. Also as just an old metal sign. Maybe.

CHAPTER 3
The Capitol of Nowhere

Driving on into Columbia, Zeke suddenly felt the
impact of his morning adventures and the need to eat.
Why not stop there and pick up a snack? He knew
there would be hardly anything else nearby. Columbia, that small forgettable but unforgettable spot in the
very center of Virginia, of America in fact if you
consider the thirteen original colonies. There had been
little growth after the early 1800s, many buildings
dating from about that time, but with little in the way
of upkeep since. It simply sagged with age and mildew, and mostly mildew holding it together.

To the historic minded though it was (and still is)
irresistible to the eye. It was in fact once considered
for the Capitol of the United States because of it's
geographic position, hence the name, but being in the
center of a state made it unacceptable to the Foundering Fathers and so the District of Columbia was born
on the border. But this Columbia was a passed over bit
of Americana, home to but a few farmers and hangers
on from ages past. Floods from the James River had
added much insult to injury however, as Columbia
had never been able to raise federal and state funding
for a floodwall as had it's finer up-river sister town of
Scottsville had done. The old tavern, now a grocery
store always sported a pickup or two out front. A sort-
of neon sign flickered at night beside a dingy and
faded Coca Cola sign,which collectors might or might

not want to snap up. The old hardware building was sagging the most and was barely occupied except to house old piles of lumber.

Across the street was a very early but crumbling Masonic lodge with a "Square and Compass" carved as a keystone over the door under sagging columns. Unfortunately later it was allowed to fall down, a great loss to architectural historians. The two victorian churches, one connected with a saint,(St.Katherine Drexel known for educating African and Native American children),had faired better up the steep hill on the first back street, a full two houses higher than Main St.

Turning the curve around the rocky cliff into town center by the store, Zeke remembered now that it was here the 2 red tail lights had been heading that strange and fascinating night long ago. They had finally seen the car, but he could'nt remember whether it had turned out to be a Studebaker, Dodge Coronet or a Mercury. Probably a Chevy. He pulled up. A couple of hangers-on were indeed hanging about the door to the store as he pushed the old Nehi Grape door handle to get in with a long atonal *squeeeeaaak——bang!* It was the kind of place Dad always stopped at to buy blood-worms when they went fishing. But the looks that stared at him inside were deafening to the ear. Walking across the uneven wood floor, stained almost to a greyish olive drab, with more innocuous squeaks and groans, caused him to pause several times and alter his steps. All eyes followed him as he did.

The hangers-ons' faces universally had a hang-dog look, with only a bit of jaw movement here or there. Whether there was chewing tobacco inside he wasn't sure and didn't plan to ask, but a large old sign of "Chew RED MAN" over the counter gave the probability to be high. At one time there seemed to be a sort of "chain" of these kind of stores all over the South, but now they were a dying breed. The atmosphere was still strong however, and Zeke lamented their probable passing.

"Hi...uh ya got some kinda sandwich and a drink?" Zeke managed to get out.

"Drinks over thar , ham n' cheese, cheese, onion cheese, cheese turkey, an' pastrami... in the fridge," said the laconic gum chewing proprietor.

"OK, pastrami." said Zeke.

"Git cher drink, I be back.." Zeke sauntered to an old style reach-in-grab-and-slide-out metal rack Coke machine. It was good and cold. He didn't know they still made the bottles, maybe they filled and washed old ones in the back room just for atmosphere. The man behind the counter and another one had a reddish anglo complexion, while a couple seemed descended from Native Americans, commonly seen in Virginia. Then there were some African Americans both in here and outside,and some of them might've had some Native Am too.

His sandwich arrived. "I'll eat in here, s'gittin' kinda hot out..." said Zeke hesitatingly, and swigged some Coke. After chewin' and swallerin' a while he asked, " Not much happen'n round here is it?"

"Never is.." replied the man behind the counter, accompanied by smiles and head jerks all around.

"Any..thing strange ever happen, in a place like this..you know of ?"

"Strange?"

Zeke nodded yes nervously.

"Yeah..ever now an' then we git a city feller lak yew!"

"Ha ha ha.." went all the wall hanging guys. One by the ice cream freezer piped up, "Course we git them flyin' whirly gigs ever so often..tarrin' up the country.."

Zeke's eyes widened."W-Whirly gigs?"

"Yeah, them tarnaders, seems we git more'n our share o' them, one tore up my barn yeeah befo' las."

"I 'member that! That'uz a baddun'!" chimed the proprietor. Zeke decided to just come out with it.

"Any...UFOs?"

"Heh heh!.. Flyin' Saucers!? Oh I dunno 'bout that..heh heh..Hey Jonah, tell 'im your story ..you know, 'bout the big pie plate!" More laughter as heads turned to the old black man by the Coke machine, but he wasn't laughing. Old Jonah stared them all down with wide eyed seriousness.

"De Ol'Pie Plate? Yeah..yeah I seed it..dey call 'um saucers, but it were mo' lak a big huge pie plate upside down, shinin'...hangin' out passed my hog pen...den it goin' on down the low ground to the Rivah..it like the Rivah..on up to the rivah fork of th' Rivanna, an' it hover..up war de ol time graves are.."

"Graves?"

"Yah, ol' Injun graves, bur'l mounds, bout 20 feet high..it like ta go up dere..." There was a long pause of silence. Jonah had said his say, so Zeke picked up the ball.

"Isn't that where Thomas Jefferson did the first archeology in America?"

"He did?" asked the proprietor.

"I think so..pretty sure...that's up near Rivanna Bluffs isn't it? Ya know my great grandfather was the builder of that. They made it a historic landmark", (which was perfectly true).

The proprietor starred a bit, "Yeah, that's Mr.Chenoweth's place now, he bought it while back.."

"Well, the sandwich was good..thank ya..I best be goin'..."said Zeke, easing out of the place as nothing much more seemed to be said. As he passed the drink machine Jonah spoke again, "Whut yo' name son?"

"Me? I'm Zeke!"

"Zeke? Dats short fo' ZuhZeekel..Ezekiel ..."

"That's right!"

"In de Bible it say..Z'Zekiel saw a wheel..'a wheel way up in de middle of the air...a wheel within a wheel...and they went straight forward...and whither they was ta go, and they turned not when they went!" Zeke smiled and kept heading for the door, but Old Jonah grabbed him not only with his hand but with his eye. Zeke couldn't move. "And I looked an' behold, a whirlwind came out of the North...and the rings, they were so high they were dreadful... And their rings were full of eyes round about them four!" Zeke broke away, heading for his car, but Jonah followed him outdoors, clapping and singing the old time gospel country hymn- " Ezekiel saw a Wheeeel, a Wheel way up in de middle of de air," The hangers on at the sidewalk joined in too, making a fine Gospel choir to see Zeke off as he sped up the road in a cloud of dust, (even though the road was well paved). "A Wheel within a Wheeeel, a Wheel way up in de middle of the air!"

CHAPTER 4
In the House of the Forefathers

Zeke had a heavy foot for a bit, flustered as he was, and broke speed limits out of Columbia. Good sense and slower speed prevailed again however, as soon as he was in pleasant pasture land once more, and crossing the Rivanna River with it's rocky cliffs on the far side, and clear shale bottom water that just made you yearn to put in a canoe if you had one. This was the stream,along with stretches of canal that Jefferson had floated Italian marble up toward Albemarle for the columned porticos of Monticello.

"It's all crazy," he thought, reflecting over his morning's escapades, "but then..I dunno.." came other thoughts hot on the heels of the first. Back and forth so it went, around and round in his head, along with dark nights and far off lights of his childhood. He had another comic strip to start on tomorrow for that regional-cyber newsletter,but how to use the remains of this country day? "It's a shame to waste it.." he thought. Then came the answer. At the first turn off, attached to the stop sign with streamers and balloons, was a sign written in magic marker.on a large piece of pink cardboard in a somewhat flowery hand--

RURITAN PICNIC AND WATERMELON FESTIVAL

RIVANNA BLUFFS

Ah, a good excuse to visit the old place again, and take part in country home cooking at a modest price. He fondly remembered when the place had been declared a national landmark and he, his Aunt Nadine and others from his family had been invited to the ceremony, and the college historian who had written her paper on it gave a talk. Good chicken and potato salad had been on hand that day, and it promised to be so again, along with juicy watermelon...mmm.

The winding narrow lane of sandy tracks with thick grass in the middle went through stands of close-hugging cedar trees, sumac and other rich country roadside growth until opening upon a pleasant and rich green sward which led the eye past quaint white-washed farm buildings and on up to the grand oak shaded house, also whitewashed, rustic with an aura of early Americana, long settled in to place, and oozing an invitation of cool country comfort. The driveway wound around the oak trees to where a laconic smiling attendant pointed to the left. Cars were parked out into a lower cow pasture, duly cleaned and decorated with the same style of streamers and balloons, with the small herd of cattle well behind a fence in another pasture that led up a rocky hill to the woods. One lonely hereford however looked at you over the fence, longing for the rich sedge upon which you parked, while she patiently chewed her cud. Zeke smilingly gave her a chunk of grass and a long "MOOOO" as he marched up past the smoke house to the big house.

The driveway attendant smiled at him again. Zeke couldn't decide whether the guy was spiritually "at one" with himself, or just sort of simple minded, not that it made any difference visually.

"Mission's three," he said.

"What?" said Zeke until he saw the outstretched hand. "Oh, admission three dollars.." The odd man grinned and nodded as he received the money. Tables were spread under the trees with taped down sheets of Dupont Tyvek for table cloths, along with numerous folding chairs, coolers and serving burners in festive picnic readiness, but most people were mingling at the front of the house. The only people in the backyard were various children running, playing and chasing each other, most wearing masks or false heads of different super heros, fantasy commercial figures and other pop culture icons, available from the local big box store. Evidently it was a planned child activity as a woman attempted to corral them more or less (mostly less) with playtime instruction. The kids ran in and out of the many out buildings, historic servant's and slave quarters, chicken coops and barns that made a sort of frontier village effect.

"John! Not so fast!, Debbie, take your time dear, don't get your dress dirty..Steven! *Stop that!*" With so many places to hide and dodge, the woman had her work cut out for sure. "I want you all to line up on this side of the hog pen to play 'Red Rover', you know you *love* Red Rover..." The kids ignored her and ran the other way. "OK, *behind* the hog pen!" The pigs kept looking back and forth, having it seemed as much fun as the kids.

As Zeke approached the house he again felt a warm emotion at seeing the hand-hewn solidity of his great grandfather's work, the clapboard siding, the square columns supporting two stories of porches, an 'A' frame roof comprising a rustic portico of back country Palladian influence and especially the foundation, built of rough local stones. As he reached the clutch of people at the front steps a woman rushed out to greet him.

"Ezekiel Landover! I'm so *glad* you could come!" It was Minnie Lee McFeeney, whom Zeke had known from some of his other historic junkets up the country. At one festival or another, he'd recieved much info about his forebears from Minnie and her capacity as chairman of the Fluvanna County Historic Resource Center at Palmyra, housed in the old jail. Always fun, largely due to her bubbly personality, which included an interest in anything a bit or even a lot "out there".

"Ezekiel, I've been keeping my eye peeled to thc driveway..I just knew you were coming I just *knew!*"

"I would'nt be anywhere else Minnie..." Zeke smiled, covering his surprise at seeing her.

"That's exactly what I told Mrs.Fahvner, I said Mrs. Fahvner, (I call her Julia) I said Julie, he *won't* let me down! It's going to be such a beautiful day, those thunder clouds will hold off 'til later won't they, because we *say so* don't we?"

She turned to the crowd. "Everybody I want you to meet Mr. Ezekiel Landover, his grandfather built the house!"

"Uh..*great* grandfath.."injected Zeke.

"oh..Oh! ..wonderful!..." came back various responses.

"But Minnie, did you invite me? I just happened to be driving by...."

"Oh, we *know* don't we, that the 'Hand of Providential Powers leads the Time and Tides of Men', and 'His Mysterious Ways' are *performed* are they not? Sympatico synchronity is it not? And all coincidences are ...shall we say..*co-inside-all!?*"

"Uh, Ex..Exactly!" agreed Zeke and wisely let Ms. McFeeney's eager arm lead the way.

After an explanation of the period and style of grass roots Virginia architecture of the mid 1800's, the graduate student called the group's attention to the hand hewn bannister of the staircase done in Captain John B. Gunderson's, (that is Zeke's great grandfather's) shop and assembled here as the house was built with the aid of his sons as well as his slaves who he'd trained in wood working. Various built-in chairs and cabinets were included in the structure, sort of a multi-service form of building. Attention was called to the beaded weatherboarding and lintels, considered a desirable luxury at the time, as well as the rustic "trickle down Palladianism" of the structure as a whole,indicating the influence on Gunderson of Jefferson's men whom he had surely worked with.

Note was also taken (at Zeke's suggestion) of the bay windows, also rare at the time, pointing to the possible input of his youngest son (Zeke's grandfather), D.Early Gunderson who went on to become a noted Virginia architect of the early 20th Century.

As much as such vocal ramblings swelled Zeke's pride in his heritage, he'd been there before and it soon wore thin as his mind wandered to simply enjoying the afternoon. Along with a few other stragglers, (mostly husbands in tow), he sauntered into rooms less packed with people.

In the front parlour, leaning against a mantel with pipe in hand was one Jeremy Snoad. "I've gotta talk to this guy", thought Zeke, "he reminds me of a character on 'Leave It To Beaver'." He had a thin frame, big feet, and a quick mischievous humour about him with elbows that seemed to paddle as he walked. A full aquiline nose and flowing white blondish hair gave one the impression of a wild uncontrolled philosopher man-of-letters, a sort of professorial Ichabod Crane. The men quickly exchanged pleasantries, occupations and family backgrounds. Snoad, was himself kin to a noted Virginia family once notably ensconced in a notably known book, "The Snoads of Cumberland County", a family which had in fact once commissioned a plantation house from Zeke's Great Grandpa himself. "My wife really grooves on this stuff.." he said, "Me, I'd rather sit around and enjoy the thing, the house itself...whatever.."

"I think I know what you mean!" said Zeke, using the old 'gubernatorial accent'. "In the gret Stet of Virginyuh , it's not who ya areuh, but who yoah ancestors wuh...", whereby they struck up a fairly humourous conversation about anything but architecture. "Yeah, I've got real Virginia roots, but half comes from New York, so I've got the Civil War fight'n in my genes. Makes me kind of biologically schizophrenic. But, I was raised in the South, which

means I carry my history around like a giant turtle
shell on my back, and if I lose it I'll die.." Sitting in
the window box of a front bay window, they watched
the grounds and the cows beyond, one with an extreme load of milk.

"Ah yes," Jerry expounded suddenly, "the bovine
propensities are quite exuberant here in the hinterland!
Strictly Grade A...and double D..." said Snoad, hissing
through his teeth. They descended rather quickly into
off color W.C. Fields imitations and outhouse sex
humour, so healthy for the male animal when women
aren't around, especially in the country for some
reason.

"An utterly amazing utterance!", returned Zeke
with crooked smiled glee,whereupon he launched into
his own Fieldsian quote of the story of Ol' Tom, "The
only common house fly, to graduate with honors from
the Harvard Medical School....I loved that fly...", and
shedding a mock tear. The conversation went thusly
until settling into more mundane matters.

"No, I doubt if they use chemical fertilizer here,
it's all natural, strictly manure.."said Snoad.

"A self sustaining system..the circle of life." added
Zeke philosophically.

"A wheel within a wheel.." said Snoad.

"*Hmm?*" Zeke did a double take.

"Book of Ezekiel...damnedest fine book in the
Bible.." Zeke was a bit perturbed at what seemed to
be a synchronistic conspiracy surrounding him.

"Yes, I suppose.."

"That is, this side of Revelation of course, that's a
regular acid trip, not that I ever touched the stuff, but
mentally you know, cutting loose of the daily

grind...great visionary stuff.." Here Jerry emphasized his pithy statement with a loud, habitual and nose twitching *sniff.*

"Y, yes, fascinating .." returned Zeke with a curious look.

"More likely a big fat close encounter of the worst kind! Don't cha think?" said Jerry leaning far over his pipe.

"Oh..uh...yes!"

"Don't you believe in them? A cartoon fellow like you? Goes without saying hmm? UFOs? It all makes perfect sense..we're not alone in this galaxy..preposterous.."

"Oh I agree absolutely..." asserted Zeke, not so assertively.

"Of course you can't go around talking this stuff all the time...people think you're *nuts!*"

"Uh...right!" Zeke nervously nodded as Jerry droned on.

"Of course the Government knows...it's a conspiracy..but unless they're the right sort to talk to, forget it. Those ultra practical grindstone types will grind you into the ground if you let them..but not *us* right?" Zeke managed a faint nod but kept his mouth shut.

"I *knew* you were a believer when you came in! I don't do it all the time..not at work, can you imagine me selling insurance while talking about flying saucers!?? Ha! Talk about sales dropping off! Uh.. *quiet,* here comes a rarified curmudgeon now.."

A thick, stodgy type came in, "Man I'll be glad when the wife gits her belly full of this, eh? I've got to get back and mow the lawn!"

Snoad winked knowingly in Zeke's direction "Yes! Time to cut grass!", he said loudly to get the man's attention, "Mind you, we might get a storm this evening so might 'swell put it off to when..."

"*Not me!*" exploded the stodgy man, "I fight it all the way! Keep it straight and flat or it'll *take over!*"

"Yes it will, why I know a man was eaten alive by his lawn.." said Zeke, tonque completely in cheek.

"What? *What?!*" puffed the man, while Snoad smirked to himself as they passed out of the room, leaving the stodgy man to scour at Rivanna Bluff's extensive and threatening grass land.

"I always wonder how his type won World War II," said Jeremy, "and yet ended up cutting their grass like Hitler." Zeke had to laugh a little. "Of course many locals here about swear they've seen 'em..." he continued,once safely in the hall.

" Hmm??" said Zeke,(thinking he meant Hitlers).

" UFOs, aliens..otherworldly stuff..you know...only thing keeps one going sometime..." Zeke suddenly decided to open up to the man.

"Uh, Mr. Snoad, I was wondering if you had ever seen a..."

" JERRY!", suddenly came a sharp cry from the far dining room.

"Ah, that's the wife." smirked Snoad, "She'll be wanting me to display my historic heritage for the crowd..I'm actually from Minnesota, just kin to all this on my Mama's side..who married my Dad of course...gotta go, look, it was damn nice talking, philosophying etc... must do it again! Ta ta!" And thus ended the conversation with Mr.Snoad to Zeke's consternation, just when he was likely to give up more

otherworldly info than he could possibly handle,and
so left him alone to wander up his Great Grandpa's
staircase instead.

The bannister was of simple design, but of an
innate quality of character, similar to those of the
Shakers, that brought forth an emotion of old American beauty and grass roots strength. It was indeed "the
gift to be simple", as sung in the old hymn.

"And when we find ourselves in the place just
right, t'will be in the valley of love and delight.."
Zeke sang quietly as he strode upward. The wood was
cool and smooth and curved so expertly from a single
piece, but maintaining itself as the expression
goes,"straight as a die" all the way to the top. "Imagine, under my hands pass my own great grandfather's
work!" He thought. " How did they cut and sand it so
straight with the simple wooden tools they had? I can
draw plans for this but not the first thing do I know
about cutting it." Arriving at the landing he looked
around at the various bedrooms, all bathed in the same
cool light from the tall hand-blown windows.

At the rear of the upstairs, a man stepped out of a
corner room. He had a towel around his shoulders and
was breathing heavily from working out.

" Hi!", he said, " I'm the owner, John Chenoweth."
He was small and pleasant with sort of a 'Pa Walton'
haircut. After a few moments exchanging niceties and
hereditary backgrounds, Zeke revealed he was 'kin to
the house'. "Oh *you're* the one!" said Chenoweth,
" I'm descended from the original owner, Clyde
Egelston. I bought the house back into the family."

" So my great grandfather was working for your
great grandfather!" Zeke exclaimed, as they went on

with more pleasantries before they parted ways, as he had to get dressed. Zeke peeked into the small corner room and saw some equally small sets of weights and barbells where he had been working out. On the wall in front was a gigantic poster of Arnold Schwarzenegger in his early bulbous muscular glory.

After a disquieting surprise wave of attraction swept over him, Zeke quickly turned to the window overlooking the backyard outbuildings, still processing the days events and what the heck he was doing generally.

Around the servants quarters and kitchen, in and out of the boxwood shrubs, still ran the kids wearing their masks, fantasy and superhero crazy-heads, chasing each other. The lady activities coordinator, hadn't had much luck controlling them but she was still trying.

"Jimmy, stay out of there! I'll tell your mother! Janie, stay away from the chickens dear...JIMMY!!" It was a roiling bubble of pastoral pandemonium that excitedly graced the quiet historic grounds, which although exasperating to the lady below, brought a peaceful smile to Zeke. At the far corner of the servant's quarters the kids were like amoeba under a microscope, dodging in out and around in a never ending swirl of motion that was hypnotic and restful as he stared. But one child, one of the "bobbleheads" stood rock still, peeping around the corner of the whitewashed building. The head it wore was grey, with huge black eyes with craggy lifelike wrinkles. It was frozen with a grotesque and knowing, almost maniacal smile. It was the face commonly represented as an alien, one of "the greys", and it was staring directly at him.

Zeke was frozen for what seemed a minor eternity, "It certainly looks realistic.." he thought. He also slowly leaned and staggered backward over the bar-bells at his feet. The grinning alien never moved but continued staring directly through his mind and soul. Suddenly, the clink of equipment on the floor broke Zeke's concentration and caused him to stumble, but with the lightning reflexes he was famous for he whirled in a flurry of footwork, which placed him once again facing Arnold in close up. Just as quick he flung himself back to the window. The 'alien' was gone. After another pause of confusion he zoomed around and down his great grandpa's stairs and out the back door to the yard. He rushed straight among the children, who took it right in stride as if Zeke was part of the game. However the activities lady took extreme umbrage.

"Excuse me, Excuse me! What are you doing? *Sir!!??*" Zeke looked frantically about, especially around the corner of the building.

"I.. I was looking for a child...he was wearing sort of an alien head!..or mask..something.."

"Oh! *Your* child?...alien head? ...are you sure it wasn't Spiderman? I always mix them up..we do have a red and blue Spidey outfit..over.. There! See?

"No that's not it... are you sure?"

"Oh yes..I've had to keep track of them all day! Perhaps you were..."

"Uh..sorry..thank you very much!" Zeke broke off and hurried around behind the building—nothing. He rushed onward, in and out of the farm buildings. Nothing but farm tools and a few chickens that scattered, making huge clucks and squawks. Back to the house, the tour guide and people were filing out the back door.

"Take note of the unique 'H' frame structure of the rear, creating two separate wings.." said the graduate student.

"We should make an addition like this at home George..." said an excited prim looking woman to the stodgy man from the parlour,who mumbled grudgingly. Zeke tried to compose himself and dust off the chicken feathers.

"Mr. Landover!Mr. Landover!", came the voice of Minnie Lee from among the crowd. "*There* you are!"

"Minnie! I..was taking a bit of fresh country air..."

"Oh I can understand that! Isn't it wonderful? I think you missed most of our talk, but then again you already know all about it. It is a wonderful afternoon isn't it?"

The last few minutes of Zeke's life had been a whirlwind of adrenaline. Minnie seemed to sense his flushed state and was quite attracted by it. Zeke was still reeling from seeing what he thought was an alien as well as suddenly finding Schwarzenegger's bulges appealing. But now here came Minnie who had quite different bulges which he found thankfully even more attractive. He had known her years before and liked her, but now suddenly it seemed so much more so. She was so wonderfully feminine, which made the eternal swirl of yin and yang spin feverishly within him. That swirl which seems to generate nothing less than the power of the Universe itself, and with it she effortlessly smiled as she strode across the thick grass and swooshed her creative skirt,(or was it skirts?) like a happy cloud skipping across the sea.

Minnie wasn't young but neither was she old and quite well preserved as the canners in the country would say. Her heaving fullness of feminine pulchritude (to continue in the antique farmyard parlance, that is, "behind the barn talk"), was a great relief to Zeke as he found himself blissfully and heart-poundingly attracted to it. It shrank his anxieties while increasing the ol' blood pressure to produce nothing but Health.

As they walked and talked, this exuberance spilled over as well toward a flouncingly flirtatious filly in the parlour, the daughter of a couple in the crowd who's eyes were on anything but woodwork. All of which kept Zeke's head shamelessly turning. He knew this was not "acceptable" behavior, especially back in the overly P.C. West End suburbs of Richmond, but after all he had been part of the New Age movement from it's beginnings, and wasn't political correctness nothing but "trickle down New Age" with corporate and governmental re-writes? (Minus all the post 60's passion of course).They had siphoned much of the fun out of it in a reality-talk show pundit spin-rush to perfection while also building an industry out of smiley-faced gossip scandal, and paparazzi junk instead of inspiring entertainment. It seemed actually that nothing brought him him closer to a feeling of Nirvana than sex, nature ,and food, and here in the country your senses were bombarded with a healthy dose of all of it. So Zeke happily said "to hell with" all suburban TV culture and decided just to enjoy himself. He and Minnie again strolled across the lawn, Minnie doing most of the talking.

The tour crowd was somewhat dispersing, although a clutch of folks were still in rapt attention to the graduate student's explanation of the finer points of the outbuildings. The children's activities lady was now free as the parents collected their kids, and was walking to converge on Minnie and Zeke.

"Bye Minnie, I'll see you next week, I can't stay for the picnic.."

"OK, Laura! Thank you so much!" Laura, who was now in a humorous mood,leaned over to Zeke.

"Did you find your little grey alien?"

"Not quite!"said Zeke nervously, as she chuckled off over the lawn.

"Grey alien?", quizzed Minnie.

"Oh, it was nothing.."

"Oh, I wouldn't dismiss it so quickly Zeke. You know Rivanna Bluffs does have it's ghost!"

"Ghost?"

"Mmm hmm, a little boy in grey that roams the grounds...so maybe what you saw was.." but then another female voice called from across the yard.

"Minnie! Are you going to serve the baked beans??"

"Y..YES!! I'll be there right away!" Then to Zeke, "Com'on, it's time to eat!" Before Zeke could think, conjecture, or scan his eye round the farm once more, he found himself swept into that time honored and irresistible gravitational vortex known as a country Ruritan picnic. Soon he was grabbing a paper plate and bumbling in line with many happy jabbering people large and small, talking and laughing and moving down the piles of food and on to the Tyvek covered tables under the oaks.

CHAPTER 5
Peculiar Picnicing

The clacking of plastic forks and squeaking metal folding chairs washed over Zeke's consciousness now, and his mind was full of potato salad. Jerry Snoad plopped down opposite him,continuing in his Fieldsian furor, "Hay Haay! Some spread ay? Ah yesss...A mellifluous melanange of malleable....uh, malleable..."

" Macaroni!" added Zeke continuing in the vaudeville vernacular, while hoisting a fine glob of the yellow and orange stuff on his fork.

" Ah yaaas..a perfection of pastamazoo.." returned Snoad, " I found some in my pajamas one night...mistook it for an elephaaaahnt..." Zeke feigned a laugh and a few full mouthed expressions before returning to his food, hoping Snoad would take the hint that he was in dire need of a good comedy writer, so he might as well shut up and eat.

Talking indeed rose to a fevered pitch at the tables now,with food entering mouths at equal speed and at every other sentence. Soon they were joined by Mrs.Snoad and Minnie who sat by Zeke. Everyone dove in with quick comments of how good was this and how good was that,(some people spend more time

talking about food than eating it) and what a good job
the Ruritan does with it's picnics etc., to which
Minnie piped up that it was also the Fluvanna Historic
Council did a lot of it too.

A black couple sat down, who turned out to be Mr.
and Mrs. Lamb. They smiled and also made comments about how good the food was. The sound of
chomping corn cobs and spoon scrapes of beans and
casserole was a continuous soothing symphony for
many minutes, much like a summer rain storm. Zeke
finally broke the ice with, "Everybody enjoy the
house?", feeling somewhat like a host himself because
of it being built by his ancestors. "Oh yes I just love
it! Perfectly lovely! Love the handmade furniture!"
came various comments.

Then Mrs. Lamb said, " Oh, I feel so right at home
here!" Which brought a few looks from the table.

"That's wonderful, I'm glad.." returned Zeke.
Another pregnant pause, then Minnie said,

"Zeke's great grandfather built the house."

"Oh really? You must be so proud!" Said Mrs.
Lamb.

"Well yeah, it's fun, playin' around with history..."

"You know, we're sort of related, my great grandmother was a slave on this plantation!" This time
every white person within earshot turned to look.

"Really!?" said Zeke. Another pause, and a lot
more pregnant. "Oh..my great grandfather didn't own
this house, he just built it!...he did have slaves
though..we just discovered it a few years back...he
taught them woodworking and they went around
building houses...I used to play on one of the chairs
they made..."

"Really!?" said Mrs.Lamb.

"Yeah..the evidence is that he was a good master though, he divided most of his land up between his slaves after the war...many are buried just behind our family plot up near Scottsville..." The table now stared at Zeke, until Minnie broke ice again.

"Gosh, you know some years ago we wouldn't be having this conversation...now it's really nice..just a bunch of Americans talking about their past!" She laughed nervously.

"Yes it is!" said Mrs. Lamb.

"Yeah!" chimed Zeke. Laughter spread now, happy and healthy.

"We've actually bought a plantation house and are restoring it!"

"Really? That's wonderful!" said various diners.

"Yeeesss, isn't it?" She said proudly.

"Like I always say," smiled Zeke, "I don't care who lives in the big house as long as they take care of the big house...uh, respect the architecture..you know.." this comment brought Zeke many more looks and some laughter.

"To History!" added Mr.Snoad, lifting a glass of lemonade. The general hum of outdoor eating and talking resumed, rising to a muffled outdoor roar.

Finally Zeke noticed the actual and true host of the proceedings. The man from the staircase,the owner John Chenoweth was advancing and smiling himself toward their table, after making the rounds of greetings and 'how are you enjoying' to everyone in attendance. "How are you enjoying the farm?!" he said in his best Jimmy Carterish smile, and people responded with a barrage of Southern hospitality and friendly

nothings all meant to be heard but not really under-
stood. Zeke smiled to himself that it was one of those
situations like a White House social event where you
could say practically anything ,such as "my what a
piss poor place you have here" and actually get away
with it. He tried to think of which president he read
actually did it, was it FDR, Teddy Roosvelt, Warren
G. Harding...Grover Cleveland?? He'd always wanted
to try it out himself, but would'nt dare do it now,at
least not here anyway.

He smiled and added his own "Oh fantastic! Really
splendid!", but winced and gritted his teeth when
someone actually said "Awesome!" And it wasn't
even a younger person, it was an older distinguished
gentleman who should've known better. Zeke could'nt
stand it, he almost told the man that "The Grand Canyon is 'awesome', *this* is not! Stop degenerating the
English Language! The Great Pyramids of Giza are
awesome but a hamburger is...", oh why bother, just
shut it out he thought. It was stuff like this that made
him want to shoot his television like Elvis did.

Being a cartoonist, he spent too much time at home
and got frustrated watching what he considered cultural deterioration. Well anyway he thought, " I'm just
no good at small talk...I'd rather exchange bad jokes
with Snoad here. I notice he's right smart with the chit
chat." Actually Zeke had quite a few insightful and
interesting comments to make, but again he got
snowed under by this type of talk, so he just nodded
and looked off into the distance of the ever pleasant
grounds of the graceful old estate.

While staring off across the yard, the verbal banter
fading out of his inner ear, Zeke remembered he had a

deadline coming up, so he tried to go over some plot ideas for his strip to be ready when he sat down to draw tomorrow.

Melvin the Gunk and Stupid the cat were as usual traveling cross country in their '39 Ford. OK, he had that much, then what? Suddenly Stupid looked directly at Zeke and said, "Seek ye not abroad what may be found in your own front yard..." Zeke's eyes quizzed up. "What? That's an old quote we learned in high school..I can't use that...besides it's not front yard but back.." Then Melvin spoke up, "Why does the chicken cross the road?"

This was no good, thought Zeke, "I can't be creative now, gotta wait 'til later.." But still in a mesmerized state from the drone all around him, he blankly stared far across the lawn beyond the tables, out by the outbuildings leading past the barn where the woods met the road. Chickens were strutting and pecking lazily about. "Seek ye not....front yard.." He mulled the thought again. The chickens continued to bob about along the rounded rise of the lawn just in front of the woods. They were now joined by a big fat grey goose, her big butt wobbling as it skimmed the grass, up and down, in and out of sight beyond the rise. Up and down, up and down.

" Man I betcha there's 10 kinds a chicken here today!" Snoad was talking loudly at Zeke, "They got five flavors of fried ,three broiled...did you taste the bar-be-que? Oh ya gotta try it!"

"Huh? oh..." now his mind was firmly back on food.

"Yaas indeed..a veritable feast of fricazeee..Ha ha

haa yaaas!", Snoad was back as Fields, having a field day.

"Yeah, it's great!" agreed Zeke, as he too chomped down on a drumstick. Then his eyes roamed back to the chickens on the hill. They were still there but he didn't see the goose. He idly looked for it until again came the grey bobbing blob of the big rear end just over the hill. But this time it was moving sideways, quite swiftly and in a very un-goosely fashion. His eye for odd detail naturally followed it until it emerged as the hill sank toward the road. But it wasn't a goose's behind, it was the head of a figure. It turned and smiled at him. The alien! And it was holding the goose! With a few deft leaps and half a honk from the goose it disappeared into the forest across the road!

"DID YOU SEE IT!? Did you *see it!?*" Zeke jumped up pointing and stumbling.

"WHAT!? see what?!! Came various reactions.

"That little grey.....*thing!* Crossing the road..." Zeke suddenly realized the folly of saying he saw an alien on the lawn at a large social gathering, and simply stopped but still pointed. Minnie quickly took up his slack.

"I'm afraid Mr.Landover has been witnessing the famous Rivana Bluffs ghost!" To this however many people were ready and willing to listen with interest, drawing near with questions, excitement and comments. Zeke actually became the celebrity of the moment, while gathering his flustered self close beside Minnie. Mr.Chenoweth then spoke.

"That's a fact, we do have a ghost, but I happened to see this too... what you saw was a deer jumping out of the woods...very common 'round here, see it ever so often.."

"Deer!!?" thought Zeke, glaring him in the eye but saying nothing. He knew well his Whitley Strieber lexicon of mental supplanted images for alien encounters, (that a deer was as good as an owl).

"Yes," continued Chenoweth, "their coats sometime even appear grey, something to do with their diets or dew on their backs I think, trick of the light...normal occurence around here, they head down to the river for water....you know.." Everyone else stared too, at the woods and at the let down he had brought to what had been such an energetic metaphysical conversation. Soon all were back to eating, but with a bit of sharing of other people's ghost stories, grandmothers appearing at their own funerals, that sort of thing.

Later there were a few Ruritan presentations and announcements from the podium, where Minnie actually recieved an appreciation plaque for her historic preservation work. Then homemade ice cream was served before a blooming thunderstorm in the distance urged many of the crowd to make moves toward going home.

CHAPTER 6
Ghostly Plans and Alien Agreements

"I'll bet you did see the ghost, at least once anyway.." said Minnie as she helped clear the tables and
Zeke worked on the chairs. "We could do a reading
after while and try to contact it!" Her smiling enthusiasm made Zeke smile and gave him a burst of energy.
He'd been alone a long time, and the day's events, the
feel of adventure,the rural atmosphere,and Minnie
were quite a tonic for him. He was in a mood to let
matters take their course, but also felt the looming
pressure of his deadline. Minnie, New Age bead
swinging maven that she was, had kept Zeke in the
back of her mind for some time since their earlier
encounters, and energetically played her hand now.

After a shimmering and cooling thundershower,
they watched a new born rainbow suffuse and wash
out in all it's pastoral drama from the front porch
swing, with a view down the slopes to the low
grounds and the river. The great grey and white giants
marched off to the east down the James River against
a deep blue sky, like a gentle mash potato parade
tinged with orange au gratin sauce in the evening sun,

stepping high over luscious green broccoli tree clumps, reaching odd shaped arms aloft in marching rhythm at the shear joy of being a cloud.

"This day has been so wonderful.." said Zeke as Minnie rested her head on his shoulder, "...and so strange.." She lifted her head. "Oh not you, you're the wonderful part."

Minnie smiled. "Oh, ghosts are'nt really so strange, just people who've passed on and..say, why don't you stay the night? That's what I'm going to do, some of the others too..."

"Well, I've got that deadline..."

"Oh do you have to? Hey, maybe they've got some art supplies here.. I'll just..."

"Uh.. no, that wouldn't work I....hey ya know? I'm only writing at this stage, all I really need is a pad of paper and a pen..for scribbling and sketching ya know?"

"That's wonderful! Then we'll have time to look for our little ghost! I could try some channeling..."

"Uh..Minnie, I didn't mean a ghost actually...I..." Mrs. Chenoweth was suddenly at the screen door.

"Minnie, would you give me a hand with the ice cream? It's a lot to clean and put away.."

"Oh certainly Delores, why didn't you mention it earlier?!" She got up, leaving the old swing squeaking with Zeke still in it.

"Well I didn't want to interrupt," said Delores as they walked off, "..besides I was rounding up the chickens. Strange, we can't seem to find our old goose...but he'll turn up." Zeke's attention perked right up at the goose news, but just then a puff of pipe smoke from the screen door revealed the presence of

Jerry Snoad.

" A fiiine special evening! And I mean *special!*"
He came out and sat by Zeke.

" Yep..pretty special.." agreed Zeke, as they started
to swing gently, the grey smoke wafting back and
forth into Snoad's eyes, making him blink.

"Yep.. pretty special...understand you're staying
over..." Zeke gave him a quick look. "Oh, I'm afraid I
was eavesdropping on you and Minnie there..not
intentionally understand, just starin' into the
evening..."

"Yes, it's special.." glowered Zeke.

"It is! That's the word precisely.., special.." his
pipe smoke now billowed up into more settled, cloud-
like patterns.

"I was hoping I'd find you out here somewhere.."

"Well you did .." Zeke was still a bit peeved at the
pushy intrusion.

"Yes, that Minnie's a fine gal.."

"Yes, we go back a ways.."

"Oh yeah? She and my wife do too! Lots of com-
mittees, ladie's auxillary, historic, regional,
Ruritan...uh like this one..very nice...Of course I've
known her too, right along with my wife of course..."

"What was he getting at?" fumed Zeke to himself.
Snoad took a deep breath.

"As I was saying about aliens.."

"*What?*"

"You know this afternoon in the parlour there..."

"Oh yes..." Zeke was somehow relieved and
piqued at the same time. "Aliens..." he said with a
distinct lack of enthusiasm.

"As I was saying earlier, a lot of people 'round

here claim to have seen 'em.." Zeke just stared, but Jerry quickly turned on him with a great puff of grey smoke. "It could'nt be that maybe *you've* seen one, could it?"

"How'd you know??" Now he came quite alive.

"Well.. you've got the look...plus I was listening to what you said to Minnie...but mainly you got the look!"

"I do huh?...and you believe me?"

"I sure do, yes this here abouts is a special place!"

"Have *you* seen one?"

"Nope, wish I had, but I've seen enough stuff to know it ain't no stuff! I mean..you know..."

"Well, what am I supposed to do?"

"Well , start with today. What happened, what did you see?" So Zeke recounted best he could the day's strange events, as well as some of the early life experiences that brought him here in the first place. Jerry sat thoughtful for sometime.

"Why don't we go..you know, *look* for him?"

"What..now?..how?"

"No, I mean tomorrow...follow his trail...can't hurt..can it?"

"Guess not, might be fun walking in those woods anyway, but now I've got some writing to do.." They agreed to reconnoiter later to make plans.

"You writ'n right now? Where's ya pen and paper?"

"Believe it or not I do some of my best writing in nothing but thin air..if I'm not disturbed." Snoad finally got the hint and returned inside through the slow squeaking screen door, leaving a wafting trail of sweet smelling cheroot pipe smoke, followed by the muted wooden screen door sound of... 'ba-bang'.

CHAPTER 7
Evening Extraordinaire

Zeke stared into the approaching dense country evening for some time. The lightning bugs were everywhere, like a thousand swimming stars, floating up and up to some unknown surface in a lake of the cosmos. Whippoorwills could be heard in a great loud symphony with crickets both far and near, some so close he thought they were speaking to him a repetitive but profound message. The occasional multitoned moan of a coal train came along the river in the distance, the clacking of the rails echoing far up the fields to the bluffs, as if they were just next door. A final grand relaxation settled on Zeke after such an incident-filled day that his mind drifted far into the depths of that Universe we all know so intimately, but which we forget and struggle again to find, once we wake up. At last he shook off these cobwebs and went in through the friendly screen door which also double banged behind him, to find a pad and set up for doodling in the parlour by a single lamp.

He finally was getting something done. Ideas were taking shape, he doodled quick little panels of action. Once he had a good storyline down the rest would be sort of mechanical. That is, he could turn on the classical music back at the studio and concentrate on good drawing, inking,lettering and such things. He stared at the drawings on the pad.

Melvin the Earth-marooned alien and Stupid the Cat were driving through a surreal Route 66-like landscape made of desert rock formations and weird roadside Americana. They were doggedly tailed by a flying saucer that could easily flip-change into an ordinary looking vehicle, but not quite, always leaving some bit of alien looking technology exposed for the quick of eye.

" Where are we headed Stupid? I fell asleep back there a ways.." said Melvin,yawning.

" A fact on which you might well inquire!" pontificated Stupid in his usual pontificatory tone. "I noticed you were in an altered state of recharging your neurons and synapses,(that's brain cells to the less educated of you in the audience), so I decided to provide you with a sudden sensory input of divertissement upon your awakening for a healthy recovery thereof!"

"You mean you wanted to surprise me?"

"That is precisely where the common piece of hardware makes percussive impact on the metalic driving wedge!"

"Hit's the nail on the head?"

"Uh, yes..."

"So where are we?"

"I have no idea.." All during this exchange they had been driving in out and around old sign boards,trees, clotheslines, fences, barns and rusting farm machinery, followed closely by the saucer which sprouted hands to grab and push it's way to safety as the brave comic duo blithely left the highway, careening cross-country. It was well known that Stupid the Cat, as highly scintillating an intellect as he was, could never concentrate on more than one thing at a time such as driving, especially when he was on a great and curious roll of grand verbosity, as he often was. After all, a large percentage of mental energy would necessarily be absorbed by his quite theatrical hand gestures alone, let alone keeping them on the wheel.

Periodically the saucer would reach out with a vacuum cleaner like attachment labeled "Abduct-o-Vac" with which to suck up Melvin, which if you were a loyal reader of Zeke's comic strip you would know was the sworn duty of this intergalactic emissary from a politically unfriendly planet of distinct thick-headedness which considered Melvin a "person of extreme obsessive interest" due to his having inadvertently witnessed certain activities so as to compromise their entire I.T.(or was it E.T. ?) Techno Propaganda Conundrum, (so he just *had* to be got).

But by the usual advent of a divine cartoon providence, the saucer would get impossibly tangled up in off-road objects such as the clotheslines and/or cream separators while Stupid's 39 Ford managed to wander back onto the road as it entered a small hamlet with a general store and gas station, so the UFO made itself scarce. Stupid now fully alert,(at least that is for Stupid) let the car rumble to a stop at this provider of roadside necessaries, when out from behind the gas pump popped a very distinct character with a pipe, looking much like actor Jason Robards and staring at him intently. Stupid immediately hit the brakes.

Zeke squinted and looked up from his work, adjusting his focus. A light colored blob emerged from the darkness near the parlour door. It was Snoad.

"Hey, Zekey boy! How's it goin'? Got some cartoonery goin'?" Zeke showed him his stuff.

"It's just the rough ideas, I'll clean it up later.." Snoad showed great interest—for about five seconds, then he changed the subject. "Hey , that Minnie sure is a nice gal!"

"You *said* that!"

"Yeah, but I just wanted to kinda warn ya, not to go right in on talkin' about alien's and stuff with her.. or even Mr.and Mrs.Chenoweth!"

"Uh, why not?"

"Don't get me wrong she's a swell gal like I said, and she's all spiritual and likes ghosts and all...but alien's might be..uh a bit outre' for her ya see? Strong practical streak ya know..don't get me wrong, good wife material there..but a strong streak of Calvinism..like a lot here about..."

"Oh well, I'm used to tha—"

"It's the English blood ..no I think she's Irish..Mc Feeney..I'm Scottish ya know...got some of the Blackadder line in me.."

"Really?" said Zeke trying to look interested.

"But we got the second sight ya know..just like Minnie!...but practical...." They stared at each other through the by now extravagant curls of Jerry's pipe smoke as he continued. "Hey, I can't wait to get on the trail of that alien in the morning.. Hey, maybe we'll run into some Men in Black or Government Agents-- maybe even Illuminati!"

"In Fluvanna County?"

"Never can tell! Didn't you say your great grandfather was a big Masonic something or other?"

"Well yeah, but he was also a *real* mason, he built buildings.."

"Well, there ya are!" Zeke began to think in light of Jerry's over-the-top glib enthusiasm for all things bizarre, that he himself may have been getting self delusional. And what was Jerry *really* up to? He seemed to have an agenda, but it was constantly changing directions.

"Well, we'll see... it'll be a nice jaunt in the woods--good exercise."

"See there? How'd you know I was planning to look in the woods? We must be in a..you know, psychic simpatico!

" No, you *mentioned* it an *hour ago*.."

" Well, perhaps other forces are at work....beyond our ken ya know??" Boy, Jerry could really pour it on, his eyes rolled large in that thin big-nosed head. With the obtuse lighting from the lamp, it gave the impression of either Huntz Hall in a B-grade Bowery Boys mystery or 'The Madness of King George', who he also favored greatly.

"Good *night* Jerry!" Again Snoad got the message, tip toeing away with wary eyes cast in seven different directions. Zeke sat on for a while by the lamp, unwinding. If he had smoked, he would've. As it was he did enjoy Jerry's lingering cheroot aroma. Thunder rumbled once more in the distance, promising an even cooler night to come. He was'nt sure how long it had been, but soon he was aware of another presence slowly emerging from doorway shadows. It was

Minnie.

"Still creating?"

"No, I'm done for the night..."

"What a pity..."

"Oh I don't know..." The softness in her eyes was equal to that of the evening.

"Hey, remember the Lotus Center?" she said.

"How could I forget! Those were good times were'nt they?"

"And strange times!"

"Strange and good times! They're my favorite!" Soon they picked up where old times had left off, saying silly things of no consequence which meant the whole world. Zeke smiled a fond memory, "You remember those 'spiritual rescues' you did?"

"Oh yes.."

"I remember we sat there in your living room, and your spirit was traveling all over Chesterfield County or something..and you found a poor bum behind a dumpster..who was actually dead and didn't know it. And you coaxed him over to the other side, toward the Light..."

"Yes yes, I remember him quite well!"

"To be honest, I wasn't sure it was real or not, but it felt so real, like watching a great movie or something..it had me in tears..at least afterward whenever I thought about it.."

"We actually confirmed that one with the police a little afterward..at least the case really matched my, uh..our description..you know, my spirit workers.." Zeke felt the old magic between them returning. Her rounded free spirit beauty with flowing tresses and swishy dresses merged with the warm light like a Pre-

Raphealite painting. No ceremony was stood on, and meaningless conversation soon gave away to passionate embrace.

"It's all so intoxicating, this night, this place.."

"Your eyes, your face..are second nature to me now.." (He sang a tune from 'My Fair Lady').

"Who are you? Rex Harrison?"

"Damn damn damn damn damn!.." They twirled slowly together on each other's necks.

"You're lucky I don't wear one of those 'My Fair Lady' hats, you could get hurt!"

"Then you'd have to just..wrap me up and take me to the millinerer..millin..er...hat making lady.."

"Oh I would'nt dare leave you with her.."

"Hmmm?"

"Those milliner girls are notoriously good looking..like in that movie with Shirley Booth.."

"Shirley Booth? How'd she get in here? Anyway it was Barbara Streisand..."

"No that was the remake..."

"I'd like to remake you." She tugged at him until they mounted the stairs, his great grandfather's stairs, but he wasn't thinking of his great grandfather. Up and around to her room they climbed and entwined, into her feminine bower, a flower, decorated with crepe like curtains wafting on the wind, with a plungey poofy country comforter and big mushy pillows.

"Love is a vortex,into which one falls,you don't see the windows,the doors or the halls...One just falls...."

"What's that?" asked Minnie.

"Oh it's a song by this pub band in Richmond,

'The Moody Magoos' I think is their name..."
On to the bed they sat as clothing dropped effortlessly away. Big fat rain drops started to fall on the tin roof, as they both lowered gently on to the poofy comforter in the coolness of the rain blown breeze through the big screen window.

Oh sex sex sex! That Nivanna of Life that can lead also to so many problems, but without it you waste away. You can speak of love and search for God, but sooner or later it comes back to this plunging, embracing, breathing, exploding, caressing, smiling, relaxing, laughing, and soothing. Is this love? Love is friendship, and a very fine thing. But good sex with a good friend is the best there is in life. Well, good food is good too, a cool breeze, beauty, fun, whatever and money,at least enough money...but even then.

I guess it depends on the moment. Life is one moment after the next, one desire, one need after the next. Why, when you're sitting on the john trying to take a really big dump, that IS the most important thing in the Universe! At that point in time at least. But what is time? Time is..but who gives a damn when you're having sex sex *sex SEX!*

Minnie looked up. "What are you talking about!?"

"Huh? was I talking? I don't talk during sex.."

"Yes you do! About the meaning of the Universe and going to the bathroom and.."

"But I was thinking.."

"But it came out as talking! Can't you just say 'Fuck fuck fuck' or something?"

"But I can see my Dad wincing at that..he didn't approve of profanity...he was a good Baptist.."

"I thought you were Episcopalian ?"

"Well we switched churches when I was going through puberty..it was very traumatic...anyway I'm sorry.."

"Oh I don't care..I just thought it strange...but strange can be good...MMmmmm."

"Mmmmm" and so they resumed their universal plunging and caressing and yes, talking, reaching ever new heights of climactic fervor. Zeke's intercourse intercourse, that is, dialogue, became less creative and more simplistic as they approached a rousing orgasm together. " Uh uuuh Huh Huh..Ahh Ahhh FUCK! FUCK! FUCK! Uh fucka fucka burnin' love!!"

"Ha HAA! There you go! A fine old Anglo Saxon word!" cried Minnie with delight.

"Yes, but not suitable for the dinner table.."

"Well no, I should say not..hey I liked that little Elvis thing you threw in there..except I'm afraid of getting sequens in the bed." More quips and giggles ensued, as well as erogenous stimulations and other attractions. " Oh OH ..Ah AAh Ah Ah yes YES! YES!" She cried over and over. Lightning cracked and walked it's giant power steps around them.BOOM! CAH-RUMBLE Bumble mumble...

They rode on a wave of ecstatic ecstasy swirling into space like Captain Kirk in his chair not giving a damn that Scotty's having trouble in the engine room because he sees a kaleidoscopic vision before him on the screen which hypnotizes him while Uhura is in his lap and a green woman dancing before him. "Shields up Mr.Sulu, Scotty...I need more power!" Minnie felt something similar but since we don't have her exact testimony you can leave that to your imagination, or hers, or whatever. Be that as it may, or were, or whatever it was, they were finally settling down.

This was another great thing in life, the aftermath of love making (now was the time to use the "L" word) with someone you really liked being with. This was perfection, or the closest thing to it, if it actually exists which is doubtful, for who can stand a perfect person? However long it might last, this was happiness.(He wouldn't mention it, but somehow it was similar to the sensation of petting a cat) "Ah yes! A fine little pussy!", he could hear Jerry pronouncing in his Fields voice, but he quickly shook it off.

For so long Zeke had run from love because of his crazy marriage. But heck, this was about as happy as it gets. He seriously started thinking about the "M" word with Minnie.

"Why did we drift apart anyway?"she asked.

"Oh, I was being super picky I guess...

"Picky! Well I like *that!*"

"No, I don't mean it that way, I was afraid of getting deeply involved with anybody...still shell shocked from my ex I guess..but you were always great. I mean..." Minnie put her finger to Zeke's mouth.

"Shhhh...." They kissed in the most tender of ways, loving, tender, blissful. "It was just our Karma catching up to us.."

"Oh, like 'Instant Karma's Gonna Get You'?"

"Yeah, sort of..like the Lennon song, but it can ebb and flow gently too, it always is, from incarnation to reincarnation, a never ending flow.."

"Yeah, but sometimes with sharp turns and eddys, even rapids, like that old river out there..." added Zeke.

"I like that," said Minnie, "I'll have to write that

one down.."

"Yeah, but not now.."

"No, not now..." And so embracing and kissing continued.

The evening breeze had been blowing cool but was colder now. Flashes came quick but silent in the sky, thunder following after by several seconds. Zeke stared out the window.

"Why does country grass, red clay and the smell or wood burning make me so fantastically happy?"

" I dunno, maybe that's *another* lifetime..hey, I thought it was *me* made you happy..."

" Well yeah, but I love this other stuff too, only differ--"

"Hey, it feels cold, could you get the window?"

"Yeah sure.." Zeke got up slowly. He wasn't using his eyes so much, nor did he need to, but his peripheral vision revealed his reflection in the old window panes, which is normal. But an unusual anomaly in it's movement caused him to focus on it.The flashing outside with the light from the lamp made wavey patterns in the handmade glass as he might have expected, but not the large grinning face of the Alien he saw staring back!

"WAAH!! G,*GET OUTTA HERE!!*"

"What!??" Minnie shot a startled look at Zeke, who was turning on a dime enough to make ten pennies.

"It's him! *It's him!!*"

"Who? Oh you mean the ghost?" She grabbed for her robe to get up. The Alien was still grinning and sort of bobbing up and down. No, it was *air humping!* It did a garish imitation of what he and Minnie had been doing! Zeke was paralyzed,wide eyed and pointing.

"NO! NOoo!!!" he yelled. Minnie ran to the window, but not before the thing hunched up and zipped downward out of sight.Zeke plastered his face to the window,but could see nothing.

"Where's the ghost! I wanna see!"

"No! No! It's not a ghost! It's an alien!"

"An alien!? Oh Zeke come on...a ghost makes sense..this old house...the history.."

"No!—*Alien!* It has to be!...S, Snoad said you'd react like this...It's..you don't know...it's ...what I've been through!" He rushed to the door.

"Where are you going?"

"To find it!"

"In your *underpants??*"

"Come...come back to bed...please..it...It'll..It'll keep...come to bed." This he did, but he did not sleep soundly.

CHAPTER 8
Breakfast of Champions

Farm murmurings and other country noises brought the house happily and healthfully awake. Even Zeke had managed finally to sink into his quota of rapid eye movement. Jerry however, had slept soundly as a board and was tip toeing down the hall excitedly, deciding whether or not to knock on Minnie and Zeke's door. But before he could the door squeaked open. It was Zeke.

"Hey! I've gotta talk to you!" whispered Snoad.

"But I'm going to the *bathroom!*"

"OK OK..but how was last night?"

"That's MY business thank you!"

"Yeah but the whole house heard you! Pretty good huh? I mean Minnie, she's all right ay? Know what I mean? "

"How's your *wife?*"

"Oh she's asleep, she sleeps through everything..but did you all, uh.. have a good time?"

"Yes yes, except I saw it in the window!" Snoad stopped dead. "It ...? In the window? I'm sorry ol' boy that's a new one on me..."

"No NO, the *Alien* in the window! It was *watching!*"

"Huh ? It ,it..but that's the second floor! How?"

"It just was, now let me go!"

"Ok, hey remember after breakfast we're gonna track it!"

"Yes, yes.." Zeke agreed through the bathroom door.

"Maybe we can find footprinnts under the window..like Sherlock Holmes!"

"I doubt seriously if you'll find any..it rained last night." The shower started running and Jerry wandered off with his peculiar sidewinder walk, all the time looking over each shoulder.

At breakfast the tone was hushed, but with muted snickering, while their host was serving hot biscuits and white gravy. Zeke and Minnie pretended nothing was amiss, and even Jerry worked hard to keep quiet.

"My what a stormy evening, I could feel the house shudder, could'nt you?" asked Mrs.Chenoweth as she dished out delicious grits and scrambled eggs.

"Yeah, the ol' floorboards were squeaking up a storm.." said Mr.Chenoweth over his paper.

"You sure it was the floor boards?"

"Uh, I doubt it," said Zeke, "My great grandfather built things sturdy with those wooden pegs...it should'nt shake...uh..". Minnie blushed and smiled. Jerry however picked up the ball of conversation.

"Uh..Zeke and I thought we'd do some exploring around the countryside this morning...if it's alright.." Mr. Chenoweth looked up.

"S' Alright with me..just watch out for things that bite..chiggers an' such..."

"W,What about across the road,... those woods?"

"That's not my land...belongs to one of the old families 'round here...don't think they'd mind...hardly anyone goes in there except at hunting season..lotta deer ya know..." Zeke and Jerry looked at each other approvingly.

"Not goin' lookin' for that ghost are ya?" said Chenoweth.

"Oh..well, just foolin' around.." said Zeke. Minnie rolled her eyes and went on eating.

"Oh I don't blame ya, we did it ourselves when we first moved here, didn't we Hun?"

"Yes we did..."said Mrs. Chenoweth, pouring more delicious coffee. "..nice and pretty over there, I collected nice leaves and wild flowers, Lady Slippers..I planted under the trees...nothin' unusual though.."

"Except that Indian burial mound.." added Chenoweth. At that Jerry perked up.

"Mound!??"

"Yes, Monacan I believe...Jefferson did some excavation over there...first archeology done in the New World they say...he used to own this land..."

Zeke perked up. "Hey, I'm part Monacan myself.. on my Mama's side.."

"Wow,"said Jerry, "That's just the ticket ay Zeke!? That's worth a stomp in the woods!"

"I don't mind stomp'n, s'long as it's not in the bedroom..." graveled Chenoweth with a smirk over his paper, while Zeke and Minnie focused all the more on their food.

CHAPTER 9
Mound of Evidence

Early mid morning found the guys crossing the road out front. Minnie had given Zeke a kiss at the front door. "Have a busy day little man, finding your little men.." He smirked back as she patted him on the head.

"Keep a pumpkin burning in the window.." he added.

Green-yellow light radiated in soft multiple lines through the leaves from the sun above. Amazingly giant and tropic looking ground plants awaited their feet to tread through sweet smelling sedge,and rotting leaves of yesteryear. After crossing the sandy tracked cedar lined lane, they stepped through a broken down "V" shape in an aged wooden fence,evidently built originally to let humans through but to keep cattle in.

"I didn't see no tracks anywhere." said Jerry, watching the ground.

"I told ya.." said Zeke with a straight lipped cynical expression.

"Well, just give it a chance, this place has a good

eerie vibe! I can feel it in my finger tips.."

"Is *that* where it is?"

"Well sometimes in my nose..*sniff*, or on my ear fuzz.."

"Nose sounds right...that thing could recieve all kinds of signals...like one of the S.E.T.I. dishes..."

"Ha..that's a good one..maybe if I flare my nostrils it'll improve reception...."

"Hey, we better be quiet.."

"OK..."

This remaining wedge of old growth Virginia "virgin" forest unwound before them, enormous poplar trees, some dropping pre-fall giant yellow leaves at their feet to mix with older ones which they kicked their way through, like stacks of paper in a very messy office of the 18th Century, because the "paper" was heavier and sounded more like parchment. Thick coiling vines wound around great smooth trunks in wonderful pulp magazine fashion. You half expected some N.C. Wyeth style pirates or swashbucklers to come running by, swashing their buckles. They felt like explorers of millenia ago in a time warp B-movie with giant birds and reptiles ready to pounce around every corner.

"We shoulda brought some pith helmets.." said Jerry.

"Now you're pithing me off..be quiet!"

Soon the ground grew rocky and an opening of sky appeared before them. Suddenly a steep cliff chasm of grey-green shale and sliding rock yawned before them with little pebbles splashing far below to a shallow narrow river. Rippling coolness reflected striped bits of light across table top rock as they looked from way on high, holding on to trees to assuage their sudden vertigo. On the far side was by contrast a low gently rolling farm land with gentle pastel colors of uncultivated brush, with yellowish purple and greens in profusion. In the distance was a happy field of milk cows bobbing among stumps and cedar trees beyond where the road crossed the river on an old metal "erector set" style truss bridge.

"The bluffs of the Rivana..." said Zeke. "Keep over this way to the right down to the point...where the two rivers merge..." The high rocky ground soon peaked and then sloped downward to more hospitable and fertile ground. Blue Jays screeched and swooped around a huge chestnut tree, looking for goodies. "The big ones are Japanese Chestnuts, the small ones are American, but don't get any bigger because of the blight.

"Ah yaas.." went Jerry in Fields voice, "one of our classic calamities of horticulture.."

"Ha!" said Zeke, "One of the first of many! Now we got snake head fish from China in our rivers, millions of illegal Mexicans while the rich class down there pays them a dollar or so a day. It's modern day feudalism down there! Not to mention the wealth and class problems up here, and who knows what diseases are coming in on airplanes from overseas..meanwhile the Earth is burning up from Global Warming and asteroids are poised to strike the planet and kill everybody, which is probably good because there are too many people anyway! Congress does nothing because everybody thinks it's either the Democrats or the Republicans fault, who don't believe the warming exists and wanna burn more coal and oil, while it's really everybody's!..fault that is...but what is everybody fighting over? Abortion and Religion!

"It's the economy stupid.."ventured Jerry.

"No it's a lot more complicated, we need fairness all around, starting with America! Borders, trade yes,health care,quality of life for all! Gotta defeat terrorism yes, but we gotta control growth! We only have so much Earth! I'll give terrorists one thing, they do slow down progress a bit, which we need!"

" You don't like to rant much do you Zeke? Sounds like a pretty good editorial, send it in..."

" Aw, I spend too much time alone thinking...used to be big into New Age philosophy..love for everybody...still am I guess, but the way everything's going, the stuff on the news..mostly I get mad and frustrated...what d' ya do?

" So you're a conservative..no, a liberal?"

" Neither, I'm a *flaming moderate!* Life..or the ship of state if you will, has a steering wheel, and you have to go right sometime, or sometime left in order to avoid the sand bars and not run aground! We're in a new paradigm! The old issues of left and right have changed! We have to do what works for a healthy world, the right mix of things! Oh I get so mad when I watch TV..."

"Well, that's one reason I come to the woods," Jerry was gazing fondly upward, "..to forget about it...sure is beautiful isn't it?"

"And that's another thing, tearing down too much woods! Awww, I'm sorry, just read my rants on Facebook... I guess we forgot about our alien...and being quiet!"

"Oh well..hey, what's that over *there?*" They saw a

strange dark mass off to their right. Jerry strode energetically toward an abrupt rise in the forest floor. "It
must be Jefferson's Indian mound!

"Yes! Wowww..! This *must* be it!"
The mound was about 15 feet high and forty feet
across. Here was history for and of the ages. As they
walked around, a self-imposed hush fell upon them, or
did it come from elsewhere? Zeke had felt the "hallowed ground feeling" many times when exploring
Civil War trenches, but it was nothing like this. They
were suddenly in direct connection with age upon age
of people, some even perhaps, his own forebears.
They had chipped stones, built huts, hunted and fished
the hills and rivers day in day out for millennia, while
the great sky rolled over them, loving, fighting, playing, eating, huddling against the cold and thrilling to
the springtime, and not a cell phone in sight.

"Hey look.." Zeke pointed out a worn down slice
near one end, sort of a rounded trench in the mound.
"This must be where Jefferson dug."

"First archeology in America..I wonder if there's
anything exposed.."

"What, you mean a skull? I doubt it, that was
covered over long ago...

" Hey, don't go digging, the Monacan's consider
this sacred...like any grave..I'd be real careful.."

"Yeah but it's so ancient...besides I'm part Monacan, I don't think they'd mind..." He reached into the
leaves and scurried things around with a stick.

"I, I don't like it Zeke..it might bring bad luck..you
know Jefferson was the victim of more campaign
slurs than any U.S. President, he almost lost the elec-
tion to Aaron Burr by one vote!"

"Oh Jerry, go on--what could that possibly have to
do with—"
Suddenly a strange buzzing rattle sound burst out near
by, then stopped just as quickly.

"Wazzat?? *A rattlesnake!!??*"

"I don't think you get rattlers down this
low..they're up in the mountains..." But again, a sudden sound startled them. A buzzing that became a
rhythmic droning, growing ever louder into a whirring, a whistling, a whining high pitched multi-voiced
roaring. The vibration took on a strobing electronic all
engulfing high decibel sound most normally identified
with sci-fi movies.

"*What is it!!?*" yelled Jerry, covering his ears.

"God! ..it.. sounds-- like a *flying saucer!!*"

"Ya think??"

The sound enveloped them from all directions. They
couldn't tell if it emanated from the trees, the sky or
the mound. It made Zeke sort of dizzy. He reeled, and
saw a brilliant flash from above. What was it, the sun?
A ship?? Suddenly the guys felt themselves being
pelted by small objects--not painful, just nerve wrack-
ing. They were in a sea of small orange and black-
blue things with vibrating orange wings! And red
eyes! Zeke knew what these were. " Cicadas!..the 17
year Locusts! It's the year for them!!"

"You're kidding! You're right!! Cicadas! Ha ha
haha!!" Jerry danced around with glee. "Oops,don't
wanna step on 'em!" Indeed they were settling and
dropping on the ground everywhere. They crawled on
their shirt sleeves, staring them eye to eye. After
experiencing this unforgettable but natural phenom-
enon, the boys made their way out further down hill,

their senses calming down, as did the the bugs themselves.

"I guess the Native Elders got their way after all" joshed Jerry.

"Maybe so! Let's go down to the river and wash our hands, I've got sticky goo everywhere!I think they were mating!"

" A little cicada DNAaay..." droned Jerry.

At the point of land where the James and the Rivana rivers meet, Zeke Landover and Jeremy Snoad baptized their hands in the ever flowing waters of eternity. If it sounds like a religious experience lacking real meaning, so it was for the two adventurers. For what is a religious experience except an encounter with the beautiful or unexplained, and having been washed in a vibrant experience that leaves one refreshed? By now they had largely forgot the object of their outing and were simply laughing and enjoying the day.

"Wow, was that something or not?" said Zeke, drying his hands on some fern leaves.

"Yeah, something!" smiled Jerry, "But what a beautiful view!" Before them was the sunlit sparkling James, quite broad but shallow with table rocks and gentle rapids. In the middle distance stood a fly fisherman,with mosaic-like shimmering reflections, casting his line back and forth.

"Quite the idyllic pictorial my dear Jeremy..could paint a picture right here.."

"Hey, this must be where the Indian village was..they always built at the fork of streams.."

"And they must've raised their crops on the same low grounds up that way, where Chenoweth does today!"

"Yeah, I 'spec so!"

While the two lads were taking in the scenery, they undid their shoes and waded in for maximum refreshment. But what they failed to notice, was that the fisherman, behind dark glasses, was watching. After a few more rhythmical whips of his rod and line with it's hypnotic and restful effect, he suddenly cast once more, but strongly downward, and the front of the rod separated, dropping into the water. This last movement fortunately gained at least some of the boys attention, because it revealed a long barreled pistol with a silencer, which was being "cast" in *their* direction! BA-ZING!

"What's that?" said Jerry, more bugs? BA-ZING!

"*No!* He's shooting at us!!" Wildly splopping and sloshing, they galumphed their way ashore, balancing socks and shoes above them in waving arms. BAZING! Through the mud and more shots they ran for a miniature eternity into the brush and trees, across the little peninsula. Now hopping and trying to get their things back on, they stumbled out of site of their assailant. "What's his *problem!!?*"

"No time to ask!" answered Zeke. They continued over to the Rivana River side and along the upstream shore heading toward the bluffs. They could hear the sure splashes and stomps of well heeled water boots behind them as the fisherman was coming ashore, but as they ran, the steep landscape and water were conspiring to trap them. Onward they scrambled. "We'll have to swim!"

"We'll be too slow!"

"No! Look, a canoe!"

"Must be his, come on!" They grabbed it fast and pushed off up stream, Jerry in front, Zeke in back, paddling fast as they could. It was oddly enough, an old style wooden canoe. Zeke thought it strange, but was glad for the increased swiftness of it's light hull in the water. They stuck close to the inward wooded shore which gave cover under the overhanging trees. Now they heard the fisherman stomping along the hill and through the brush. "Get as much distance as we can, then we'll make for the other shore..", said Zeke in hushed urgent tones.

"But then he'll see us!"

"You wanna climb those rocks??" He indicated the steep shale bluffs approaching fast on their left.

"I don't hear anything..I don't like it.."

"Shuddap and keep paddling!"

They were now quite under the quickly rising bluffs, trying to be swift but silent as the saying goes. But a quick scrabble of stones caught their attention. There he was on the bluff above and taking careful aim!

" Evasive maneuvers! Head for the shore!" Luckily there were still trees between he and them.BAZING— Bloip! A bullet came far too close. They paddled for all they were worth, zig zagging as much as they could muster. BAZING! Ga-BLAP!

" It hit the boat!"

" Keep going and keep low!" BLAP! BLAP! Water began to bubble between them.

" Why couldn't he get an aluminum canoe?"

" Traditionalist I guess!" BAZZING! A piece of the upper gunnel cracked near Jerry's hand!

BAZ-ZING! Another hole in the boat, fortunately they didn't need it anymore as they slid around into a little inlet behind cover. As more shots came they kept low, making their way through the cattails and brush up toward the road.

On the roadway of Route 6, they realized the need to get back to the farm, but that took them on a converging course with that of their mad gunman. They had to cross back over the Rivana River bridge for one thing, and their pursuer was closing in up on the bluffs.

"I don't think he's gonna give up that easily.." puffed Jerry.

"But we gotta get across!" A car was zooming their way, but flagging it was no use, it actually sped up to avoid them. Next came a farm truck, surely he'd let them ride in the back. They waved and yelled. He waved and yelled back but didn't stop.

"Drunk.." said Jerry

"Com'on, we gotta make for the bridge." They puffed along with wayward shots at intervals buzzing around but not too near them. At the bridge it was a different story, there the bluffs narrowed in close and they could see their enemy's face, except for the parts behind a baseball hat and dark glasses. From the roadside brush cover they darted to the iron girders and superstructure of the old metal bridge, so fondly a part of rural Americana. TINK! A bullet hit an upright. TWONG! (That piece was kinda loose). The guys darted again to another load bearing girder. *Be-TONG!!* Looking across the bridge to the lower pasture beyond, they saw a large cow staring at them and chewing it's cud. It was oblivious to what was happening and with each TWONG it simply twitched it's ear.

" Oh to be a Guernsey and just go...nobody shoots at a cow.." bemoaned Jerry.

" Uh..that's a Hereford..."corrected Zeke.

" Ok, I heard of Hereford.." *Pa-DING!!* " Hey we gotta do sump'm!!" They could see their assailant inching ever nearer along the ridge. Some rocks fell into the river and a duck went flying, QUA-QUAA-QUACK!—under the bridge and far up stream. The boys looked back and forth for some opportunity. Just then, a large motor started up. They looked as a large yellow piece of rusted farm machinery pulled out of the field down the road and started toward them.

" Oh, forget it, it's a backhoe.." said Jerry dejectedly.

Zeke's face lit up." No, wait a minute... when it gets here, follow me!" Gunshots kept coming as Jerry looked scary. The backhoe came closer and closer with it's deafening roar. It was crossing the bridge, which began to bump and rattle under the vibration. The driver smiled and waved at the boys hunkered along the bridge rail.

" Catchin' anything? " he yelled above the engine. The boys smiled and made a nebulous gesture while the machine started to pass them.Then Zeke tugged Jerry and went running with his friend twitching after, his big eyes rolling every which way. Bullets came flying thick and fast, ricochetting off everything. The big metal scoop at the rear of the backhoe hung invitingly in front of them as they swung up and inside—PA-TING PA-TING! They had a bullet proof shield!

" Stay low!" yelled Zeke.

" Uh, yeah..I think I will.."smirked Jerry. As the view behind revealed more and more river, and then

the ridge, the sunglasses fly fisher popped his head
out of some brush above and took aim. They saw little
poofs beside his weapon and then more PA-TINGS!
bounced off the machinery. Jerry and Zeke hugged the
bottom of the scooper as the tractor began the steep
uphill grade, trying to keep their legs and butts from
sliding out. Suddenly the driver put on the breaks! He
got out, looking at the engine.

"Never heard it do that before..." he rubbed his
head under his baseball cap. Jerry and Zeke huddled
with totally indescribable expressions.They did however manage a look at the ridge and saw that Sunglasses was nowhere to be seen. They let out a breath
as the driver got in and started up hill. The ridge was
falling behind with much woodland coming between
them for almost a quarter of a mile. The turnoff road
to Rivana Bluffs was soon approaching, and they
easily rolled off and skedaddled to the left and uphill
towards the farm.

Finally Zeke and Jerry puffed steadily up the familiar cedar lined driveway, having made a grand
circle back to their point of origin for their morning
exercise.

"Think he'll come up this far?" puffed Jerry.

"Hope not..don't think so.." said Zeke,nearly
staggering, "he seems to want to avoid attention.."

"Yeah, except from us!" They finally rounded the
bend which revealed the kindly old farm house with
it's clucking hens, lazy hogs and staring cows, safe
and secure in the warm late morning sun as if nothing
had happened. They plodded, grateful but depleted up
the rolling lawn, when out of the trees, a grinding

whizzing sound pierced their ears, winding up ever louder as it approached . The boys jerked into frozen statues and dropped to the ground.

" Cicadas..." said Zeke.

"Yeah,..cicadas..." said Jerry, as they picked themselves up and dragged on toward the house.

CHAPTER 10
Don't Muck with the Muckety Mucks

Jerry began to whisper. "Zeke, I would'nt mention any of this in the house."

Incredulous, Zeke stared at him blankly. "Are you *kidding?* We've been attacked, and I mean violently! I think we should call the police! That serial killer is out there in the woods, and.."

" No, I don't think so.."

" What!?"

" I..I mean he's not what you think he is.."

" Well then *what* is he??"

Jerry shooshed him. "Men in Black...Shadow Government, high muckety mucks... you name it.."

" Jerry, you've been reading too many books from the wrong section of the book store..."

" No, no, just think about all that's been going on..that little man we were following...do you really think the police would help us? And what would people think if you told 'em? You know how that goes...no, this is something high up..Area 51 maybe..."

" *That's* in Nevada!"

" Who cares? They got the power! *Foosh!* Be here in a minute!"

" Aw com'on.." Zeke started toward the porch. Just then the air was shattered by a terrible and loud beating that push into their eardrums. BAP BAP BAP BAP BOW BOW Bow bow bow... a great dark shape zoomed over the trees.

" What is it??" Zeke jumped backward. " Aw, it's helicopter, boy those things really can..."

" No! A *black* helicopter!" Jerry pointed upward, his big eyes rolling, "Muckety Mucks!" Zeke shook his head and kept walking up the porch as the screen door squeaked open.

" Where have you boys been? Having fun? You look like it.." It was Blanche, Jerry's wife who liked to sleep late.

" Oh we had fun alright..." Jerry joked.

" Well we better get ready to go Hon.."

" Oh yeah, gotta hit the road..first I gotta wash these shoes..."

" Yes,"continued Blanche, "and put on your shorts, they're in the car.." Zeke moved past them.

"Excuse me, I gotta make a phone call." Jerry shot him a look but Blanche was blasé.

" Ya can't, the line's dead.." The boys were stock still. " Yeah, Chenoweth's been tryin' it all morning, now he's gone to town somewhere to find out about it...cel phones don't work either...really strange! May have been the lightning.."

" Yeah, lightning..." agreed Jerry and Zeke, not smiling. Inside, Zeke went upstairs to his room where he ran into Minnie.

"Hey.."

"Hey.."

"I've gotta get back..got this deadline you know..."

"Yeah..I know.."

"You still at the same place on the North Side of Richmond?"

"Yeah,"replied Minnie with soft inviting eyes, "it's really comfy, I like it..."

"Well I'll give you a call then.."

Mrs. Chenoweth popped in the door carrying clean sheets.

"Well hello! I'm sorry but Minnie be will up here a couple more days finishing our project, but *then* you can have her back!"

Zeke and Minnie blushed and started saying goodbye. He became suddenly protective. "Hey, you be careful driving out, somebody was shooting this morning, these locals like their target practise ya know.."

" Yeah I know..Hey, you be careful too! Keep your doors locked."

" Oh I'll be alright..."

" I mean it!" Minnie noticed the nervousness in Zeke's eyes as they parted, and he noticed that she noticed.

"Look, as strange and horrific as this..visit has been, it's been really wonderful..and I don't want to lose.."

" I know Zeke, it's the same for me..but strange and horrific?"

" Oh something has been happening..look, I've got to get to Richmond, please catch up to me as soon as you can...You got my cel phone?

" Yes, of course but.."

" Call me..or I'll call you..but we must stay together..uh, in touch..I think..I mean I really feel it..I've gotta go! Remember!" He started off.

" Of course Zeke, I will! And don't worry!" She watched him down his great grandfather's stairs. " Now I'm worried.."

Outside he ran into Jerry by the spigot washing. A mockingbird was singing overhead and the water plashed happily, making orange streams and puddles below his shoes caked with good ol' Virginia red clay. As he watched, this made Zeke look off over the low grounds to the distant view of the James, near where the fly fisherman was first standing.

" I don't like leaving them here Jerry."

" Oh, it's not them you gotta worry about, it's us! We're the ones that know something, whatever that is... Now you get on the road in a hurry—I'll do the same!"

" Well, I guess.."

Zeke got in his car. " Look, I'll call ya when we get back to town." With that they somewhat nervously parted company. He pulled out of the pasture and down the driveway, but still watching the woods.

CHAPTER 11
Gunk in the Road

Naturally Zeke was jittery as he re-covered the ground
of their recent terrifying escapade, especially when
crossing the bridge, but ducking below the dashboard
helped. " We should've called the police.." he
thought..."That Jerry..."

Mainly, the thought of his deadline for this week's
episode of "Melvin the Gunk" drove him onward.
He'd never missed a deadline and he didn't plan on
starting now. At his first chance on reaching Colombia, he turned North on route 659 , thus avoiding
again the sight of his long ago "abduction vision", but
also heading toward I 64 and the fastest route home.
"Deadline"—the literal meaning of the phrase impressed itself upon his brain the more he replayed the
morning's events in his head. In fact they were on
instant automatic replay, and nearly impossible to
erase or shift traks. But what a time it all was in retro-
spect. Good Friends, good love, good food, fine country, adventure, and now he was racing back to the
grind.

If only people who "wished they were artists"
knew what it was like, the sitting, the cranking out,
the business, or the lack of it, the exaltation of new
ideas, the depression or "postpartum creative syn-

drome" after finishing, not knowing what to do next. The decompression of the brain, the feeling of utter idiocy, not able to decide which socks to put on, or even to get up, without his characters to tug him, tug him, always toward the drawing board and the next turn in their story. But hell, there's a grunt side to every occupation.

That's life. But if you're doing what you love you'll have the energy to go through it all in a healthy way, (if you get wise about the practical side as well). Inspiration, emotion, motion,planning, putting on the brakes, relaxing,and downloading your brain. It's a process. What does a surgeon do when he gets home? Ask one sometime, but then again he's got a huge support system at his back and a great salary to boot. Zeke remembered how many doctors he knew admired his artistic ability. Then, logic would follow, why doesn't society pay him a comparable salary and provide him decent health care? Not gonna happen, not in America today. Maybe someday.

This was when his mind reached a negative overload of worry, and he always thought it was time to "get on the floor and get stupid". Play with a puppy or something. But he did'nt have a puppy. Sometimes with the neighbors dogs. How depressed he was getting. He must stop he told himself. Stop the visions, the thoughts, the internal videos. Hell, he's just starting a new strip, he shouldn't be having these feelings, he should be pumped at this stage of the cycle. It was all this adventure he had embarked on. It had filled his head,it was part of his life narrative now, that he dragged around with him. Close the door on it! Get clear! *"I'm an artist damn it!"* He thought stringently.

"That's what I do and I must get back to it!" However, he must not let himself get caught up in the lonely artist syndrome again, he must work it so he's continuously tasting of life, the greatest work of art of all, without which the other is nothing.

The more unfamiliar landscape he put between *it* and himself, the more normal he felt. 659 was one of his favorite types of Virginia road, which, having it's roots in old wagon days, meandered through the landscape according to which way the hill rolled,or the river cut. These old roads connected with a whole network of others like them, linking hamlet to farm to church to crossroads. He knew from old family stories that his great grandfather Capt. Gunderson had driven them often by wagon. A true "net" it was when viewed on the map, you could get anywhere from anywhere else, and if that didn't work you could change directions and work your way over to where you could. This one he was on also had an old time name- "Stage Crossing Rd." Focusing on these roadside details helped him muchly with his mental balancing process.

Virginia's so full of quaint oddities and odd place names. A sign read, '5 miles to Willy Pie's Store!' "That's a good one! Make a note of that.." he said to himself. He had wanted a little "mini vacation" and boy had he got one. It was good to feel like an ordinary cartoonist working stiff again, living from coffee to coffee. "Wow, an actual set of old Burma-Shave signs--still standing!, 'Thirty days, Hath September, April June, And the Speed Offender'...Ha ha" he read. By now he had gotten off on the wrong road, but he headed steady to North, knowing he'd have to hit I 64 or at least U.S. 250 before long, and then a straight shot back to Richmond.

Before long as was their habit, Stupid and Melvin began to talk to him. Some of his best ideas for the strip came this way,while behind the wheel. A little refining or re-shuffling and he had a decent story line. Sometimes, they just "acted themselves out" for him, before his eyes, in pantomime. Sometimes with music soundtrak from the radio or whatever. Now Melvin appeared before him in the road ahead, just skipping and dancing along. But soon he became less coherent and coordinated. He just bumped along like a balloon on a string, hands by his side. What was this? "Come on subconscious, do me some good." He had his hand at the ready with a pencil and a brown paper bag at his side. He knew it was dangerous, but he planned to pull over and sketch it as soon as he could figure what it was. Finally he stopped and sketched Melvin. He realized it was incredibly close to the image of the owl in the road that his brother had mentioned, as well as the cartoon Dad had first drawn for him after that seemingly fateful trip of long ago. He crumpled it up onto the floor and drove on, focused and determined.

The engine had a ping going, a little knock-clockety clock sound. Clockety clock..mockety mock..muckety mucks..ah, Jerry and his talk. What was he going to do with all the stuff that just hap-pened to him? Where to store it in his brain so it wouldn't drive him crazy? Worry about it later...worry about it later...put it on a shelf, close the door. Muck-Muck-muck-muck-muck-muck..a deep fast chopping sound.

"Huh , there's a helicopter... so? There's a helicopter, so what? I can't even tell if it's black or not with the angle of the sun..it's pretty far off anyway...Mmm could be black.." Anyway, it flew off toward Charlottesville. Now the only thing to concentrate on were the pleasant curves of the rolling hill road, the pleasing smell of autumn roadside corn shucks, that pink blob rising and falling in his rearview mirror. What? A small car, looked to be a P.T. Cruiser, was on the road behind him, painted totally pink. Must be a Daisy Ray Cosmetics car or something. You see them every so often. Some housewife sets up a side business with a franchise...

Zeke decided he needed some lunchtime sustenance so he actually pulled in at Willy Pie's Store when he got there. It was what passed most often these days for the old general store at the crossroads. This one was in an original general store building, but most of it's "innards" as Dad would say bespoke mostly of convenience store. Still, the old floorboards were the same and the barefoot girl behind the counter was far from citified. He started to get a Slim Jim jerky stick but instead went whole hog and got him a steak sandwich from the cooler in the back and put it in the microwave. While he waited he noticed the pink P.T. pull up and park outside by the natural gas tanks. "Yep, a Daisy Ray car" he said to himself, noticing the familiar logo.

"Willy Pie ever come around?" he asked the counter girl curiously.

"Naw, he died ten year ago...mah Daddy bought it an' runs it, but he kept the same name. That thar's

Willy". She pointed to an old black and white photo near the cash register. An amazingly huge fat man with an equally broad grin smiled out at him over the years. "Ever'body loved Willy...but he *wuz* big..had ta come in through the load'n dock.."

While Zeke was appreciating this fascinating saga, he noticed no one had come in from the Daisy Ray car. He took his food outside to eat and listen to the radio. From behind his steering wheel he noticed the windows of the Pink P.T. were completely dark. It just sat there. "Of course it sits there, it's a car you idiot.." he thought. Just the same Zeke decided he needed more mayonnaise for his sandwich. "Uh, does your Daisy Ray distributor always just sit in the car like that?" he asked the girl.

" Oh, I 'spec she's tallyin' up her tally sheet 'er sump'm...but I don't know what she's doin' here in the first place cuz I din't order nuth'n an' she usually don't show up before next week.."

CHAPTER 12
Peril in Pink

Back outside Zeke gingerly got in his car and ate his sandwich. No change from the little pink car. As soon as he was down to just his drink he hit the ignition and spun off up the road. Damn! He was heading the wrong way, *West* from the crossroad instead of *North*. He knew he had been flustered for a reason, but a glimpse in the mirror confirmed his suspicion, the pink PT Cruiser was pulling out straight after him. He sped up, but that little four cylinder must have been hopped up something crazy the way it kept pace right behind him.

The winding curves got windier as they rose higher and higher toward the foothill country of Virginia's Piedmont region, heading toward Palmyra. Beautiful as it was Zeke had no time to take it in. That car meant business and he had no desire to partake in the transaction. He felt somehow it must be that damn fly fisherman with the sunglasses. On a straight away this too was confirmed when it pulled up alongside and the driver opened his window and took aim. PA-TING! "There goes the paint on my Buick" Zeke thought. "I mean I've heard of jealously guarding fishing holes but this—SCREEECH!

Avoiding a pot hole, he began zig-zagging from side to side over the bumpy old macadamized surface. The pink car did the same, trying to get another shot. Pa-TOW! There went his side view mirror. Damn, what a lucky shot. Now his rear vision was compromised as well. Then came a surprise curve after a sharp rise, one of the casualties of this area, giving one the same sensation as an express elevator in a tall building, plus that of a Tilt-a-Whirl at the State Fair, but he took it better than his pursuer who almost went off the road. "At least I have some home court advantage," smiled Zeke in the mirror.

He also made a quick mental note to include this material in a future episode of Melvin the Gunk, although he wasn't sure how a 39 Ford coup' would take the turns. Damn, was he an obsessive compulsive cartoonist, worrying about plots at a time like this! Pinky was getting close again. He'd have liked to get a look under that hood, but not just now. Zeke hit the pedal to put more distance between them. Down and around, over a creek, through woods and uphill they went. Up onto a long and clear plateau of open farm land, the road lay on a long straightaway. Zeke knew the pink car would gain advantage here. There was a large dark dot in the distance, which soon became a tractor pulling a load of hay at 3 miles per hour. They both swerved and dodged around it, scattering red clay dirt from the shoulder, tires bumping back to the pavement.

"Hmm," he thought, there was something familiar about that farmer on the tractor. " Yes, we're nearing ol' Toady Stankmore's place! And that was his son, Juney Coon Dog on the tractor!" Dad had brought him and brother Buzz up here many a time to go fishing, they were almost cousins by marriage on Mom's side from up at Scottsville. Their driveway was along here somewhere, but that was no use, Pinky was closing in fast. Lots of straightaway lie ahead and now 'Sunglasses' made his move. Gunning that supercharged engine, he started coming along side. Too late to swerve, Zeke thought about countless scenes like this in the movies. The next thing would be a gunshot from window to window.

But why, Zeke had always thought while watching Steve McQueen or whoever, did not the hero simply slam on brakes and let the bad guy go zooming forward? They *never* did this! So Zeke, just to be different, was gonna do it now. SCREEEEEECH! He held onto the wheel tight as he could swerving slightly to a stop.Sure enough the assailant zoomed passed just as he fired a shot, which went wide, at least it sounded like...

Popping it into reverse, Zeke ground his way back, gears whining, to where he thought Toady's driveway was, a little ways back. He could see Pinky hitting his brakes and spinning wildly in the distance. Zeke hit the small bumpy farm road at 40, almost missing the bumps from memory, so little had the road changed. The only problem was the wide open nature of the country, and pretty soon he saw the Pink blob bumpily joining him on the road. By now he was up among the farm house complex, spinning through the oak trees and momentarily out of sight.

The only place to go was the cow pasture beyond

the barn. The old wooden gate was shut but he'd have to crash it and settle with Toady or rather Juney later, bein' as how Toady was probably dead and planted over in the field in the family plot, his ghost turning flip flops as Zeke made a shambles of the farm. Dodging cows was an interesting way to drive and might make a good video game he thought, (yet another stupid mental note). "MOOoo MMMOOOOOOOoo!!" At least he was hidden from view, but Zeke knew he'd have to somehow dodge Pinky and circle back to the road, as there was no way out back here that he knew of. Curving back to the right he crossed an open space which revealed the PT Cruiser already in the pasture and also dodging cows.

All at once a childhood memory came back, there in the distance before him was an old cement and yellow tile silo far out in the field. He remembered how they used to play around there. But now Good ol' Pinko had spotted him and was breaking away from the herd straight toward him, bumping over the clumpy thick grass like a pink porpoise. Zeke therefore quickly doubled back behind the beef, zig zagging between the great mooing undulates, and worried that he might hit one. Suddenly his cartoon friends Melvin and Stupid appeared before him, jumping and diving down among the heifers, like going off a diving board. What were they about? Here and there he'd also catch a pink glimpse of his assailant with his ominously determined dark plastic eyes and pugnacious stare, bumping by during visual breaks in the black cattle herd, which by the way was getting nervous. Zeke was afraid of a stampede, but utterly relieved to see again the farmyard fence. He curved and worked his way left again, and soon saw the silo once more.

There was some sort of distant mental inkling in his brain connected with that smooth tiled structure in the grass. What was it? A glance backward showed the pink car still struggling with cows. Zeke headed toward the silo, not knowing exactly why, but then a very odd childhood word popped into his brain-- "Gluckwater". What? It was a made-up game he and his brother and Dad had played, which required the presence of some water, (usually a creek), and an energetic barking dog. They had played in the silo, pretending it was a castle, and then throwing rocks and broom straw clogs in some water sending knaves to the dungeon. A dog was on hand to bark as you tried to splash your opponent on the other side. This, was Gluckwater.

The silo came on, looming huge. Pinko was free of the herd and speeding at him across the pasture. Funny how much info the brain can cram into a few split seconds..But no, he suddenly remembered, the water they had played at was actually an open farm cesspool! Dad had to hose down their pants afterward or Mom would lay down the law at the smell and they couldn't come back to go fishing. A visual plan of defense suddenly appeared from an on-high camera angle in Zeke's brain. Would It work? It was worth the chance. He had to time it right though, by slowing down enough to make the turn as well as encouraging his foe to speed up.

Now came the moment of truth as he slowed around the curved yellow tower. Pink PT was closing in swiftly from behind. There it was, the cesspool!

Not environmentally healthy but very helpful at the moment. Zeke cut his wheels sharply left, sliding and spinning. But the PT maintained speed as he rounded the silo—Baba deBUMPa de BUMP-BLOMP!!—he hit the last large clump of earthy silage before going airborne and SpeeLOOMPH!! Pisshoo!!Blub blub blub—down into the muck! Brown delicacies were thrown every which way as the wheels spun and the obnoxious occupant banged on door and glass.

Zeke circled back enough to see his handy work, and saw the cute and fancy logo for Daisy Ray's Cosmetics sink beneath the crud. Never had that Apple Chancery text font brought such a tear to his eye. He then drove laughingly back towards the road.

He did stop briefly at the Stankmore's back porch long enough to grab his brown bag and pencil to write-

JUNEY - I'll PAY 4 THE GATE-
ZEKE LANDOVER

He stuck it in the inside railing of the screen door with the drawing of Melvin the Gunk showing.Let Juney puzzle over *that*. He then sped fast as he could for I 64.

CHAPTER 13
Revelation on the Road to Richmond

Pushing onward, Zeke turned west instead of east, in the direction they'd been heading before the detour through the farm.For some reason it felt right.Maybe because if Sunglasses could somehow still chase him, he Zeke would be headed in the opposite direction than expected,or maybe not. Logic wasn't really part of his agenda, so he followed his nose through the various winding turn-offs until he ran into Route 15 at Palmyra.

There he thought briefly of his great great uncle the Civil War hero with his name ensconced on the monument on the hill across from the historic court house, known for it's Jeffersonian greek temple style architecture and called by historians the "Acropolis of Palmyra". But he stopped only a moment, because now he had a straight shot north to Zion Crossroads and 64. By the time he got there though he was over-come with a sudden exhaustion, so he pulled into a large truck stop by the McDonalds and parked, safely hidden among the many vehicles large and small. Without exactly meaning to, he slept.

Minnie was tied to a railroad track and a black heli-copter was bearing down on her. Helpless to get at her to save her, Jerry was holding Zeke back saying, "No! This is a job for the government, you don't have the proper clarence!"

"Clarence!?" Zeke yelled, " I'll give ya clarence!"

"No *you're Clearance*, I'm giving you clarence!" Jerry argued while shaking him. "Don't you get it?" He broke away and ran up along the track to the oncoming copter, but the ground spun under him like a rounded cartoon landscape. He looked at his feet and saw he was walking on a spinning globe of the Earth, not 10 feet in diameter. He somehow gained the cockpit of the helicopter and swung aboard ready to put on the breaks and save Minnie. But through the windshield he saw Minnie was not there, and neither were the tracks. It was just a road at nighttime. In the middle was Melvin dancing a Scottish jig backward, but wearing cinderblocks on his feet which crumbled as he went. (It was very messy). He then began to morf and change shape. Jerry then poked his head above the front, becoming the hood ornament,(which by now belonged to a 39 Ford) snarling, " OK, if you don't like Clarence I'll give you Richard!"

"What? Jerry!! Wait!" said Zeke, "Can you do a '51 Dodge??" He looked back at the road. Melvin had turned into the little owl in that old Tex Avery cartoon, singing— "I love ta singa, 'bout the moona and the June-a and the Spring-a...I love ta Singa..." Then lightning crashed and water washed over the road." BOOM CRASH! Rumble..."

Zeke woke to find himself in an actual thunderstorm, with great long tadpoles of rain wobbling down the windshield. Huge windswept grey, black and white wafts of cloud were speeding across the landscape, and a brilliant pink-orange flaming sunset blazed strange and amazing in the West against cobalt blue shadows, patches of light blue and even green,with bits of broken rainbow in the East contrasted against the dark bluish grey. The sky was dreaming too.

The rain was letting up, so Zeke shook himself and staggered into Mac D's for a couple of cheeseburgers and a cup of coffee for road.

"WelcometoMacDonald'scanItakeyourorder?" went the girl with hardly a head bob. As he looked around the crowded room Zeke saw many trucker types, some with sunglasses. Were they looking at him? That one..no that one.. "I've got to stop this.." he thought, "settle down.." Finding a small wall seat he began to relax. Finally he called Minnie's cel phone and got the answering service.

"Hi, this is Minnie McFeeney! Believe it or not I know why you're calling!...So talk to me silly, wait for the beep!"

"Hello Minnie, this is Zeke..I guess you're still working on that project..what was it, a spiritual house cleaning? Or is it cleansing..anyway..I just wanted to talk..and tell you how much I enjoyed everything..uh..and also that there's a lot more to this little grey alien thing..I dunno..it's something big and terrible..well maybe not that..but bad..anyway be careful..and let me know as soon as you get to town..and maybe ask Jerry if he's still there..uh..but keep quiet about it.."

His voice went silent as he looked and saw a really menacing looking trucker in sunglasses coming straight for him with 3 Big Macs and 4 things of fries.

He was breathing heavy as he blumped down heavy right next to him.

" Uh, well I gotta go an' git on th' road..uh..bye..Love you..bye.." Zeke hung up and sat still, trying unsuccessfully to look relaxed. The big trucker turned slowly and stared at him. He smiled quite warmly with great wrinkly cracks in his face, revealing a somewhat toothless palette.

" I can't hep' it," the man growled, "I'm just a real watcha call romantic!" It seemed Zeke's conversation had reminded him of his ex-girlfriend. He smiled back as they talked a bit about trucks they'd known and loved, from semis to pickups, and even a dog or two before Zeke got up to leave. Soon he was coasting down the entrance ramp to I 64 East, and there was nothing but the familiar sight of white lines on the highway in the headlights.

He was in a drowsy work mode now, at least for the dull parts, figuring which pieces of the comic strip job he would need to have done by when, pacing it out for the end of the week and delivery to his publisher. Getting home now was the priority. Getting home and putting the last two days events out of his head. He knew Jerry would bother him about it soon enough, Jerry was that type. He would let all that stuff ride for now while he got back to Melvin and Stupid on the road.

On the road, on the road, white line-white line-white line,(what, no Willie Nelson?).His mind was a broken record as he tried to focus on the interstate monotony. Normally he prefered small windy roads but not now. The coffee and cheeseburgers helped, but soon he was wondering how to keep his eyes open

with toothpicks or scotch tape. Fear also gave him
little boosts, thoughts of his insidious assailant and
what it all meant. What could it mean in a larger
sense? Because it made no sense, unless he bought
into Jerry's conspiracy theories,which after all were'nt
all that organized,(at least the way he talked about it.)
Suddenly the nicely controlled world he had become
used to had turned into a gigantic universal jungle of
beasts and things mostly unknown.

What? He saw something. Up the road in the growing darkness was a blooming flash of light. This
worried him all the more, but he was on the Interstate,
what could he do but keep going? As he passed the
exit to Shannon Hill, the light grew large, but it came
from the far side of the expressway. As he came from
under the overpass, he saw it's source. On the uphill
exit ramp a car was rolling to a stop at the top, totally
ablaze in fire. So amazed and shocked was Zeke that
he could only look with dropped jaw. So weird and
surreal but so terrible and silent. The older model car
must've had some fault in the fuel system or something. The people, they must already be dead. He must
call 911 at least. But his phone was suddenly dead too.
Must need charging he thought---perhaps.

Soon the terrible dreamlike sight faded again into
his dozy attempt to stay awake with coffee. He
could'nt be sure if he had actually seen it. Then he
had a thought. Had it been meant for him? Had *what*
been meant for him? A laser blast? That's silly. More
coffee....coffee...He turned on the radio. His usual
choice, WCVE FM - PBS was playing the Brahms
Requiem, normally a great favorite, which he loved to
hear as he lay in bed trying to sleep. He may stay up

to the end, but after that, sleep was good and sound. Sound..sleep...sound.-white lines.-white lines..NO! He needed something loud and abrasive to keep awake! Another slug of Mac D's coffee and he went digital dial searching. Blip Blip Blup—— "RICHMOND RACING! BaZOOOW! Today at the International Raceway the action was unbelievable as —Blip"..No that's too abrasive...Rap music..Punk Rock...Country Rock..cute girl 'Uh-Oh Rock'--these he just didn't like..blip blup— "JEEEEESUS!" went an exuberantly happy voice. Ahh, a crazy preacher, he could deal with this. The human voice jazz riff surreality appealed to him.

" Now as we read in Jeremiah.. 'The heart is deceitful above all things, and desperately wicked! *Who* can *know* it?' Now look here Beloved, now stay with me..It says, 'As the partridge sitteth on eggs and hatcheth them not, so he that getteth riches, and not by right, shall leave them....and be a FOOL!' Hear that Beloved? Shall BE a FOOL! Now just what does this say to us today Beloved? Shall we start raising partridge eggs to find out? Anybody know the price of partridge eggs?" He laughed to himself. "No I think not.. Ol' Brother Bob was making a joke Beloved, but it is said *laughter* is the sound most favored by *angels*, so *amen* to that..can I hear an amen?"

"AMEN" went the congregation.

"Now as we turn over to uh..to page..we have a bit of a breeze here in the studio Beloved..or perhaps the Lord made me lose my place.." Zeke smiled to himself. "Uh..(flip flip)..his wonderous works..in mysterious ways ..to perform..uh..OK, in the book of *Ezekiel* we read, 'By the river of Chebar..and when the

cheribims went, the wheels went by them... and when
the cherubims lifted up their wings to mount from the
earth, the same wheels also turned not from beside
them...', Beloved, I wish my Cadilac would do *that!*"

This momentarily awakened Zeke's mind,but then
it drifted off into his childhood church days with his
parents in an Episcopal pew, and him drawing on the
bulletin with his Dad's ballpoint pen, but mesmerized
by words of the mysterious Communion hymn...

"Rank on rank the six winged seraphs,
Cherubim with sleepless eye..."

What strange hypnotic imagery appeared in his boy-
brain, and it came out in his drawings. The lady sitting
next to him seemed to think he was possessed. No
wonder he'd turned out like he did.

"Uh..now," continued the radio preacher, "when it
says it turned not from beside them.."(By now he was
quite page-flustered). "it uh..is telling us that..if we
turn to the gospel of Paul...we shall see that...(flip flap
flip)..wheels..uh.. within wheels..uh..."

With a frown Zeke turned it off with a jerk and just
concentrated on the road. He told himself he was
dream-hallucinating, no radio preacher would say
such—then he slugged more cold coffee. Even at that
his eyelids still were getting droopy. Finally he decided to pull off on the exit at Gum Spring, a regular
half way point from C-ville to Richmond, with at least
one convenience store or gas station, he could'nt
remember which.

Just off the interstate he pulled into a mom and pop
store where they sell name brand gas but make their

own sandwiches. He just *had* to get home and get to work. Well, that would have to wait 'til morning he guessed. In the parking space he rested and rubbed his eyes, contemplating another cup of coffee. It's usually good in these places he thought, as a woman came out with some kids, getting into a truck camper. Not bothering to look, he just listened, imagining their faces, as his ears soaked up the patois of your basic po-white people of the road.

" Mama, I ain't changed my underwear since the Maypole, so why I gotta do it now?"

" You better git in that truck an' stop tellin' all th' neighborhood!" she answered. Then a little girl spoke.

" Mama, I wanna yaller Moon Pie, cuz the choc'lit ones look like a new moon which ain't no moon a'tall, Mama why do they make a moon that ain't no moon? I mean it taste good but it ain't no moon, huh Mama? Are you gonna git me a yaller moon pie er ain't cha?" Zeke was smiling at the dialogue as well as his mental pictures.

" No I ain't! Yew had enough now git in the truck lak I tol' ya!" An adult male voice spoke, obviously the father.

"Yew don't want no moon Jamie, it might come roamin' round through the trees lak it did over ta' Patsy's place one night.." Zeke's eyelid twitched.

"Jake, don't tell that story agin..it's awful..that thing like ta skeered Patsy half ta death! Now come on kids I said git in the truck!!" They were running around yelling and screaming, "I'm a big moon an' I'm agonna gitcha! Ahh! EEEEeek!" Suddenly something went BADUMP!—on Zeke's door window. He looked and the boy was spraddled all over the glass, right in his face. That wasn't so much, it was what he was wearing, a big Spiderman mask. Zeke overreacted and fell down on the seat, covering his eyes.

" Jamie! What did I tell yew about botherin' strangers!!?? I'm so sorry sir these yung'uns is a handful sometime.."

" It's alright.." Zeke answered, "I was asleep is all.." He tried to hide his nervous sweat. Thoroughly ill at ease, he started his car quickly, but the woman was rushing back to him. "Here, I want to give yew this, if yew ever are in need of some good fellership where people love ta sing an jes' praise th' Lord..well come on by! We'll be glad ta have ya...I'm sorry 'bout the boy-- *Jamie!* I said GIT IN THE TRUCK!!" Zeke took the little paper flyer and crumpled it on the floor as he lit out of the parking lot, just as another cloud burst crashed and came flooding down, making every-thing bleary in the green and blue neon lights. He was out on the road and driving fast before he realized he didn't know which way he was going. And besides, he never did get his coffee.

He plowed onward through the rain, looking for a sign to see where he was. He should cross Rt.250, unless he was going the wrong way, or maybe he missed it. How far should he keep going like this? He should turn around, (if he could find a good place), find that store and get his coffee. Funny how he al-ways got sleepy halfway between Charlottesville and Richmond—why was that? That was a good way to lose a chunk of time and maybe get—no don't think of that either. His head was nodding, the rain kept pouring, the narrow road winding.

WOOSH!, he just missed that oncoming truck,

better...get off..road. He saw a gravel parking lot appear on the right and pulled in. His head nodded up and down at the dark building before him, he leaned his head against the window as rivers of water distorted his view in the lightning flashes. A small white building with a point on it...must be a church. He remembered a Slim Jim he had stashed away in the glove compartment. Trouble was the door always came lose. After struggling with it, he was more awake and he chewed pleasantly. It helped give him energy. He reached for that damn glove compartment door. You had to slam it shut over and over until the latch would catch. BANG! BANG! BANG! Ba-BANG! BaROOOOOM! Lightning struck very close! The floor before him was illuminated. Words appeared on the crumpled paper the lady had given him.

ALL BELIEVERS NOW
Inter-Faith Tabernacle

Zeke instantly recognized the odd religious organization from the even more oddly placed sign of coincidence he had seen directly opposite the "owl abduction site" on Route 6 outside Colombia, which had spelt out "Alien Tera tera" because of the covering leaves. He sat up-BOOM! CRASH! Another strike, right on the steeple of the little church before him. For a second all was bright as day. The sign over the door read—

ALL BELIEVERS NOW
Inter-Faith Tabernacle

On both it and the flyer were also the same blue logo
of 2 praying hands with starched cuffs and "glowing
radiance" lines around it, and above that, an eyeball
like on the back of the dollar bill, all copied from the
cheapest old clip art which had been around since the
back of 50's comic books. Zeke could do nothing but
stare as the wind and rain howled.

Why were all these crazy coincidences as well as
incidents constantly pursuing him, ever since his visit
to the site of a possible but implausible occurrence in
his early childhood? He had come looking for some
confirmation. Well, he seemed to have gotten that. But
so much else was involved that either did or did not
make sense, depending on what theories you were
espousing.

More thunder and flashing. He simply had to get
back to the main road and get going. But out of the
parking lot's darkness there suddenly shown a light. A
white circle was roaming right and left, up and down
at some distance. Then suddenly it swooped around to
the church and into Zeke's face. A somewhat mechanical voice came over a speaker.

" Please get out of your car with your HANDS
UP!" Zeke stared like a deer. "I REPEAT! GET OUT
OF THE CAR.." Zeke was getting. "Hands over your
head!" A shadowy form with a big hat walked toward
him pointing a gun. "May I ask what you're doing
here?" the officer said.

" I..I was sleeping.." Zeke stammered, and fitfully
reconstructed best he could his attempt to get home as
well as stay awake and getting lost.

" Well ok..see, we've had reports of vandalism at
this church.." the officer said while checking the back

seat of Zeke's car. Being so close with reflections off
his dark glasses, Zeke could now finally make out the
details of his face.

" Sunglasses!" he shouted, "You're wearing sunglasses!"

" Stand still!" The cop waved his weapon close.
"You got a problem with sunglasses?" Zeke thought
quickly of Jerry's warnings.

" N,No..it's just a bad reaction..childhood memory,
a bully I knew wore 'em.."

" Well, I'll take 'em off then...guess it is kinda silly
wearing'em at night..stupid habit..watched too many
Hitchcock pictures or something. Do it for effect I
guess...listen, you take it easy and get yourself a cup
of coffee up by the Interstate..." He was actually very
nice and gave Zeke good directions. Soon he was
healthily heading back on his last leg toward home,
even if his hands did shake a might.

CHAPTER 14
Fandom

Zeke awoke in his familiar ramshackle Fan District apartment full of character that people expect from an artist. Little did they know he dreamed of great immaculate gorgeous halls full of wonders wherein he floated about on an Art Deco hovercraft giving lectures or directing great masterpieces. At least these things were in his mind. The physical reality of his studio to him was not that important, it's what gets on the paper or canvas that's important. At least the place was cozy, and there were his little friends on the drawing board calling to him to bring them to life.

"After coffee and a bagel-" he thought, "hold on to your thought balloons, I'll be back". But over coffee and NPR radio, thoughts came flooding back of his recent experiences. Thankfully the night had been dreamless which was rare for him. He still could'nt quite believe it and worked hard at ratcheting up his mind and drawing hand for a flamboyant ramble by Stupid the Cat.

Stupid stood in the rumble seat of his shiny red 39 Ford, in the middle of nowhere, with Melvin the Gunk

at his side, staring into space. A few roadside stragglers listened to his happy harangue, eating junk food
from a nearby gas station.

" Ladies and gentlemen, fellow creatures and tiny
microbes. *Why are we here?* Why this tiny rock hurl-
ing through space, spiraling around on a galaxy?
Planets and planetoids swirling, electrons buzzing
'round neutrons—to what end? To get to Cleveland in
time for the big game? Then what? Off to the mall? Is
that all? A wise man once said, 'where ever you go in
life, there you are!'"

" Ahem..." Melvin rose a finger.

" Ah,listen fellow travelers! My associate Melvin,
a pilgrim of the cosmos, pitifully marooned on our
ignominious planet deigns to speak! Deigns, I say, and
he's not even Scandinavian! But when he speaks he
speaks volumes! May we all deign to listen!"

" Ahem.." Melvin gurgled his throat and gently
thumped his chest. "The Universe is always right in
front of you."

" Did you hear *that* my friends?" Stupid enthused
enthusiastically, " The Universe is always right in
front of you! What style what grace, what a beautiful
face! Such as it is..What grandiloquence, what leger-
demain! With pearls such as these one can coast to the
middle of next week, and hardly need bread! Surely a
small gift or gratuity is worthy from you my brethren,
for such a nugget, such a gift as, 'The Universe is
always right before you!'" At this point-SPLAT!
Stupid was hit by a hot apple pie. So he turned the
other way. "The Universe is always right before
you!"—SPLAT! This was a peach pie.

Stupid turned again. "Start the car Melvin, we've

had our desert, now we must seek our daily bread!"
The Ford pulled off down the highway, Stupid saving
face while gaining his balance.

Happy with his pencil drawings, Zeke hit the classical
music station and began to ink. Unfortunately the
telephone rang— it was Jerry. Could he come over?
Yes, they needed to talk, but a bit later please?, OK.

"Hey HEY!" greeted Jerry when he finally showed
up. "Wow, this whatcha working on? That's really
cool!" He admired Zeke's cartoon rubber toy collection, art on the wall, and his Grandfather Landover's
wooden patent model for a special kind of hibachi
style barbecue with turning kabob skewers dating
from 1925. Then Jerry saw the painting. "What's
this?" Leaning among the junk, on canvas was the
image of 5 year old Zeke, frozen in time with either
wonder, (or was it dread?) on his face,and standing in
his back yard with giant planets hanging in the sky. It
really caught Jerry's attention.

"Actually the red planet is the moon,"explained
Zeke, "in it's primordial state at the time of the forming of the earth, the other of course is Saturn. It was
painting this, earlier this year that started me on this
whole big escapade...of course the vision itself goes
back to my childhood." Jerry studied it intently.

Finally, over coffee they got down to "the topic".
Jerry was amazed at Zeke's problems on the road, and
agreed something monstrous and all encompassing
was after him, but especially if it was conspiratorial.
Then he went off on his own tangent, "There were
these big buzzards in the road on the way over here
that had a suspicious look. It may mean something."

Zeke stared at him and shook his head, but the two friends continued to rack their brains over various theories.

" It must have to do with the alien I saw," said Zeke, " but was he really an alien?" Jerry was all for it being the government, men in black stuff, with super escalated plastic surgery procedures designed to shock the population into submission. "Wasn't that on the 'Outer Limits'?" Zeke asked.

"Uh, I dunno, but it could still be true, one of those Hollywood writers could've been out driving near Area 51 and these government men stopped him and..uh injected his brain and.." Jerry stopped talking, his face deep in quizzical thought, but soon, after Zeke's cesspool-chase story he re-thought the matter.

" Men in Pink?" he conjectured.

" Look," Zeke said, rousing himself to reality, " I need to get these panels over to my publisher off Broad St., wanna come along?" Jerry was eager as always to be going anywhere. As they made their way to his back alley garage, he thought out loud.

" I wonder just what it could be... I still say the government..Hey we better watch what we say, huh?!" He looked around in all directions. As they reached the corner restaurant, a man with sunglasses suddenly jumped out at them, followed by the tap tap tap of his white red-tipped cane on the sidewalk.

" Hey Rick!"

" Ohhh hi, Zeke! Nice day we're havin' ya think?"

" Oh yes I do!" The blind man passed on, then he muttered, "Com'on Jerry, get a grip!" His friend's legs were now rubberized down to sidewalk level where he clung madly to the wall. They turned the corner of the alley, and Jerry jumped again, for there were 3 cool, more or less artsy guys, one wearing an extraordinarily floppy hat,and another in a bright blue 50's style blazer and golf shoes, with a stand up comic delivery.

" Hey Zeke! How's it goin! Didn't see ya at the Folk Festival!"

" Oh, hi Kevin.."

" Uh, this is my friend Al and his friend Thump!" said Kevin, "He can't always remember his real name so he goes by the sound he makes when he get's up!You know, you gotta get some floor cushions Thump! I can getcha a deal.."

" Thump." said Thump sleepily.

" Anyway Zeke, you goin' to the opening at the 1014 Gallery? Lotsa free food and girls! Hey, ever wonder why so many Galleries these days are named after numbers? They're a bunch of *artists!* They can't *spell!* Ha ha ha!"

" Yeah, I heard that Kevin.."smirked Zeke. "Uh, this is Jerry..."

" Hi ya Pally!" Kevin called anyone he didn't know 'Pally',(and sometimes even those he did, that way he was immediately on intimate terms enough to tell them a joke).He also appeared regularly on a local public access TV talk show with "Immaculate Harold ", under the stage name of Kevin Creosote (a well preserved personality he said), and as a hobby, posed for pictures with anybody and everybody, celebrity or not, real or made of wax. He was doing selfies all by himself 20 years before people thought of the term for themselves.

"Yeah, we gotta go to a meetin'..." continued Zeke, trying to break off the distracted conversation.

" OK, I gotcha..maybe I'll see ya there..hey, don't mind the artist joke..I know you don't take it personally...that is unless you're appearing in person!"

" No..are you kidding?"returned Zeke, taking aim back verbally-- "By the way, was that a joke or just patter?"

" Hey, whattsa matter with patter?"grinned Kevin, " I ordered a whole platter of patter just yesterday..but it's high in cholesterol! Ha ha, you know me, anything for a laugh! Hell, anything for an audience! I even go through alleys!"

" Yeah, check that dumpster back there.."

" Good idea! I hear rats like one liners with their cheese! Good one eh? Maybe I'll use it on the show!"

" Hey, how's Harold doing?"

" He's still Immaculate, but that's *his* conception! Get it?... It's a Catholic joke..see ya!"

Zeke turned heavy lidded to Jerry, "Denizens of the Fan...it's a long story..."

Opening Zeke's alley garage door revealed an avalanche of boxes full of drawings which partially surrounded his car.

" I used to do quite a bit of animation work..." He grabbed a wayward falling cartoon cel. " Here, have a free Scooby-do, I did that for a TV commercial for Zagway Stores that was never made...God, I'm glad I could hide this car off the street.."

" Wow, this is neat! Uh, yeah," agreed Jerry, eagerly grabbing the cel, "Me too, not that there aren't plenty of green '99 Buick Centurys on the road, but who knows what technology the Muckety Mucks got..they can prob'ly read car paint prints,or maybe rust carbon 14 depreciation patterns..or"

"..or even license plates.."

" Yeah, that too.." Jerry shut up for a while as they pulled out and drove through the Fan towards downtown.

They passed through the brightly painted "Uptown" section of town including the Lost Sock Laundry, above which Zeke had got lost many times in the eccentric but legendary parties thrown by Kevin. Then they came to the VCU campus, dominated by the pleasing dome of the Cathedral of the Sacred Heart, and nearby the minarets of "The Mosque", an amazing old theatre built by the Shriners. They made you call it the "Landmark Theatre" these days, or some other name which seemed to change every 10 years or so, but to real Richmonders it was always The Mosque, and had little to do with Islam unless something like "Scheherazade" was being performed.

" Richmond really is a great town, so much character..." mused Jerry looking out the window.

" Yeah, and characters!" added Zeke. "But you're right,so much happened here, I like to call it 'The Crossroads of American History'".

" Hey, I like that.."

" I pitched that idea to City Hall once but they didn't go for it.."

" Well that sounds typical."

" Yeah, maybe it's all for the best, if Council ever got their act together and actually accomplished something they'd probably ruin the place!"

" I'm still getting to know downtown.." said Jerry, " but it's got history going way back doesn't it?."

" Back to the forming of America and beyond... the

first explorations and settlements in the continent.."

" Wow..the Illuminati..I mean the visions they must've had sailing up the James..." Jerry gazed as if into a metaphysical mist.

" Huh?" Zeke had to catch up with his friend's mind, which wasn't always easy. "Oh.. yeah, they've got the oldest Masonic lodge in America,1780 something..and still in continuous operation!"

" Really!!??" Jerry's pop eyes were really popping.

" Yeah, it's down in Shockoe Bottom where all the bars are...you can even have an Illuminati Toddy!" Laughing together,they also passed the large Branch Cabell Library on the VCU campus.

" God ,the hours I've spent in there, what a collection of art books, and everything else.." reminised Zeke.

Jerry's brain lit up. "Hey, *that's* what we need! Since we're doing our own sleuthing, we should do some research!"

" But I'm going downtown, besides what would you look for in there?"

" I dunno, records of close encounters in the Old Dominion I supposed.."

" Hey, you gotta know where to look...you're from Minneapolis, this is my town, lemme think...the Main Public library has a great collection of old newspapers, but you gotta search them yourself...but the State Library..that's the thing, they've got all kinds of obscure records and they're cross referenced..very professional, and they search it for you!"

" OK, great!" Jerry rubbed his hands.

" And, it's near where we're going.." added Zeke, incidentally saving himself some time. They soon passed through the very historic Jackson Ward,passing Maggie Walker's house and museum, and pulled up near the "Milk Bottle Building", which was once the Richmond Dairy with giant bottles on each corner.

Jerry was into the 'pasteurized architecture'. "Don't you miss those old specially built milk trucks?"

" Miss 'em?" answered Zeke, " I designed an intergalactic space vehicle based on one for my strip! I just added these cool fins and.."

" Oh? I didn't catch that issue.." Jerry was suddenly disinterested.

" You haven't caught *any* issue..I'll pick up a few at the publisher's and elucidate you..."

" Ah yes.. I love to be elucidated...much better than water..." said Jerry once again doing Fields. Zeke pointed out the Library up the street as he dashed into the publishers, relieved to be off on business.

" Go on ahead, I'll meet you in the lobby in a few.." Jerry cheerfully started chugging up Marshall Street arms akimbo, his flamboyant reddish-white hair blazing, his aquiline nose furled on high like George Washington's embarrassing younger brother, or like a 19th century vaudeville actor with a pinch too much of snuff, just back from a tour of "the sticks".

CHAPTER 15
In the Halls of Chief Justice

" Boy this is gettin' ta be fun!" Jerry said out loud to himself, oblivious to people staring at him. His enthusiasm carried him along, dissolving all unpleasant recent memories. "Lotsa Founding Father stuff around here! Bet there's Illuminati symbolism at every turn! Better take note of all architectural angles... Hmmm just look at these old bricks..." Actually he had started to trip over the uneven sidewalk, but turned it into historical fascination. There were a few aged buildings interspersed between the modern office towers and parking decks. It was a bright day and still at the lunch hour rush. Many people were out wearing sunglasses. Jerry finally looked up from the bricks and gave a scramble-footed start, not knowing which way to turn. A whole army of sunglassed working stiffs was marching straight toward him! He tried this way—an iron fence, that way--- more people— he'll dash across the street he thought. Finally he settled down, gathering his nerves. After all it was late Summer, and people do wear sunglasses.

Just then a tour bus pulled up and dumped a clutch

of passengers in his face. The crush pushed him diagonally past the sunglassed workers who stopped and
stared after the tour guide blew a little metal pipe,
similar in appearance to a dog whistle.

"This way to the *John Marshall House*." she
yelled. Jerry perked up. "John Marshall House!? Our
first Chief Justice!?" He followed the crowd, smiling
with shrugged shoulders at the halted men on the
sidewalk. The whistle blew again, audible and
weird,but not unpleasant. But one man was holding
his gloved hands to his ears in excruciating pain. Jerry
was just coming abreast to him. The man jerked his
face in recognition. It was the same man! The fly
fisherman! Jerry jostled onward through the gate and
'Sunglasses' pushed violently to get close after him,
but the whistle blew once more,and he grabbed his
ears and fell back as Jerry was swept spinning among
the tourists up the steps and into the house.

The old Federalist style brick structure was instantly
quiet within, except for the clonking of shoes on the
ancient oak floor. The interior was amazingly light
and spacious. As high as the ceilings were, the front
door was small by comparison, equal to modern
ones,with a small vestibule for an entrance way. This
caused a bottleneck for which Jerry was exceedingly
thankful, as he worked to get as much distance between he and that man as possible, while the on-duty
docent took charge of guiding the tour.

" Welcome to the John Marshall House!" she
beamed in a slightly base nasal tone. "I'm Ginny and
I'll be your tour guide.." Jerry put on his widest grin
while sidling over among the tightly packed crowd to

the farthest part of the room. " This two story brick house was built in the 'Federalist' period of architecture, which is known as the first true period or style of the then young nation of the United States of America..." Jerry was up against a door in the far corner, and gently tried the knob which clicked with a minute squeak.

" Oh, sir please wait, we'll be going to the dining room in a minute!" Jerry raised his hands with an apologetic grin. The bottle neck from outside was still funneling through the tiny vestibule and into the large parlour. He could now see Sunglasses jostling and glaring at him with an emotionless scowl beneath his bull dog nose.

" Uh, Welcome to the John Marshall House! Please keep moving..This large house is located in the heart of old Richmond's fashionable 'Court End' district which includes the Valentine Museum, the White House of the Confederacy and other historic buildings about a block or two away...yes come right in.. there's plenty of room.." Sunglasses was making his way to the front of the crowd which would give him freer access to cross the parlour. Jerry doubted he would pay attention to the docent's warnings, so felt again for the door, luckily it was now cracked open, which relieved him no end.

Peeking to the other side of the door in the dining room, he saw another group was moving on to the library. Another docent was straightening a plastic chicken on the dining table and saw the open door. She quickly pushed it shut with a loud CLACK! Jerry jerked his fingers away and checked if they were all still there. The parlour docent gave him a look as she

continued. " John Marshall is best known as the
'Great Chief Justice' for his role in creating the modern Supreme Court. He lived here with his wife Polly
and their family from1790 until his death in—" Sunglasses was getting excited like a cat about to pounce,
which made Jerry try to jump out of his own skin with
nervous gestures, causing perturbed reactions from the
people close around him. The docent raised her voice
to a menacing pitch.

"His *Death in 1835!*" The docent triumphantly
finished her sentence. She glared at Jerry, then back at
Sunglasses who was creating his own disturbance as
he jostled once more. "Damn the noise," thought
Jerry, and forced himself through the door. He whirled
into the dining room, picking up plastic food and
dropping it as he flailed about for his balance.
He ended up in the hallway by the stairs. There he
saw a door opening toward the rear kitchen serving
area, but between him and it was a woman dressed in
a huge bustle style historic gown that totally filled the
doorway. The side door was locked, but before him
was one to the library, partially filled with the other
tour group.

The docent in this room was also talking about the
Chief Justice. "In fact Mr. Marshall was so unassum-
ing in his appearance and belief in equality and the
common man, that once a high toned merchant saw
him at the market in Richmond, tossed him a copper
and asked him carry a huge turkey on his back for
several blocks. This Mr. Marshall did without com-
plaint, the merchant learning only later that his turkey
had been delivered by the Chief Justice of the United
States!" Jerry was intrigued and joined in the laughter,

when he noticed Sunglasses shoving slowly into the room from the opposite door. He ducked back to the hall but noticed his pursuer did the same going the other way, obviously intending to catch him by way of the dining room.

At a loss as to which way to go, he tip toed up the uniquely quaint and attractive staircase. At the top landing he was met by a man with dark hair and heavy eyebrows in historic dress and bearing an uncanny resemblance to the Chief Justice's portrait on the wall.

"How do! And what may I inquire my good sir, are you in search of?"

" Uh.. I guess you could say my freedom.." stammered Jerry.

" *Freedom!*" shouted the man, " A most marvelous word as well as a goal, an idea, *and* a birthright! One which every man should seek! Of course freedom is relative, it always is. And *Justice!* The handmaiden of Freedom, (she is quite blind you know, as to who you are), but!—holds aloft her scales with which to weigh the evidence as it applies to the *law!* Of Gravity! A little joke there you see, uh... very little..but Justice is no laughing matter! Nor is Freedom! Now I perceive the freedom you seek sir is of the most urgent kind!?" Jerry nodded eagerly,if not paranoiacally. "Is it a call from nature? No I thought not, come my dear sir, and I shall show you a special egress from this structure which may be of service!"

He led him around the corner to a smallish door in the wall which opened on a tightly crooked back stairway. "Get thee hense..as I myself have an entrance to make, poor actor-reenactor that I am, groveling among the citizens for me daily bread!" With this he reached behind a door and hoisted a huge plastic turkey upon his back and proceeded grandly down the stairs. "Ahem! *Polly!!* Do I perceive we have visitors?" Jerry was placing his foot through the doorway when he caught a glimpse of Sunglasses starting up the main stairs. But his nibs Mr. Marshall shouted at him with vigor as he brandished his turkey.

"Avast thar ye vandal! What business have ye upon the stairwell of me own house!!? *Be off!!*" It was a loud and terrible scuffle, which perfectly covered the clumsy rattles Jerry made on his way down the dark stairs. At first a few twists and blind snags going down, his eyes finally adjusted until THUMP! He hit bottom. Not only had he gone to the first floor but all the way to the wine cellar. This was even more private, thought Jerry as he found the stairs to the cellar door leading up to the backyard. He could still hear Justice John wacking Sunglasses with the turkey.

Even so he rushed out back through the garden to a modern office building just next door. A great screeching from above startled him, as if a vengeful eagle was on the attack. But soon he realized it was an electronic digi-recording designed to keep pigeons off Mr. Marshall's house, (not that he seemed to need much help where birds were concerned).

The steps up to the office building were on a strange modern artsy angle with pointed edges, but he entered it undercover amid a small crowd of business men. Suddenly a lady in uniform accosted him, "Put your valuables in the box! NO CELL PHONES! Put'em back in your car!" Before him was a security lineup for walking through a scanning device.

"Hey!"Where am I?" said Jerry.

"What case are you with sir?"

"Case? I don't have any luggage..is this the State Library?"

"It's the John Marshal Courts Building sir..step outside to your left, go 2 blocks South and turn to your left..NO CELL PHONES I SAID !!" Jerry stumbled back out, tippy toeing down and around the pointy stairs, and hurried up the block. On Broad St., he found the impressive facade of the Virginia State Library and hurried up the steps.

CHAPTER 16
In a State of Libraryness

Zeke paced back and forth near the circulation desk of the State Library. What was keeping Jerry? Suddenly his familiar spraddle legged form was hurrying toward him.

"You would'nt believe what just happened to me!"

" Hey, remember who you're talking too.." They quickly found a table and Jerry reenacted it all, blow by blow. Anybody watching would think he was giving a Punch and Judy show without the puppets.

" We better watch out for him showing up in here.." said Zeke.

" Don't I know it! We better do what we're doing quick!"

" What are we doing?"

" You know..research...But where do we start?"

" Com'on, these guys at the desk are incredibly helpful." They got up and went over. A very organized and efficient gentleman listened as the boys posed as your basic pie-eyed UFO enthusiasts looking for old reports of sightings and other encounters over the years in Central Virginia. Jerry mostly nodded and looked over both shoulders.

"Oh..UFOs..," replied the laconic librarian, " yes we have a number of records on the subject..but shouldn't you be heading for Roswell?" He caught their looks of consternation and shifted his tone. "Actually it *is* incredibly interesting, I watch those things on History Channel all the time!" He went off to the stacks, while Zeke and Jerry did some searching on a nearby computer.

" Ya know, my cousin saw one out in Sandston in the East End, back in the 60s...I wanna try searching that..." Nothing came up. " He never reported it. It's hard to get him to talk about it even to this day.."

" Maybe we could interview him!"enthused Jerry.

" Yeah..maybe.."

SCHHHhhhhhhGLUMP! Jerry jumped and Zeke whipped around. It was a vacuum tube delivery behind the desk, with a sort of cart containing a book.

" Huh..space age technology.." grinned Jerry.

" I think it's neat, I'm glad they still have those.."

" I guess I'm still a bit jumpy..." Jerry had the jitters and also began to sniff.

" Yeah, maybe we can wait over there, in case of you-know-who..." They found a table behind a bookshelf, and Jerry went over to a street window to keep an eye out.

" No sign of him yet, but I never realized how many sunglasses people wore! *SNIFF!*" All the patrons in the area gave him a stern look, so he tried sniffing quietly.

" Hopefully no more than one pair at a time.." Zeke added as he picked up a newspaper.

His eye landed on an article in the "Science Today" segment--

"Astronomers and astro physicists agree
 that all stars and galaxies that can be seen today
represent just 4.9% of the Universe. The other 95.1%
percent cannot be accounted for, but can be inferred
by the gravitational influence on the bits we can
see, planets, stars etc. These mysterious substances
are often referred to as dark matter and dark energy."

"Ha!"said Zeke out loud, but quickly got quiet
when people looked up. "I had a conversation with a
scientist over lunch about this once at NASA when
my uncle was giving me a tour of the place. This guy
told me about this missing 96 percent,and I said,'Well,
it looks like you've discovered God!' Know what he
said? '*Now* you sound like *Oral Roberts!*' I repeat—
Ha!"

Jerry was interested. "You like Oral Roberts? Or
liked ...he's dead isn't he?"

" 'Like' is correct, he's still around somewhere,
just in another dimension I'm sure, giving those wild
sermons of his I suppose...probably with spectacular
visual aids, such as inflating his head or turning
green..I wonder who his congregation is? No, as much
as I like to make fun of goofy hell fire preachers, I
usually respect them for their intense spirit and
belief..and *faith* in that belief. At least they're not
afraid to seek for truth! What did Jesus call it? 'Thirst-
ing for Righteousness'? And 'blessed are they'? You
know...and everybody today on TV talks about faith,
or faith based whatever..it's not just faith, *that* can
mean anything, but faith in *what?* Hell, Hitler had
faith! But these scientists, are so damned rational,

they say everything's in the brain...just neurons flashing or something..even with all the facts they have in front of them, can you get even *one* of them to at least speculate on what lies in the Great Beyond? No! So again I say HA!"

Other patrons of the library were casting perturbed looks in their direction, so Jerry was now trying to get Zeke to shush. "Oh, sorry...ha.." he added softly, smiling apologetically to the other tables.

" Boy you got some rants in you..ever think of having your own talk show?"

" No, I don't like talking that much...vocal chords get tired..seems everyone's always talking at *me!* "

" Dustin Hoffman! Jon Voight!"

" Yeah, I like that movie..I dunno..I think a lot..and the world seems to be going madder and madder, I just react to it sometime.....and explode!"

" Me, I talk all the time.." mused Jerry, "but don't say anything..I'm sort of a flow-er out-er..I guess you're more of a bottler upper...with fizz!"

"Hey it looks like our books are ready!" said Zeke. They got up to leave, but Jerry looked again at the window. There he saw Sunglasses's head peering in with a determined smirky grin. But that was 20 feet up! He looked again and he was gone.Jerry nervously went over to the window and checked anyway. Nothing. His face twitched all over.

" I've got too much imagination too..." he said with a sniff. The books proved interesting but inconclusive. As they flipped through them taking notes, Jerry said, "Ya know, I don't think that Sunglasses guy is real!"

" I dunno, he seemed pretty real to me.."

" I mean not human..and it's like we know something he doesn't want us to know..."

Zeke looked up from his writing. "But why us?"

" We're on to something.."

" But what? My feelings about *them* have always been good..strange and mysterious, but basically good...I think..I hope.."

" Maybe these are the *bad* ones!" said Jerry, leaning over with his big eyes. Zeke's mental images of what might have happened on that shrouded night of early memory on the road came back to him. A greyish glowing light in the farm land beyond the railroad tracks and the car. He and his family somehow trundled off, or levitated over the tractor road and the grass...to what? Unspeakable experiments? Protuberant probes? He preferred not to dwell on it.

They jotted down several interesting cases from the books, including an amazing one Zeke remembered, about a giant pyramidal shaped ship of multicolored lights that was seen over I 95 south of town. He then told Jerry about his cousin Tommy, and what happened in Sandston out near the airport, how a giant bright light about 100 ft. across, came down on he and his teenaged friends who were out smoking in a field one night.."

" What were they smoking?" said Jerry.

" *Marlboros*.." glared Zeke. "Anyway, it was so bright you could pick up a pin. There was no sound except a faint whirring or humming. They stood dumbfounded a few seconds, staring up at the huge round shape, then they lit out running as fast as they could. He came to the front door yelling-- 'Mama come look at this thing!'" Zeke's Aunt Lavinia saw it too, she'd told him later she saw a light whooshing across the sky. Zeke could always get his aunt to talk about it, though she was slightly dismissive, not knowing exactly what she saw. But Tommy, he was now very closed mouthed about the whole thing. Thing is, both he and his Mom were people that normally loved to talk.

Finally the boys were losing energy for research, and Zeke suggested that Jerry take the books back to the desk. "Don't we get to take them home?"

" No, is this strictly a reference library.." Jerry carried them back to the librarian.

" Well..did we obtain some stimulating findings?" smirked the librarian.

" Yes we did, thank you..."

" Are you enjoying Richmond? You're not from around here are you.."

" Does it show that much? Actually I've been here 9 years..but yes I'm enjoying it very much..the history! I was just over at the John Marshall house, fascinating!"

" Oh! My wife works there as a docent..I volunteer myself sometime with some of the programs..."

Jerry lit up. "Ya know, I was really impressed with their historic reenactors, especially John Marshall himself, so lifelike! Very entertaining! Be sure and tell your wife.."

" Reenactors? But there *are no* reenactors at the Marshall House!"

" No?.. But I just spoke to him..you must be mistaken.."

" Well I think I should know..we've been there for years..I spoke to her a moment ago during lunch, she

said there was a minor disturbance in the hall, someone had low blood sugar I believe..might that've been
you?" Jerry made his excuses and hurried after Zeke
who was near the exit.

"Zeke..Zeke, wait up!" he shouted, which was
followed by a resounding *SHUSH!* from everyone in
the library.

CHAPTER 17
A Bill on the Hill

Zeke and Jerry nervously made their way back to the
car. Jerry felt danger lurked at every turn but Zeke
was more at ease in the city, feeling protected by the
crowds. He was most amazed by what the librarian
had said to Jerry, in fact he wasn't sure what to think.
He did get a cell phone call from Minnie, who was
still up the country but said she was coming back to
town.

" What's all this stuff about?" she asked, "I
couldn't get much out of Jerry.. you got me frightened!"

" Well nothing to worry too much about...yet,
anyway, we'll explain it tonight.."

" I'm pulling out of the driveway now, maybe I can
try to pick up some impressions!"

" Well maybe..hey, you're not going to channel
while driving are you!!?"

" Oh silly, it's not like using a cel phone..I just may
get some intuitive thoughts..don't worry! It's very
relaxing!"

" Well, don't get too relaxed..it's bad believe me..and watch out for pink cars!"

" Whaaat??"

" It's just something..never mind I'll tell you later.."

" Oh pooie, you guys have fun and I'll see you soon." They planned to get together that evening. That made Zeke quite happy, taking his mind off things somewhat. They turned on the radio. In 2 minutes they were informed about crazy politics, riots, murders, celebrities' slip-ups, earthquakes, Middle East warfare, and terrorist threats in the U.S., plus a very short blurb about Global Warming.

"Ahhh, everything's going kablooie, not just us..somehow comforting in a weird way.." He smacked off the dial.

" Hey, let's drive around Capitol Hill!" said Jerry as they got back along Broad Street.

" What for? It's out of our way!"

" I want to check for Masonic symbolism!"

" Boy you sure get over your post traumatic stress quick!"

" Well look at you! And you a knee jerk New Age believer! But I tell ya, this stuff excites me, now if we could just get our own reality show..."

" Well..yeah, but sometime I'd like to just forget about it..crawl up in a shell at my drawing board..." They passed by Mr. Jefferson's Capitol, another "American Acropolis", in fact, the first one.

" Just look at the apex of the Capitol roof! I'm sure it aligns with something!" drooled Jerry.

Zeke stared at him. "There's an apex alright...but it's not on the roof..sure it points, it points over the 9th

St. Bridge to Southside! Look, if the Senate and the House of Delegates would just keep *themselves* in line I'd be happy.." But Zeke couldn't help admiring it as they drove by below the "Hill" on Bank St.

" Ya know, they did do a pretty good job of remodeling the old place, although I do miss the old magnolia trees that once stood—AAAHH!" A flash of early afternoon sun reflected off a Capitol window and into Zeke's eyes. The car spun out of control.

" I gotcha!"shouted Jerry, grabbing the wheel.Then Zeke, regaining his sight, reacted and grabbed it back.

"Hey whaddya doing!!" He shouted,while swerving and struggling, as well as avoiding an oncoming sprinkler truck,which resulted in them turning suddenly into a parking deck. Before they could back up, another car pulled in behind them.They had no choice but to take a ticket from the machine thingy, raising the cross bar and drive inside.

"Wow! What caused *that?*" said Jerry. Zeke explained about the window flash but with all that had happened, wondered if it had been somehow by design.

Jerry wiped his brow. "You mean a near miss design!" After sitting still for a while in a quiet parking space with nothing else happening, Jerry said he'd always wanted to tour the State Capitol building, and having a big chunk of the afternoon left to fill, that's what they did.

Since 911 the Capitol had undergone extensive renovation,adding much space and security to the complex, but all underground. On the surface Jefferson's historic architecture was undisturbed, but now one had to enter down the hill on Bank St.,

through a vault-like chamber of multiple and highly
polished security. This made for a long subterranean
staircase and escalator rising tier upon tier through
modern high tech "alabaster halls", like a slightly
futuristic Egyptian tomb. This of course inflamed
Jerry's imagination into a high octane burn.

" Wow, this is amazing--Holy of Holies! Do you
suppose there is a forbidden throne room? Probably
this floor opens up and..and ,an all seeing Eye looks at
you and.."

" Oh Jerry, cut it out..It's all depressing to me!"

" Depressing??"

" Yeah! I used to just walk up the hill on my lunch
hour, say hi to a state trooper by a door, walk down
the hall past grinning senators glad handing on the
way out of the marble latrine, a laid back guide or
two, and step into "Chicken's Cafe" and get a chicken
salad sandwich while politicians joked, smoked and
laughed with reporters or whoever. There'd be some
wise and wrinkled old doorman standing around, and
you felt like the good ol' country was bopping
along...more like a visit to a country courthouse,
than....I dunno..this is a Xanadu's Crypt-slash-vault-
slash parking deck ..."

" Oh," said Jerry.

" Yeah, that's the way it was..and sleepy people on
their lunch breaks lying under the trees. Did you know
a baby squirrel climbed in my pants pocket one time?"

" HA HA ha ha! Was he after your nuts!?

" No, seriously, he crawled right in,like I was his
favorite log...it was..beautiful.."

"Really? Uh...Well, that's some sort of sign don't
ya think?"

" Sign? No, it was just good 'ol home town America!"

" But built by Illuminati Foundering..uh Founding Fathers eh?!"

" Ha..you had it more right the first time! Did you know Patrick Henry had a mad wife he kept in the cellar? Or that Ben Franklin joined the "Go to Hell" club?

" What?"

" You know, a bunch of lads hire a prostitute and.....yeah I met Franklin's direct descendant in the Y locker room, he told me..he looked like him too.."

They passed through an ultra modern/post modern glass-inclosed rampway affair and suddenly found themselves inside the old building, just as it had always been. "This is more like it..I just mean I like some *warts* with my history..some down-to-earthness and age in my country, I wanna smell the horse manure and the boxwoods..*that's* America.."

" Ya mean like George Washington's wooden tceth?"

" Yeah.. sorta.." continued Zeke, " but this 21st Century keeps slicking things up with plastic, high tech and world power military deployment..aps and SUVs..over-crowded sub divisions ..build build build, smart phones video games...Where's *Nature* for God's sake!!"

" I can go along with that, I think.." agreed Jerry.

" Speaking of Nature, let's use the giant porcelain urinals...nothing like it." They proceeded into the black and white tiled room.(Actually the hall they'd been walking down was tiled the same way but with bigger tiles). There before them with welcoming

grace, stood a row of full length, down to the floor
early 20th century style porcelain receptacles with
appropriately cute chrome levers on top with brass
collars, perfect for complete relaxation in the downtown stress of the urban environment. While doing
their thing, Jerry was looking all around except where
it was not a good idea to look.

An old Senatorial type with iron grey hair was
finishing up and washing his hands. He puffed and
blowed at the mirror in his rumpled grey suit which he
adjusted with many a creative motion, gave them a
deep toned "How yall t'day!", and with a rye, crinkled
and yellow toothed grin, which must have seen many
a down-home fund raiser barbecue or shad planking.

"Yall boys be sure an vote now *heah?*" He snorted
loudly and headed toward the door.

" Uh, we're in the booth right now!" said Jerry.

" Right you are! Heh heh heh!" The old guy's face
lit up. "Be sure an' pull the lever and close up when
yer through! Heh, heh Heh!"

The boys vociferously agreed as the old politician
wiped his hands on the circular towel gizmo and
slammed the big door on the way out.

" Nobody wearing sunglasses in here!" said Jerry.

" Nope!" said Zeke.

After ascending the small old stone spiral stairway
which was tucked tightly in the corridor wall,(a
Jefferson design feature no doubt) the boys found
themselves on the main floor. Several political and
legal types are moving past in one direction.

"The House must be in session.." said Zeke,
"let's check it out.." They hurried along with the
crowd.

"I *think* it's the House..or maybe it's the Senate..no that's back that way.."

" One's as good as the other!" Said Jerry.

" But the House is more fun to watch..more theatrical!" Indeed it was the House as they saw from the sign above the door while the guards directed them upstairs to the gallery. As they took their seats, words of oratory rose from the floor below.

" The chair recognizes Delegate Hanneran..."

" Mista Speaker, in reference to House Bill 743-B, I wish to add that in my humble opinion as a delegate, I have for many yeeahs seen many attempts by the legislachore... to effectively secure drinking water for the region in question, and to make viable in a timely fashion the construction of dams and spillways et-cet'tra et-cet'tra for the service of owah ever growing communities in the south eastern portion of the State.."

Zeke and Jerry recognized their iron-grey-haired and rumpled suited politician from the men's room, making this impassioned harangue. Jerry was so excited to be within such an hallowed hall of potential Illuminati-ish conspiracy laden intrigue, not to mention the halls of governmment itself, that he was like a kid on a school trip. He twitched and sniffed himself into such a frenzy that he suddenly let out an enormous--BELCH.

"Sorry, I didn't mean to bring that up!" He whispered.

"Bring it up again and we'll vote on it!"returned Zeke, also in a giggly mood. The gallery guards stared meanly at them with an intense "shush" motion in their fingers. The boys also became aware of several

people with environmental posters not far from them
in the gallery. One nearby smiled and handed them
some literature about their cause to save an entire
system of river wetlands from being destroyed. They
smiled back and looked at the pamphlets which, while
being interesting also seemed bogged down with more
legalese than the boys were really ready to digest.
Meanwhile the iron grey delegate continued.

"We cannot allow, nor should we allow the interests of a few uh... *tree huggers*, nor the lives of a few
obscure short tailed owls..or purple eared galoots et-
cet'tra et- cet'tra to dissuade us from owah duty to an
important industry or the sug'nifigunt and ever expanding public that it serves, or will need to serve
later in this century! Growth is *key* heah!

" HA!!" exploded Zeke, with no control over his
mouth. Black stares were shot from the gallery
guards, making it clear such out bursts would not be
tolerated. However several among the environmental-
ist delegation were smiling broadly and nodding
toward him. Meanwhile Delegate Hanneran regained
his oratorical composure after a brief moment of
beflusterment.

" Uhh.... Ever expanding growth is how our
economy..well..grows! So I further move that we quit
shilly- shallyin' and bush-beat'n and a lot of other
funny folderol an' take a vote to defeat this new in-
junction which will do nothing but further..uh..dam up
the damn project so to speak...(sporatic laughter from
the floor)..." Zeke was holding his mouth hard while
Jerry smiled wide-eyed at the guards.

Hanneran continued, " What is our land, owah
forests and streams, owah resources, except just that!

Resources!..to be used and exploited as we see fit for owah Commonwealth's domestic and industrial improvement, just as God has given us *dominion* over the beasts of the field, so must the Old *Dominion* dominate it's resources as it sees fit!..uh, For the public good of course!" At this Zeke let out a terrific barrage of coughing and hacking so bad that the entire assembly stared up at him, and Hanneran lost his audience completely. While the guards glared, Zeke and Jerry hurried off the gallery floor, Jerry apologetically waving as well as patting Zeke on the back and handing him a tissue.

Out in the hall Jerry was greatly relieved, "Boy, I thought the Men in Black would come through a secret panel any minute and get us!" Zeke however was steaming.

" I'd like to sick them on Hanneran..imagine the crap coming out his mouth..dominion over beasts of the field..I'd like ta make him sit in a *cow flop!*"

" Quiet! Remember where we are!" whispered Jerry, "Halls of government et-cetera et-ceteraaah...."

" So what?" Zeke shouted, "I'm a citizen..a tax payer!" Jerry tried hard to shush him, as they were approaching a blase' looking guard at the information booth.

" The way I see it," he continued, "it's my God Given Right to stand in the halls of my Capitol and complain about it! *Right!?*" he said to the guard as they passed.

Who, without batting an eye said, " Yessir..as long as you don't throw a hissy fit, then we have to arrest you..." With a couple of double takes, the boys proceeded to the main rotunda.

CHAPTER 18
In Hallowed Halls with Talking Walls

Jefferson's fine "internal dome room" opened before them. Zeke's architect grandfather had once proposed adding an external cupola to the roof thus continuing the dome theme to the roof, but as much as Zeke admired his work, he was glad the plan had not been adopted, thus preserving the purity of Jefferson's greco-roman temple concept, emblematic of democracy and worthy of the grand new experiment known as America.

A tour guide was finishing her talk on Houdon's famous statue of Washington in the center, considered an exact likeness, which had been carved to exact measurements of the General himself.

"In later years when Lafayette returned as an old man in 1824 and saw it he said, 'That *was* the man'." She took them into the old assembly hall. "Before you is a statue of Robert E. Lee, facing north and standing on the exact spot where he received the leadership of the armies of the Confederacy..." Zeke and Jerry hung back and assumed sole audience of the now hushed rotunda, the better to bathe in it's historic aura. The amber gold rounded ceiling with elegant aged decorative motifs of brown and blue framed Washington as you looked up, standing erect as the perfect example of the responsible and responsive citizen of this new invention, a republic. He was the man who had been cheerfully offered a crown but had refused it in favor of being a servant of the People.

The artistry of the marble sculpture was equal to it's subject. You felt almost as if you were meeting the man, who might just as easily be a highly regarded uncle or grandfather figure of your own home town, even a next door neighbor. Zeke naturally thought of his own next door neighbor when he was a kid, "Mr. G" who looked the part, and who filled in the roll of grandfather in his young life because his own had died long before he was born. " Hi Sonny Boy!" He would always say cheerfully, and teach him earthy wisdom while hoeing his garden. He was a member of one of those Masonic spin-off organizations, "The Woodmen of the World", and had worked at the Federal Reserve.

When Jerry heard of this his eyes widened, full of delicious conspiracy expectations. But to Zeke, these things bespoke of an old time shining quality of upright goodness and fair play that you naturally felt when you met such a man. Those times were not perfect but there was a lot to recommend them, especially when you had known people who had kept such flames alive. Although the cultural upheaval of the 60's had tarnished such realms as old and stogy, even in some eyes corrupt or evil, it was also a link to the spirit of 76, and good yeomen of the land who had lived by it.

This room with it's fine design and the surrounding

statuary naturally imparted this feeling to whoever stood there through an unspoken language of beauty and balance, that needed no speech. Even Jerry's pop culture giddiness was quelled as he approached another Houdon piece facing his old friend Washington, a fine bust of the French General, "America's bon ami".

" Hey! It's Lafayette!" he said as if he were real. "..says here that Virginia commissioned two of 'em, one for us, one for them, but one was destroyed in the French Revolution!"

The thought brought home to Zeke just how fragile Liberty can be. " 'You have a Republic Madam, if you can keep it!'" he said aloud.

"Who said that? Washington?" asked Jerry, assuming Zeke was reading an inscription.

"No, Franklin, at Independence Hall.."

"Oh yeah, I've been there..."

The two continued to scrutinize each sculpture as they stood in comparative silence. As Zeke read the details of the carved inscription, including Washington's exactly replicated height of 6' 2.5", he could 've sworn he heard a whispered voice.

"*We're on a mission..*"

He looked up and over at Jerry, who turned and looked at him.

"You say something?"

"No, did you?"

They went back to their reading, but Zeke glanced at Washington's head as he did. It seemed to be turning back into position, as if it had been looking at him. Zeke shook his head and looked over at Jerry, who was also staring quizzically at him. They drew closer, and soon realized they had heard the same thing. While looking about Jerry pointed to a man smiling down at them from the upstairs gallery.

"It's J-John Marshall!" he shouted, as the leaning figure disappeared. He suddenly ran toward the stairs. Zeke could do nothing but follow. They had to slow down near the guard, but soon were rushing up the tightly winding stairwell. On the upper floor gallery were many painted portraits but no live people. They immediately circled the gallery and roamed about the various corridors available. Upon returning to the spot where Mr. Marshall had been standing there now stood an ordinary looking man in clerical collar.

" Reverend Wall!" exclaimed Zeke.

" Why if it isn't Ezekiel, what a pleasure to see you, how is your mother?"

" Oh, very well..she still remembers your visit to St. Barnabas."

" And I her visit to St.Timothy's along with you and your charming aunt who was quite up in years I believe?

" About 99 I think, she's since passed on at 102 and a half!"

" Really, well she didn't look it..."
Jerry held his tongue with a very arched eyebrow as Zeke exchanged these surprising pleasantries.

" Oh, Rev. Wall, this is my friend Jerry."
Jerry shook hands, "Hello Wall.."
Ensuing laughter and expressions of "I get that a lot" from the reverend, led to talk about his little church in Fluvanna which Zeke's grandfather, (son of the one that did the plantation house) had designed, and further remembrance of the charming visit, and how

things were around Bremo Bluff, not far from Colombia. Finally he invited Zeke and his friends to an
ecumenical religious jamboree and cook out in a few
weeks, to be held at the church grounds including the
historic Slave Chapel nearby, which was now a landmark.

" We're actually joining forces with some of the
evangelical churches for this, to celebrate the uh,
cross culture of Christianity shall we say..you know,
God is God, the same God made us all, whatever you
call him...or her!..and just have a good time with
prayer and good music...and *food!* Don't forget the
food!"

" Hey, sounds good! Should be some nice fall
weather by then.." said Zeke, smiling blandly, but also
half interested.

" Yes! Here, I have a flyer! There will be gather-
ings all over Fluvanna and Albemarle throughout the
month!" Zeke took it into his pocket with barely a
glance. After saying polite farewells, the boys decided
it was time to start heading home. Outside they
walked downhill through the Capitol Hill grounds.

Zeke shook the flyer in Jerry's direction, "You
might like to come to this..my grandfather's little
church is very pretty, stained glass, brick, columns,
and an octagonal steeple.."

" Ahhh, octagons! Another Masonic motif!!" They
walked on down in silence as the hallowed halls re-
ceded behind them in the gathering gold of the afternoon sun.

" Well, I'm not sure what this visit was all about,"
said Jerry, "but it was kinda fun.."

" Yeah..these 'signs' or 'events' we keep having..

sometimes I'm not sure.."

" Yeah, me too, it's like something's trying to reach out to us..."

" I still don't know if it's real..." said Zeke.

" But it's happening to *both* of us..."

" Mass hypnosis?" They were now passing the Edgar Allan Poe monument. "Maybe *he* could explain it.." Further down the hill they passed the aged bell tower, once used to ring the alarm or call to meetings for old Richmond.

" Maybe we've been hypnotising ourselves, together." said Zeke, "I remember as a college student sneaking through a fence into old Hollywood Cemetery at night with a friend. Boy, we got ourselves worked into a fright frenzy! You know how Gothic that place is, well there was a bright moon, but there was also this deep deep shadow on the walk way. Well, we got to calling it a "dark void", and saying 'who knows what' was waiting in there.."

" Yeah! There's a similar cemetery in Pittsburg!" enthused Jerry, "All Victorian...just like a Dracula picture!..or was that 'Night of the living Dead'?"

" Well, we got so frozen and worked up about this 'Black Void'...I don't think we ever went in there..in fact I don't even remember getting out!" All this time Zeke was gesticulating with wild hand gestures while holding the flyer. "We ought to go to this jamboree of Rev. Wall's. It will be something fine and sane for a change, well organized and.."

" And don't forget the *food!*" added Jerry with zest.

" Right, the food!"

As Zeke gestured enthusiastically to the sky, an evening gust of breeze caught the flyer out of his hand, and it angled off, up and down onto the walk-way before them. Rushing to get it, the crumpling of the paper unfolded just enough to reveal the bold text of one of the group participants in the ecumenical jamboree. There again was that blue ink logo of the praying hands and the all seeing eye. It read of course:

ALL BELIEVERS NOW
Inter-Faith Tabernacle

Zeke stood rock still. "It's starting again."

CHAPTER 19
Uncommon Communication

The Fan looked splendid in the afternoon September light as they drove back. Late Victorian houses looked their red bricked best, like stained glass windows in the slanting sun. Tree lined cobblestone shadows defined a depth of richness to the neighborhood's ambiance. Students were everywhere around VCU, mostly freshmen getting acclimated to their first semester world, over dressed and carrying superfluous art supplies they may never use. However, Jerry and Zeke mostly stared straight forward trying to think of what to do.

" Makes ya wish for simpler times.." mused Jerry as some particularly cute co-eds crossed their path at a stop light.

" Yeah.. but I'm looking forward to seeing Minnie tonight, it was really great to get back with her again..like good ol' times.."

Jerry got excited all at once " Hey! That's right! She could maybe do one of her psychic things..and contact one of *our* things!..Or beings whatever... They're supposed to be extremely pyschic! And she's *good* ya know! But of course you know.."

" Yeah... I guess.. I'll have to ask her." Zeke agreed reluctantly. He had other things on his mind.

At Zeke's garage, Minnie walked up as they were putting away his car.

" I remember this garage, it hasn't changed a bit!" Surprised, Zeke dove into a hug while Jerry stood by slightly embarrassed. " Zeke gave me a Scooby Do!" He said proudly as he held up his cartoon cel.

" I want one too!" shouted Minnie.

" Are you kidding, you want the entire garage to fall down? I was lucky to grab that one!"

" Awww.."

" Let's get inside, I'll draw ya a Care Bear or something..."

" Where'd you get your talent Zeke?" asked Jerry.

" People always ask that..it was pretty much always there..I watched Dad paint of course, but it always came naturally, it's improved over the years, but I was always 'the kid who could draw'".

" That's because you did it in previous lives.." said Minnie nonchalantly.

" Yeah, I guess so.."

" What, reincarnation?" Jerry's eyes were bugging. " Now I don't believe in *that!*"

" Of course we do!" Minnie shot back defensively, " Many many lives in many places, races and different sexes!"

" Whoa now that's going a bit *far!*" Zeke stood by with a wry smile as his friends' metaphysical argument heated up in quite comic fashion, there in the light of a truly otherworldly sunset which shone down the old garages and trash cans of the alley. But on a surge of near-rant energy he suddenly raised is voice.

" *Wait*, wait a minute Jerry! You mean to tell me, that you believe in aliens, UFOs, shadow government,

Masonic conspiracies, men in black,and who knows what, even android chipmunks probably, but you can't get that brain of yours to even consider the transmigration of the soul?"

" No!"

" Jerry, if everybody believed in reincarnation there'd be a lot less fear, greed, hatred..and, and other problems!"

" Well *I'm* not greedy!"

" I didn't say you were!"

" I'm not gonna come back as a toad or cat..I, I, *don't* wanna be a *toad!*"

" That's not how it works! It's *all energy!*" voiced Minnie.

" Look!" Zeke turned Jerry's shoulders toward the sunset. "Look at THAT! See that miracle? If the Universe or God can manufacture that, why is it so hard to believe that..." But then Jerry's natural attention deficit brain kicked in.

" Uh oh! Look at the time! Blanche will have dinner on..and I have to be back here to meet the ghosts!"

" What?" said Minnie.

" Zeke said you were gonna talk to the ghosts tonight!"

" I said I *might* ask her!" snarled Zeke,visibly perturbed.

" It's OK, I don't mind...let's do it!" said Minnie, quite perky.

" So *they're* OK ?" questioned Zeke to Jerry.

" Oh yeah! I believe in ghosts! "

" But not that they can be reborn in a new body.."

" Well, I dunno..I just don't wanna be a toad, one

peed on me once.."

" Goodbye Jerry," waved Minnie emphatically,
"Be here at eight and you'll meet plenty of ghosts..uh
spirits!"

" But no toads!?"

" No toads!"

" How 'bout lizards?"

" She can't promise that!!" shouted Zeke.
The two walked arm in arm through the sunset shaking their heads and smiling. "What does he think you
are, a witch?"

" Well, they used to burn people at the stake for
just this kind of stuff..." said Minnie.

" And guys like Jerry?"

" Oh, they'd dunk them in the river to see if they'd
float."

" He'd float alright...without water.."

They went inside the old townhouse at sunset on
Grove Ave., with bricks aflame as if God had been
toasting them a cozy nest all day. God it seems usually
doesn't provide great opulence or an extensive bank
account and a limo. He says, "You've got a roof over
your head, it's cozy, here are some pretty streets full
of interesting characters, some cuddly little sparrows
hopping around and quite an amazing sky. What else
do you need?"

Minnie insisted on working up a fine stew from
"found objects" in Zeke's fridge, which indeed began
to smell wonderful, while Zeke pondered and
sketched at his drawing table.

Melvin and Stupid had parked beside an idyllic stream
at sunset on their cross-country cartoon ramble. They

had improvised a lean-to tent along side the 39 Ford
roadster coupe', and were cooking dinner as best they
could. An old "Ma and Pa" couple pulled up in their
amazing but ramshackle homemade airstream camper,
and insisted the boys share in their cooked up bounty
of hog jowls, greens and sassafras gizzards (which
they never completely explained) along with carrots,
taters, and onions which fleshed out the menu, all
served on various tinker toy, erector set Rube
Goldberg devices that automatically brought food
from stove to table, more or less. Sort of a "Maw and
Paw Kettle on Wheels" they were.

Paw laid back in his hammock talking, "Yep, the
world is full of new innovation, always has been. But
it'll drive ya nuts if ya let it! Ya gotta pick and choose
the gadgets ya really like, but stay slow and natural,
that's the way ta happiness!" He puffed his pipe and
swung slowly back and forth.

"He allus says that!" chimed Maw while she ladled
the stew, "But I can't say as I blame him..he's right!
Usually is..." The evening progressed into a muted
multicolored splendor of nature, roadside rubble, and
fantastic things appearing in the sky. Melvin cut some
garlic and sang strange songs from across the Galaxy,
especially one that went, "Oh Wertlebaum, Oh
Wertlebaum, ten thousand years ago..." Meanwhile
Paw happily twanged an old guitar with handmade
rhythm attachments from bits of junk. It also con-
tained a reed and brass blowing device with alterna-
tive bellows, all of which made surprisingly strange
and vibratory overtones, but also a beautiful blending,
and no questions asked. Maw hummed and shelled
snaps while Stupid either yodeled or philosophied on

the expansiveness of the Universe, both outside and inside his own brain, as well as why Einstein's Theory of Relativity was a nice parlour trick but not of any practical worth.

Zeke updated Minnie on all their strange and danger-ous happenings. They argued a bit over her getting involved with her psychic abilities, but with her assur-ance that she knew how to do it with safety, and since they were all sort of "in it up to their necks" and needed all the help they could get, Zeke finally agreed.

" Discernment is the key.." said Minnie, "Just because you contact beings from beyond, that doesn't mean you buy into whatever anybody says...there are all types over there, just as there are here." This made good sense to Zeke. He reasoned how he wouldn't necessarily walk up to a stranger on the street and trust him, so it seemed the old saying "so below, so above", held true.

"Besides", said Minnie, "I use various prayers and procedures for protection."

About 8 PM found Minnie, Zeke and Jerry sitting in a glowsome pool of light on the old persian rug with frazzled edges in the "living room segment" of Zeke's apartment. From the shadows above peered an array of pale staring faces, all members of Zeke's unique and collectable manikin and dummy head collection.

" Shall we invite them to join us?" asked Jerry.

" They're just leftovers from previous seances.." smirked Zeke.

" Oh boy, I can't wait.." giggled Jerry, " Hey, are

we really gonna 'see-ants'? Get it?"

" Com'on boys settle down, and the correct term is channeling...here, give me your hands.." She then, surprisingly, said the Lord's Prayer. After that, a few more pronouncements asking for guidance and safety from her spirit guides concluding with, "and we now open the Psychic Door."

They sat in darkened silence for some few minutes, trying not to breath too heavily. Then, from over head a swirling green light undulated down and around the room, then abruptly was gone. But almost as soon as it left it came back again. "Do you see it?" hissed Jerry.

"Oh, that? It's the street sweeper", said Zeke, " it has a revolving green light."

"Huh..awful spooky for a public utility."

"How spooky are they supposed to be?"

"Com'on boys, settle down, or the spirits won't take us seriously.." They settled, and pretty soon Minnie started speaking in an altered voice. "mmm Yyyee Yes! *we will!*"

Minnie then answered in her own voice, "Will what? Who is this please?.." Jerry was surprised that she didn't go into a trance,but just sat there, eyes closed at least most of the time, basically talking.

"Wuu...Wuuhh seriously! Take them *seriously!*"

"Where is Judy?" Minnie asked,then turning to the boys, "she's my guide.."

" J..J..*Judy* is here! *Judy* is here!.. *Messages!*.. mm..many *messages!*"

" Hi Judy!, say hi to Judy.."

" Hi Judy"..said the boys, somewhat reluctantly. It went on like this for while, like various employees at a supermarket playing with the intercom after hours. Minnie said it's actually quite similar to that, with spirits anxious to communicate but many have little experience and need help, "stepping up to the mike" so to speak. Even Minnie's great Uncle Gordy showed up telling bad jokes like he was drunk, (or pretended to be). Finally another guide took over, a large and stern Indian chief named Standing Bear, who brought order and solemnity to the proceedings. He thanked Minnie for her recent work in leading a poor victim of robbery and murder, into the light from out in the woods. Minnie returned his thanks and added this was a case she had just been working on. After an abrupt silence,Standing Bear said, "There is one of great age..who wishes to speak..this we will allow..." Then a long silence.

"Ezeek—!" Came a voice, loud and strong but with echoes of time and distance. "*Ezekiel!*"

"Ye..yes?" Zeke stammered.

"...I have been..watching you..."
Jerry and even Zeke became quite nervous and fidgety, but Minnie urged them to be calm.

" The first time..." came the voice again, " long ago..long ago..before the..highway..the...choo choo tracks.."
The boys again looked wildly incredulous, although Zeke's eyebrows perked up.

" The road...red lights..you thought it a car...but it was me..it was we..the owl..the little owl...we who know you...love you...your family has..." Zeke was suddenly a true believer, he felt a surge of elation. He had told no one about his strange childhood memory.

Suddenly Minnie's head began to plunge, her face

to grimace. Zeke was upset and nearly "broke" the circle, but something made him hold his ground. Her voice changed to a deep grumble. "Mmmm Mmm No...*NO!* We...are..here..there are many plans..for the Planet..." Minnie then spoke in her own voice.

"I feel I'm on..the dark side of the moo..the moon!" Then the deep voice returned, "Mmm mmm but the best laid plans..often..often..Mmm mmm WE WON'T LET IT HAPPEN! We will..."

" *What* won't happen!?" shouted Zeke, "What plans!??" The voice went on at some length as to their plans and how they were deadly determined to carry them out, yet not revealing enough detail to pin point anything.

" The Earth is our oyster.." it continued, "we will *crack*..it.." You could utterly feel the sinister intent in the voice. You felt it watching you as if nothing could stop it from getting to you no matter how far away. It then addressed itself specifically to Zeke.

" This one has power...we can work with him...let us show you how...we will...we will.."

Minnie's head began to shake, she whipped it back and forth, as if waking from a stupor.

"*Judy* is here! This is *Judy!*...The instrument is tired..she needs rest.." Then Minnie shook herself.

"No, I'm alright...I'll continue..I'm fine.." There followed a more "normal" episode in Minnie's channeling, a staggering drunk had fallen in an alley nearby in the Fan. His head was bashed in. He was dieing. Minnie continually worked with him to "down the long tunnel to the light", and leave his used up shell behind, until happily he did. The boys were fascinated with this and nearly forgot the earlier communication, so disjointed but compelling was the whole process.

Finally Standing Bear returned to restore order and announce that "energies were ebbing" and the session was coming to a close. Minnie said her closing prayer which ended with, "May thee Lord watch between me and thee while we are absent one from the other, and we now close the Psychic Door." Normally she would "wake up" at this point, but suddenly a voice shouted from within her- " Zeke! Zeke! *It's important!* I have *proof!* We must...meet me tomorrow morning..old park house..picnic..tables! Bird..Bird.. May.. mountain..park...come.." Then it broke off and Minnie was her normal self.

"Wow!" was the universal expression given by all present. Then came a flood of questions and discussion. Minnie pulled out a small tape recorder she had wisely placed beside her pocket book on the floor.They began playing it back with great interest. The words of the strange character who had been friendly to Zeke they dubbed the "Wise Alien", because of Minnie and Zeke's impressions of him. The voice had been amazing to hear and somehow powerfully uplifting. But the other, with the gravely grumpy disposition, was chilling to the bone. It was hard to give a name to this entity (or entities) without a terrible shudder of fear, so they just referred to them as, "The Others".

The strange intensity of the experience subsided as they all came thankfully back to the feelings of "normal life". While raiding the fridge for a much needed snack, they played it all back again and talked far into the night.

CHAPTER 20
A Rarefied Rendezvous

Examining the messages on tape raised further questions. Who was doing the speaking, and when? The "alien" voices definitely sounded like two different entities, one wise and benevolent,which Zeke was sure was the same being he had chased at the farm, and one shall we say "iffy" to be polite. And this last minute "invitation", was this for real? And where exactly? A bit of deductive reasoning pinned the location down to a picnic pavilion in either Byrd or Maymont Park. Since both of these magnificent city landscapes sat side by each and were essentially one park, except for a high fence to enclose the zoological exhibits inside Maymont, they decided it must be near the border of both. Should they follow up on this strange and mysterious summons? It was one thing to see lights on a road, chase fleeting anomalies through a farmyard, or even to dodge bullets from sinister assailants. But to respond to an invitation received at night in a seance to a secluded place where one was to have a face to face meeting with who knows what from who knows where generated an entirely different set of emotions.

After much fear and trepidation however about whether to "keep the date", the next morning found Zeke and Jerry circling "Swan Lake" in Byrd Park. They crossed the causeway and little stone bridge straddling a damn and spillway separating it from yet another lake, one of three in fact in this sprawling late 19th, turn of the 20th Century park complex.

Jerry had insisted on driving, which meant riding low in his orange and black Mini Cooper, with much of his signature sniffing and elbow flipping while he shifted the four-in-the-floor. Zeke for his part enjoyed navigating from this low, close to the ground view-point.

" Minnie's going to try and catch up to us on her lunch hour, if she can get away from work.."

" Oh, great!" shouted Jerry over the roar of the little engine,while sniffing furiously. They first drove to a grove of oaks and pine trees at the northeast corner of Maymont. Here was an old time picnic area, but which had been crowded in by a new nature center, a constant attraction to kids, parents and school groups. Clearly this couldn't be it. The only good candidate was the picnic pavilion on the west side of Byrd Park, across the Boulevard. Winding their way over, they caught a glimpse of the Buffalo enclosure. Inside the great beasts could be seen galloping in frenzied circles, something Zeke had never known them to do. Jerry down shifted to a head bobbing stop at the Boulevard traffic, then on to a sputtering zoom as they crossed over and on to the rutted dirt and gravel parking area near the Carillon, a great towering memorial to World War I. They parked near " 'Barker Field, where a dog can be a dog' ", which was printed on a sign by a chain link enclosure with many canine pals gazing at them with wagglely smiling tails.

In the distance was the pavilion, made of stone brick and wood and sheltered among huge pine trees, to which they'd have to go on foot. A chain blocked the driveway which would've been removed had they reserved it for a family barbecue, which was often the case on Sunday. The slow walk up the path to the empty looming building added lumps to their throats. The only sound was distant barking and traffic. Normally the 30's style WPA rustic style structure would bring feelings of childhood pleasure and hotdogs, but now there was only forboding and perhaps doom. Each crack of a twig or scutter of gravel seemed to echo twice as loud as normal, while Jerry and Zeke's feet seemed to step slower and slower.

"Whaddya think?" asked Jerry.

"Seems innocent enough to me...probably nothing there..we'll feel like fools..then go get a corn dog at that little stand by the Carilon, maybe check out the animals for a while..."

"Yeah, that sounds good.." The irregular granite stones and wooden beams of the pavilion rotated by their field of vision, as they strained to see inside from one end to the other. Empty. Just the tables and large stone fireplaces stared back. The echo of their steps on the concrete floor heightened their senses to every corner of detail. They even checked up the large chimneys, but only a clear rectangle of sky and bits of trash were found.

BLAM! A projectile hit the table.They jumped a mile high until they saw the odd bouncing of a football at their feet. A lanky boy rushed in. "Hey! Thanks

man!" he said as Zeke tossed it to him. " Hey man!
Go for it!" He threw it to his friend and ran after
across the lawn. Somewhat disgusted, the guys
walked outside. All there was of note was a distant
fireplace,the woods beyond and the old bath house not
far away on the left.

"Wanna check that out?"

"We could at least take a whiz.." said Jerry.

"Maybe...I'd just as soon hit that snack stand..." By
now the football boys had crashed recklessly into the
woods.

"Hey man, watch it!" one yelled, but just after, a
deer came springing out of the brush and galloped
across the yard, disappearing behind the bath house.

Zeke remembered his symbolism. "Com'on!" The
two friends rushed quietly to the little brick and stone
house. They checked the men's and women's doors,
both locked. Then they stepped gingerly around to the
back. Looking slowly around the corner—there he
was! A little grey alien with a wise and smiling face,
and an amazing amount of expression surrounding
those large black eyes. The boys stood speechless.
The creature raised his hand as if to speak.

"No!" it said. A rustle behind them caught there
attention, from the woods was emerging Sunglasses!
He carried a briefcase in one hand and a gun in the
other. PHHhphT!— went the silencer. PA-TING!—
went the bullet off the bricks. The boys turned back
but the alien was gone! Around the next corner of the
bath house? He'd simply vanished! Bullets were
coming fast now, and all they could do was run, keeping the bath house as a shield until they got to the big
trees on the hill descending to the Boulevard. PA-Fft!

PA-Ffft! From tree to tree they dodged until they got down to the traffic.

Knowing Sunglasses's habits, they knew they'd be relatively safe in a crowd. There before them was the toll booth complex of the well known "Nickel Bridge" of Richmond, which of course now cost 35 cents. Cars and trucks were backed up to pay, and Zeke tried to get one to give them a ride. A trucker cussed at him, while a little old lady was so scared she rushed through with out paying toll. People were shouting, a normally polite toll lady was yelling about calling the police, so the boys whirled and staggered their way to a strip of trees on the other side of the street.Crashing through these,they came up against a high fence.

"It's Maymont Park!" said Zeke, "Quick, climb over!" This was fairly easy even with the bit of barbed wire at the top, for the fence was made for keeping animals in mostly, namely elk.

The boys flumped onto the other side and there was a prime specimen starring down at them, a giant stag. He rolled his eyes, cocked his great horny head and stamped his foot.

" I hope it's not the mating season!" said Jerry. Evidently it wasn't because it then turned and galloped off down the hill. But before they could get on their feet, half a herd followed after him from up the hill, along with some very cute miniature "dic dics", a tiny deer from Africa, who bounced by bleating pitifully. Zeke and Jerry scurried across the pasture compound to the farther fence beneath the observation deck. There they ducked behind a water trough.

Watching the open expanse they'd just crossed, they saw no sign of Sunglasses. Perhaps they were safe, (as soon as they could get out of the elk pen that is). But then from above them came a faint electronic whine. From over the large oak trees by the corral appeared Sunglasses, who was flying it seemed by the aid of his briefcase! He would tilt it forward or back to stabilize himself, or sideways to move over and downward etc. He seemed to be playing with magnetic fields to manipulate gravity around him.

" Looks like some sort of anti-grav segue thingy! I *want one!*" said Jerry excitedly. Zeke made a sour grimace in his direction.

" Well," returned Jerry, "I'll bet you'll be able to order them in a year or two, at least on the Black Market.."

" What if he's from *outer space?*" smirked Zeke.

" Well, that might take a little longer.."
Meanwhile Sunglasses had floated his way down to the rear of the corral, followed by an ungodly screeching sound (but somehow melodic). AY OOWWwwwah!!! AAAOOWWwwwah!!

" What in the world??" said Jerry.

" He must've landed on the Maymont peacock!"

" Huh, those things must be from outer space too!"
Then Sunglasses came scuffling and immerging around the other side of the building, briefcase normally in hand and dusting off his jacket as he joined the rest of the tourists at the animal barn. The boys could watch him from their low place through the fence and vines,as he tipped his hat to a kid and his mom, patting him on the head as they fed the goats. He couldn't fool the goats however. They ran away bleating nervously.

Zeke and Jerry waited until the area was deserted,

then quickly clambered up the wall to the platform. As they straightened out there clothes, they noticed a little boy standing and staring at them. "Are you an elk?" he asked.

"Uh..yes I am," said Jerry, " I used to be a Moose but their fezzes were too tight." He shook his hair proudly.

"*I'm* a Moose!" answered Zeke, " and my fez fits juuust right!" and walked away, leaving the kid with a deeply searching look on his face.

The farm animal compound consisted of various fenced in areas with paths running in between. They suddenly caught sight of Sunglasses, down at the far end where open park land began, with tall trees and grass sweeping down to a creek bottom.

He was slowly scanning the distance. Just then, a nearby mule started to HEE HAW. This started many kids to laughing, but also made Sunglasses turn around. When he did, he jerked up his head as he caught sight of Zeke and Jerry. He slowly walked to the right around the pens, so the boys moved to the left. For a while, it was a stand off, back and forth. Then they took off back and to their right, which led them through a zig zag of pens down the hill. By now pigs goats and chickens were in an uproar as the boys jumped over fences as they went and Sunglasses followed doggedly on foot, unable to use his briefcase in public.

On a lower level,they came to a side fence with nothing much behind it. They jumped it, and found themselves back in the elk compound. Meanwhile Sunglasses stopped by a bush-engulfed tree, and looking quickly around like Superman outside the

Daily Planet store room, turned on his briefcase and started floating, wobbly at first, then up and through the bushes.

The elk and deer got spooked by the boys again and ran back up to the barn. Then Sunglasses hopped over the shrubbery and was buzzing along in the pasture,undulating unseen and close to the ground, like a snake doing flying push ups. This spooked the elk again back down the hill. People were starting to stop and watch the exciting little spectacle, unaware of the weird two-footed espionage occurring along the ground below the observation fence.

"At least he can't shoot us like that!" said Zeke, "His hands are full." But just then Sunglasses manipulated his legs so he now sat on the floating case, causing him to lose some maneuverability, but allowing him to reach for his gun. He got off a few ill aimed shots with his silencer that cracked on the trees and dirt. The boys scrambled and finally got out of the elk pen further down hill and headed through the oak trees and around other exhibits. They could see Sunglasses trying to maneuver and follow, but with very wobbly success, while also avoiding the gaze of the tourists. He was not missed however by the Bald Eagle in his enclosure nor the Fox sunning himself on a rock.

Zeke and Jerry gained distance now on a straightaway path that led into a small but steep valley with granite cliffs and a high fence below surrounding a pond. One of the more picturesque sections of Maymont, Zeke knew it well and ducked in close by the fence behind a maintenance building. Sunglasses, having seen them, came swiftly but not so surely forward as he dodged behind tree limbs to avoid being seen. The quiet whine of the briefcase device grew louder overhead as Zeke and Jerry held tight behind a dumpster. Sunglasses made his landing where Zeke had hoped, on the other side of the high fence, which just happened to house an energetic but cranky black bear. AWWRRAWrrr! went a growl from the feeding trough which was unfortunately quite close to his landing spot. The surprise made Sunglasses lose his equilibrium however before he touched ground, and went spraddle legged through the air, all the time trying not to go any lower, as the bear came after his feet.

Evidently the bear was tired of his feeder pellets and found him much more appetizing, or at least interesting. Finally, his cheap imitation Gucci shoed legs went flying up as Sunglasses flipped over, splashing into the pond, and came bobbing to surface, now trying to hang on to the floating case which seemed to have a life of it's own. He and it finally came sputtering and scrabbling to a stop at the base of the granite cliff on the farther shore, with the bear growling and closing in, but not sure what to do with him. By then Zeke and Jerry were laughing hysterically with comments about "well that was brief", and "that wraps up another case", as well as "lots of trouble a-bruin" as they headed hastily up the hill.

CHAPTER 21
Parkside Relativity

After an exhaustive running climb, Zeke and Jerry arrived back at the farmyard exhibit. Jerry gulped down some fountain water.

" We've got to get to my car.."

Zeke for some reason was suddenly pensive, " You know Jerry, I think Einstein was wrong..."

" You think *what?*"

" Yeah, he was a nice guy and all, and brilliant, but all that relativity, it's just a matter of how things look from a certain viewpoint. So light bends because of gravity, so what? What does a clock appearing to slow down have to do with time? That's just special effects! Optical illusion, a visual doppler effect!"

" Hey Zeke, you realize that character, thing whatever he is, will be after us again?"

" I think Chester Gould had it right.. 'The nation that controls magnetism will control the Universe!' "

Jerry just stared.

"You know..Dick Tracy!"

" We gotta *move!*" insisted Jerry.

" Exactly! What is a time-space continuum? How can it exist? But that briefcase of his, it's manipulating magnetic fields! Makes perfect sense!"

" Ok, great, so let's make sense and manipulate ourselves outta here to my car!" They made their way toward the Boulevard entrance of Maymont. Across the traffic they could see the cars parked by the dog park. How happy and tranquil things looked over there. Just people and their dogs, playing and relaxing, simply *dwelling*. In the foreground was a huge oak tree. A figure dropped from its branches hovering, and began lurking around it's trunk. Sunglasses was already back on the job and waiting for them. The boys were hustling back towards the barn when a voice called out.

"What are you two characters up to as if I didn't know?" Minnie had driven up as if by special order! Piling into her plain looking sedan, they sped out of the parking lot while trying to explain. How to get to Jerry's car? The only way seemed a round about trip through Byrd Park and to sneak up from an unexpected direction, then jump into his car, but hidden by Minnie's large sedan.

"Do you think we can make it?" said Minnie.

"I dunno, it's gonna be close, Sunglasses is waiting very near Jerry's car!" said Zeke.

"At least he does'nt know which car...I hope..." added Jerry with a gulp. The three drove on north through Byrd Park at an ever slowing speed. "Hey, you guys could take me home and I'll come back later and get my car when he's gone!"

" Yeah, that would work..except.." said Zeke oddly.

" Except what?"

" Except he's already gone..and following us!" They looked behind them, and saw their assailant furtively floating in and around the park farther back, like a June Bug searching to land in the grass."

Minnie looked in her rearview, "What's he doing?"

" I think he's sensing us somehow...at least that's the sense I get." said Zeke.

" *Now* who's the psychic?" she answered.

" Well, the brain does produce a type of radio wave I believe, it's bio-electronic..maybe he picks us up on a receiver or something.." They continued driving slow, lest they call undo attention to themselves.

" Me I'm just sickic.." mumbled Jerry. They stopped again near Swan Lake.There also was a tranquil scene devoutly to be wished, flocks of ducks, geese and swans swimming and waddling around it's small and wooded "Duck Island" in the center. Placid people on shore were relaxing and feeding them. Oh to be simply there instead of here, was the trio's common thought.

The field of view behind them now seemed tranquil too, but they knew better than to relax. "Keep the car running, I want to get out and have a look see..." said Zeke.

But Minnie was concerned, "You think you should?"

" Yes, I've just got to get a better sense of things..I think it's the metal of the car.."

" Maybe the metal is protecting us from him!" said Jerry with trepidation.

" May be, but I gotta get out, for just a minute..here, gimme that grungy old hat on the floor." Jerry handed him an old vacation bucket hat from the back.

" I happen to love that hat!" exclaimed Minnie, " I

sit on the beach with it and nobody bothers me.."

" Exactly!" said Zeke, putting it on, "How do I look?"

" Totally repulsive...uh, adorable!" smirked Jerry.

" I'm coming with you!" said Minnie.

" No!...oh OK.."yielded Zeke, "I never could stop you from getting into trouble could I ?"

" I'm already in it! Besides as a couple we're a better disguise." They got out cautiously while Jerry parked under a tree. Proceeding down the long slope to the lake Minnie and Zeke could see a wide swath around them, from Swan Lake and beyond to wooded park land and fine old turn-of-century houses on the left, to the curving road with the small stone bridge on the right and Shields Lake and Maymont beyond that. The main hazard at the moment was not watching your feet, which were most likely to step on goose turds, a slippery proposition at best. Before them were a wide array of people relaxing on the bank. They sat down between a man with a very inventive hand-painted beach umbrella doing watercolors, and an old lady wrapped in voluminous scarves, a flowery dress and a huge straw hat. She seemed to be knitting.

"Well, I don't see anything, what happens now?" murmured Minnie.

"Just wait, something will..it always does." Ducks were quacking and children laughing as they both cast there eyes around the quaint and peaceful scene, sort of a Richmond version of Seurat's painting, 'A Sunday on La Grande Jatte'.

"Say Minnie, do you think Relativity is just media propaganda?"

"Will you shush? *Pay attention!*"

"Knit one..pearl two..no pearl two..one..knit, oh dear.." The old woman seemed to be having trouble.

"May I help?"said Minnie,"I used to crochet a bit."

"A bit?" laughed Zeke, " She knitted me a stuffed Humpback whale once for my bed, except I could'nt get in to go to sleep....flippers kept me awake..."

"That was *macrame'!*"

"Whatever, I still say it was life size!" Zeke squinted around the park as Minnie helped the old lady.

"Thank you Dear..it is so confusing without the factory instructions..." Over by the embankment near the bridge Zeke saw crossing the road a quite proper gentleman in a small Homberg hat with very reflec-tive glasses. He sat by himself very far off, opened his briefcase and appeared to start working on his laptop.

Meanwhile the umbrella artist, whose demeanor simply screamed "I'm gay and proud of it", turned to Zeke.

" Hello..didn't I see you at Art Parts? I used to work there.." He wore stylish mini-sunglasses shaped like musical notes which gave Zeke a start, but then he lifted them for him to see his face.

"Oh yeah..I was buying some gouache...how's it going.."

" Just fine..and did you?"

" Did I what?"

" Go wash! Get it?"

" Oh yeah! Yes I did! Gouache..ha ha ha..."

" It's an old art store joke..so how've you been?" He was obviously coming on to Zeke, and Minnie glared at him.

" What?" said Zeke defensively under his breath.

" Nothing..if that's the direction you want to go, far be it from me.."

" Hey, I'm just talking..aren't we supposed to be highly evolved New Age people?"

"Pardon me?" said the umbrella guy with emphasis.

"Oh, it's nothing," said Zeke, "by the way this is Minnie...So tell me, which way are you going?"

"Who me? Oh I'm going over to Bob and Norman's in a while, they have a nice chipoltle club sandwich..would you be interested?"

"No, what I want to know is which way you're going..it's a metaphysical survey I'm doing..obviously you're gay, which means you're probably on an incarnation that's half way between male and female soul polarities..so what I want to know is which way you're going, from female to male, or male to female?" The man was flabbergasted.

" I..I hadn't given the matter much thought!"

" Well it's very interesting..you see I'm also a writer.."

" Oh!" The man enthused, "That *is* interesting!"

" Yes, and I might want to include your experiences in.."

" Your *book?* This is so exciting!"

" Yes, well actually it's a comic book, but I think you'll find tha—"

" A COMIC BOOK! Hmmph! You know where you can put your comic book!" He got up and stalked off, nearly dropping his water colors.

" No..I don't..think..." said Zeke, non-plussed. "What did I say?" He turned as Minnie glared at him.

" That was extremely rude! How could you do

that?"

" Hey, I thought I was being *scientific!* Jeez, just when you think we've come so far.."

" Honestly Zeke I don't know about you some-times.." Minnie shook her head in exasperation. But as Zeke looked at her, he saw something in the distance.

"Look!!" He pointed to the Homberg man on the far off grass. He was using his silvery glasses to reflect sun in their direction. A multi-fractaled spot of psychedelic light flitted all around them and then vanished.

Then the old woman on Minnie's right turned and said, "I think we better conclude our meeting at the little arch beyond the island..."

" What??" They both looked at her with incongruity. She then lifted the large scarf from off her hat and there sat the Wise Alien, smiling gently.

While Minnie and Zeke sat with mouths open, the strange light reappeared and danced on the top of the 'lady's'huge straw hat, which after a second or two suddenly caught fire! Flames were leaping all around that wonderful friendly face! In the speed of the moment Zeke saw the Homberg man aiming intently. Quickly he was up and beating the hat with whatever he could grab, which was Minnie's big macrame' pocket book, flopping all over. Minnie did the same with Zeke's bucket hat. They tried to grab the flaming hat and toss it but it seemed pinned to the old lady clothing. "Stop it! Stop it!" Minnie yelled at any and everything including Sunglasses's Homberg whoever. But before they could do anything else, the bulk of the lady, that is alien, clothes and fire sunk straight to the ground. There was nothing there!

" Here we go again—Let's go Minnie!" Zeke grabbed her by the hand as they ran off toward the grove of big oaks up the hill.

" Why do I always feel like I'm in a cartoon?" She blurted.

" Because I'm a cartoonist!" Over their shoulders they caught a glimpse of Homberg-whoever steadfastly striding after them with briefcase swinging, as if late to a big corporate meeting. Jerry was very beside himself in the car, not understanding what had happened but savy enough to know it was bad. With much lunging and elbowing at a gear shift strange to him, he started Minnie's car leaping and spinning around.

Somehow, as he ran, Zeke's consciousness chose this very moment to shift, as he saw again his characters, Melvin and Stupid, running before them, backward and forward, twirling and doing jigs while leaping over the landscape,which seemed simply to whiz beneath their feet, giving them super speed. Because it was in Zeke's "mind's eye" so to speak, it seemed to have the same effect on he and Minnie. Suddenly they found themselves up under the oaks, where the only possible refuge before them was an old octagonally shaped park activities building that was usually locked. But today there were cars and people around it.

" I don't believe it.." said Zeke staring at the park house, "I've always wanted to see this!"

" See what!?"

" A meeting of the Richmond Whirling Dervish Society! A very rare occurrence, they're very secretive

you know.." Minnie didn't question him further, she
was aware of the ancient Muslim religious fraternity
with strong roots in Sufism. They were known for
their whirling form of meditation which would trans-
form them into a state of ecstacy. But to Zeke and
Minnie it was refuge, so they bowed briefly to some
men near the door with hands clasped in prayerful
attitude, then rushed in before anyone could say anything.

On the wooden octagonal dance floor, the ceremony was just beginning. The tall hats of the participants bobbed as their long draperies twirled outward
like upside down Art Nouveau mushrooms. Minnie
and Zeke made their way in their best balletic manner
through the group which didn't notice as the two
staggered and bounced off each other, so deep in
trance were they. The two decided it best to flatten
themselves against the far wall to avoid any more
whirly accidents.

Zeke caught sight of their assailant approaching
through a window, and motioned Minnie to grab a
couple of Dervish robes hanging on the wall. The
strange monotone chant of their ritual was speeding
faster now, as was their sacred spinning. It was amazing how these human tops spun around and around, in
and out with eyes closed, yet never touched one another. Zeke and Minnie took no such chance,and
joined the wild dance with eyes wide open. At that
moment Homberg barged in like he owned the place,
ignoring the entreaties of the men at the door. He tried
in vain to insert himself into the fray, getting whacked
again and again against the wall, by the blinded danc-
ers' hands,which somehow sensed the presence of evil

among them. Meanwhile Zeke and Minnie did their best to keep to the opposite side of the room, which wasn't all that large actually.

Suddenly the evil alien-whatever threw caution to the wind and turned on his briefcase. He lifted up and over the Dervishes and spotted his targets dancing far too clumsily in the far corner. But he didn't reckon on the great faith of the ancient brotherhood, whose upward held spinning arms of jubilation hit against his legs and began spinning him even faster, and in many more directions. Zeke and Minnie saw their opportunity and made for the door, while Homberg bounced and spun from wall to wall, finally catching his coat on the large ceiling fan which although turned off at the moment, spun him faster it seemed then it ever had. And the timeless dance of eternity went on.

Outside they ran to the car where Jerry was honking, but first dropped off their costumes and hats on the heads of some very bewildered doorkeepers of the Dervish.

Wide eyed and twitching, Jerry stepped on the gas, "What the heck happened?"

" You wouldn't believe it!" They answered.

" Hey, did you notice that building's a perfect octagon?"

" *We noticed!*"

They spun round and through the little park roads, back toward the dog park,which soon was in sight. Zeke had suddenly assumed a wise and all knowning pose. "You know, they say the Dervish acquire a truly Zen like state in the motion of spinning round and round and.."

" Hey-- zip up yer *Zen!*" said Minnie.

Zeke looked and gulped. "Hey look, Sunglasses—he's *still* by the tree! There must be more than one of these glasses guys!"

"I thought so!" said Jerry as he spun the car again, bumping over the park puddle holes.

"No, go *slow*...he doesn't know this car.."

"I sure hope not!" added Minnie. "Besides,we have to meet the old alien."

"Meet?" asked Jerry.

"Yes, at the little arch beyond the island!"

"Yes that's what he said.."agreed Zeke, " but what he meant I don't know.."

They reluctantly drove back to the area of their most recent troubles. All seemed quiet, but they were sure to "watch the skies", in particular those near the trees. They turned right of Swan Lake however and stopped in the middle of the little stone bridge over the spillway. What little arch? And why was it so quiet? There was Duck Island in the middle of Swan Lake, and to the left was the bank they had been sitting on. Then they looked to the right.

"Look, at the gateway to that cul-de-sac of old gingerbread houses!" said Zeke.

"Yes, over the sidewalk, a little archway.." And as they stared at it, a rainbow flash of sunlight sprang out at their eyes. "What's that?!"

" *Get Down!*" They shouted and dropped to the upholstery. All was calm for a moment, until a bright spot of reflection began to play over the windshield.

" Oh no, it'll burn my car!" shouted Minnie.

" And us in it!" shouted Zeke. But nothing really happened. It flashed away and back a few times and then stopped. They all laid deadly still. " Touch the glass, see if it's hot."

" You do it mister hero!" said Minnie. Zeke reached up with a quick tap. Nothing. Looking out once more, all was calm except for quick intermittent flashes from the arch.

" I think it's a signal." said Zeke. They drove slowly around the lake toward the cul-de-sac. At the turn-of-the-century ornate gate way, all seemed normal, so they drove inside. The small loop took them around what appeared as an old Hollywood movie set, with various houses in different architectural styles, from Spanish, to Swiss, to French, German and English, an eclectic mix of whatever.

" Hey, I'd like to live in here.." mused Minnie.

Zeke more or less agreed. "It is kinda cute, with or without mutant alien invasions.." But where was the alien? As they circled around they were now approaching the side with the little decorative stucco arch over the sidewalk. The only unusual things were a few trash bags placed at the curb for pick up. But one of them was wiggling. Plastic fell away and the now familiar smiling face was before them. It nodded with implied wisdom. They all stared in silence, but then suddenly burst forth with questions.

" What's going on?"

" Why are you here?"

" Where do you come from?"

" Do you really reverse in time as you approach the speed of light?" This last came from Zeke of course,as they all stared at him, including the alien, who then spoke.

" In your dreams.." What?—a street smart rude comeback from a highly evolved intergalactic being?

But his eyes indicated otherwise.He was looking
toward the nearby lake. A rustling of tree branches
from the thicket on Duck Island, and a chorus of
flapping quacks and honks soon revealed Homberg
immerging to the narrow bank. He was aware of them,
and began to manipulate his briefcase.

Suddenly the Wise Alien whispered with urgency,
"Turn sharp right at 609 Westover Rd, keep going no
matter *what!*" He then sunk into the trash bag which
in turn sunk flat to the ground, empty.

"What? How does he *do* that?"

"Westover Rd.? What does he mean?"

"He means shut up and drive!" hissed Jerry as he
peeled out of the cul-de-sac. Homberg was now in
briefcase-hover mode and followed after, trailing bits
of pond water. The friends sped around Duck Lake,
not sure where to go. Their anxiety and questions all
converged into pure adrenaline.

" Go right!"

" No Left!"

" Use the GPS!"shouted Minnie from the back
seat.

" I'll have you know I drive a vintage reproduction
Mini Cooper,and I read maps!"

"And I draw maps and drive a 99 Buick Century!"
added Zeke.

" I would'nt brag so much.." she added while the
boys frantically searched her dashboard.

" Guys, it's that button there!"
Jerry managed to start the mechanical voice talking.

" Turn left here..turn right here.."
Jerry really whigged out. "Doesn't this thing know
we're in a park? There are *5 intersections* here!"

" Just turn the damn thing off and head for those houses!" said Zeke, pointing. They approached another row of Edwardian mansions along the road leading back to Maymont. There was a street sign— Westover Rd. "*Quick,* check the addresses!" They craned their necks passing the ornate lawns, not given to ostentatious display of numerical signage, while behind them Homberg's legs wobbled in mid air as he rounded a sharp corner. He steadied his reflective glasses best he could and shot out the odd laser-like blast which sporadically hit the road around them.

"Watch out!!" Along the curb ahead of them were several very thick bushes, well rounded with horticultural fervor, some of which burst into flames and psychedelic light particles. But as they passed, a fine ceramic inlaid pillar was revealed with old English text- 603. A set of over hanging juniper trees ,a burst of cultivated sea oats, some bulbous azalea and then in white painted brick with Times Roman text--609.

"This is it! *Turn!*" yelled Zeke. Jerry slammed on brakes, skidding round as to line up with the very narrow brick walled and cement drive way, designed for carriages and 1920's cars. He spun out, but before them, at the long end of the small tracks with angled bricks to fit old tires, was a completely closed and well manicured garage! Jerry began to slow down. Behind them Homberg was spinning in the air, gaining his balance to follow. "*Keep going! Keep going!*" they shouted.

Jerry was stymied, but one look at the briefcase floating weirdo behind him decided his mind. As he speeded toward the garage door it suddenly opened up and they plunged into darkness. A green pulsing field of ectoplasmic fog swept over and past them, with an accompanied feeling of intensifying speed. There then came a loud KLUNK--followed by an OOF and a splattering on pavement.

" I guess Homberg hit the door!" said Zeke looking back.

" Yes, but where *is* the door?!" added Minnie, as they plunged further into a distorted realm of flashing, stretched imagery which included bits of visual data somehow gathered from the surrounding city and park they had just left and with which they were quite familiar, but also broken and disjointed like an ex- ploding jig-saw puzzle spinning and flying repeatedly past their eyes.

"Hey!"said Zeke, "this is like that ride at the New York World's Fair!" The both stared at him. " I think it was the Ford Pavilion.." The effect soon made them dizzy, to the point of losing consciousness, when suddenly a large door flopped down and they bumped happily down a ramp to the ground.

"More like 'Mr.Toad's Wild Ride'.."said Jerry. They were facing the Carillon in the other half of Byrd Park across the Boulevard. The dog park was not far away. Looking back at from where they had come, they saw only an ordinary landscaping truck with it's back door open, and gardeners working nearby. They had instantly traversed a quarter of a mile without road, plane or bridge.

"But that *still* doesn't prove Einstien was right.." mumbled Zeke.

Jerry headed Minnie's car toward the parking area next to Barker Field, but sure enough Sunglasses was still stationed, now standing under the large oak tree.

"Let me drive," said Minnie "He doesn't know me, and Jerry can get out." In their new positions, the boys ducked down as Minnie drove pleasantly past the oak tree, smiling largely with batted eye lids.

" Don't over do it.." said Zeke, while Sunglasses blankly followed her gaze. Several cars were between them now, and Jerry's Mini Coop was to the right. He scrambled out promising to catch them up later. But as was Jerry's want, he fumbled loudly as he searched for his keys. Sunglasses began to show attention, and started walking over. "Hurry up!" growled Zeke. Just then however, the dog gate squeaked open and a stylish female owner of two Afghan Hounds was striding gallantly over. One look at Sunglasses and the hairy lanky pooches went ballistic. Jerry dove into his Mini kicking up dirt, while Minnie spun out back toward the park entrance. The last they saw of Sunglasses, he was taunted round and round the oak tree by both dogs and owner, he shoving his briefcase at the dogs, she claiming he doesn't understand or love canines. All the while he scrambled and-or floated up among the branches several of which he threw at the dogs. When this didn't work, for some reason he reached in his pocket and began to write checks which he floated down to the groveling Afghans,which of course the chic woman started to pick up. Go fathom the alien mind, but it worked. Zeke smiled at Minnie as they reached the Boulevard.

"Another fine day in the park..."

CHAPTER 22
Dutiful Dreamer

Most of the afternoon lay before them when Zeke and Minnie returned to his apartment. He glanced at his drawing board, and saw Stupid and Melvin making sheepish doe eyes at each other like in an old time musical. Zeke made doe eyes at Minnie. Minnie made dove eyes at Zeke. The release from all the excitement plus their need to catch up with one another led to them making love. "One thing about all this confusion," Zeke said, "is I found you again.."

"And I you.." replied Minnie. "We whirl and twirl and tumble like feathers, but fate as always brings us together..." But before they started a second round, Zeke actually rummaged through his junk and put a 45 RPM copy of "Afternoon Delight" on his record player.

"You actually *have* that old record?" she quizzed with raised eyebrows.

" Yeah..I like it..."

" So do I..." Their arms blended around each other. As the afternoon advanced and shadows were growing longer, they were both exhausted, as well as thoughtful.

"What's been happening Minnie?" murmured Zeke.

"Hey you tell me!"

"No, I don't mean just to us, or these strange..occurrences. I mean, I started out to solve a riddle from my childhood...but it's sprung out of control. Like some vast unleashed vortex."

" That's a fun word, vortex..."

" Yeah, it's been goin' around.."

" And around!" They laughed.

" But as crazy and dangerous as these chases have been..I actually love it..It's adventure..it's 'The Hunt'..definitely not sitting behind a desk, which I'm so tired of..it all feels so healthy somehow, to get out and fight for one's life..."

Minnie caressed his chest,"My primordial man.."

"God bless you Minnie, for being so...happily feminine. So many women are trying so hard to be men. And what for? Being a man isn't so much fun, you spend most of your time wanting women!"

"Why should I?" Minnie replied, " I know soon enough when I need it I'll reincarnate as a man, or whatever mixture of genders I desire..or need..so I play whatever role I'm playing to the hilt. What else is there?"

"Ahh..that's my girl..she's so wise.." He stroked her hair as he began to doze off. Minnie got up and wandered around the apartment. Approaching Zeke's closet door, she wasn't sure if she should open it, but did anyway.Suddenly a giant blob lunged and sprung out, knocking her to the floor! " Oh I see you found your macrame' whale..." Zeke mumbled, "You can have it back if you want..put it in one of your gallery shows..."

"Thanks, I might do that!" Minnie puffed beneath frazzled hair. Settling down, she casually flipped on the TV. It was a news show called 'The Condition Room', where you were bombarded with all the world's problems at once, usually with 6 other pundits to argue their opinions and guess what some tidbit of news meant and will mean, repeating it over and over all day, instead of just waiting for more facts to come in. The host, Wolf Kruger, droned on and with controlled urgency about terrorism, threatening epidemics, global warming, scandals both personal and public, political tension, racial protests, police controversies, immigration conflicts,wars and rumors of wars and atrocities galore—

Again she clicked the remote. Another news channel had six more pundits in their various boxes parsing out the latest political scandal in ever so thickly smooth P.C. language, each one sounding like the next, as if all were reading from the same teleprompter prepared by the same lawyers.

" This informs the narrative that speaks to the relevance of the polls with respect to the demographics of the candidacy in terms of diversity while flying in the face of conventional wisdom which has evolved a more nuanced approach to situations and or conflicts of this nature so as to put a spin on the topic which takes it to a whole new level. It's just not who we are as a nation..."

" *Oh turn it off!*" shouted Zeke, rolling up in the sheets. "I can't stand it! It just makes me mad! Why can't they talk like people! All that blather and nothing is fair, clear,or even communicated! And nothing changes or gets done! Why can't they let people talk like people again? I used to enjoy news commentary, it once was an art form! Walter Cronkite..Harry

Reasoner..Eric Severalsides..uh, Eric..oh *this* is like
that 'Newspeak' language in Orwell's '1984'!..and so
much MESS! I...I just want to sleep.."

Minnie looked quizzical. "But I remember you as
being so involved in so many causes!"

" I did, I mean I was.. but I need a vacation! I need
work, I need rest! Just Life! We fought so hard for a
better world, but it keeps getting worse! PLEASE turn
it off!" She clicked the picture black and silent.
"Thank you..I just want to sleep..I just want the
world..to be healthy..and to..go away...we'll go out
later and get some dinner..and some...sleep.." Minnie
looked thoughtfully at her new-old love. Then she
smiled a little smile and got up to putter around the
apartment, while Zeke zonked off into a very deep
zone.

Stupid and Melvin drove their 39 Ford off of Route 66
into the dirt and stopped opposite some very unique
rock formations in the desert. They ran energetically
like kids into an odd but beautiful 'rock window'with
a hidden grotto, with a flickering pool capturing the
setting rays of the Sun and opalescent colored lights
swimming and reflecting off the curved ceilings.
Another more strange light emanated from a single
source, an old 50's style Sylvania television carved of
red stone and imbedded in the rock.

"It's time for our favorite show!" shouted Melvin
as he bounced up and down, morphing into various
objects, a plumber's helper, a kitchen sink, a pressure
cooker, a commode, all in 50's commercial semi-art
deco style. But instead of the expected cartoon show,
or Howdy Doody or whatever, there appeared on the

screen news footage of war and other calamities throughout the world. At first it was accompanied by news reel and show music and many reporter voice-overs that Zeke could'nt quite comprehend, except for occasional words such as "intensive, military strikes, drones, international response, The president said.." Endless marching men seemed to be walking by.

Then Zeke found himself within the TV scene--and then suddenly standing in the backyard of his boy-hood home. He was 5 years old again on a bright late summer afternoon, the family was having a typically maddening game of croquet. His Mom was on one of her rolls, knocking ball after ball through the wickets, banging away opponents while getting free turns. Ol' Mr. Madden from across the street, in his suspenders and broad brimmed hat, looked like a crooked South-ern old time politician, shoving his own ball along with his foot when he thought nobody was watching, laughing quietly to himself, "Heh, heh,heh...", his mallet on his shoulder.

Zeke happily saw his favorite red petal tractor close at hand. He reached out to touch it but found the distance daunting. It was somehow far below him and looked like a small toy. A great flapping and buzzing sound was in his ear. Suddenly an enormous yellow swallowtail butterfly and a June Bug the size of a small pumpkin hovered by his face, its jewel-like surface glittering in the strong sun like Egyptian jewelry, the very image of a scarab, symbol of rebirth and regeneration. Zeke now realized he had grown to gigantic size. Below the family never noticed, so intent were they upon their grassy game. Looking around at the tops of trees and the distant curvature of the earth, he was now noticing again those giant close-up planets floating near him to the north in a cool blue sky, Saturn and a great angry Red Moon.

Turning his head south and west, he was shrinking again as he stepped into the street and over to the subdivision beyond. Finally at normal size, he realized he was on a long street that was once part of his boyhood paper route. As usual in such dreams, he had the sudden paranoia of having forgot to deliver papers for the past 20 years and they had been piling up to the size of a small mountain at the paper truck stop. (Never mind that for decades the paper routes had been taken over by adults driving cars).

Finally he noticed a disheveled man, a bum or homeless person whatever, trudging aimlessly down the hill toward him. Zeke knew he could'nt avoid the man, because he now had papers to deliver, a large sack of which was slung on his back,even though he hadn't actually gone to pick them up, such being dream logic. Nor was his bicycle anywhere in sight which had been his usual method of delivery. He walked with stoic trepidation toward the troubled, stumbling man who now wavered back and forth across the road, weaving from side to side. This troubled Zeke as he was anxious to avoid a confrontation, but now wasn't sure how he'd do it. To his astonishment, as the man passed from left to right,he was now leaving behind him a series of "copies" or clones of himself, so that gradually the road was filling up with staggering disheveled men,plodding forward all in step with one another.

Soon enough there was virtually an army of men marching toward him. News reelish Souza-like march

music filled the air. So tightly did they fill the road
that Zeke was obliged to jump the ditch to watch them
pass. As he did he began to recognize many of the
throng. Amazingly enough there was John Wayne! He
was wearing an 1870s Calvary outfit and appeared to
be in command in his usual gung-ho screen manner,
of at least a large group of the men, which included
many recognizable figures, such as FDR walking
jauntily without aid of a wheelchair (but pushing one),
with pince-nez glasses and cigarette holder firmly in
place.Also on horseback were Crazy Horse, Iron Eyes
Cody and Chief Dan George. There was Dr.Martin
Luther King, and Robert Kennedy looking very firm
and resolute.There was Jimmy Stewart and Henry
Fonda, joshing with each other but striving to maintain attention, and Abraham Lincoln,with stove pipe
hat towering above all in a lanky stride. Beside him,
walking solemn but wistful was Robert E. Lee. For
some reason Lincoln had trouble keeping in step, but
no one tried to reprimand him, even the spit and pol-
ish soldier to his right who shocked Zeke when he
realized he was staring into the face of General
George S. Patton.

He also realized that they all weren't men. There
were various First Ladies like Dolly Madison, Eleanor
Roosevelt, who oddly enough walked with her uncle
Teddy. Jackie Kennedy hung close to her husband
John, almost subconsciously protective of him. The
Temptations danced by in profusion singing what
else? "Ball of Confusion". Roy Acuff with his fiddle
kept singin' "Listen to the Jingle,the Rumble and the
Roar!" James Brown was dancing, amazing wild and
crazy and carrying a bag that looked totally new. Also

Katharine Hepburn marched smilingly with Spencer Tracy, her chin high in the air, raaally she was..., Aaron Copeland marched by with Billy the Kid, both wearing cowboy outfits and throwing lassos to the strains of "Rodeo", while Aaron also chomped on a corned beef and rye sandwich from the deli. These were but a few of what seemed a complete and crowded host from over the years, a river of American culture from the political, entertainment and media world. Pat Nixon waved shyly while her hubby Dick waved and gave the "V" symbol with his fingers. Robert Redford and Dustin Hoffmann as Woodward and Bernstein kept throwing globs of recording tape at him and he kept sluffing it off, all the while waving and smiling. Believe it or not there was Edgar Allan Poe, staring hauntingly ahead, arms stiffly by his side, but for some reason every so often he'd break out into some very spectacular karate moves.

Along with these were many beings not actually human, but very real in their own way. Bugs Bunny along with Daffy Duck, who had trouble paying attention, were exuberant in their cartoony enthusiasm, even though Daffy periodically stepped on a land mine and Bugs was unscathed. Howdy Doody had trouble keeping in step, or even stepping at all.

Just then Zeke noticed Chuck Jones in a very "animated" discussion with Tex Avery and Bob Clampett, their bodies stretching and squashing like their characters, while Friz Freleng rode by on a player piano doing the 2nd Hungarian Rhapsody. Mel Blanc jumped his place in line to talk to Bugs as if asking him to coach him on something. The road was simply packed with icons of our peculiarly American civilization. Zeke wished he had a camera as the amazingly odd or surrealistic moments unfolded.

The Marx Brothers were perfectly serious as they portrayed Washington Crossing the Delaware in a boat with training wheels and honk horns. Salvador Dali lay nearly naked on a walking couch as he posed to be painted by a melted watch with a beret on it's head. Zeke couldn't fail to stare at Jane Mansfield, as lovely and voluptuous as ever, but with a coltish sense of humour as she kept grabbing her head and turning it around 180 degrees to wink backwards at the soldiers behind her.

Indeed also there were many ordinary soldiers or people he didn't know who just enjoyed marching. What was that march they were playing? He knew it so well, but from where? Then he suddenly remembered as he saw George Reeves as Superman not complaining at all in that tight woolen union suit he had to wear, marching to his marvelous TV theme music. Perry White, wearing laurel leaves rolled by behind his desk yelling "Great Ceasar's Ghost!"

From among the "unknown soldiers" Zeke recognized one. "Walter!" He shouted at an older guy he knew from church when he was younger, who loved swing music.

"Hey! Zeke! How's it goin' boy! Git with th' beat!" he then produced a slide trombone and started riffing on the Superman March. Nearby was Fats Waller and Count Basie playing miniature floating pianos with little propellers as the music really got up and scat.

" Say hi to Fats and the Count!" shouted Walter while he waved back in enthusiastic approval.

Then Fats chimed in, "I'm Fats in name only now!

Yas Yas!", as he suddenly lost 200 hundred pounds before his eyes.

"What's going on?" Zeke thought to himself. Then the now familiar figure of Chief Justice John Marshall road up on a Harley shouting happily, "It's a Spiritual Army! A *Spiritual Army!*" He then threw away the motorcycle as if it were a balloon and took his place in the rear of the march, proudly waving the American Flag. They marched off and off into the distance,disappearing into thin air while Zeke just stood in the road....watching.

The pavement beneath him suddenly started to tremble. "*An earthquake!* What to do?" Zeke thought as he tried to keep his balance. Then Minnie's voice intruded from the sky.

"Zeke! *Zeke!* You gonna sleep all afternoon?" He roused himself and wobbly stared from the bed. "Don't you want to go to dinner?" she said.

" I'm in the Army! All they have is K- rations! ...Dinner? Oh..yeah..." Zeke dropped his head back on his pillow, and gradually got up.

As they drove out they made an attempt at analyzing his dream, as well as the recent "mission" oriented visions received on and around Capitol Hill. They determined that whatever was happening or "communicating" to them was connected somehow with spirits of the Dead, as well as the fate of America it seemed. Something large was afoot in the World, that was sure. One could easily see *that* if they only used their eyes and ears and paid attention to the media. But just now a much greater and more urgent mission impressed itself upon the consciousness of Zeke and Minnie. Their stomachs.

CHAPTER 23
Bobble Heads, a Sandwich and Thou

Evening was descending on the Fan as the couple
drove toward Carytown, site of many good
restaurants,boutiques and the classic old movie
palace,the Byrd Theatre. Colorful neon lights and dark
silhouettes of the shops shown out in contrast to a
comforting and flaming sky. Soon Venus was competing with the street lights like an air bound night light
without a cord.This reminded Zeke of star-like light
that he, his brother and their science enthusiast neighbor Will Stinson saw shining in the East one evening
when they were kids. They struggled for a full 30
minutes to focus Willy's impressive but wobbly
homemade telescope, but when it was finally crisp
and sharp in the lens, the thing simply moved away.

"An alien with a sense of humour?" said Minnie,
"It was playing a trick on you!"

"Yeah, I guess.."

They finally decided on one of Zeke's favorite places
next to the Theatre, the New York Deli. As they
walked up toward the Byrd they noticed a couple
historic films were playing for a sci-fi festival. On
The marquis was "It Came From Outer Space" and
"Aelita Queen of Mars", that amazing weird silent

Soviet film from the early 20s, also with big lettering
that read "WEAVEY EDWARDS at the MIGHTY
WURLITZER ORGAN!" A great Richmond favorite,
this last was above all the titles,(the Byrd knew it's
advertising priorities).

"We can check out the show after we eat!" enthused Zeke, now totally psyched up for an evening of
good chow and show biz diversion. As they came near
the door of the theatre, up walked Zeke's cousin
Tommy. As he approached, Zeke whispered to
Minnie, "He's the one I told you about with the big
UFO in Sandston remember?"

"Hey cuzzin Ernest!"

"Cuzzin Ernest! Whut chall dewin'?" began a
round of old family jokes which both relatives always
recited as a ritual, (with special mentions of Uncle
Ralph as always). They always started by callin' each
other Ernest, but the real cousin Ernest was probably
going to bed up the country just now and knew nothing about it. "Hey, yall goin' ta see this *thang?*" said
Tommy pointing to the wall poster.

" Yeah, are you? We can sit togeth—"

" NOooeew that's a message from the *Devil!!*"
Zeke's eyes rolled. "Hey Tommy just because you
married an evangelical girl doesn't mean now
everything's demonic!"

" Oh yes it does! I mean some of it..read your
Bible! It's in there...Hey! You wanna go for pizza?"

" No, we're going to the deli and the movie..."

" Secular Humanist propaganda..."

" It's Ray Bradbury! It's a *classic!*"

" Uh uh...Hey don't go in there it's *evil!*" he said to
two theatre patrons who smiled and kept walking

inside.

" But Tommy, you were almost abducted by a UFO! Remember?"

" Naw, that was the Devil!"

" God you're frustrating, you're usually a lot of fun but.."

" Don't take the Lord's name in vain!" Tommy took a preacherly stance with loud oratory, " As it says in Revelation Chapter 13, 'And I stood upon the sand and saw a beast rise up out of the sea, having seven heads and ten horns, and'..." Just then a couple of enthusiastic young guys walked past on the way to the ticket office.

" Hey Dude! I saw that one too! Awesome!!— Great special effects!" Tommy just looked at them a moment, totally nonplussed.

" But why do you still go to that church?" continued Zeke, "You're divorced! And she didn't even take it seriously!"

" I can't help that, if she wants to burn in hell let her go!"

" And what about *me!*"

" You will too! You sure yall don't wanna go for pizza? Or maybe Chinese?"

" Naw, we'll see ya later...give my love to Aunt Linny Boo!"

" Yeah, say hi to ya Mama!"
They waved each other off like at a family reunion, then Zeke shook his head. " See what I mean? See what I have to deal with? "

Just then the movie started to let out and the audience spilled onto the sidewalk, talking and laughing. Among them were many of the usual "Richmond

characters" that you'd meet if you stayed away from
the suburbs and attended the various civic, artistic and
cultural functions available in our fair city (especially
the ones that provided free food). Immediately visible
was Kevin Kreosote, who Zeke introduced to Minnie.

"Hay! Hi ya Pally!" grinned Kevin as he saw them.
" Ya know, Zeke and I go so far back that we both
have Alzheimer's and it seems like we just met!"

" Yes, do I know you?" said Zeke.

" Ha! He's forgotten already! Hey, when we were
kids , we didn't have baseball cards, so we traded
fossils!" Zeke rolled his eyes and decided on a come
back.

"Yeah, the doctor told Kevin here he has short term
memory loss, so Kevin asked if he could come back
tomorrow for another opinion."

"Is that a joke?" asked Kevin.

"Sure it is, you told it to me yesterday!"

"Oh yeah.. Gimme a pen so I can right it down!"

"Hey, how was 'Aelita'?"

"I really loved the Outer Deco sets!"

"Oh you mean Outer Space Deco?"

"No, I mean Out On the Deck Deco! It was a really
cheap movie!" Minnie rolled her eyes.

"Boy you guys with the jokes.."

"Eh, it's a living!" They both answered simultaneously.

"But what sort of name is that?" asked Minnie,
"Kreasote, like the stuff they put on telephone poles?"

"No, no no, It's pronounced Kreaso-tay!"

"You don't say?"

"Well, I figure if my jokes stink, I can blame it on
my name!"

"You gotta change that.." murmured Zeke.

"Yeah..I know..but ya gotta admit I'm well preserved!"

"You did that joke already day before yesterday..."

"Oh yeah, that's right..."

It seemed they were all heading to the New York Deli.
Soon a group naturally formed there along with more
scintillating conversation. It was actually becoming a
party. As they sat down Zeke ordered his favorite, a
Reuben. Jokes were flying, (mainly between Kevin
and Stan, another comic minded fellow with an over
preponderance of puns per minute (if such a thing was
p-p-possible), all relating to the movies they just saw.

" Hey was it just me, or did Queen Aelita's triple
brassiere drive you crazy!?"quipped Stan. "Va Va
Voom!"

Kevin turned quickly on his heels. "But should'nt
that be *Va Va Va* Voom??"

" She should've gotten the oscar for breast ac-
tress.." said Stan.

"Yeah, but the trouble is,when I was mentally
undressing her, I had to do it one and a half times!"
He nearly choked on his drink from laughing at his
own joke. "Hey, she gave me the hiccups!"

" And that Barbara really gave me a rush! Get it?
Barbara Rush?" Kevin got it. Several other film fans
came by and introduced themselves or just smiled
without saying much out of shyness, but the creative
artifacts they wore such as plastic tail fins, or flying
saucer hats spoke for them. One wore a "Bradbury
Forever" sweatshirt.

" That's right," said Zeke, " he wrote the story for
'It Came' didn't he?"

"It was channeled..." returned the sweat shirt wearer rather pompously, "Higher intelligences would visit him in his basement while he sat in a meditative state drinking beer. When he woke the typewriter was still warm, and the text perfectly printed, with no corrections needed whatsoever..."

" But what I wanna know," laughed Zeke, "is what brand of beer he was drinking?!" To which the sweatshirt nerd looked indignantly down his nose, so Zeke went back to his Rueben. Ah, thick corned beef, bulging squirming tendrils of sauerkraut, melted cheese and rye—it made him sigh,(as well as high).

"You've got to admit there's atmosphere.." laughed Minnie.

"That ain't the word for it.."
Soon a familiar figure sidled up and sat down at the next table. It was Bud Basinski, an older Jewish TV repairman from Poland with a knack for enjoying life, jokes, flirting and artsy events. He was a well installed Richmond character who Zeke knew well. But if the subject turned to the horrors of WWII, he might roll up his sleeve and show you his Holocaust serial number, and talk serious, telling you some of his story, but mostly he wore a congenial smile and told old Borscht Belt jokes.

" You like ze Flyink Zauzers? Let me tell you, on zome nights I tink I *am* one! I start out on one side of the street, but zoon I'm on ze odder zide, an' sev'ral miles furder on! How izzit dis happen?"

"Maybe you had a close encounter.." ventured Zeke.

"Oh yes, I tink you right, but it vas a close encounter vit Jack Daniels I tink!" Again with the joke as

usual, so he and Zeke laughed heartily and exchanged
a few more. But after showing Minnie his tatoo, for a
while they both stared silently. He was but a boy when
his parents were killed, but he survived.

Several of the group on the floor were doing a sort-
of high tech broken down robot break dance to the
60's hit "Telstar", played on the Deli's retro-restored
jukebox, when Bud suddenly spoke again. "Yah, it'z
someting sim'lar to de Lamed-Vavnik.."

" The Whatnik Whonik?" responded Zeke with a
start.

" Lamed-Vavnik, you know vit de aliens comink to
Ert und ze people are schcared un ze aliens hidink vit
super future knowledge, but some'o dem know more,
und talk wit dem and schtop ze world from blowink
up etc..."

" Oh you mean like 'It Came from Outer Space?'"

" Ya ya, same ting.. more or less.."

" But the Lamal.."

" Lahmed-Vavnik. Is mystic esoteric Hebrew
Kabala ting, ze teaching of ze 36 Righteous Ones
living on Earth, and thereby the earth is saved..same
ting.."

" How is that? " asked Zeke.

" Oh, ven ze wurld is in turmoil which is nearly
always, their mystic powers of prayer and good deeds
keep God from destroying it for their sake, or
zomehow they save the wurld..is old old legend.."

" Do they speak to aliens?" asked Minnie excitedly.

" Speak wit wat??" Bud was mockingly incredulous. "Dose tings? You jokink right?" He saw that
they weren't. " Oh maybe, who knows..it's such a

strange world you know...poof!" He shrugged in typical yiddish philosophical fashion.

Just then more film fest sci-fi fans arrived dressed in even wilder home-made garb, in futuristic outfits with spikey protuberances,or wearing grotesque alien heads of paper mache, bobbing and tilting, nearly knocking things over as they grinningly stared at people through bulbous eyes.

" Maybe that's what *we* are!" Minnie suddenly exclaimed. "So many weird things have been happening to us.." Zeke tried to shush her up but Bud caught on.

"Vat--you talk to schpace sships? Vit de beep beep?"

"Yes!"

"Maybe you left your funny hat at home?" Pointing at a nearby bobble head. "Go Vay, I Zzap you— PIISSCHT! Anyway, nobody knows ze Lamed-Vavniks, even they don't know demselves! Dey very humble and dey do good, but zey are powerful und save ze wurld, but zey don't know it..and if somebody says he's Lamed-Vavnik, you know for sure zat he's not!"

" Oh.." said Zeke, not really understanding.

" And it's always 36, just 36, enough to keep ze wurlt from hexploding..if one dies, there's another take his place..or her place..it can be anybody, but nobody knows..even *dem* you zee?", pointing at the bobble heads. At that he excused himself to go get another drink, leaving Zeke and Minnie in a pondering stare.

Zeke watched the pointy people and the intersecting bobble heads in a foreshortened view down through the narrow room as he munched on his juicy thick Reuben and fries. The situation was somewhat familiar, and he unconsciously started to scrutinize the dimly lit space with a lighted rectangle by the bathrooms in the distance. One bobble head evidently had had too much to drink, and was dizzyingly making his way to the gents when it stopped, stood erect with perfect composure and turned around toward Zeke. The face was incredibly life like and familiar. It smiled and winked at him with a very real eyelid, between intermittent viewpoints among the criss-crossing partying bodies. But a moment and it was gone.

"*That's* not paper mache'!!" Immediately Zeke got up and rushed best he could to the back corridor. By the time he got through the crowd and bobble heads there was nothing to be seen, so he checked the men's room——nothing. He was about to risk checking the ladie's when two giggly girls came out looking at Zeke either as if he was a celebrity or from another planet, he wasn't sure. Again he had self doubts about hallucinations and his sanity. Out the back door into the alley, but there of course all was vacant. He'd been this route one too many times. Back inside he confessed his frustration with everything to Minnie. "I'm about sick of all these wild occurrences..who can you tell about them? I think I need therapy!"

" Well, you've got me and Jerry.." she answered, "besides, a shrink will probably make you worse, put you on pills or something.."

" I know..it's not that..it's..such a wild goose chase...and most people think you're either crazy or a marginal dim-wit if you speak of it. Where's society?

Where's normality?"

"*Here* is normality you goose!" she retorted. "People everywhere, and not very normal at that! These are *our* people Zeke, artists, freaks and weirdos! *Creatives!* They won't laugh I wager, at least not all of 'em. Besides we have a marvelous secret, like being spies! It's adventure! You said yourself you yearned for it, now you've got it!"

" Yeah, but I'm becoming a nervous wreck! I set out to find an answer to the strange visions of my childhood and.."

" Well, that will come..but let us relax and enjoy, we need the rest!" Zeke could'nt really argue with her, so they got up to dance.

As stated, it was a lively crowd, as well as a bit weird and quite creative. Zeke ran into Kevin's friend Thump. He asked him how he was doing, to which he replied, "Thump!"and kept on thumping.Then came "Horace the Hat", a playwright who was never, *ever* seen without cranial coverage, dancing ever so smoothly with his wife.(Rumour had it that someone once yanked off his chapeau and simply found a smaller hat underneath). There was also his old friend of many "dos" and functions by the name of Shade Tree McSmith, a quirky black guy from the Virginia Dept.Of Taxation, who never talked about his work, but always talked about Popeye and Bluto, and was very knowledgable on cartoons and showbiz, especially horror and sci-fi. He also had a habit of going "Ug gug gug gug gug" when dancing, which he now was doing zestfully with his girlfriend Amethyst.

The choices from the jukebox tended to fit the gathering, so after classic hits like "Purple People

Eater", further jumps and gyrations were even more..shall we say-"out there". Many of the gang sang the words, either that or replaced them with some of their own. Zeke and Minnie were soon "in the mood",(especially when that particular tune was played). When "People Eater " was repeated, they laughed and sang—

> "It was a one eyed one horned
> Lama Lamed Vava-nik!
> Sure looked strange to me..."

And when the Pointer Sister's "Neutron Dance" came on-

> "Oh, I'm just burn'n
> Doin' th' Vava-nik Dance!"

Just at this moment Bud Buzinski came waltzing by with a rather nice looking blonde. As if on que, Bud winked at Zeke. Somewhat non-plussed, Zeke dug in his brain for an appropriate quip. "Who's the lady?" was all he could come up with.

Bud was quick on the uptake. "Dat's no lady..dat's my wife!"

"It really is! I mean I am!"added the blonde.

Similar variations and fun flibbeter-jibberish was done to "Rock Lobster" and other notable jazz, like Squirrel Nut Zipper's "Put a Lid on It" and "Hell", as well as a number of "Big 80s" tunes. Drinks were being handed round and Zeke and Minnie got a bit tipsy. A fun and freaky time was had by all, even while avoiding collision with the bouncing cardboard heads. Someone put on a local record by the pub crawling Richmond band, Reefus Boceefus and their lead singer Keithy Britches—

" Do you want to be an alien?
" Yes I want to be an alien,
" I'll bet you can be an alien too!
" *And you!*

" If you find your feet have been failin'
" Just jump and jive and get into wailin'
" And you will see that you're an alien through!
" *---and through!*"

" Don't sit wishin' you were Pygmalion
" Jump and morf with arms a flail'n and
" You will see that you're an alien too!
" Yes *YOU!*"

In the thoroughly swingin' and syncopated words of Fats Waller, "The Joint was Jumpin'!...yas yas!"

Things were finally winding down a bit and some were making their way out to the street. Here Kevin Kreosote came bouncing up, drink in hand, to Zeke and Minnie. "Hey Pally, are you leaving? Hey so am I! We're all leaving..wanna know where?"

"To bed I hope.." said Zeke.

"No, after that! Tomorrow!" He rambled on, revealing that he and several of his friends were going to be extras in that big movie they were shooting outside of town, that he and Minnie should come, they need more people and that he, Kevin could get them in! "Why not?" they thought, fitting snuggly as it did into their get-away-from-it-all plans. So away home went Zeke and Minnie making songs and rhymes about being in the movies.

As they drove back through the historic old townhouses and apartment buildings along the Boulevard, some of which Zeke's grandfather had designed, (which he was quick to point out), they turned for a shortcut along Idlewood Ave., back toward Zeke's place in the Fan. The vista suddenly opened up as they drove past the big paddle boat lake at the north edge of Byrd Park. In the water was an odd orange ball of a reflection. They looked up and beheld a perfect eclipse of the Moon, almost a scarlet red. They stopped and watched awhile, enjoying the eerie beauty of the night and each other. Then Minnie remembered something.

" Wasn't there a prophecy about a blood moon?"

" Yeah,I remember...was it a New Age thing?"

" Sort of, but I think mainly it's in the Bible.. something about the Apocalypse or the Tribulation..."

" Oooo, that sounds like fun, just when I was in the mood to relax and enjoy myself..."

" Well, you never know, these things are usually will-o-the-wisps...let's just be laid back and look forward to a different kind of day tomorrow."

" After all," said Zeke, "it can't be any stranger than our regular life."

CHAPTER 24
Round Up the Usual Extras

Early morning found Zeke and Minnie driving out
Patterson Ave. and toward the same stretch of Route 6
that had started Zeke on his rather odd quest, which
had so far borne such exciting but bizarre fruit.
Minnie drove while Zeke slouched in the passenger
seat. Behind them in his Mini was Jerry, who was
thrilled to join this new adventure of being extras
(excuse me, background artists) in this big glossy high
budget costume action thriller Civil War/Sci-fi epic
tentatively titled, "Glory, Guts and Robots."

" I wish we could've gotten away earlier..but we
had to go to Northside to your house.."said Zeke
grumpily.

" Well, I had to get a change of clothes and pack
away that whale.."

"Heck, they'll be giving us 19th century costumes
to wear all day. And *then* we had to stop on Fauquier
Ave. to pay homage to Shirley MacLaine's birth-
place..."

"Well, I like to say a prayer to 'Saint Shirley'
every so often..."

"Saint? She gets a bit cantankerous for a saint doesn't she?"

" Have you *read* about some of those saints?"

" Yeah well...she *did* really kick off the modern New Age movement...maybe they could do a monument to her on Monument Ave., with little Machu Picchus and flying saucers around her head..."

" Huh?" said Minnie.

" But what about her brother Warren Beatty? What does *he* get?"

"I don't kno--"

"Oh, that's right, he's a film director, he doesn't need to be a saint.."

Minnie threw her sweater in Zeke's face.

"OK, he can be on the other side of the statue.." As she drove on, she heard him mumble, " I could've been a great film director too, but I never got the chance..." After some napping silence, Zeke spoke longingly again of the shadowy childhood visions and memories that had so haunted him along this idyllic ribbon of road.

Turning on PBS classical radio, there was Mendelssohn's overture, "Fingal's Cave" which suited his mood. It also reminded him of those Warner's "Inky and the Minah Bird" cartoons but that was beside the point. Waxing strange and wistful as he stared into the sky, he longed again for the rich cool growth of the countryside "up home". Trees protruding upward from the rich ground below, buzzing bees and cicadas and an occasional Monarch butterfly floating by. This was the feeling he and Jerry had been under the sway of that morning at Rivana Bluffs before they'd been rudely interrupted, and sent ping-ponging off on a breathless chase cross country. Oh, to simply be searching for an odd little alien 'neath those primordial trees leading down to the river.

"GOD FUCK'N DAMN IT!" The air burst with Zeke's sudden expletive as they passed another ultra suburban mushroomed development of "McMansions" full of plastic and concrete prefabricated trash,which blighted his beloved traditional landscape of farms, flora and fauna. Minnie tried to calm him down, and indeed as soon as the view before him changed again and suited his sensibilities, he'd again waxed poetic,wistful and wondering.

"Red tail light, in the night, what make of car is in my sight.." With such gibberish she knew he was calm. She let him dream, watch and ramble, the hypnotic two lane yellow lined asphalt snakeing dreamily before them. His eyes half closed, he mumbled snatches of incongruous dialogue, but would suddenly awake with some clear commentary of the passing visions in his head.

"I hope they do it!"

"Do what?" smiled Minnie.

"It..whatever..the world's in such a mess..Global Warming, species dying, destruction, over population,technocracy,poverty,terrorism..we better *hope* they're helping..." then he murmered off again to unconciousness.

" I'm sure they are Hunny Bun.."she soothed, "don't worry.."

" They're watching..We know that..why would'nt they help?" He dozed under again.

"Yes Dear.." They drove on a few miles without speaking.

"But not *all of 'em!* " Zeke burst out so suddenly it made Minnie swerve. She righted the car with no trouble, but she almost missed the turnoff.

The first sign/symbol to turn off toward the movie set was a piece of pink paper with the letters "G G R" on it. These they followed until they came to an obscure gate in a pastoral fence, leading to a winding dirt road over rolling fields topped by copses of oak trees and brush. This they found out was State Farm property, cared for by prison trustees, but the visual effect was wonderful, giving it the aspect of agrarian 19th Century America, so free from technical intrusion. That was to change they found, as soon their little roadside guide flyers became light blue, with silhouettes of a cannon and a robot facing each other with exclamation marks coming from each, indicating they were nearing the great artistic brotherhood of the movie set.

Looming on the horizon of the peaceful rustic road was now a great bulbous headed giant robot, gleaming of brassious coppery metal and somewhat victorian in it's style of construction,with many plates and rivets as well as flanged collar pieces and wheels, giving the appearance of a higher intelligence having raided a Civil War railroad yard for parts in it's insidious plan to invade Richmond before Grant could get there or Lee could retreat from Petersburg, thereby taking advantage of civil unrest and setting up it's own puppet earthly kingdom in the midst of the coming industrial revolution with a surplus of metal goodies to play with and crash about. Or so Zeke surmised to Minnie on their approach, but they would soon be surprised just how close the actual plot (a very loose usage of the word at best) would follow that very assumption.

Now could be seen trailers, trucks and tents set up for the crew and mobs of milling about extras, who also stood in long lines to be fitted for costumes. But then beyond that—BOOM! A great balloon of smoke surged upward, while extras ran into each other or hit the dirt. Obviously the effects boys were up and at'em already, adjusting their explosive devices to a high degree of precision, (it was devoutly to be hoped).

Jerry, who'd been swerving and bumping over the ruts in his low down Mini Cooper, ran into a marshy ditch full of cattails, nearly drenching himself, but came out with only a messy Mini and increased sniffing and twitching on his face. They were now being directed where to park up a far hill, on a field so vast the walk back would about equal what they'd already driven. But hey, it was showbiz!

"Hey listen!" said Zeke excitedly, "That's a quail, a Bob White! You never hear them anymore, but up here on State Prison land they're flourishing! And over there, a tortise! You don't see them any more back in the suburbs either! It's all this god damn growth and development that's killing them off! Growth growth growth! What's that got to do with progress? The Earth ain't but so big!! Whadda they gonna do, build a deck out behind Siberia?"

Minnie jumped on him, "Now don't get onto one of your self righteous rants! Even if you're right, we're here to have some *fun..*"

As they parked their cars they found they had company. Kevin's familiar "Hiya Pally!" greeted them along with others of his usual entourage from Cary St. Also there was the beaming face of Bud Basinski.

Zeke smiled and pointed, "Hey! Lahmed Vavnik!"

"You know 'bout dem? You must'nt speak—izt a zecret!" grinned Bud, perking up from his sleepy ride. "Oh, you de fellow fum las' night...zo, you gon' be movie star too? You must got talent!" It was a good spirited start to a long day's shoot as they walked downhill through the tall grass. At each and every junction was a production functionary with a walkie-talkie, a badge and a t-shirt with a robot and an alien beating the hell out of each other. They were being directed, lowly extras that they were, to a huge hold-ing tent marked "BACKGROUND", with another graphic of giant explosions, aliens and robots slugging it out with hoards of miniature 19th Century people running beneath them screaming.

"Hey cool!" said Kevin, "We get to be stepped on by monsters! Maybe I can get Godzilla's autograph!"

"You'll need a helluva beeg vountain pen!" said Bud. Somehow Zeke didn't feel like laughing.

They entered an area marked "Orientation" where they were given forms and work sheets to fill out which they at all means MUST do, as an assistant yelled at them, "..or you will NOT GET PAID!!" So they all sat down and started writing. Jerry kept look-ing around at everybody, scrutinizing them to see if any of them was a 'star'. Before they got very far however another functionary came out and yelled at them about the vast privilege of being in this magnifi-cent Zarke-Spumoni production of a Gaylord Zarke film.

Then he shouted, " It was the TIME OF THE CIVIL WAR! A country torn asunder, brother against brother, and— ALIEN ROBOT HOARDS WERE ON

THE ATTACK!!!" He handed out another EX-
TREMELY important document of non-disclosure,
that if anyone revealed any creative material,
designs,story lines, actors etc. etc. before the film's
glorious release, they WOULD be sued, and if anyone
had a problem with this they could leave now with no
hard feelings.

Getting in yet another long line they suddenly
heard, "Soldiers in the right line, civilians in the left!"
shouted another t-shirt functionary with a big scowl.

"What if we don't know?" asked Zeke.

"Big table over there..get a roll assignment!"
Kevin showed a piece of paper and waved goodbye,

"We got ours at the casting cattle call in town, see
ya later Pally!"

Zeke, Minnie and Jerry stood in line and dutifully
received up and down glances from no nonsense
casting personnel, who then gave them slips of paper
with their roles on them. Jerry became a "civilian
gentleman", Minnie a "field hospital nurse", and
Zeke a rebel soldier. He was happy with that, being an
actual 'Son of the Confederacy', except for his Yankee half which he'd mention sometimes,sometimes
not.

The costume and makeup department was fun as
usual. Each dresser or makeup person thought of
themselves as artists and you were their canvas, but a
canvas they could talk to and which could talk back.
And talk they did. A very sexy girl named Nikki with
a few tasteful tatoos, had fun with Zeke and he with
her."You have a good look for a Johnny Reb, we'll
mess you up a bit...this battle's been rough, don't
worry, you'll still be *cute!* But I don't know where I'll

put that cannon ball hole...*Just kidding!!"*

"Ha!" Zeke jerked his head, "That might be good air conditioning on a day like this.."

She giggled, "Now look, you almost smudged up my smudge! Now where am I gonna sign my name?....Just kidding!!"

Nikki was excited to learn about Zeke's own art- work in cartoons, while he himself suddenly saw Stupid and Melvin standing nearby and getting yanked into various costumes that just didn't fit. They were cartoonily stuffed into them and made to fit one way or whatever.

Finally he and the girl settled into silence while she did his detailed face and hair work. This gave Zeke a chance to scan the immense activity of the tented room. He barely caught sight of Minnie going behind a far partition with her hoop skirt in hand. The space created by the large tent, partitions, chairs and tables was jam packed with people either sitting for, or administering to, a plethora of costumes, makeup and props. Shouts of "I need a sponge" or "got any eye- balls left?" were common. It was a scrambled beehive of a time warp, or rather the washed up tsunami debris of a section of the 19th Century, namely The 1860s. Mix that with the web of criss-crossings and shoutings of the film crew crowd with wide eyed looks from hapless newcomers and you get some idea of the endless sights to keep one solidly entertained while sitting solid in the makeup chair.

As he lazily cast his eyes about people being fitted for costumes, Zeke tried to match up "types" in his head with characters from classic costume pictures he'd known and loved. There was a Thomas Mitchell type, a Zasu Pitts, even a C. Aubrey Smith...but this one getting fitted with a Yankee soldier's hat he couldn't tell. Where had he seen such a face? If only he'd take off his sunglasses. Yes, he'd have to take them off before——Sunglasses?? Just then the man strongly resisted an attempt by his makeup girl to remove them. Evidently assuring her he would, as if he had an astigmatism or something. Turning away and downward for a moment he did remove them and push away her insistent artistic hands. Zeke then saw his eyes. And what eyes! Dark small pits with no whites and hardly a pupil to be seen, more like two bloodless gunshot wounds instead of an organ of sight. Small and in their way insignificant, but all told quite hideous, like those of an extremely vicious pit bull he knew in his neighborhood. Of course in an instant Zeke knew who or what it was, but luckily he himself remained unseen. Nervous, but gathering his composure he lost himself in the great crowd as he received his marching orders to the filming area.

From another large tent a short bulbous bug-eyed creature came gibbering and shaking it's antennae as it ran up to Zeke.

"Mm yum Bally!" It mumbled.

"Kevin is that you?"

"Meah..Mime man mMalien! Ma'int it Mool!!?"

"Here,open your..uh proboscis.." They flipped up a loose hanging access hole through the nose piece of Kevin's huge prosthetic latex head. His excited speech burst asunder.

"I'm an alien! Ain't it cool?!!"

"Yeah... I'd have never guessed!" They laughed and enjoyed their new hyper-real make believe status

as they walked toward film set. The next major obstacle to their enjoyment came in the form of the 2nd
Assistant Director, who talked more to his walkie-
talkie then to you, but barked sharp orders at you all
the same. Several more functionaries helped execute
his orders by herding about 50 extras to where they
were grouped before the 1st Assistant Director who, in
an even louder voice, proceeded to set up the scene
and what would be expected of them.

"Now I know what Hitchcock meant by actors
being cattle!" quipped Kevin.

"Yeah but remind me not to buy any of your milk!"
said Zeke, glancing at his utterly disgusting appearance.

"No talking! *We* will *tell* you when to *talk!*"
shouted the 1st AD, putting the two friends squarely
in his sites. " You must follow instructions, for they
will come swift and be somewhat complex. Sometimes you will talk, sometimes you will only appear to
talk, sometimes you will get blown up! That is, it will
appear that way to the camera, you will not be hurt, IF
you pay close attention!

"Camera, where is the camera?" Kevin's tentacles
shook terribly as he talked.

"The CAMERA is over there! Do NOT look at the
camera! My name is Jim, if you have questions, direct
them to ME, or one of the other walkie-talkied
personel!" More instructions followed about how to
inter-act with the stars which was not at all, and where
the flash pots were located and not to go there ever,(or
get severely burned). Soon however, he answered his
walkie-talkie and informed them that they were to be
privileged with some instruction from the famous

director himself, Mr. Gaylord Zarke. They waited as the 1st AD stood waiting...and waiting, and waiting. Finally a jeep came sputtering and screeching to a halt, and a small energetic personage in a pink baseball cap, a shock of blown-out-the-back blond hair, neon green shorts and silver sunglasses came striding quickly on to the set.

" Jim! Mind if I break in with a few words?"

" No Gaylord, go right ahead.."

" Ladies and Gentlemen! We are making a *film!* Why? Because we're *artists!* I'm an artist, *you're* an artist, Jim here is a *great* artist.."

" Thank you Gay.."

" Hey wait, I'm on a roll!..and *you* are *background* artists..*detail* artists..because you make the details of this picture I paint with my camera! It's gonna be *awesome*..these aliens are coming down, see?"

His unfortunate use of the "A" word brought irritation to Zeke and a moment of nervous energy, as he thought of Sunglasses,but not seriously, as the coast seemed clear. He and Kevin then tried hard to focus on the creative words of wisdom before them, being wielded from the mountain top as it were, as Mr. Zarke continued with feverish energy.

"Into the Civil War they come, these aliens, a classic time warp kinda thing..uh..like a commentary on the angst of our times..because the cannon goes off—BOOM! See? Just like a bus backfire in your own life..or maybe a tractor..And the horses scatter and this ship and giant robots are coming and BOOM FOOSH! And you start running but you have to look see? You're fascinated—— then a mortar explodes KABOOM! With shrapnel and horses flying, that'll be green screen don't worry 'bout that— But General Grant, he sees what's happening and yells retreat and..But General Lee wants to charge but his horse is gone—FOOM!

"You're not gonna kill *Traveler!??*" one anxious Virginian shouted.

"Traveler? Uh no, it's *another* horse! But all computer green screen, computer-- not to worry. The ship swoops through-(more green screen) and FOMP!! There comes a giant robot foot right in the lens!! Great composition and..and..you all are *scared* right? And then you run..FOOoooooo *BAM!*"(The director was now doing his own stunts, rolling all over the grass, regardless of horse manure) The AD tried to warn him but never had the chance.

" Pow Pow pa pa Pow! Fa-Zing! Fa-Zing! FOOossh Ka-BOOM!" Somewhere from the back of the crowd came a shrill "*Woo* woo woop woop woop!" Like Curley in the 3 Stooges.

"Who said that!!?" shouted the 1st AD , but no one answered. Gaylord Zarke finally got to his feet. "And and...and..well, do what Jim tells you..obey him as you would me..."

"Thanks Gay.." said Jim.

"No problem Jim..." and he walked off, thoroughly out of breath, brushing off his clothes,but totally unaware of 2 glaringly big brown, orange and sticky spots on the bottom of his chartreuse pants,while waving and giving several thumbs up. Some of the group swore they then heard the 1st AD mutter, "Pay no attention to that man behind the curtain.." but they were'nt sure.

Now they were being separated into new groups

and led to various parts of a field beyond some old farm buildings. On "one" this group would run left, yelling and screaming. On "two" another group with alien heads would chase them snarling (or rather mime-snarling), and waving their appendages wildly about them.

"Boy this is sure different from that courtroom scene we were in on "Range War: Stockyard of Justice"! said Kevin.

"Yeah, and there was much less manure!" Zeke agreed, while checking his feet.

"Quiet in the ranks!" yelled the 2nd AD. Zeke assumed attention and Kevin buttoned up his schnozzola thing, as he was led off with group 2, while Zeke became part of the army brigade which would charge the aliens from the rear. But somehow Kevin ended up following Zeke,what with his limited vision, but nobody seemed to care, so they didn't either. They soon found out that many of their newfound comrades were actually full time Civil War reinactors. Memories of Chancellorsville and the Battle of Sailor's Creek were flying back and forth as if they had actually been there.

"Ol' Fuss n' Feathers made us skeedaddle to a fair-the-well at our last engagement," said one old looking sergeant with great inflection of arm and limb, "I swar ta Goshen! PITOO!!" (he shifted his cudd and spat so it landed 'squar' in an old tin cup).

Another campaigner ups an' answers him, "Why, that t'ain't nothin' compared to Chickamaugee! I caught enough minnie balls ta fill a bucket an' then some!" — PITOO! (also land'n squar)

"Wow," said Zeke, "you guys oughta get some a

this dialogue into the movie!"

"Pshaw!" said one, "Why them Hollerwooders ain't got no more battle sense then ta come in out th' rain in a gully wash!"

"That's a fact!" said t'other, "but yew think they'd ask us our opine on th' subjeck? No sirree Bob! An' ussin's bein' th' ones that wuz actually *thar* too!"

Just then a group of slave reinactors were ushered over to stand by them, along with a small group of Yankee soldiers from the "U.S. Colored Brigade".

"I hope yew boys know yore place.." said one of the Rebels stroking his mustache.

"*What!?*" said a black sargent, "I have you know I'm emancipated!"

" No, excuse me, I meant the place you'll be standin' when th' shoot'n begins..you know, the motion picture apparatus..."

"Oh..yes, yes, we do.." Just then a man playing Frederick Douglas walked up.

"Is there some problem soldiers?" he said.

"Oh no, we're all emancipated and happy here!" After he left the Southern soldier said,"Uh, did you know we have uh, colored soldiers in the Confederacy?"

"Yeah, sure I do, I know *both* of 'em!" There was some tension, but then that got them all kind of laughing. Then Lincoln walked by, having trouble keeping his hat and beard on. He gave them a look while a make up girl came up with her kit and made over him.

" Mustn't lose your whiskers Mister President..." Zeke had been staring, watching the intriguing scene, but soon realized all these guys really believed they were *in* the Civil War itself, so he stopped talking except to Kevin.

" Maybe they're 'reincarnactors'.." mumbled Kevin through his bulbous head.

" Yeah, I met a lady who wrote a book about that, they did all these past life regressions on the battle-fields and—

" Hey look, it's Bob Finch!" Kevin was pointing.

" You mean the guy from your parties? Is he still a Libertarian?"

" Just look!"

Sure enough Bob was parading in front of the troops in his wide eyed smile, full beard and waxed up mus-tache, enthusiastically handing out flyers.

" It's the only platform that makes sense! Why should we pay taxes? Who are you fighting for? It doesn't matter who wins, it's still the State! The ob-jective is not Objectivism! But subjective objectivism which is truly objective in the subjective sense! Only *then* can we be truly autonomous!" Then the 2nd AD ran up and jerked him by the collar.

" I thought I told you to stop this crap!"

" See? The omnipotence of the State once again tramples our Civil Liberties!—Oh, hi Kevin! Hi Zeke!" Zeke and Kevin meekly waved but tried to melt into the crowd, while the 2nd AD barked into his walkie-talkie for security, and poor Bob was whisked away in an olive drab golf cart, but not before he threw a boat load of flyers into the air. "Power to the People!!" he yelled into the distance.

A broad pregnant pause descended over the crowd, as if an unseen but impending doom hung in the air above them. That fake "effects atmosphere smoke" they were spraying sort of made Zeke a bit nauseous, and he thought of those wild gory Civil War trading cards he and his friend Larry used to play with when they were kids playing war. They'd toss a coin and the loser had to be a Yankee. But this smell, if he had been really 'back there' on a battlefield, it would be a smell of wood smoke and gunpowder. *That* he could handle, that would be good.

Soon the crowd was back to it's normal self, fidgeting and chatting, heads bobbing everywhere. But one head across the way was stock still, it's union cap bent to the ground, which caught Zeke's eye. Then it slowly rose upward, revealing those same hideous pit-bullet hole eyes, staring directly at Zeke. Immediately the man fingered under his hat and snapped down his sunglasses into their accustomed place. Zeke froze, surrounded tightly by his fellow extras, not knowing what to do or where to go. But that problem was immediately solved by the 2nd AD who suddenly came trouncing past with an excited air, listening intently to his walkie-talkie.

"OK you people! We're going for a take!!" he screamed and ran quickly away. "Remember your places!" People everywhere were activated. Some scurried here and there, others, such as Zeke and Kevin's group made scurrying motions but didn't really go anywhere.

" Do we have places?" said Zeke.

" I don't think so.." said Kevin.

" Well then, let's *go* there!"

" Right!"

CHAPTER 25
Huzzah for the Horror!

Somewhere somebody yelled "Speed!", and soon after
that they heard "Action!" A few union soldiers ran by
out of nowhere followed by a few horses. Gunfire
could be heard farther up out of site. A walkie-talkie
squawked, "Forward on ONE". On a far hill was a
camera tower for shooting long shots, waving pink
and green flags. Somewhere some people were moving.

"Are we s'posed to follow them?" said Kevin,
wiggling his antenna at anyone who'd listen.

"Oh just make it look good!", said Zeke, "We're
actors aren't we?"

"First rule o' the Army, don't volunteer fer nuthin!"
said one reinactor, a grizzled looking sergeant, who
had to dodge Kevin's head as he swung around.

"Are we one or two?" said Zeke.

"I ain't got no number!"said Kevin inside his head.

"Oh tay Buh'wheat.." said Zeke. "We like the
Little Rascals..", he explained to the sergeant,who
nodded while chewin' his cud. "Ready on TWO!"
came a loud voice from behind.

"That must be us!" said Zeke, "they don't have

anymore numbers than 2.." and everybody sort of gathered themselves together, while Zeke sneaked a look across the way at Sunglasses so he could be sure to avoid him, but the soldier he thought was him was now somebody else, so he didn't have a handle to go on. What if during the battle he—BOOOOM!! He never finished the thought because a gigantic blast erupted just behind and sent everyone, union, rebel, alien, and civilian running and screaming in utter chaos!

Civil War soldiers and alien heads ran into each other while horses reared, dropping officers as cavalries charged and/or retreated simultaneously, no one knew for sure. Kevin frantically tried to negotiate his way by lifting his proboscis, shouting " 'scuse me! 'scuse me!" Zeke looked every which way at once, worrying about Minnie, possibly Jerry, but mostly looking for pit bull eyes in the crowd.

More explosions--BABOOM..BAbulBloOOoom— as fuller's earth, (the effects dirt of choice) and fodder of various types rained from on high while white-grey smoke rolled over them, obscuring what view and place orientation they had which was none. Suddenly on the horizon, through the smoke appeared a bulbous head and towering coppery edifice with waving arms and making a machinish grinding sound like a giant hand-cranked french horn with a steam induced bellows.

"Mad Robot! Mad Robot!" shouted a Rebel commander on his charger, "Head for the hills! Uh..the barn! ..THAT WAY!!", waving his sword he led the stampede at his General Custerish best. They all were moving more or less in one direction at last, except for

Kevin, who could'nt see very well and finally ripped off his alien head and started hitting people with it. Suddenly a roving cameraman came up on him, so he slapped it back on, acting with wobbling head as if going for the Oscar. The big robot finally went by, pulled on wheels by grips, nearly teetering over as it rumbled over the rocks.

" I thought everything was gonna be green screen!" shouted Zeke,(showing off a bit of his CGI computer effects knowledge).

"Some of it will be,"said a grip, as confused as anybody, "but a lot of it won't and they'll combine it later. It's the director's own patented style, he calls it 'Cinema Gravitas'."

" Hey, *quiet on the set!*" shouted the 2nd AD, also confused.

" You *know* we're not shooting sound!" Shot back the grip. Just then the entire mock giant robot hit an unexpected bump and toppled over side ways ,just missing the scrambling extras. "Now look what you made me do you stupid fuck!" yelled a robot grip, and he and the 2nd AD went at it, cussing and fighting. Just then Kevin ran by blubbering under his latex head, which was on backwards.

" CUT!" came a call from somewhere beyond the jumble of misshapen showbiz. Everyone more or less stopped what they were doing, whatever that was. ADs ,1st ,2nd and 3rd repeated "CUT" and "Standby to go to One!"

" One? What one? One what?" agreed both Zeke and Kevin.

" One is the first position,where we started.." said a rather condescending extra, " It means we're gonna do another take."

" ANOTHER ONE? Like that?? Nobody told us
anything!!" blurted Kevin from under layers of floppy
latex.

" Who are you? Are you SAG?" said the extra.

" Yeah, I'm sagging all over!!"

" Hmmph, non-union..." murmured the extra to his
friend. Just then the pink hatted director buzzed by in
his jeep.

" Great stuff people! Good motivation! Very authentic! I could really *feel* your paranoia! But next
time I want you to push it even further, think outside
the box! OK now people? You're *beautiful*, I love you
all...and thank you, for being human.." Faces now
looked at each other in wonderment, whether they
looked human or not.

" Back to One!" shouted the 1st AD. Now the giant
robot was back on it's wheels and being towed back
up the hill from whence it came.

Zeke turned to Kevin, "So we're gonna do all that
again?" But before he could get an answer,"ACTION"
was shouted again.—BaBOOOM!— went a cannon,
horses came running and troops were moving.

" Hey, it's different this time!" yelled Kevin, "I
thought it was Take Two!"

" Oh, take it which ever way it comes!" said Zeke
and dove into the battle. Kevin began slapping anyone
who came near with his big octopus tenacles. Zeke
parried and thrusted with his bayonet,(which was
rubber) while Kevin learned he could twirl around,
making his tenacles spin out like helicopter blades,
(just like he used to watch Saturday morning on
'Squiddly Diddly'). Zeke was also really getting into

it, losing himself in the role, with many a "Damn Yankee!", "The South Foh-evah!" And "Avast there Matey, ye scurvy swab!" thrown in for good measure.

Again the sky was engulfed in smoke and robots rolled around. Again all the directions seemed new and totally improvised, that is if you could call them directions. Who was on which side? Which way *was* his or who's side? The sun above, a grey inundated disc was Zeke's only guide, so he just ran in the path of least resistance. This must be a lot like real battle he thought, total pandemonium.

Now his body was getting tepid and clammy within the layers of imitation woolen clothing. He tried to think of that old joke about the "damp yankee",but suddenly the back of his neck felt hot. He looked around, his eyes came to rest on those two familiar bullet black dots in a pugnacious face, staring straight at him,the black eyes now glowing a deep orange. Immediately Zeke's eyes burned like fire. Ducking and turning away he staggered and ran with his head tucked down, plowing through or around any obstacle he encountered. Cannons growled and rolled around him, shouts and even screams that sounded too real for comfort. War-like phrases were mixed with stray and futile production directives from equally futile assistant directors. Occasionally a pink hat with yellow hair rose above the din as the director flung his arms and yelled for more authenticity, and to "feel the pain", "feel the atrocity of war", and to *Become the horror!", "Become the cannonball!"* He even re-warded Zeke himself with a face to face instruction.

"Here's your motivation soldier!—BOOM! CRASH ! POW! Make it AWESOME!" Zeke winced

at that hated word, (even though it's usage here was
pretty correct) then Pink Hat staggered away into the
dirty billowing clouds, laughing joyfully as well as
groaning like he was shot, (soon he'd be smoked ham,
thought Zeke). That encounter with fame however,
stimulated Zeke and reawakened within him his latent
filmmaking ambitions from college, so now he
charged ahead into the melee.

" *I am the cannonball, I AM the cannonball!*" He
repeated to himself like a mantra. But the main thing
he could think of was his high school book report on
"The Red Badge of Courage", for which he got an
"A". The main character, a young soldier,first time in
battle had run petrified into the woods, all the while
convincing himself he was just lost, and wrestling
with guilt,until he met with the "Raggedy Man", or
was it the "Tattered Soldier"?, (played in the movie by
that gaunt looking old TV character actor that looked
like John Carradine but wasn't). Anyway, he must
"find the Raggedy Man, the Raggedy Man..." His
eyes grew wild as he dodged his way through the
brouhaha, chanting to himself his odd mental
ramblings...(It seemed to help).

   He found himself at one point on a hilltop perceiv-
ing all below him.In a hypnotic stupor he stood trans-
fixed while the panorama swirled below him, like one
of those far flung medieval battle paintings com-
memorating a famous victory. The maggot like mass
moved, engulfed in smoke,uproar,bayonets, bobble
heads and teetering robot giants while filtering a
mysterious redness from the sun which was now a
dirty orange ball. All things below were writhing,
undulating shapes of clashing futile human endeavor,

while even so, he knew the old Earth turned beneath, oblivious to the all-intensive matters of men.

Or..did Mother Earth somehow feel the millions of pin pricks thrust upon her from her own tiny creations? But after all, this was a mere mock up for the cameras, he was worrying too much, he must relax and enjoy, as had been their intention that morning. Zeke was still standing, hypnotized by the whirling vortex of life imitating life before him, when again he saw another figure standing, still with glowing orange eyes in the smoke. Aimed straight at him, he recognized the overall humanoid shape, but now it seemed rougher and somehow encrusted with ash, like the grey powdered turds you dig out of your kitty's litterbox, but with arms and legs. He reacted with a start, then the pit bullish alien bounded up the hill toward him with immense strides, not on two but on four legs,like a pumped up hyena. Zeke quickly sank again into the battle around him.Now he again dodged and ran, but constantly looking over his shoulder for the evil orange eyes in the smoke, which appeared every so often it seemed, off and on between the rushing battling shapes around him. What a sickening, dizzying and nauseous vision!

Again Zeke doubted his sanity or his reality vs. dream awareness. Was what he saw the true appearance of the evil Sunglassed aliens? He continued moving through the mass of insanity which was itself unreal enough. What was reality? Is what's in your mind unreal? It's certainly real to you, and after all, that's the only way we experience anything, through our mind or *whatever* it is. The mind within the body, the soul within the mind. He couldn't believe he was philosophying and waxing intellectual like this in the midst of such sweeping agitation, where each step or lunge was a life changing decision.

Did these filmmakers actually know what they were doing? He heard one production person he passed say to another, "Don't worry, we'll fix it in the mix." (Cement mixer was more like it.), and "Wait 'til the CGI guys in post get a hold of it, it'll be OK..yeah sure, it'll be alright..."

Zeke's sinuses began acting up, snorting and spitting as the smoke clogged his passages. Some soldiers where cussing at each other. Another couple of production people were saying something about being 12 days over schedule and 20 million over budget. Zeke found himself more and more nonplussed by the whole experience and took to making up whatever dialogue he could think of for himself regardless of sense or logic, such as "Now is the time for all good men to come to the aid of their party" and "Four score and seven years ago..," "And God said, let there be light.." What *was* creation? Life? Each life form needs some point of reference in which to live, a pool, a shore, a cliff, a hole, a cave, a strange out cropping, clouds passing over, legs to walk on, wings to flap, eyes to contemplate the next horizon, which may in fact be a bump on a giant's thumb from a parallel universe. But of course what the hell, *he* was *here*.

More horses rattled by, one dragging some poor background actor who sounded too real to be a stunt double. "Let there be Light...", "*and* darkness", added Zeke to himself, footnoting the famous quote, for without darkness what is light? Contrast defines our reality, even while we sleep. Sleep, perchance to dream, shake..spear..rattle sabor..with many mortal coils to shuffle off of...and mortal nostrils to sniffle.. Take Sominex tonight and sleep, safe and restful, sleep sleep sleeeep."(He was now actually singing commercials from his childhood.) "New Ajax, laundry detergent is *stronger than dirt!*...Oh Marvel the Mustang, he's almost for real, just saddle him up, with spurs on your heels..."

"Orange eyes? Orange eyes? Did he see them?"he thought,with poleaxing bodies running and slamming and shouting. He was sure now there were actual casualties in this great swarming mess. The groans were too real. Was this history? Was this Art? Greatness? *Showbiz?*

The whole thing was making Zeke tired and woozey. Somewhere below and far off, bullhorns were barking orders, and the huge fighting-crowd-beast slowly came to a stop. Grey sooty Robots wobbled listlessly. Everybody was looking around. Zeke was again on a hilltop so he got a good broad view. A couple of ADs were storming up the open corridor more or less separating two halves of the crowd. Flags were waving weakly from the camera tower.

Smoke was dissipating as the pink baseball hat zoomed up, hunkered down in his jeep.The ADs immediately reported to the hat and talked with animation, but could not compete with the hat and it's furiously gesticulating arms. Soon the director under the hat was pacing back and forth nodding his head with quick jerky bursts as the ADs answered questions and pointed back and forth as well as "way over there". Clearly Gaylord Zarke was on a roll and quite pleased with himself. He then started making gestures with both hands chopping in unison with great decision and import,(just the way Kim Jong Un does on North Korean TV with his big hat generals when the cameras are rolling).

Suddenly a man with messed up hair and carrying an expensive looking camera came stalking up and pushed the pink hatted genius, flipping him 180 degrees around. All the ears of the hundreds of extras strained to hear what conversation transpired, but the one clear phrase that rang out to them was, *"YOU IDIOT!!"*.

"Whoever made you a director anyway?" yelled the director of photography, "Where's the continuity? You've screwed this movie up nine ways to Sunday!" But the pink hatted director gave as well as he got.

" *What the hell?* I'm shooting *coverage* you *damn putz!* In editing I'll turn this into a..a..fuckin' symbolic masterpiece that'll win the fuck'n *Oscar!"*

" Coverage? *Of what?* None of this crap we've shot will ever cut much less make sense!"

" It's what's known as a subjective-objective character driven transition introspective subjective omnipresent poetic montage!"said Zarke smugly.

" That's artsy fartsy bull shit and you *know* it!"

" Shut your face, *focus puller!"*

" Oh and who are *you?* The office fart face that sleeps with the producer's daughter...no, make that the producer!"

" Ha! That camera is so automatic it could shoot the movie by itself, go to the premiere and give a press release! You don't even know what an f-stop *is!*

" I'll show you an f-stop, come on you *twerp!"*

Suddenly the two creative heads were joined by a younger functionary with a walkie-talkie. They all quickly dropped into hushed tones as they noticed that the whole crowd of actors, extras and stunt-robot-doubles were starring at them. Assuming overly cooperative attitudes of damage control, they went back to their positions while the 1st AD conferred with the functionary who shouted, " OK! Everyone back to ONE!"

Zeke was fast realizing that despite all of his high flying fantasies about movie sets and directing films etcetera, he didn't actually have the stomach for it. Not like this. This was like fighting a military campaign with no battle plan in fast motion run through a meat grinder. Here he was in the middle of what was supposedly the pinnacle of American cultural achievement in one of the most desirable of fields, an A-list motion picture, and yet he felt like a cow turd that had been run over by a bulldozer. Where was the fun ? The excitement? The art? Excitement there was a plenty but at the price of a thousand ulcers. What about all those classic "on the set" stories told by great stars and film artisans of yesteryear?.

Clearly there was more than one way to skin a movie, but Zeke had just about decided to dodge this particular grim reaper's swing blade. Besides which he had his own outre' drama to contend with, which had a will of it's own worse than any pink hatted director with continuity problems and which was consistently discontented. Zeke started taking off his uniform and walking down the hill.

" Hey! Where are you going!?" shouted the 2nd AD. " You can't leave, you were in the last shot and now you'll disappear!"

" That's what I plan to do!" retorted Zeke.

" No! I mean.. Hey WAIT! You'll never work in this town agai— Hey!" The 2nd AD finally caught Zeke up in the crowd further along and took him aside, murmuring.

" Look, I know how you feel, I know this is another big dumb picture that doesn't need to be made but..see this is my *job!* Please..please go back to your place..please go back to One, hmm? OK?" Zeke saw the anguish in the guy's eyes and caved. He now walked slumpingly back up the hill with the 2nd AD's hand over his shoulder posing like "nothing's wrong here", and a big coat hanger-stuck-in-his-mouth smile.

Soon they were set for another take. The air was actually quite clear now, the choking pollution of battle gone. A crisp blue sky shone to the Southwest.

"This shouldn't be so bad this time" thought Zeke.

" SMOKE!! WHERE'S MY SMOKE?!!" yelled ol' "Pink Hat n' Feathers" as he ran down the lane in a full blown conniption. Then came a truck blowing thick stuff in the air with people coughing and some union extras grumbling that the smoke they were using was illegal since 1996. They swore they'd sue the production company, and were soliciting support from other extras including Zeke, who could only cough and nod. Now came another take, more cannon fire and charging chaos.

"BAROOOM!" "HUZZAH!" "WHAT THE FUCK!?" SHIT!!" "AAAAAAHH!"came the various barrage of sounds as bodies ran and tumbled in the orange and brown pulsing horror. Finally somebody somewhere was yelling "CUT!" A groaning sigh of relief all 'round, then— "Back to One!" The groan was turning to snarls and threats.

Zeke began trudging up the hill again with head hung low, when he suddenly stopped short. There before him on the ground was something at first beautiful in his peripheral vision which caught his eye, a love since childhood, a flash of patterned yellow, orange and black in the thick green grass at his feet. It was what he thought, but was in fact a squashed, cracked, and trampled tortise. All the turtle friends of Zeke's childhood cried out to him, along with the creatures he had played with on the porch, animals he had caught, birds, baby rabbits etc., played with, wondered over, loved and then let go as his Dad had taught him.

All his overpowering love for nature and it's creations, memories from an emotional youth, running out on the golf driving range at the Dupont picnic because of a far distant silhouette on the horizon of a tortise walking across, picking him up and carrying to safety, (like his Dad, a safety engineer).That beautiful shell, the cracked orange reptilian smile as the head "fooshed" back in it's shell, the round scaly feet left showing that you could touch, all this now poured back to and through his soul from those pitiful red-yellow eyes on the ground, and the once plodding reptile friend was now gushing forth in several directions from within that once fine "house on his back". Formidable,impregnable to natural predators such as fox and coon, but a mere shattered eggshell before the onslaught of boot-heeled Man and his ever increasing wonders of technology.

Zeke snapped. He didn't go back to One, he didn't

stand still, he started walking wherever the mood took him and the mood was one long explosive rant to the world.

"God Fucking Damn it! *God Damn it!*"

"Don't take the name of the Lord in vain brother!" piped a nearby reinactor totally lost in his role. "We must except his righteous judgement upon our bereft native land! Vengence is his alone! He hath trampled out the vintage where.."

" I'll damn anything I want, and do it *in* HIS name dammit! Look at that beautiful turtle! Where's the righteousness in *that!??* What the *Hell* are we doing?? What is all this?! The World is dieing! And all they do is BOOM! CRASH! BLEEEH! All this damn technology—it's TOO MUCH!! The *TAIL IS WAGGING THE DOG!!*"

" What? Hey man, shut up and sit down ,you'll get us in *trouble!*" came the voice of another extra.

" We're already *IN* trouble!!" yelled Zeke, his voice straining. " Don't you get it? The TAIL IS WAGGING THE DOG!" Already in the distance a walkie-talkie man was moving this way, but he kept on yelling. "You see, WE are the Dog,and *we* created technology, to make life *BETTER* see? It grew out of *us*! But now the TAIL is WAGGING THE DOG!! SEE?? It's shaking us to bits!! And all this...this...". He was waving arms at the intricate workings of the modern day action motion picture, while the Walkie-Talkies were converging, squawking about a disturbance and requesting back-up. More people were either shushing Zeke or urging him to take a hike or something—mostly something.

" And all we do is yell and bash our heads together!, driving SUVs, talking on our cel phones, tearing down civilization, tearing down nature, stomping on *turtles dammit!*" He was staggering along with tears in his eyes and hardly able to see. Just then Kevin noticed him and ran over.

" Don't mind him everybody! He's just getting into character! Method actor ya know-- Stanislavski!"

" But I don't *know* any Stanislavski..." returned Zeke.

" Yes you do..come on, I'm gittin' you out of here!" Somewhat quieted, the two started moving down the lane between the crowds of extras, just as the Walkie-Talkies arrived. Luckily no one gave them away and they passed unnoticed. Kevin still had his prosthetic head on and no one was going to interrupt a lunatic escorted by an alien. Besides, extras have to stick together.

Then Zeke started up again. " Growth Growth Growth! That's all they talk about, everything's got to be bigger and bigger! And then they've got to blow it up! Meanwhile *polar bears are dieing!* Too many people! The earth's not getting any smaller you know! And Mexicans pouring over the border because the rich Mexicans pay them a dollar a day!Or is it 2 dollars? It's modern day feudalism! I actually *like* Mexicans, it's what they've done I don't like, the rich class especially! The Conquistadors are still in control down there! They need minimum wage laws! And the Politically Correct newscasters and PC media, too afraid to say the truth because they're too apologetic and nice and afraid of lawsuits, meanwhile the networks pour disgusting violent depressing filth all over the television!"

" We've got a right to defend our borders! Hell,the Mexicans usually have good taste at least! They sure defend *theirs!* Save our culture! But what good will that do? We're all gonna burn up! Everybody can't come here! And the middle class is disappearing! Why does America have to give up their culture while everybody else preserves theirs? They need to develop democracy *there* instead of always coming here! We're full up! But even if they get democracy then THEY will want growth growth growth, because businesses must grow or die they say, but we're all dieing from GROWTH! And meanwhile we fight over religion! What good is *that!?* Arabs trying to blow up everything for Allah! God! What's that to do with God's work! There! There's one now!" He was pointing at a dark haired and bearded man controlling a rather large electronic device.

" Hold on mate! I'm Jewish from Australia!"

" Oh.. so sorry, you're lovely people..But none of this will do any good because asteroids are going to hit the earth! And we're not paying attention! You better pray the *aliens* are! Somewhere in a hollowed out volcano! In the old Sci Fi movies everybody got together by the end to save the World! With the leaders and the countries and the scientists..the guys with white coats and glasses and smoking pipes! Played by Walter Pidgeon and Whit Bissell!! Yes! We need our men with pipes!! *GOD,where are our men with pipes!!??*" By now Zeke was crying and sobbing and flailing about. Kevin was still guiding him to safety best he could and apologizing for him.

" Don't mind him he's just a cartoonist.."

" Yeah, and the cartoons are no good anymore

either!" Zeke was sort of media-rant punch drunk now
and easily led. Soon Minnie came up helping and
asking what was what.

"I sensed a super rant was getting ready to blow.
He'll be fine if we get him quiet and away from modern things..lay him in the grass somewhere.." But just
then the infamous pink hat bobbed into view through
the crowd, and his nibs, the imminent Gaylord Zarke
himself was tearing up hill on a rant of his own.

" OK! We're going again and I want major thrusting! A whirlwind mass of militant mayhem! Hey,
write that down, we can use it in the ad campaign",
(he muttered to his assitant). " And cannon! I want
lots of BOOM BOOM BOOOM! You know!? And a
charging *thrust* you people! Tumbling down and down
like Niagara Falls! What? Not enough stunt men?
Don't worry, it's only a movie! You'll all be great! Ha
Ha! Thumbs up! Just kidding...You got the helicop-
ters?" (Again to his assistant) "I want AWESOME!
Lots of AWESOME..*AWESOMENESS!!*" Zeke suddenly stared wide eyed as the pink hat passed near
him.

" *YOU!!*" yelled Zeke pointing him in the face.
Zarke turned on him, with indignant indignation, but
speechless.

" Uhh..yes..what.."

" *YOU* are *he!* "

" Look I'll be glad to sign autographs later but just
now I'm too—"

" The Mark of the *Beast* is upon your brow! Remove that hat so that all may see!" Zarke started
calling for security." So that all MAY *SEE!!*" Zeke
grabbed for his hat, there was a tussle, but the hat

gave way—revealing a head full of hair plugs! Both
gasps and snickers were heard all round, but Zeke
pointed like abolitionist John Brown before his raid.
"BEHOLD! THE MARK OF THE BEAST! *Smite*
him upon his brow!"

" Git him out of here!! *Get him!*" Zarke yelled,
snatching back his hat. Security was wending through
the crowd while Kevin and Minnie pulled and jostled
Zeke to melt further away when-BOOM!! There went
the cannon. " CUT!!" yelled the director, "I mean I
didn't yell cut! I mean action..NO! Back to one!"—
BOOOM!— "*Stop it! Stop it!*" —BOOOM!—
"GODDAMMIT I SAID—" Zarke stopped in his
tracks when he saw one of his cannon squads innocently leaning against their weapon, awaiting his
instructions. BAARROOOM! RUMBLE RUMBLE—
Everyone looked overhead to the West. Huge black
clouds were billowing up and over them, as if Zeus
himself was about to attack. ADs were shouting for
everyone to go to the tents and cover the cameras.

"No!" yelled Gaylord Zarke, "This is great! We
can get some shots before it arrives! We can *use* this!
Everybody back to one! *Hurry!*" Some people
obeyed, some grumbled, but many yelled in protest.
Many just ran, while the rest just panicked.

The new pandemonium of course was a boon to
Zeke and company. They wound their way surely but
calmly through the crowd, accustomed as they were to
being chased on all sides, except for Kevin, who was
new to it all, as well as frantically trying to remove his
alien head. "Lemme outta hea! lemme outta hea!!" He
finally gave it a mighty tug and it blooped off his
shoulders, hitting the back of another extra, who

turned around with a menacing snarl, revealing an amazing makeup job Kevin couldn't help but admire. "Hey! Good one!" He said to the beady eyed pit bull-ish face,saliva dripping down.

" *This* way Kevin!!" It was now Zeke's turn to steer his friend to safety as fast as possible, while the Sunglasses Alien tried nastily to catch them. Again, rushing people pandemonium was in their favor, but that evil face kept thrusting at them at every other turn as it paralleled their tracks in wolf-like fashion. Meanwhile Gaylord Zarke careened around and around with his own hand-held camera shouting.

" That's it! More energy! Think with your gut! Your *gut!!*" Meanwhile various debris was blowing about as somewhere a siren was being played with-- BLOOEEEoup! BLOOOooooooo. People were rushing every which way. Mr. Zarke was laughing to himself, "Ha HAA! We may have to do a re-write but that's OK!" His camera pointed this way and that, until a spinning human being whirled up and knocked his camera in the mud. It was Jerry.

" Oh *sorry!*"and he went off calling for Zeke. The clouds were now high wide and extremely black as well as greenish purple. This did not bode well. The wind began to kick up. Paper plates and styrofoam cups were flying everywhere. Zeke knew these signs well, but held back until he knew for sure. Someone shouted "*Tornado!!*" It was echoed here and there and followed by screams. Zeke and Minnie saw the strange smooth finger of cloud extend towards the ground. The huge white tent was doing a wild dance, 19th Century figures ran hither and yon,bonnets and top hats whirling away like frisbees. Some of the

more bodacious of the local-boy Southern reinactors
were yelling "YEEE HI!" and leading charges to
nowhere, Hell bent fer leather, while some others
drank beer and fired a cannon at the funnel cloud,
while Jerry had somehow found Zeke and Minnie.

" Head for the parking lot!"

" Aren't we s'posed to git in a ditch?" yelled Zeke.

" *What ditch?*" yelled Minnie.

" I think the parking lot's over that hill!" said Jerry.

" No it's over that one!" yelled Zeke. People and
horses still criss-crossed around them, but soon a pair
of burning orange eyes smoldered at them from the
crowd and decided their direction for them—the other
way!

"EEEERRRAAAAAAAKK!" The horrible alien
gave an unearthly cry like a pterodactyl crossed with
an elephant, and ripped open his suit revealing his
steam emiting muscular cat-litter bulging body as he
leaped into the air like a demonic rottweiler. Bounding
forward in a giant leap, he was suddenly smacked by a
large mass of spinning metal. One of the huge robot
props on wheels had gotten away from it's handlers
who were frantically trying to save it from storm
damage. It went frolicking down the hill waving it's
loose arms like a big copper ginger bread man, as if
shouting "Catch me! Catch me if you can!", to the
handlers who were all the more determined to grab it's
flailing ropes.

The three friends had gained distance now and
reached the top of the hill, beyond which was not the
parking lot, but another one beyond held promise as
they got their bearings. They could see the evil alien
amid some wreckage zestfully working at putting

himself together, scooping mud and steaming crumbled parts of himself to build up arms and chest. This regenerative ability amazed them, but now the main visual attraction was the tornado, beyond the movie set in the low grounds by the river, just touching down and churning up the rich red clay of Virginia, and taking that color up into itself. It undulated grandly in the afternoon sun which reached it aslant from a western break in the clouds. As it proceeded into the dark loam of the bottom land, a chocolate swirl mixed in with the sandy red.

From behind them came a shrill voice. "*Zeke! Zeke! Minnie!*" Jerry was suddenly picked up and carried down hill,where he was now scrambling like a cat in quicksand. But now came a lateral wind of tremendous strength from the west over the ridge they stood upon, forcing them all back down the hill into a somewhat protected bowl in which much of the film had been shot.They tumbled through the weeds, trying to avoid people and horses.As Zeke managed to right himself, his eye was caught by a valiant scene, as a band of Southern and Yankee infantrymen charged up the ridge for safety, colliding and arguing with heroic fervor as they in a sense tried to "take" the hill.

"*Take that fer Manassas!* Yew filthy hash slingin'cussed thunder-jug field pirate Rebs!"

"We call it *Bull Run* , an' that's fer Gettysburg ya karn sarned pig sloppin' Blue Bellies!"

Despite the dialogue, if you "turned down the sound" it brought to mind the heroic scene at Iwo Jima, or some of the fine sculpture on the field at Gettysburg, as they also upheld their competing flag standards as in a full pitched battle. Adding to this, a battery of artillerymen with two cannon pulled by horses was fast gaining at their rear, anxious to save their precious equipment.

However, the wind shear over the ridge was so much, that this entire assembly, as it fought for it's ground soon lost it, not horizontally but vertically, and was now treading air as they slowly but surely left the ground! Here was a magnificent battle scene worthy of a giant canvas by Remington or Russell, hanging in the Smithsonian. They were going through their paces, seemingly unaware of their strange new condition, and moving gradually backwards, completely airborne. The afternoon sun illuminated them brilliantly so that fear and amazement barely entered one's mind at the site of it, and was replaced by wonder and awe, if not a shout of--"*Huzzah!*"

The giant funnel cloud was getting angry, dirt and debris were everywhere,while humanity and horses were collecting at hill bottom in ever more swirling chaos. Zeke held on to Minnie as the broom straw blew sideways along with everything else not nailed down. All were hugging the earth for dear life with their faces in the dirt. The freight train sound was much in their ears but also the high frightening whine of high speed wind, much like old Hollywood wind machines. Zeke focused on that sound as somehow comforting, thinking of an old John Ford movie, "Hurricane" and how through storm blasted FX and devastation, Dorothy Lamour still survived (at least he thought she did).The roar and whine blended now, striking an almost pure musical note which was tuning ever upward into a whole new key.

His cartoon friends Melvin and Stupid suddenly

passed across his minds eye, one pedaling a bike, the other in a rocking chair, waving happily at him as if he Zeke was Judy Garland. The sound of her voice came to him— "Somewhere, OOOooooooveeerrr th-" but the second word turned into a beautiful harmonic tone, so heavenly sent he just had to risk looking up.

Above him was an amazing vortex of blue-grey purplish cloud. Was he seeing the inner chamber of the tornado? Swirling it was but dangerous it was not. (That is unless another funnel began to descend from it). Besides, by the sound of the roar the tornado was already receding off down river to the east, and even diminishing in strength. Debris was still flying but settling down. They laid there, frozen behind some wagon wheels while the rushing feet and hooves went around. Occasionally a horse leaped over them. The strange cloud still held Zeke's hypnotic gaze when he became aware of a bounding dark shape in his lower vision. The pit bull cat litter alien had them again in his sites and was but a few leaps away. Zeke held Minnie tight while frozen in amplified but stifling fear. The evil thing bounded and was descending upon them when of a sudden it was flipped and lifted, spinning in mid air as if caught by an invisible lasso which twirled it overhead and out of sight.

Zeke was just regaining his wits when he again looked at the cloud. It was indeed rotating but at a comparatively slower rate, and beams of light were shooting through the frothy vortex. As if in a heavenly vision the cloud began to open and the clear sky beyond could be seen. But in the middle of this great aerial window was a great shining ship, a flying saucer, awesome but immensely benevolent in it's aspect.

The sun was beaming brightly off it's metalic blueish surface, beautiful chrome trim with muted violet colored lights not unlike wonderful glass paper weights in a sunlit window or tail lights on a classic car in the evening that fascinate when you're a child. A child, tail lights. Punch drunk as he was Zeke had a sort of uplifting creative revelation that pulled him suddenly to his feet. He started to sing like in a choir of an old time gospel church.

> " Ezekiel saw a *wheel!*
> " A wheel way up in the middle of the air!
> " A wheel within a *wheel,*
> " A wheel way up in the middle of the air!"

He began to stagger forward, not looking where he was going but fixed on the spectacle in the sky. Minnie went after and tried to guide him best she could.

"What's he doing?" said Jerry.

Kevin answered. " It's very indicative of a charac-ter channeling trance, he's really quite brilliant, doesn't even need make up! He could use a good manager though..."

" Ezekiel saw a WHEEEEL!" Zeke staggered on while normalcy descended on the set.

" I didn't know the film had a Biblical message.." said one extra to another.

" Oh yes, I think it's a faith-based production, and these special effects are wonderful! You really feel you're IN the story!"

" Must be done with hologramic projection, amaz-ing what they can do.." Then came Libertarian Bob

Finch, gleamy and big eyed, his handlebar mustache grinning from ear to ear.

" Now is the time to declare our freedom! Join with me brothers, it's a New World Order!" Just then a stumbling pink-hat man came by screaming, "Did you get it?! Did anybody git it on camera? We can use it!! Does *anybody* have a camera??" Then he saw Zeke, who was hard to miss with his wild singing and jestures.

"YOU! I remember you!" yelled the director. "You put some kinda hex on this whole production! I know bad Mojo when I see it! SECURITY! *SECURITY!!*" The nearby functionaries came alive with accusing looks and walkie-talkie squawks as the friends again ducked for cover, winding their way through the crowd. Zarke then picked up where he'd left off. "OK you people! Back to One! Get going! Let's think *outside the box!*" Just then, for some unknown reason, a cardboard container hit Zarke up side the head.

" I've got to get out of here" said Zeke.

" I *know* you've got to get out of here!" said Jerry.

" *OK* I'm getting!" They pushed hurriedly along. "It's such a shame to leave our cute little countryside tribulation.."

" Call it your very own pocket apocalypse..." Suddenly remembering they were wearing Civil War regalia they made a detour to the costume tent which was as they would say in 1860's parlance, "all cattywampus" and in a frenzied state of repair, but the ever stalwart movie set workers were fast setting up shop again and were ready to process Zeke, Minnie and Jerry's movie clothes and return their own. They

were about ready to go when they noticed stealthy
security people eyeballing the wardrobe department,
phones to the ear. Just then Kevin, who'd gotten separated, ran up.

"Hey Zeke! Are you going?" They tried their best
to shush him while turning away from the guards.
"Hey, it's not over! They're gonna shoot some more
scenes! I wanna get in on it!" He smiled back with
glee as he ran off, swinging his big torn latex append-
age. "Hey, somebody said they saw a UFO! And
they're gonna fix my head!"

" What services they provide..maybe I should
stay...I could use a good shrink.."said Zeke.

" Oh no you don't!" said Minnie. "Be off with
ya..we'll catch you up later, call me on my cel.."
pushing him behind a canvas out of view. But on the
other side were more Securities and ADs all scanning
around.

" Look, *here!*" said Jerry, "Take my car keys and
give me yours, those forms we filled out probably let
them trace vehicle registration.." They agreed it was a
good idea, plus Zeke had been aching to drive Jerry's
Mini Cooper.

" Where will you go?" asked Minnie wistfully.

" I think I'll head on up to Colombia, where all this
mess began..." Zeke's eyes were already searching the
western horizon.

CHAPTER 26
Monacan Moon

Zeke felt a sudden rush of release and freedom as he trudged through the grass to the cars. On the State Farm property the onslaught of species depletion had been slowed down compared to the outside, so that he actually heard a Red Winged Blackbird for the first time in years, and the bright powerful warbling of a Meadowlark on a fence post made his heart sing like a great symphony. No more meat-grinder drudgery in the name of creativity that had descended on his soul at the movie set. That gave way to a boyish exhilaration when first he sat in Jerry's Mini.

The throaty sputter of the little engine and the bouncy quick-steering ride through the country lanes was like a ride at the fair, until he suddenly slowed for a movie set check point, where a guard gave him a stern once over. His staring sunglasses brought back some worry to his spine, but then he was waved on and he was free. Free like a wayward starling to weave and roam once again. Soon again the undulating ribbon of Route 6 lay before him.

He playfully zig-zagged across the yellow lines, tempting oncoming traffic in his exhilaration,

watching ahead all the same. Soon thoughts of where
he was heading overcame him. Memories of that
strange night long ago rose before him, as he approached once again the area where it had occured.

But also his mind was full of complexities, not
only the ramifications of the strange labyrinth of
events to which he and his friends had recently been
subjected, a vortex of mystery and violence, of weird
wonder and partial revelations, but thoughts of the
world at large and all the confusing swirl of not only
events, but the continuous clash of voices, idealogies,
mindsets, awarenesses and cultural view points which
had been set on an ever increasing collision course
since around the year 2000. It was like all the splits of
life and doctrine so strongly associated with the 60s
and 70s, had resurfaced like a giant hurricane of excited confusion,with all parties shrieking their various
viewpoints and yes, physical attacks, even while some
who had fervently searched for peace and fulfillment
and had become as a result smiling and complacently
mellow (often that is, if they had money for such
indulgences), also flared up in righteous rage or teary
eyed rants to equal the energy of the others.

The result being the world resembled more and
more a gigantic Tower of Babel, while immediate
dangers were left mostly unattended to. The cultural
revolution of Western Civilization had come full
cycle. All the bright new ideas were now getting
muddled, and some sort of cleaning up and fix it
campaign was in order. But how would it all work
out?

As always Zeke had to shake his head out of the
immense depression such thoughts brought on.

He had, (because of his feeling for his family which was old and full of beloved characters), tried to always except both sides of cultural arguments, right and left, even if he didn't always agree with them from either or both sides of the ongoing political debate that is America. It seemed ever since the 1860s, that we were always in a way re-fighting the Civil War, (while also being nostalgic for it!) The answer as always was to be found in both directions, and many side avenues. Ever since the great divide of the 60s this stance of his often made him feel like a rubber doll torn asunder,trying to hold his family and even the nation together internally. What he wanted to feel like was just a kid, at those family reunions he remembered with such fondness on the lawn of the old home place up at Scottsville. What he hated most were extremists who can't take a clear multi-sided look at any situation. He had always hoped to contribute to this approach somehow in his art. But now as most days, he must try to get his head into a feel-good place for his own health and well being.That is until the next time he turned on the news.

That place now was his old country road and childhood mystery of possible alien abduction, which oddly enough gave him a peaceful warm glow. Again he was approaching "the place" just outside of Colombia. The turn-off spot by the railroad tracks, the partially obscured sign reading "Alien, tera tera". It was all still there, except the leaves had shifted slightly to now read, "Ali, tera ter". Sounded like a foriegn boxing match from the 60s hosted by Howard Cosell. Driving through town, the place looked de-

serted so he kept on going. What stimulated his adventurous vision-quest gland most now
was the old farm, Rivana Bluffs, where all the recent strangeness and excitement had started. It should be quiet there now, and quiet was what he sought, that and possible answers. Something...

As he pulled up the sandy, grass-lined cedar sheltered drive to the house it all came back to him. There was the place in the aged fence where he and Jerry had gone seeking the alien that bright morning not long ago, only a few days. But also somehow long ago. It seemed nobody was home, so Zeke just parked in the grassy parking lot, figuring to explain his presence later as hoping for another tour or having forgotten his reading glasses or something. Then there was always the angle of his great grandfather, doing research etc. But now he headed immediately for the "V" shaped gate in the old log fence.

Again his feet sloughed through big yellow and orange Beech and Poplar leaves on the ground, sounding like someone shoveling loose trash. The overhead cathedral tree arches filtering yellow sun passed over him as the old forest embraced him once more. The ridge of slippery shale again revealed itself beetling over the Rivana River far below, and he knew to follow the dim trail to the right, down, down toward the point where it merged with the mighty James. Thoughts of the Indian village that once populated the point came to mind, but more ominous came those of the rude interruption upon his and Jerry's adventurous reverie by the "fisherman" who had so turned their lives upside down.

But today, the original sublime feeling had returned and Zeke felt safe and secure in his "up the country" rapture as of old, and again felt the wondrous pull of the ancient burial mound above on the high plateau. Just then a large shadow passed over Zeke's face to his right and he knew that it was near. The woods were suddenly dark as he turned up a narrow deer trail, fending off prickly branches and holly leaves from his face. Finally the sun peeped through again like a sunset in the sky even though it was only about 3:30. The hulking form above and before him showed that he had found again the great mound of the Monacans. This place had drawn him back just as it had the day of the picnic, as well as from his childhood and the stories recited each time on the way up home to his grandmother's by his Dad and others. The Monacan mound, Jefferson's mound, site of the first archeological dig in America. All these thoughts were one and the same with the fresh country air, family memories,and the sense of and love for, "The Land".

These boxcars on his train of thought naturally led to the cut, the slice in the mound that Jefferson had dug in his investigation of the ways of the Monacans. It was along here somewhere. Zeke then remembered the strange but brief happenings at this ditch before the violence at the river below which had nearly wiped all memory before it. The cicadas, with wild whirring noise that had so rattled he and Jerry, was uppermost—but before that— a light? No, that was just the sun surely, but hadn't there been a distorted dark outline floating amid that blazing glimpse? Just before he averted his eyes and began dealing with the dropping, dripping bugs? Zeke knitted his brow.

There were no such distractions now. The afternoon was mild and pleasant, so he might as well enjoy
it and keep exploring. Perhaps he should seek a vision, or some message from his own native ancestors.
But the old weathered cut wasn't revealing itself. He
must have the wrong deer path he thought, so Zeke's
attention turned instead to climbing to the top of the
mound.

Once there the view was clear, as if some one had
kept it manicured all along the top. Why would that
be? No trees, only nicely cropped but clumpy-soft
grass along the top as if grazed by goats or something.
Oh yes, the deer. There was a nice view as well, down
to the James River. And looking back, the top of the
old Rivana Bluff's chicken house could just be seen.
Taking all this in, Zeke instinctively looked up to the
clear afternoon sky with it's pleasant breeze, hoping,
even willing something to land. The too-bright sun
was enough visual excitement however, so he looked
back to the ground, yellow and cyan-blue lights on his
optic nerves still swimming inside his orbs.

Momentarily dizzy, he looked along the mound top
toward the river. To his surprise, a vision *did* now
appear before him, a puff of pure white smoke billowed and undulated out of the ground, and as soon as
it assumed a goodly and bulbous shape, a rainbow
burst of light appeared within it, also undulating in
quivering shape with bright yellow beams alternating
with oddly stratified spectrums of color. "What's
this?" Thought Zeke, "Am I truly hallucinating? —
losing my mind? I've got to get away back home and
settle into the reality of my apartment and drawing
board—but not this."

But the strange shapes and light continued up before him as he moved toward it. He smelled a fire. A drum started beating, beating, beating. Of course it was all coming from the Jefferson cut in the mound which he now saw sloping before him. But who? Why? Now from below and inside the drumming came a voice singing rhythmically like Indian chanting, "Ai Yi yi yi Ai Yi yi...", but then it morfed into the old African American spiritual and words from the Old Testament.

> " 'Zekiel saw a WHEEL...
> A wheel way up in de middle of de air,
> A Wheel within a wheel..
> A Wheel way up in de middle of de air.."

Zeke knew that voice! The old black guy from the store that day in Colombia. There he was on the slope below, burning a fire, beating on an old can and dangling a very shiny pie pan on the end of a stick,which reflected sun in his face.

" If I build it, they will come..that what they say, but instead I get *you!*"

" And you! You're..".

" Well my name ain't *Jonah!* Sum o'dem in da town call me dat cuz dey say I act like I was throw'd up by a whale..an' cuz I sing 'bout da whale sum time, preacha an de bear an wut not..or dey think I'm crazy or bad luck...but dey don't *know!* I fox 'em! I watch an' I wait! I see an' I *know!* Wut goes on 'round hea..an out deah too.." He pointed to the sky.

" Well who are ya?" asked Zeke, "And what are ya doin.."

" Ol' Manny Moon...das who I is! Always have, always will be, least til I'm *dead!* Den I might jes git a brand new name, and a brand new body *too!*"

Zeke smiled. "I think you're right..."

" I *know* I'm right!"

" But how'd you know I'd be here?"

" I didn't! I jes knew it was time...

" Time for what?"

" Time for *sump'm!*"

Zeke asked if he came here often and he said that he did, because this is where "They" came the most. This led to a retelling of his stories of seeing "pie plates" flying on his farm, and general prolonged sightings in the area.

"Dey tend to follow families around, over hunderds o' year! Been followin' us, my mama, grandpa, great gran—so on from way far back, even when we wuz Indian! Some as buried in deze mound right chere! We's got some Monacan in us, jus' like yo family!"

" My family!?"

" Yeah, I know'd it furst time I seed ya!"

Zeke admitted as much, or his suspicion of it,- as well as his general interest in UFOs, Native Americans and the mounds. Deep discussion was difficult with the old man because of his lack of education, but he sensed a great worth of truth and richness to what he had to say. The afternoon was advancing and he was feeling the need to get back on the road. It had been very interesting, but he felt more of the answers he sought lay elsewhere, but where?

" OK Dad, time to go home." Came a voice from behind him. Zeke turned to see a congenial looking black man about his age, professionally dressed but casual.

" Oh dat my son George, he come t'git me, he worry too much. But he can't hep it, he a doctor!"

" Can't I look after my Pop a little bit?" The man smirked. After pleasantries and introductions, Zeke offered to give them a ride back to the father's farmhouse which was just down the road. While the old man gathered his paraphernalia they talked their way down the path. The doctor, Moon and Zeke found they had similar interests, such as local country lore and ancestry, always a common subject when Virginians get together. On mention of the Zeke's Mama's people the Gundersons, the doctor's face lit up. Seems his family was kin to their slaves over at Scottsville.

Did he remember Aunt Lizzy Lambert? Did he!— Zeke told as she was like a legend in his family, used to make cookies for his Mom and her sisters! Turned out they found she was actually the last slave born at the Gunderson plantation just before emancipation. Great Grandpa Capt.Gunderson had divided most of his land between his slaves, and many like Aunt Lizzy had lived just down the road. It might have been an awkward conversation for some, but "down-homeness" prevalied and actually it was a bit like old home week, sharing connections and memories.

" Dat why de saucers follow both our families too. It's all connected!" chimed in ol' Manny Moon. Zeke had to admit it meant something. When he mentioned his cousin Helen had recently told him of an old slave graveyard on the old Gunderson place behind his family graves, old Mr. Moon perked up again.

"Dat's sacred ground! Don' let'em ruin it!"

Zeke assured him the county would'nt allow that, but it set him to wondering. He admitted his Aunt Charlotte, when she lived on the place alone before the family sold it, had seen a strange moon shaped light wandering above the trees. This got old Moon excited again. "See? Dat proves it! Dey're up dere watchin' *too!*"

As they got scrunched down in Jerry's Mini, his son George smiled wryly at his Dad's comments. "He's on a roll now, I should get out my tape recorder..if I could reach it"

" Dat right! I'm tellin' privilege stuff! Say, dis car made fo' sardines or sump'm?!" They laughed their way down the road with jokes and comments about the car. "It handle good though", Ol' Moon had to admit. Zeke was letting them out at their shady front yard gate when he looked up to a shock. Coming right at him down the dusty dirt road was that pink PT Cruiser! The Daisy Ray Cosmetics logo on the hood was bearing down upon him as Zeke, so utterly surprised, shook and fumbled at the controls of the unfamiliar car like a toy robot with a faulty battery. Ol Moon stared at him.

"You all right Mista Zeke? Dat's just Hazel Poindexter comin' over ta sell my wife some face smudgin' stuff. Don' know if it helps much none, I like her fine way she is.." Zeke began calming down as a very friendly woman got out waving and smiling.

" Sorry I'm late Mr. Moon!" Then to Zeke, "Hello, are you married? I'll be glad to show you my catalog!"

" Dat's alright Hazel, he gotta go..Muriel's in da kitchen wait'n for ya.." Moon turned and looked Zeke

sharp in the face. "You thought she was someone else didn't ya? Mo' like some *thing* else, am I right?."
Zeke managed a weak nod.

"I knowed it. I know dat look. You gotta go I know, but lemme tell you sump'm! When you do see *dem others* agin, in yo head, jus crawl up like a ball, like a turtle in his shell! Like a lil' kid dat wants de world ta jus' go away, see? An' if you do it right, dem bad things can't see ya! I did it to 'em *mysef'!* Sump'm 'bout their eyes or they brain. You 'member whut I said—now git on up de road!"

Zeke did just that, making a wide circle around the little pink car by the cute little gate, his face stock still, but hiding in his body a volcanic rumble of trembling. At the entrance to RT. 6 again, he was at a loss as to where to go. All he could think of was "go home", but not his home— the old family home. Even with his sudden irrational wave of fright, he felt impelled toward the old places, so he turned west up the road to Scottsville.

CHAPTER 27
When Cousins Collide

The road was ever more mountain like from here on out. Up one long big hill and down the other, but also some interesting plateaus of grazing and grain land. Zeke knew at one point the Blue Ridge would start peeping up in the distance, that fabled mountain range that more than lived up to it's colorful name. Zeke called also to mind the warm memory of their appearance in just the right sunset at just the right time when they actually appeared a deep purple, exactly like in the song "America the Beautiful", and some fine slides he had taken as a teenager, pestering Dad to stop as he bounced around in the back seat searching fine landscapes at 45 miles an hour. Dad didn't mind because he was an artist and photog too. It was always Mom to worry about schedules, but eventually she got a camera too.

All the usual warm feelings followed him into town, this early American village nestled on a great bend of the James, with a very healthy collection of Federalist architecture,and terraced lanes laying on steep hillsides. Zeke stopped for a sandwich at the convenience store on the corner at the bottom of Valley Street. Leaning by his car and munching, he took in the evening air and the friendly quaint beauty of the town. There, across the street among the old row of buildings, situated near "Miss Mollie's Doll House" and the "Dew Drop Inn" was Thomas Jefferson's old law office very little changed, but lacking an historic plaque because nobody had thought of it or at least gotten around to it.

His brother Capt. Randolph Jefferson had lived here most of his life, farming "Snowden Plantation" just across the river in Buckingham county. Like his famous brother, he also played the fiddle, often with his slaves as they sang and danced. Scottsville was once the biggest canal boat trading center of the area, the Virginia frontier center of the universe long before Charlottesville was thought of.

Zeke eyed the friendly country locals with his caricaturist's cartoon eye. People of the land, they who had that open way of smiling or passing the time. People who's people had known his people. Many fine horse farms and other well heeled people also called it home. As in ol' Tom's day, a high esthetic of beauty, philosophy, and art could live side by side with wisened farm knowledge as well as johnny house humour (as in the case of his Dad and his brothers on occasion) and an incredibly natural expression of life, love and sex,(at least it always felt that way to Zeke),but with a strong dose of religion on Sundays. Sweet country air was infused with the lush life force of the thick roadside sedge and beginnings of pumpkiny harvest decorations as Indian Summer advanced.

This was an attitude he had grown up with naturally from his parents, but which often wasn't appreciated in his sometimes upturned nose and cliquish home town of Richmond. But then that old history-encrusted town as Zeke well knew, had it's own substantial way of bubbling up with passion and creativity as well, worthy of volumes itself. But what the high society types often fail to realize is that true talent for art, drama, music etc. always begins with the sophomoric urge to caricaturize, to "act up" behind the barn of respectability. Even the proponents of Zeke's grandfather D. Early Gunderson, who made a name for himself in Victorian-Edwardian architecture, usually failed to appreciate his vaudevillian humour and playfulness.

Along the far sidewalk Zeke saw Stupid and Melvin promenading proudly, one wearing a "topper" and the other a three cornered hat. He smiled in recognition for not having seen his little drawing board friends very much of late. But now a wrangly middle-aged white country couple was coming his way.

"Nice evenin' ain't it?" said the man with a John Deere tractor hat. A somewhat disheveled smirky woman in a patterned dress trailed behind him. "But don't ask her," he added, "she's havin' a hissy fit!"

"Oh shut up Junior!" the woman spat, "No I ain't!", back slapping him on the head with her floppy pocket book like a Grand Ole Opry comedienne, and then again on his rump, "I'm have'n a *fissy hit!*"

" Don' believe her!," answered the man, "She gits everthang bass ackward!" She grinned and swatted him again as they passed, but slowed down enough to smile prettily at Zeke. She then whipped her head back to her husband, "Do you want your double bucket of Slurple or not!? Com'on, I gotta coupon!" They hurried on into the convenience store, but were followed by a very artsy and educated lady handing out flyers for the Scottsville Art Center.

"Won't you come to the Concert Art Show? Music combined with art! At the old Excelsior Theatre! Paintings on wheels while the string ensemble plays along with Billy Bodkin's Banjo Bach and Bell Band, plus the Children's Choir singing authentic American Shape Note hymns...*and* homemade food!" She beamed with an infectious high flown spiritual enthusiasm. "I made the streusel, also on wheels, a truly *movable feast!* Only a dollar, but we take contributions! Here!" Zeke took the flyer and was strongly considering going. He looked up at the makings of a beautiful sunset coming up and wished he had his camera. He smiled at the utter down to earth fresh-aired normalcy of it all. There was nothing to disrupt his mood of true peace and tranquility. But then something did disrupt it.

It was his cousin Tommy, arm flingin' his way down the street and lookin' from side to side in a humourous scowl. But when he saw Zeke his knee jerk jokes were turned on.

" Cousin Ernest! Whut all yew doin' this neck'o th' woods?"

" Wal Cousin Ernest, I was about ta shoot the same flap jawed flap doodle back in yore die-rection!" Returned Zeke in like mode.

" Shoot, that sounds like a mess a corn chittlins' ta me!"

" How do ya make corn chittlin's anyway?"

" Well ya git a big chit see..and..." finally settling into normal conversation, it was revealed cousin Tom had just come from the town cemetery, putting flowers on family graves, a somewhat regular ritual.

"Those damn caretakers give me a fit, saying it's their grass cuttin' season, so I snuck back after they left and put down the flowers."

" They'll just throw 'em off again.."

" And I'll just put 'em right back!"

" How long you gonna do that?"

" A few days, I'm stayin' at the boardin' house. I promised Mama there'd be flowers for her birthday."

" Next month they'll stop cuttin'.."

" I don't care..."

Zeke soon mentioned his interest in the old family cemetary on "Olavana", the old home place outside of town. Tommy's eyes perked up.

"Hey, *that's* what I'd like ta do! We could put all the left over flowers out there! That would please Mama. I may not be able ta put flowers on the grandparents and aunts and uncles, but who's ta stop me puttin' 'em on the *great* grand parents!?"

"Well there's the current owner.."

"Hey it's a *law!*" raved Tommy, "He's gotta give the family access!"

"Yeah but I'd like to show him respect and get his permission.."

"So we'll git permission! Com'on." Soon Zeke's older cousin had him by the arm, moving him up the street. "We'll stop by the boarding house an' git my bags o' flowers.."

"B-bags?" said Zeke, unable to resist elder family

protocol. Soon they were headed out of town in the Mini, with the back seat stewing over with bulging multi-colored plastic and artificial silk which fluttered out the little windows. It was always something like this, getting flowers to the graves from down in Richmond, where most of the family was. Who's going up there, what needs to be done, when to do it, dealing with whatever mortuary rules, (that is if anybody knew them). No real organization about any of it, just a sudden flurry of activity from one aunt, cousin or another,who might be traveling in that direction. Zeke had done it often himself, glad for an excuse to go up the country. And of course there'd be big discussions about who's doing or paying for what, before or after the fact, which often led to arguments between aunts ending with somebody stuffing dollar bills in a car window as somebody was heading out the driveway.

" No Lavinia I *insist*! Take this money! Lavinia come *back* here!" he could hear his mama now.

The two cousins passed by the town commercial cemetery on the way out of town. "Daggone idiots," Tommy grumbled as he saw the lawnsmen still working. Zeke caught quick sight of all four of his grandparents graves laid out nearly next to each other, or as Dad would've said, "side by each".

Tom turned quickly on Zeke, "Hey, you know where Great Grandpa's graves *are?*"

"Oh yeah, I found them by accident when I was a kid while out with my dog, I never forgot it."

"Oh you mean Ol' Blue?"

"No, Dusty.."

"Oh yeah, I loved Dusty..." They passed various family related land marks which elicited automatic

family comment, such as Driver's Hill where the girls
had to get out and push the Model T, while brother
George would ride up front, ready to pop the clutch
and get it going again on the other side. The place
where Aunt Lizzy Lambert's old house once stood,
but now was replaced with a sturdy white cinder block
one, and still owned by her descendents, her son
Robert and his people. "There's the old Stubbs
place.." said Tommy. Which was actually colonial
architecture complete with exterior kitchen and other
buildings. It was now nicely fixed up and restored,
quite authentic. Soon they were heading down to the
Hardware River past The Gunderson's old spring
house, and up the long uphill drive through the woods
to Olavana.

    "The graves are over down past that ridge."
pointed Zeke to the east as they rounded the hilltop
into pasture land approaching the house. The long
circular driveway revealed no cars and knocks at the
door suggested no one was home. They fell into
standing around talking, perfectly "at home up home"
again. Both remembered the beautiful smiling face of
Mama Gunderson as she would often come to the
door of long ago, either in happy greeting or in fond
goodbye as family members would leave for home
after heartfelt visits. Also there was much of the usual
discussion about places, people, trips down to the
spring house and the river, the Ohio relatives that
came 500 miles driving an old Kaiser, ol' cousin
Grover across the river who would call on the phone
just to say hi, and actually just said "hi" and then hang
up, other cousin capers and all things Gunderson, as
well the new additions to the house which were either

sacrilege or rather nice according to your point of view.(Tommy took the former, Zeke took the latter).

The late afternoon sun was shining aslant fine iridescent autumnal angles of foliage across the lawn which was about to spawn more memories of chicken fried family reunions, until Zeke reminded Tommy that they were losing time and had better leave.

" Hell no, we're gonna go to the *graves!*" insisted Tommy.

" But I dunno.." conjectured Zeke.

" Com'on it's the *Law!* They're our *ancestors!* Besides if anybody says anything, tell'um we didn't know, com'on.."

It was hard to say no to Tommy, even when Zeke pointed out the brambles they'd have to negotiate. So leaving the car on the hill in the pasture, they tromped on in by Zeke's dead reckoning, down the long sloping hillside of broom straw and cedar trees, and various other growths. They had just passed the site of the old barn and pig pen long since gone. It was there out back that Dad had taught his petite little mother-in-law Mama Gunderson to shoot a pistol. Dad was always proud of how well she did, saying "she was game for anything!". Atop the far hill a half a mile away and over the river could be seen Great Grandpa Captain Gunderson's old house, peeping up white above the slopes of trees and far off farm land.

This was the way Zeke had found the graves the first time, by just following a "certain feeling" down the hill through the brambles, that something was there and he had found it, on a golden afternoon of childhood's wonder, but now, although this afternoon was also full of splendor, Zeke's brain was full of apprehension , not only over what might happen, but by his imbalance caused by big floppy bags of flowers while tripping over Virginia Creepers and pushing back dry honeysuckle and sumac. Zeke wondered if now would be a good time to reference his newly found UFO connections with these hallowed family grounds, but somehow he couldn't get around to it, knowing Tommy's likely A.D.D.-ish evangelical reaction to it. He made a quick comment however.

"Ya know, Aunt Charlotte's supposed to have seen some sort of UFO up here.."

" Ha!" snorted Tommy, "More like envoys of Beelzebub! Demons of Satan! They'll come at you in a moment of weakness or fear on a cold night or sump'm, but if you're saved and say the name of Lord Jesus Christ, you ain't got nuthin' ta worry about!"

" But,what if they come from somewhere else and don't even know Jesus *or* Satan?"

" Well if you believe that they're gonna *gitcha!* An' I ain't got no sympathy for ya!!"

The cousins trudged on a while in silence. What were these dead inter-twinning curvy things that kept grabbing and tangling his feet? They looked like psychedelic alien mangrove swamp plants. If you were teeny tiny, you could have a hell of a roller coaster ride on it. If Mom were here she could tell you just what kind of plant it was.Probably Sumac or Honeysuckle. Zeke mentioned all this to Tommy, but all he answered was "Yeaaaah.."

Zeke started to imagine Melvin and Stupid taking a ride on it but stopped himself. It was getting quite thick now, but the golden shafts of sun spotlighted the way to the old miniature cedar grove he knew was their destination. " Hey, don't get the flowers caught, them thangs cost money!" said Tommy. They struggled and trudged their way ever closer, teetering way left and way right, each cousin juggling and catching the bags as they went.

"Is anybody gonna care if we get there?" asked Zeke.

"Quiet, our ancestors are watching from the spirit world..." said Tommy. Zeke had to agree, if only because of the rich Halloweenish autumn atmosphere, with it's brilliant colors light and dark, the brisk healthy air—also the scenery was right for it. The perfect place to play as a kid, fall in love when you're older, or just to run away from wailing banshees. "And besides it's tradition..we always bring flowers on---" *BAA DA DA DA BOO BOOM* Bum bum bum!! A large greyish thing exploded into the air from their feet and flower bags went flying. "What the HELL was that!!??" yelled Tommy.

" Hey! It's a Ruffled Grouse!"shouted Zeke, "I haven't seen one since I was kid!"

" Well he sure got me ruffled..is it some kinda quail?"

" Sort of, but bigger..."

" Yeah, more like a flying watermelon! Damn, the flowers are ruined!"

" No they're not, they're plastic!"

" Half of 'em are silk!"

" Same difference.." Zeke started reaching for a bag when a large shadow suddenly blotted the sunny patch of field before him. "What was that?"

" Might be that damn bird again!"

" Naw, that would'nt happen, might be a buzzard.

Can't see him though.." answered Zeke, searching the sky.

Tommy beamed suddenly, "God it's beautiful up here, I love it! Hey, remind me to git Mama one of them cute little pumpkin baskets they make when we go back ta town, you know, with the little fuzzy goblin bunny things? She loves 'em.."

Zeke's eyebrows narrowed. "Now how can you talk like that one minute, and be against saving the environment and little creatures of the Earth the next?"

"The Earth is gonna burn in Hell! It belongs ta Satan! The Bible says so! 'Satan ,who is the god of this world, has blinded the minds of those that don't believe.'-Second Corinthians four four! All I care about is bein' caught up in the sky with the Lord! Git saved an' you can too!"

" Alright, you wanna do scripture, how 'bout Revelation seven three? 'Hurt not the earth, neither the sea, nor the trees', Huh??"

" You're takin' it out of context, it then says, 'until we have sealed the servants of God in their foreheads'.."

" Well what does *that* mean??? Listen Tommy, you were raised a good Episcopalian just like me and your Mom and my Mom!"

"They're the worst ones! Did you know most politicians in Washington go to the Episcopal Church? It's all Secular Humanist propaganda! They're all gonna *burn!*" Tommy trudged on determinedly, and Zeke made a face to himself, but kept quiet after that. Family was family after all.

They finally made their way to the bramble and

cedar grove, burrowing into a tunnel-like blob of vines as best they could, but soon they pushed through the brown shadows to see suddenly revealed a 7 foot stone obelisk with a large Masonic symbol carved on it, the Square and Compass with a great capital "G" in the middle, proudly radiating in a spot of afternoon sun.

"Wow! It's just like Indiana Jones or sump'm!" grinned Cousin Tom. Great Grandpa Gunderson had been the leading Mason in the county, and D. Early had made the monument according to his wishes. 'Lord, the old man loved Masonry, and the church too,' said Cousin Grover in a little book he'd written about the family and old times gone by, 'He used to haul the hand pump organ in a wagon to church every Sunday. A gruff and blunt man, but a good and fair one.' He was born before Jefferson had died. This was long forgotten stuff and covered by time, but now wonderfully revealed, along with Great Grandma's grave and others within what was left of a stone and iron fence. "Here, let's clear some room.." said Tommy.

"Only spirits and chipmunks are gonna see this.." said Zeke.

" That's good enough for me... chipmunks are cute!" said Tommy, adorning flowers wherever they would fit. Zeke rolled his eyes to himself.

"I'll bet the birds use some of this for a nest."

"They do and I'll come back and *bop 'em!*" Tommy finished with a flair. The flowers were oddly strewn, more like a Christmas tree than anything. Zeke noticed rows of somewhat sunken depressions in the wooded area just behind the monument.

" Those must be the graves of the Gunderson slaves cousin Helen told me about!"

" Yeah, those go way back," said Tommy, "I guess Great Grandpa wanted to be buried over here across the river too."

" Very foresighted since this was the last piece of Gunderson farm after he died, guess they planned it that way.." A cool breeze began blowing with leaves wafting by. Zeke eyed the winking sun through the far trees.

" It'll be gettin' dark soon.." The two started their way back up the hill, but suddenly Zeke's foot sunk into a soft spot and he twisted his ankle. Cringing with pain, he could hardly move much less make it back through those brambles. It was decided that Tommy should go back to town and get an Ace bandage from the drugstore. " I always bounce back quick with one of those things...and make sure you bring a flash-light!" added Zeke as Tommy nervously stumbled away, saying "an' I'll git some Ben Gay!", assuring Zeke he "wouldn't be no time!" Meantime Zeke fished about for a stick to use for a cane, but down as he was, he instead started experimenting with the numerous Virginia Creeper vines on the ground, wrapping one about his sock, like a make-shift ace.

Tommy jumped and stumbled up hill, but then slowed down, "Hey I better not sprain *my* ankle, that would really tear it.." Swearin' and snortin' his way out of the field and up to the Mini, he fumbled with the strange car keys in the increasing dark. His eyes were getting large, as he nervously looked over his shoulder. He could hardly make out the house, just a black shape against the twilight sky, and all those fingery branches of the trees. Soon a small high pitched whine began to play in his ears. Not sure where it came from, he held up the keys and pressed buttons on the remote.It made several noises but none of them a whine.

" Damn foreign cars.." Back at work, he hunched over close to the key hole, jingingly everything. Thup thup-thup-thup-THUP! Something flew over his head.

" Must be a bat...they're envoys of Satan too..." He jingled ever more nervously. "Come On, God damn it!..OOPs! Sorry Lord, I didn't *mean it!*" Then came that high pitch whine again. He knew it wasn't the remote this time. Off toward the house and the big oak trees, he could make out a small number of white dots, swirling and floating, and moving this way. "Lightn'n Bugs..it's *gotta* be!" Tommy fumbled ever more furiously. Golf ball sized orbs were closing in, circling around him and the car, making WEEee WEEee sounds as they buzzed down and close. He gritted his teeth, twirling a flurry of key metal between his hands which bit and scratched like a chainsaw of tiny bells. *"These* ain't no bugs!"

Finally the door jerked open and Tommy got in, cranking the engine but fumbling with the gearshift. "God damn European straight stick!— Sorry Lord!" It wasn't the car's fault, but Tommy's, however the orange and black Mini Cooper sputtered to life, and Tommy jerked it out around the pasture, bumping back around to find the road. Lighted orbs about the size of soft balls now swooped and banged against the windows, making odd swishing and doll-baby cry noises each time they did. Tommy struggled and steered best he could, while muttering under his breath, "demons, demons, *demons!*" The road was supposed to descend down through the woods towards the river but instead, in his headlights he saw the large oaks of the circular driveway in front of the old Gunderson farm house, it's darkened windows staring blankly back at him. "*Where are the owners!!?*" He shouted in frustration.

Then, from the side of the house and the boxwood bushes emerged several crouching black humanoid-canine or otherwise hunched figures, furtively darting across the drive, running like wildebeests. Wide eyed with terror, he did the only thing he could do—step on the gas. Circling back and around he finally found the drive to the river, down the long hill through the woods. The orbs picked him up again, now the size of cantaloupes, darting in and out of the trees. One splatted on the windshield directly in front of him, again with that sickening noise, but now revealing from within it's gelatinous interior a bulbous shape that sloshed to the fore, and looked at him with an intense and hideous face! The nose was flattened sideways at an incredible angle while dagger black eyes stared out of a gargoyle and bulldogish counte-nance. Tommy lost control momentarily and got stuck in some mud on the road side. Gunning the engine, wheels spinning and spinning, all the time the thing made faces at him as if to say, "*Your soul is mine, and I'll eat you for supper!*" With a great roar the little car gained the road and spun off, the orb creature sliding quickly away, but leaving a smear hard to see through. Finally Tommy bumped to the bottom at the state maintenance road, circling about in a dizzying confu-sion, but finally heading off toward town.

The orbs seemed to have gone away, no longer interested in him. Thanking God and sweating profusely, Tommy tried to calm himself by turning on Christian radio. An old time gospel choir was singing, which put a smile back on his face.

> Now one a deez mornin's bright and fair
> Way in de middle of de air—
> I'm gonna take my wings an' cleave de air
> Way in de middle of de air
>
> Now I tell you one thing you can't do,
> Is serve the Lord and the Devil too—
> Way in de middle of de air,
>
> Ezekiel saw a wheel
> A wheel way up in de middle of de air...
> The big wheel run by Faith...
> And the little wheel run by the grace of God...

Tommy started feeling dizzy again as the announcer came on.

"That was some of the sounds of old time gospel, 'Ezekiel Saw a Wheel' by the Charioteers right here on WJEZ HD, Charlottesville..." Tommy smacked off the radio and hurried on down the road.

CHAPTER 28
Earth of God and Field of Demons

Meanwhile, back at the graves, Zeke sat helpless with his thoughts, and actually contemplated that very term, "meanwhile". So stereotypical, basically the same indication as cross cutting in movie language as in "Meanwhile back at the ranch." It had fascinated him in his early boy-artist days of drawing comic stories, not only as a useful device, but as a somewhat mysterious and sinister feeling, as in "while things got mean".

He had heard many sounds in the distance, odd whoops and whines which he took to be some kind of bird, a Screech Owl or possibly a Bob Cat. Both can make ungodly sounds, seemingly from another world. Also mainly, there was Cousin Tommy in the car speeding away, but not exactly away, but around and around stopping and starting, spinning out. He figured Tommy had trouble driving the different gearshift, and only prayed Jerry's car wasn't damaged. Sitting alone in the deepening darkness between the little grave grove and the woods behind, he had continued working on his "vine ace" bandage and it seemed to help.

He could get up and walk a few steps with the aid of a stick, but he preferred to sit and wait for Tommy. Vines can be incredibly strong if you work them right, as our primitive ancestors well knew. Those animal sounds didn't bother him, in fact they were a comfort, until he remembered stories of Mountain Lions who had made their way down from the hills, following the creeks and rivers. This did give him pause. The Hardware River was not far away down the hill, an approximately 20 ft. wide stream that varied widely during the infrequent floods.

Not far below the driveway entrance the road crossed the bridge to his great grandfather's old farm property. Capt.Gunderson as he was known had built the original bridge after the Civil War, even though a flood had almost saved his home from marauding Yankees. He, like his brother the war hero had "turned his heart to healing the Nation's wounds" after the war. His brother had served as delegate at the Capitol in Richmond and gotten legislation passed for a covered bridge further down stream on the main road, now Rt.6.

The Captain had gotten the contract himself and done a fine job. That bridge had become a favorite spot for mass baptizings of both black and white, with famous anti-liquor preachings given from the little balcony window over looking the river, later giving the little picnic area they built the name of "Temperance Wayside". Even so he could never get the county to build a bridge on the road that ran through his own farm, so he finally got mad and built it himself and then presented Fluvanna County with a bill for supplies minus labor. "By Gum, my word is my bond sir, take it or leave it!" was his favorite expression.

It was with family stories like this that Zeke kept his mind occupied while laying on the ground between the graves and the clear cold sky above him. It was mostly quiet now, except for periodic little toots and peeps every now and then, scattered over the hills. Every so often a little step or lunging *crunch* could be heard over yonder in the leaves. "Must be a deer.." thought Zeke. " Yeah, it has to be a deer. They feed mostly at night." Yeah, ol' Capt. Gunderson was quite a character. Had a big workshop and taught his slaves wood working. They'd go around the county in the spring building houses and churches and such, as well as the furnishings. Zeke used to play on one of those old dining room chairs that sat in Mama Gunderson's kitchen. He loved that old hand hewn chair, running his fingers over the rustic decorative grooves and the exposed wood grain from more than a century's worth of wear, while his grandma cooked a delicious pot of beans and ham. Grandma's pretty calico cat played with him too on that chair. He and cousin Davy later put it in the Scottsville Museum.

"Yeah, that's a deer. Has ta be..." It seemed though that on the open ridge above him he could see dark shapes every now and then popping up and down. "Could be a trick of the light.." he thought. "Or lack thereof..." A fine pumpkin moon had risen just at sunset and was now climbing the sky in the East. Pretty soon shadows and objects would be more distinct.

"Yeah, Great Grandpa must've treated his slaves alright, there was much evidence to point to it. Him dividin' so much of his land for 'em after emancipation." Then there was Aunt Lizzy Lambert and her son who were pretty close to his family. The Captain always believed in the Law, following the rules. 40 acres and a mule. There were several old black families in the area that had at least that much land. Land which was once the Gunderson plantation. The Captain had once been the richest man in these parts, but he died in near poverty. Knowin' him, he must've supplied the mules too, just as the Government said. But a lot of those plantation owners didn't keep the bargain.

Zeke turned to look at the slave graves behind him. The shadows made it seem a tad ominous, but all was quiet. The only apprehension he felt was from that ridge in the field up above where he and Tommy had been trudging a few hours ago.

Zeke looked at some rocks on the ground, which brought him to think of the old tomahawk head Dad had found up here, and how he had wrapped it up with rawhide on an strong handle cut from a tree as a gift for Zeke, which he treasured. This led his thoughts to the old log cabin that Mom's Uncle Bill's house was built around, later cousin Grover's house down near the other side of the river. And the story that an Indian who once lived there who gave a tomahawk to a child when he died, to hang by her bed for protection. Yeah, no matter what you could say about this land, it *was* America. He still wondered who was that Indian? Were they kin? But what was *that?* Not only was there another crunch but also a strange guttural growl, somewhere midway up the ridge.

Yeah, Great Grandpa was quite a character, married his second wife by stopping his wagon in front of her house on the way to Colombia, said if she were of a mind to marry, to be ready when he came back. Zeke could see him smiling in his long beard and big grey broad brimmed hat from the old photograph, just like the ghost a little girl in recent years claimed to have seen in the cellar of his old house. More shuffling. A low growl. Yes, his spirit was bright and friendly...he told the little girl she could call him "Capt.Jack", that she and her family were welcome there. Asked her if she like squash, that the land around there was good for raising— *Thump Thump!* Pat pat pat pat- Crunch! Zeke could see the shape of sort of a hyena ape-like being bouncing about, sniffing the air. It's eyes glowed like orange embers in a camp fire. It stood up, and pieces seemed to fall off of it. Then it growled quick and deep and lunged into a fevered hunt, back and forth among the brambles, searching for a scent it seemed, back and forth down the ridge toward the bottom, just where Zeke lay, breathing nervously.

Where now were his comforting down home thoughts? His last refuge of sanity—Schlump *Schlump!* He couldn't summon them, his obsession with the past had given riotously away to the now-now-*Now!---Survival!* But where could he go? The thing's nozzle nose now snorted and inhaled the air as it came. What was Zeke to do? He couldn't move much if he wanted to. He could make out it's rearing head and graveled breathing now, not twenty feet away, it's overhanging crumbling brows in the sharp relief light of the rising moon. It slowly lowered it's steaming head and waved it slightly back and forth, as if it were honing in on the source of his scent, or perhaps body heat. Zeke knew it was a matter of seconds before it pounced.

"What was it Ol' Manny Moon had said?" he suddenly thought. Something like—become a turtle, crawl up in your shell. The thing was rocking quickly on the balls of its forelegs. It's shoulder blades, such as they could be discerned, were shifting up and down like a cat does before jumping a bird. The burning orange eyes brightened to yellow. It pounced! Zeke rolled quick as he could to one side, wishing he was deep inside something, a dead tree, down in the earth, away away, anywhere but here, wish the world away! ...*Away!* The great sulphorous stench and gravel growl passed above and beside him. He heard the galloping pads of it's appendages retreating down the woods through the slave cemetery. He opened his eyes and looked about. It had worked! Somehow..Ol' Manny Moon knew what he was about! God Bless him!

Again there were pieces of smoking cat litterish material strewn about. Strange...he thought, staring for a moment, it was as if a sort of internal lava made the beast move and live. But enough of that, he must go! He wasn't out of the woods yet, how could he be? (There were trees everywhere around him—he joked to himself) But that was a positive sign, it meant his wits were intact and it gave Zeke forward moving adrenalin, even if it was a very nervous form of it.

He felt now like getting to his feet and trying for a getaway, but just then came a wild whirring and sluff-sliding sound, somehow coming from the air atop the far trees, which stopped him from all action. There over the ridge now appeared the same darting and swarming orbs of light and ectoplasm (for want of a better term) that Cousin Tommy had encountered.

They were gathering in size shape and speed, floating and filling the sky before him, also ranging back and forth over the field as the black crumbly creature had done— searching, searching, and drawing ever closer.

Even with the success of his "disappearing act", Zeke felt the need to cover himself somehow. He grabbed his dull green jacket and pulled it over him, crawling bit by bit to the stone grave enclosure. He heard again that thumping, crunching sound and knew what was coming, but now in greater numbers. Below the line of the broomstraw he made his way around to the front of the graves, somewhat inside the little thicket grove. He still had a view of the sweeping bramble-blown ridge above, and what he saw didn't please him.

Those luminous gelatinous orbs were swarming closer and closer together over the field until they nearly formed a ball. Then they summoned great strength from their common vibrations, creating a fantastic hum of dissonant sounds like so many bass, tenor and treble harmonicas all out of tune and ready to kill each other. They backed up in anticipation, then FLOOM! They collided in one quivering mass, creating a giant shining orb, floating in the air with hundreds of evil head-ball faces slithering within, making scream-like faces and all working through the jellified substance, struggling to get out.

Soon black protuberances emerged from the huge globe, like so many dead tree branches put out like feelers. Many of these reached the ground and helped the thing to in a sense walk along, pulling and picking at the ground like a great sea urchin, in it's unending and odious search. The sound now reached a deep fluteish base, an otherworldly pitch vibration as the thing seemed to pause in it's progression, appearing to squat. Many of the glob heads inside seemed to swirl down to the base and mass together into dark shapes. Steam emitted from the globe as chunks of crusty "turds" hit the ground, springing up to become more hyena-cat-litter-rottweiler apes. Bounding forward through the weeds, more globes were flying furiously as well, closer and closer to the graves.

Zeke had seen more than enough. Turning his head around he saw what might be his last sight in this life, the moonlight illuminating the large "G" of the Masonic insignia on his great grandfather's grave, which stood for God. How he wanted to reach and grasp it close to him, but instead he ducked his shivering head down as far as he could go, under jacket, through brambles, down in the leaves. He only wished he was a mole with powerful baseball glove claws for digging swiftly into the ground, just like a "pet mole" he and brother Buzz once kept in a bucket of dirt. He thought and thought of good things, his family memories with warm feelings connected with this old farm, now turned into a land of horror. His tightly held nervous shaking became a rhythm as he slightly rocked back and forth. Wish it all away—Pray it go away—Wish it all away. He tried imagining God in his dizzy stupor while the creatures whined and raged above him, making fluttering, crumbling, up-chucking noises, hot breath upon him, quick hunting steps, padding over his back, then giant grunting lunges—sometimes landing heavy and crumbling upon him, with a breathing, pulsing and unbearable stench, hissing of polluted steam.

He thought of Michelangelo's figure of God the
Father on the Sistene Chapel ceiling with its flowing
beard. But just as often he thought of Matthias
Grunewald's altarpiece of "The Temptation of St.
Anthony" tormented by fantastic demons with multi-
species hybridized heads, wings and claws trying to
tear the poor saint asunder.

But somehow, in the midst of all this, Zeke felt a
strong urge to do the least desirable thing in the Universe, to roll over belly up, exposing himself to the
torrent of evil above him. Despite his clinging tightly
to Mother Earth, he felt his inner self, a spirit body
within the body, somehow turning over or rather *being*
turned so that now he was gazing upward through his
back from within his own body. Above him he indeed
saw a man with a long flowing grey beard, but also
on his head a grey broad-brimmed hat, and a friendly
face smiling down at him with warmth, love and
determination. It was Captain Gunderson, his own
hallowed ancestor!

Looking outward, he raised his old Civil War
sword, which Zeke recognized from having played
with it at his uncle's house as a boy. The captain made
a motion for a charge, then he and an army of old time
slaves, farmers, and tattered soldiers surged silently
over him through the air. Even Aunt Lizzy Lambert
came marching forward, rolling up her sleeves. There
were many other "Old Fluvanians" as well that he
didn't recognize, but who felt like old friends and
relatives somehow, all joining the great woosh of
wind and sounds above him with sickles and pitch-
forks and muskets clashing and banging. He saw an
old Indian chief with a tomahawk, that he also didn't

recognize, but he did know the tomahawk. It was his own that his Dad had found and fashioned for him. Then, walking steadily with chin down and stiff upper lip came Mama Gunderson herself, pointing straight and strong with her pistol!

The drone of all these images melted somehow into a very deep and restful sleep on the ground for Zeke, hidden under his jacket and nestled in the leaves. A heavy, long and comforting blackness settled over him. Next he knew, he heard twittering birds and fussing squirrels scuffling into the brush with the sadly beautiful whistle of a white throated sparrow. Peeping out, the first sight he saw was a golden shaft of sunlight landing on the Masonic emblem on Captain John B.Gunderson's grave. All was calm and at peace, as if some ancient magic had been worked.

CHAPTER 29
Means of Transport

Zeke again felt he wasn't sure what had happened, only that it had. He felt he could walk fairly well and that he must get going. That deep and merciful sleep had also been healing.

Then catching up with himself he thought-spoke half aloud in blustering urgency, "What had happened to Tommy? And Jerry's car? Oh my God, I should call Minnie?!" But cel phone signals were somehow hard to come by. An electric static crackling invaded the audio, but finally a broken up voice of Minnie came through. "Where are.... Been trying ..get you...

"I'm in Scottsville!...Scottsville! My *grandmother's farm!*"

"Hsss sputter—Charlottesv---ssss Jerry needs..car...what?"
He finally got something about Jerry wanting to see Monticello, something about researching conspiracy Illuminati architecture...they were coming and to meet them at 11 at Mitchie's Tavern. He also managed to ask her to find Tommy's cel phone number so he could call him, but then the signal was gone and his phone went dead. Zeke knew he'd have to start walk-

ing, and the shortest and easiest route was straight down through the woods to the old Gunderson low grounds near the road. Stepping between the sunken graves in the pine tags Zeke paid silent homage to the old Gunderson slaves, whoever they were. Some of Aunt Lizzy Lambert's people surely. If only the geneology could be researched—well maybe someday.

Walking with his stick it was fairly smooth going. Soon, he heard a heavy four footed crunching through the thicket in the high weeds beyond, amid the flat and rich low grounds. He could make out a large slow moving brown animal. "Somebody's cow got loose," he thought. The closer he got to open sunshine the happier he got, taking in the dew dappled freshness of the rich old farm of his forebears. Reaching the open ground he had to maneuver over old plowed furrows and leftover regrowth of cornstalks from previous years' crops.

His hobbling step became more torturous and slow going, although he was anxious to make the road and maybe hitch a ride to town. That Tommy probably got all in a dither last night and forgot all about him was most probable."That or was just plain afraid.Still you'd think he'd drive out this morning and OOW!!" He felt a great twinge go right through his ankle muscles. Immediately he let up the pressure, holding his ground with his stick. It was so tender and the sun was getting hot, so he decided to lay down for a bit between the stalks and furrows. Getting carefully down, he sighed as he soaked up the gentle coolness and relief of the ground, and soon dozed off.

Darkness enveloped his mind, for how long he

didn't know. Strange faces stared down at him, all shifting and shaping, some with sunglasses, pouting in disappointing condemnation. A grasping hookish hand reached out to his face. It grabbed him with a thick wet blobishness that made no sense. It felt more like—a tongue! Bright yellow and green light came into focus with a big black and brownish shape snuffling his face. The cow!

Zeke blinked and gently pushed the whiskered soft muzzel away as he got to his feet. Big cow eyes stared at him, but were attached to a strange camel-like face. A *llama!* What was a llama doing in Fluvanna County? Then he remembered hearing of a farm nearby which was raising the noble South American beasts. Every so often it would haul off and spit, but not at him,(a very good sign he thought).It was quite tame, and had obviously gotten lose. His foot still hurt, so he wondered if he could hitch a ride. Pulling himself on to it's back, the llama didn't seem to mind. It just stood there, chewing it's cud." How do you drive these things?" thought Zeke. Finally, a little thump to the rump (but not a boot to the booty), and they were off.

Bouncing up and down they headed for the road which was just where Zeke wanted to go. But at the road itself the llama turned right when he wanted left, and he couldn't make it do otherwise. "Well, if it takes me home I can get help from there.." he mused, trying to plan ahead. They bounced over the Hardware River bridge and up the hill.

Holding one's place upon a llama also proved a problem, as he tended to slide off to the side. But he righted himself right enough. He then heard a small roar in the distance. Speeding down the road in a cloud of dust was that little pink car again. The good Mrs. Hazel Poindexter with more beauty products for the lonely farm wife? But no, this driver wore a little black fedora hat and sunglasses—uh oh. As the car drew near, Zeke slid over to the opposite side of his magnificent steed, almost hanging upside down under the llama's wool, hair, whatever. He heard the car rumble past and screech in the gravel down by the bridge.

It was speeding back. There was nothing to do but drop off and roll into the ditch. Hiding below the broom straw once again, Zeke saw the pink car slow down and scrutinize the laconic sad-eyed beast as it continued to bump along, intent on returning home and minding it's own business. The car sped off up hill, and Zeke hobbled across the road to the opposite pasture. Pushing through the honeysuckled old fence, he was screened from the road and kept his head low. Indeed the car came back again to the same spot , driving slow, searching for a bit until finally heading off toward town.

Zeke gazed off across the pasture he was in. It must be part of his great grandfather's old land he thought, and very beautiful it was. He felt it unwise to go back to the road, so he headed cross-country above the bend of the river, knowing he'd eventually pick up the road again. Feeling that "lucky to be alive" feeling that we tend to forget in this modern age, he breathed deeply the morning freshness while dodging cow paddies. Making another fence line and then another pasture, he could see the perfect and painterly com-posed pictorial before him sloping down to a sparkling blue patch of river with bordering old trees hanging over it. He must try to come back here some-time with his easel.

His hobbling made him breath rather heavy, but he now noticed another breathing, out of tune and out of rhythm with his own. But where could it be? He looked around and sensed it came from far off, like that of a giant dragon or something.

Slightly above and beyond a rather thick grove of oak trees he saw a bit of bulbous shape, with bright red and yellow colors, heaving up and down. Trans-fixed, he followed his fascinated eyeballs across and through the grove, until he found himself standing before none other than a hot air balloon, it's little blast furnace turning on and off periodically, keeping the great multicolored canopy afloat. It seemed to be running on automatic as no human was present. Then up the hill Zeke saw a largish garage-like structure of some age, perhaps once a barn, but now more of a hanger.

Of course! This was the source of those balloon rides he'd heard about near Scottsville, that he'd always wanted to go on. But now a man with a base-ball cap carrying a wrench was walking about and suddenly accosted him. At first Zeke was afraid, but then realized it must be the owner and that he could help him find transportation, so he waved back and hobbled up hill.

But just then came a roar from up toward the road, and then the Pink PT Cruiser came galloping down the drive toward the man at the garage. The car drove straight at him, chasing him inside. Zeke was part way up the hill but turned around and ran as fast as he could. The car circled back and started down the pasture toward Zeke. Then the owner came back outside with a rifle, shooting at the Cruiser, which started curving back and forth in evasive action. The rifle managed to hit one of the tires, blowing it out—BLAM!-blubida blubida— the car was loosing control but still making it's way toward Zeke, who made it as far as the balloon where he could do nothing but get in.

Somehow lurching with his bad leg up and over the top of the basket, then scrambling up from the floor, he reached beyond to a somewhat computerized set of buttons, and to a set of valves which obviously controlled the burners which were firing gently, off and on. The pink car was blundering back and forth in the cow pasture, spinning in mud and manure and bumping through chuck holes, but getting ever closer. The intense face of the sunglassed driver was fixed on Zeke as he tried to aim his gun at him. Zeke grabbed a valve and turned— the fire went down! He turned it the other way —it went up! He turned up the other burner too, and the balloon started skyward, but was bobbing against the earth as the car got closer and bullets zinged past. Ropes! There must be ropes! He found them, some looped over and some tied up. He fumbled and fumbled as the pink car spun into some nearby mud, fish tailing around. Sunglasses was struggling now to get out of the vehicle, but was having trouble with his slipping leather shoes. Zeke finally got the ropes loose just as the evil humanoid ran from the car. The basket soared upward with bullets shooting through it, but also the owner's rifle was firing down the hill. Zeke balled up and rolled this way and that in a blue faced panic.

The bullets finally stopped. All Zeke could hear was the wind. He ventured a look below and saw the pink car still stuck in the mud but drifting far into the distance. A man was running around shouting at his cel phone—that was the owner, very distraught. Sunglasses was no where to be seen...but, ...uh-oh he thought. His worst fear was realized as suddenly the devious alien rose into site not far off, clutching his ever-lovin' briefcase.

At this altitude there were all sorts of funny cross winds that sent the balloon in different directions, while Sunglasses would get caught on another and have to adjust. Zeke remembered a video he saw once on the internet about how the only way to steer a balloon was to catch these various winds by changing altitude. There was supposed to be a red rope which would open a vent up above so he could descend. He found it. Soon he had some measure of control, but not a lot. He saw that ballooning takes a lot of prac- tise, but this crash course was his only option just now. "OOoo don't say *that* word!", he said to himself.

At times Sunglasses came perilously close with that demonically dead stare of his. Zeke stared in- tently back showing no fear—he hoped. Then an odd ray of sun would illuminate the horrible pit-like eyes beneath the plastic lenses. He could easily have picked off Zeke with his gun but for some reason didn't do it, as if he was saving him for something. Maybe he'd have too much trouble aiming with the briefcase and holding with only one hand. He did however take pot shots at the balloon to weaken it's lift, but that was slow going, and Zeke could counter a good bit by adding more heat. The fire breathing "breath of the dragon" caught Sunglasses off guard and made him wobble. Perhaps this amazing technology was unknown on his planet. Maybe they supplied their own hot air, Zeke mused briefly with a smile.

But then the alien decided to move in close on him, obviously planning to board him like a pirate of old. Zeke instinctively looked about for a weapon in the supply pouch hanging alongside the basket. He found a large silvery wrench and flung it, but the other raised his floating briefcase and deflected it. This however caused him to lose equilibrium and he went spinning off and downward. Zeke smiled in minor triumph, but he knew his enemy would be back and soon.

Well, at last at least, he'd gotten his chance at a hot air balloon ride. The video had proved valuable and he congratulated himself on those afternoons wasting time searching Google. But at what cost this fine exciting ride? No ticket charge to be sure but...plus he would have to land it. And then there was ol' Thingamabob behind him, over, under and around. He tried to enjoy some of the view, "be in the moment" as they say. Yeah but don't be an idiot...keep track of things.

The rich green farmland, autumn colors beginning to blaze, rivers and creeks, embankments of bright red clay next to curving domed green swards all were fantastic on the eye. He did notice he was headed mainly north, with the Blue Ridge Mountains (very beautiful and very blue) to his left, the sun behind him. This was basically good for catching up with Minnie and Jerry...somehow. On watching the roads, he noticed some activity. A dull red pickup truck was speeding northward from where he'd come. It had to be the outraged balloon owner. This was encouraging, there'd be some sort of help at least. Also, a ways behind it he noticed, and also going at a decent clip was a little dot of black and orange, like a lady bug crawling over lumpy green leaves. Jerry! No— Tommy in Jerry's car! This was also good but..."OK, slow down Cousin Tommy, take care of Jerry's car!" Zeke wished to goodness he had a cel phone number for either of them, as well as a place to charge his.

Meanwhile, the wind had shifted, so he pulled the vent cord to bring him back down to find a northerly breeze. He passed over the truck which he knew was heading west to pick up the Blenheim Road north. But this made the truck stop and turn around, trying to follow him as he floated east. Back down the road toward Olavanna he roared, heading straight for Tommy! Luckily they both saw each other and skidded to a stop. They seemed to be gesticulating wildly at each other. Zeke called out and they looked, but kept on with their arm waving. He could hear their voices but not their words.

Hopefully Tommy would realize from what the owner told him that the guy in the balloon was him— But Zeke had other worries. Sunglasses was appearing on the port bow (or was it starboard?). He was coming fast up and from behind, catching the easterly moving wind. (It was easterly but coming from the west, which means it was westerly to the—or-) Zeke slapped himself in the face. He had to concentrate--on something important that is. *In the Moment!* But momentarily things were—well, confusing. People don't realize how much we depend on rocks and trees and things to tell us where we are! Let's see, what happened to North? Is this it? Or is that Northeast? He'd lost sight of the roads he knew, the Sun was on his right, so this had to east...that was right, *right?* He had a big attack of artistic A.D.D and dyslexia, the bane of his life. He thought of Jethro Bodine, "lessee, I keep my buckeyes in my right pocket.." that was no help..(great show though..) *"CONCENTRATE!"* He yelled to himself.

Melvin and Stupid now appeared before him at the dashboard of a classic 50's car. Melvin pointed from side to side and gave hand signals, while Stupid steered, tilting the car back and forth while grinning at Zeke with that hand jesture, nodding like everything was A-OK!. What was all this? Zeke screamed and wiped them from his mind. *Oh,* they were telling him something. Steering wheel on the *left,* glove compartment on the *right,* yeah, he could remember that. Anyway, he was heading East.

Rummaging further in the pouch he pulled out a laminated topographical map of the area. This would come in handy. And... a gun! He grabbed it and looked for Sunglasses. There, he was coming within range. Zeke aimed the pistol and shot—CLICK! CLICK again. Empty! But Sunglasses had veered off in evasive action, curving down below. With all the wind in his ears, Zeke couldn't tell if he'd had been shot at or not with that silencer of his. And maybe Sunglasses had the same problem and thought he, Zeke had a silencer too.. Anyway it bought him a little time. Studying the map Zeke got lost in looking for landmarks. He needed to get a handle on where he was. Reaching again into the pouch he hit on a pair of binoculars. This too would come in handy.

Getting to his feet , he was suddenly bowled over. The gondola basket had tipped nearly on it's side! The balloon was leaning over toward the landscape below which was moving by awful fast. Funny, the wind didn't feel that strong. Zeke thought a moment. Of course, he was traveling *with* the wind! Naturally he would'nt feel that much, just like a boat floating down river, as apposed to a post stuck in the mud feeling the water rushing against it. Ah ha, thought Zeke. He was learning something about ballooning! Well, a little something. He had to get to lower climes, out of this high jet stream thingy, whatever... besides it was getting quite chilly. He pulled the red rope. He began descending as well as to slow down. Whew! The balloon also righted itself, what a relief. But where was he? He scanned the landscape with the field glasses. There was a small river, but bigger than the Hardware. Beyond it on a hill was a small town with a Jeffersonian style courthouse like a cute little brick and white Parthenon on top. Palmyra! The Fluvanna County seat--10 miles in 10 minutes, he must've been doing 60!

The balloon was settling gently and moving near to the Rivanna River, which now flowed broad and blue over shallow shale rock down below the hill and under the bridge. A nice place to go fly fishing, and people often did. Somewhere around here would be a good place to land thought Zeke. There were fields nearby and plenty of people to help, plus a little convenience store by the end of the bridge where he could get to a phone.

He was moving and dropping slowly now on a gentle breeze, things were getting better, except he thought he'd caught sight of Sunglasses in the distance flying down to duck among some trees to the West. Below in front of the store was the usual little crowd of yokels, mostly kids, and a couple of biker types that like to drink sodas and beer in the parking lot as their main form of entertainment. They were noticing him now and getting excited. He was hoping to land on a good size piece of ground across Route 15 from the store, and it looked like it was to be a 3 point..uh 1 basket..a good landing. A basket case? No no no, but things were looking good and Zeke was very proud of himself.

The beer swilling crowd was cheering and yelling "Hey Yall!, Dude! Check it out, no way, freakin' A! etc." and came a running. This wasn't so bad, but the biker dudes were now in the field popping wheelies and skidding all around, coming on at 40 mile an hour. They were probably harmless but one biker drew a pistol and started shooting in the air. This was a bit much for Zeke so just as he was touching the ground he turned on the fire again full blast, and rebounded back 20 feet in the air. "Aw comon' dude, we're just funn'in! Your balloon is awesome!" To which Zeke naturally yelled back.

"The *Grand Canyon* is awesome, a balloon is fantabulous...uplifting..whatever! The Pyramids are awesome, so is the Universe! But *Not* a hamburger or a beer!"

"Hey he's a scientist or sump'm! Hey professor,we wanna see the pretty balloon, OK Mister Wizard!?"

At that, Zeke yelled, "I can't come back, I don't

know how it works! G'bye Folks!" and waved his hat like he was leaving Oz. A big "Awwww" rose from the crowd, but when they saw him floating down wind over the river and about to crash into the bridge, they started yelling warnings, "Hell man look out! Yeah Dude! *Heads up!*" Zeke caught himself just in time with another fire blast as the bridge bore down upon him. Up he went and over the top, to which the crowd went, "OOOOooo!" and "AAAhh!" as he came down on the other side with a gentle "plish" in the Rivanna River, a little way upstream. Zeke waved back to the adoring crowd. The water was shallow. Now to get out and pull it to shore.

But suddenly came a great honking from the road along shore, which was Route 53. It was the balloon owner followed by Tommy, both waving and yelling. "That's my balloon! Hey! Stop! Wait! Wait!" To which the gang on shore joined in with more cheering. Zeke was amazed as he got a leg up to get out, but the owner and everybody were now yelling wilder and louder. The basket rocked back and forth and soon he realized he was moving. Zeke shrugged his shoulders in jest, back at the crowd, but they weren't laughing. He then looked and realized he and the giant balloon were floating back towards the bridge, and that they wouldn't fit! The red pickup and orange Mini were pulling up onto the bridge now and both the owner and Cousin Tommy were beside themselves.

" Zeke! It's Tommy! We're here to help ya buddy!"

" YAAAY!" went the yokels.

" Hey! Don't ruin my envelope! Don't ruin my *envelope!*" yelled the owner. Everybody stopped and stared at him. Tommy reached in his pocket and produced a letter from his tax consultant.

" Would this help?"

" NO! The Balloon—thing—the *envelope!* He could *tear it!* It's nylon and.." But by then it was all a 70 foot tall moot point. The balloon was fast closing in on the bridge. The envelope hit the metal and concrete with a whine of nylon and splash of water as it bent over, following the basket under the bridge. Zeke was preoccupied with keeping the basket upright by counterbalancing his body on it's upper edge, leaning way over the river. It was all quite precarious, but he did manage at the same time to glance down the underside of the bridge to the north side, where trees grew along the bank. Sunglasses was making his way secretly under the roadway superstructure from the trees. He was having a bit of an anti-grav problem which caused him to bump about, bat like, along the underside as he came, nearly losing his silly little hat, and his glowing orange eyes briefly shining out from over his wobbling glasses. But he was coming too fast for comfort.

Zeke soon appeared downstream on the other side and the crowd followed him over. The balloon was squeezing back and forth as the river pulled it one way and nylon sprung it back to the other. One of the bikers, (the one with the biggest mouth) was still on the upstream side where the bulging expanse of colorful material was contorting back and forth. He watched it, mesmerized by the gigantic undulating movement.

"Hey! It looks like the balloon's fuck'n the bridge!"

"You shut up!" yelled the indignant owner, " I'll

have you know that's an 80,000 dollar *apparatus!*"

" Well it looks like the apparatus is hav'n a good time!"
Everybody laughed and hooted. "Fuck'n awesome!"

" It's NOT *AWESOME!!!*" yelled Zeke in awesome exasperation.

" My poor baby!" yelled the owner.

" Hey, I'll smack your baby!" said the biker and started smacking nylon, which made a deep roar-like vibration. The owner then pounced on him in a full tilt brouhaha.

"How *dare* you abuse a lighter than air craft!" The owner rained such blows upon the biker that he nearly ran for cover, but then his biker pride sprang back and he drew a switch blade, which made the owner all the more agitated. "Watch my envelope! Be careful my envelope!", while both used more impromptu martial arts moves than either of them had ever dreamed of.

Somebody up on the hill above yelled, "My God! It's a rumble in downtown Palmyra! Call the sheriff!" Some were attracted to the show upstream, and others to the one downstream, where Zeke was trying to balance the basket and-or push it off the river bottom with his stick, all the while giving little blasts on the propane burner. Finally the giant envelope oozed under the bridge and began righting itself and taking shape. Sunglasses had grabbed onto the side of it from under the bridge and was hanging on to the far side where most people couldn't see him. But Tommy had been watching his cousin and yelling helpful hints here and there, but now he saw something that was all too familiar and evil, something which had haunted him in his dreams ever since that UFO incident when he was a teenager. That heartless staring mug of the glaring eyes and burning crumbling flesh that sometime appeared as a strange man in suit and sunglasses. He or it was rotating upward with the floating twirl of the balloon, and was staring also at him with ravenous recognition. Tommy's throat stuck, his voice stammered, but out it finally came— "DEMON!! *DEEEMON!*" People turned with yet another look of surrealistic wonder, but then went on about their business.

" DEMON! DEMON!" Tommy jumped and pointed, "You don't understand, it's a *DEMON!*" As the balloon turned again, the face rotated back out of sight with a malicious grin. Tommy ran about like a madman trying all the harder to make them understand, but to the crowd, with all they'd witnessed in the last 15 minutes, his actions seemed normal and not that unusual.

Finally, at the other end of the bridge, the sheriff and his deputy pulled up in their patrol car down from the courthouse, where they just stopped and stared.

"What ya gonna do chief?" asked the deputy.

"Well," graveled the sheriff, taking in the bizarre circus of human endeavor on the bridge, and shifting a toothpick in his lips, " It's near lunch time, hand me a sandwich.."

"But ain't cha gonna do somethin?"

"Oh yeah, but this bears studyin'.." He took a bite. "I was plannin' ta listen to Rush Limbaugh, but this here show's a whole lot better.." Anyway, the deputy blew a big BEEYOOP blast on the siren and drove on down. The balloon was almost out from under the bridge now, and the owner was yelling confused directions at Zeke on how not to damage his $80,000 toy.

" Alright!" barked the sheriff, walking into the outre' confrontation, "Who's *responsible for all this?*"

" I'm trying to save my envelope! Uh, balloon!" went the owner.

"I'll sue! He tried to scratch my Harley with a knife!" ranted the biker, (while quickly putting his own switch blade away). Then Tommy ran up in the sheriff's face.

" It's a demon! You gotta arrest it!"

" Now, settle down sir," smiled the sheriff, "It's only a balloon, we can handle this I assure you—"

"No, the demon's *on* the balloon!"

"What?" the sheriff looked at Zeke in the basket.

"No, no, that's my cousin Zeke, we gotta help him!"

"But he's *not* a demon.."

"No, *he's* over *there!*"

"And we *shouldn't* help *him*.."

"Of *course not!*"

Now the others of the crowd demanded attention from their duly elected constabulary as well, yelling any-thing and everything. "What about my bike!??"— What about my envelope!!?--" "Are they filming a movie?" " No the bike!— No,the envelope!"

" Don't worry, the ticket comes with it's *own* enve-lope.." replied the sheriff reaching in his pocket and very, very confused. Meanwhile the deputy decided to help the situation with his shiny new bull horn.

" ATTENTION EVERYONE! This is the LAW, now CEASE and DESIST..uh, whatever it is you're doin'..."

" That's enough '*Deputy Fife!*'"shouted his boss, so he just stood by the patrol car, holding on to a drooping bull horn, but also eating a sandwich.

Through all of this Zeke was pretty much left on his own. For all his scrambling, it didn't look like he was making much headway, but now he caught sight of Sunglasses's outline through the colored nylon, creeping stealthily around it like a tree frog. But suddenly the balloon lurched upward, free and beyond the bridge, giving him an upward and optimistic tug. His now well-developed hot air reflexes came into play and he turned on both heaters full blast. The huge craft rose quickly above the frenzied scene on the bridge, carried west on the prevailing breeze. This caused another wave of excited screaming from the citizens below. All Zeke could do was wave his hat to the crowd.

The sheriff turned to the other biker, a lean deadpan fellow who had'nt said a word until now, "Hey, make him bring it down!"

The biker rolled his big sad eyes at the cop. "He can't come back, he don't know how it works."

CHAPTER 30
Beauty Below, Evil Above

Zeke once again felt relief by leaving the ground, but on second thought he didn't know why. He was very close to getting help back there. And yes, sure enough he could still see Sunglasses's silhouetted shape clinging to the outer edge of the balloon.

He was being swiftly carried west along route 53, known as the Thomas Jefferson Parkway. So he knew at least he was heading toward Monticello, and a chance to reconnoiter with everybody at Mitchie's Tavern for lunch. Maybe. He'd forgotten for a moment he wasn't exactly driving a car. But speaking of which, he was now again being chased by the pick up, the Mini,and the cop car, not to mention the two Harley's and whatever else was in the neighborhood. Despite all this, the trip was especially beautiful. 53 rose and fell over hill and dale like the perfect pictorial you learn as a kid when drawing perspective. The road (along with the telephone poles) goes over here but comes up there, patches of trees here and pastures of cows there, winding, diving and bobbing like a dreamy friendly roller coaster.

The easy sight of the road allowed Zeke to refine his "balloon steering technique", plus he could keep a better eye on his crawling upper enemy. Why wasn't he using his anti-grav briefcase? He did appear to be hunching over and fiddling with it, while trying to hang on to his little black plastic hat with the white band. "Where the heck do they get their wardrobe? Those sunglasses looked like they came from the eye doctor.." puzzled Zeke. "Hey! Maybe the briefcase is on the fritz!" Maybe this was Zeke's opportunity to somehow shake him! Even dispose of him!But what was the deal with 'sunglasses aliens' anyway? They have some frightful powers and technology, but then they were'nt but so bright, for an alien that is, or what you'd think one would be. And what did they want? (Not that he felt like taking the time to find out).

It went like this for a while, pleasant contemplation of the scenery and the art of ballooning, along with wariness and wonder at the inscrutability of the Universe. As the pleasing landscape rolled beneath him, he couldn't help thinking this is how it should be, a healthy balance of man and nature, plenty of woods and wildlife, but also the good aspects of man's stamp upon the land, and here and there a nice and very livable (but not too big) city. Agriculture and Culture, wildness, passion, beauty and refinement, fun and frolics and fiscal assurance, but not too much of any. In short just healthy life. Yes, his dreams were very Jeffersonian, happy yeoman farmers and all that, but he came by it naturally, his family coming from where it did, Albemarle and Fluvanna, in the "shadow of Monticello".

But that's utopia, not reality as reason tells us, that is, modern reasoning. Reason. The "Age of Enlightenment", the 1700s, is what gave rise to it to begin with.

The yeoman farmer living happily on the land in democracy and higher awareness. Well, it hadn't turned out exactly that way—had America. But, a lot of it had. And what's wrong with idylic dreams anyway? Without them will things ever get better?

Sure there had been destruction of pristine primordial forests, wholesale killing of Indians, and their special way of life, being one with the land, the Great Spirit. But then America had become "Great", (whatever that word means). And so many of the new ideas of the Rights of Man had taken root and given full flower here, not perfectly but in greater abundance than the world had ever seen. And great contrasts and struggles as cultures and ideas clashed on the new stage called the New World. Struggles built on the sweat and toil of free men, (more or less) ever debating how to run their communities, and also the unfree sweat of Slavery, but sweat that helped build America, and it's descendants who were gradually doing a lot better. Then more and more immigrants, culture clash after culture clash. The struggle to right these and other wrongs, desires and needs on going, imperfect but ever perfecting, hopefully, or working towards it at least.

America was built on the idea of "if it don't work fix it", which isn't a bad motto to work with. But even that can go wrong. To much success leads to unhealthiness. The ever chugging engine of industrial profit and growth takes on a momentum of it's own, like a headless monster, ever eating, eating at a planet that is only so big, and has a delicate life system of it's own of which man is part, but through his amazing creativity is capable of destroying that which created

him. If only he didn't have those apposable thumbs.
What would dolphins do if they had thumbs? Or
would they even want them?

Is it such a bad or unrealistic dream then to think
we can achieve a healthy planet? And America, which
so many tend to look to because of our "success". Is
the answer for everyone to keep coming here? Is not
the land of China as beautiful as ours? Is not Russia?
Africa? Europe? Australia? The Figi Islands , or tiny
Tristan in the mid Atlantic? Are not all the cultures
and people on these places all beautiful and worthy of
preservation? And isn't ours of America *also* worthy
of that? *All* people can't come here! Yes it's a melting
pot and land of immigrants to a degree, but aren't all
nations, when it comes to that? If they envy our free-
doms they should study them, fight for and organize
them *there*, and *We* should help or encourage them!
(Within reason).

Zeke didn't feel like an immigrant, Capt.
Gunderson's grandfather Nathan fought in the Revolution, his family had been here centuries, millenia
when you count in the "Native Am" contingent. Hell
it was just *home* to him! The ideas projected on the
U.S. from foreign climes in this modern age were
almost always strange to him. Even though he'd spent
all his artistic life soaking up world culture like a
sponge and loving it. 'The cultural smorgasbord effect' he called it, spoon fed to him by the Golden Age
of Television, Information and beyond. Years of
haunting libraries had now changed into surfing the
internet.

Isn't the real problem the organization of the gov-
ernments and economies of *each* country, that they

should be healthy, with modern representative demo-
cratic systems which also value the culture and "style"
of each one respectively? To live as a good neighbor
with all others in *fairness*, using the basic systems
developed in the Enlightenment, representative democracy, rule of law, free enterprise, none of which is
totally "free", but *relatively* free, so that hopefully all
will live in basic health and comfort while pursuing
their happiness? While also cooperating to preserve
the health of the entire world? The Gene Roddenberry
world where each party sits down and works together
on a fine futuristic 'enterprise' while still maintaining
pride in their old country origins and culture. Yeah,
Gene got it right, but we're not there yet.

It's the human ideas in force upon the land that
make it good or bad, best of times or worst of—Oh
God, thought Zeke, now he was quoting Dickens. It
was bad enough that he was borrowing heavily from
Jefferson and Star Trek. Ideas just flew from invention
to invention, but that's what this landscape did to you.

Too many people, that's the ultimate problem
today thought Zeke. But when one realizes the fact (or
belief if you insist) of reincarnation, and know that
souls are constantly entering and leaving the physical
Earth, and that scary as death is, it's really the ultimate blessing. The true goal should be maintaining
this *stage* called Earth, (to borrow also from
Shakespeare) as a well kept garden, for souls of all
species to enter and leave, pursue their needs, and life
dramas,(otherwise known as Karma), without trashing
and destroying this rare blue jewel of a planet.

Cousin Tommy said he didn't care about this
"Kingdom of the Devil" called Earth. To be saved and

sit near the throne of God in some pearly gate picture was one thing, but Zeke thought it would get plenty boring after awhile. Much better to explore and work with the vast complexities of Creation and the Universe, including the intricate and complicated mysteries of Earth. Pearly Gates might be an impressive entrance to Heaven, but how long can you stand around in the driveway?

Where was the reason that had given this country such a good start? Even so, spiritual teaching had been the great undercurrent that had guided us and given us strength from the beginning, even long before there was a drawing on the map called "America".The physical realm is an important part of the Universe, a great obstacle course, a school house, a laboratory, the great waves of fate for "Kuhunas" big and small to try their skills at surfing upon, to see how long or well they can catch a wave, and arrive at the beach by maybe a crash, or a long gentle slow down, or something inbetween, and thereby develop and strengthen their souls.

Reason is reason,but emotion and desire are more powerful and drive everything. Nothing gets done in Democracy but what it gets really popular.There is a time for expansion and great dreams, but also a time to fight and protect.(A time to throw away stones and to gather them together, to quote the Bible). A higher awareness by all is what's needed,but from where will it come? From "Them?" But what of these other beings, some strange, some wise, some deadly,which have kept invading, or rather "inter-vading" our earthly pursuits from time to odd time when we were least aware?

This brought Zeke's mental ramble back to the crashing present, of the thing above him, a worried awareness of a lurking parasite, sort like when Zeke was at his drawing board working on a particularly pleasant but strange drawing while he knew a stink bug was lurking around the edge,watching him. He would then urge the little fellow onto a ruler or pencil and put him out the window before he could stink. But this "bug" above him now could do more than stink. He must try and do *something* while the chance was upon him.

Then it hit him. What if he could make the balloon rotate back and forth by twisting the ropes, and this by rotating the basket? He started shifting his weight to test it, by running quickly from side to side, leaning and shifting, end to end and then diagonally across the middle from corner to corner, which worked best. Also across the short ends worked fairly well. If only he could build up a big rocking momentum, he might fling the blighter off. And he without his anti-grav would go crashing below!

The twisting motion grew and grew the more he ran, ramming his shoulders against the side. Rocking and swinging, he was gradually built a huge turn and shake effect on the balloon above him. Soon he heard honking and yelling from the cars below, especially from the owner, still worried about his "baby". But also, the legs of Sunglasses were indeed sloshing back and forth along the canopy. He also emitted a very odd and gravelly grunt with each rotation. Many of the chasers could also now see the strange body clinging and rocking for dear life high above them, especially the two cops.

" What is it?!!" asked the deputy with strained vision and emotion.

" Dunno," barked the sheriff,"might be some kinda sleeper cell high-tech terrorist, or maybe a lone wolf Communist! Get on the horn to State Police!" The deputy struggled with his improbable description to the Charlottesville office, which of course had a hard time interrupting *their* lunch to believe him.

" Tell them I'm pretty sure it's a terrorist," added the sheriff, "they always wear bad hats!"

The deputy gave him a look. "You really want me to say that?"

The balloon was now approaching the back side of the Monticello mountain which is actually part of Carter's Mountain known to some as "Highland". A very pleasing part of the country, this ridge of land leading finally down to the point where Jefferson watched the building of UVA and Charlottesville from his telescope, was marked by wide grazing land, a picturesque crossroads and vineyard, as well as another historic farm and home place of a founding father, that of James Monroe called "Ash Lawn",(a name which came later). Here was the perfect country for landing thought Zeke, but with "Ichabod" hanging about, it was going to be complicated. Also, he figured, who knows what kind of wind would be kicking over that ridge from the west.

All at once there was a loud CLICK. Above Sunglasses had closed his case and was on the move, crawling with confident certainty toward him like a spider to a fly, it's captive prey waiting for it wrapped in silk. Soon his mug of a face emerged below the envelope, peeking upside down at Zeke, breathing like a rattling stove of steam. Suddenly he flipped over and around and on to the floor of the gondola, brief-case firmly in hand. Zeke noticed bits of burning cat litterish crumbles scattering about his fake Gucci shoed feet.

"Grabsa Magga Bugna...", he thought he heard him-she-it-whatever say. Bits of cooking litter crumbled from the edges of its mouth, cooling as it landed below. "Grobelax jobshlah Bugna..".

" I couldn't have said it better.."droled Zeke with nervous defensive energy, suddenly imagining himself the witty equivalent of James Bond. He did notice that when the thing stopped talking, it's face became more flesh like, and the illusion of it being human was nearly complete, but when it tried to speak it began reverting to the crumbly molten lava-like substance again, as if it needed to draw on such power to com-plete the task. What gave it it's power? It's life force? It seemed to run on a mineralized metabolism, burn-ing as it went like a bionic steam engine. Clearly it used oxygen in the process, and who knew what for fuel, probably something found in dirt.

Now it stood and stared at Zeke, and Zeke stared back. It removed it's sunglasses, revealing those glow-ing deep pitted orange eyes. Zeke felt an odd, some-what blinding but also hypnotic effect, which he instinctively avoided by looking away. The thing shifted it's position, the better to aim it's laser-like gaze at his eyes, repeating, " Grabsa Magga Bugna...Grobelax jobshlah Bugna!" Then it lunged at Zeke, running quickly at his position by the gondola wall, but he was able to duck sideways, while Sun-glasses ran straight at the wall and flipped over into the air! Zeke was momentarily relieved but held to his new position at the opposite end of the basket. A wise thing it was too, because his enemy rose quickly back into sight, hovering unsteadily and clutching his brief-case.

Zeke also noticed a large open field of pasture land ahead, perfect for landing. He grabbed the red cord to release hot air. Immediately the balloon descended, leaving Sunglasses behind and surprised. He quickly corrected for it though and was closing in again on the basket. Zeke could hear the peculiar whine from the anti-grav device getting closer. Then he had an idea, while he was out of viewing range he threw the rope ladder over board so he could climb down, drop to the ground and hopefully make a get away. A good plan but too late, the alien was already upon him, grabbing hold of the gondola railing.

"*Grabsa Magga Bugna!*" it repeated with sinister vigor.

"What a single minded agenda.." said Zeke, while also thinking that somehow it planned to suck the life force right out of him. It had it's fakey plastic shoe foot on the railing and was pulling on the ropes now, while simultaneously trying to lean on and stabilize it's wobbly briefcase before turning it off. It's nor-mally homicidal expression was showing frustration and angst for just a quick moment, but Zeke seized that moment to make use of another onboard piece of balloon equipment he had been spying, the sand bags. Grabbing one with weightlifting fervor, he lunged forward and slammed it into Sunglasses—OOF! GARRRGalaga! Ga Baff *gag!*

He went down overboard and his briefcase went

spinning away by itself. Relief sprang happily to
Zeke's face, but then came a sudden jerk downward to
the entire apparatus. Looking hesitantly overboard, he
saw the snarling thing from another world holding on
to the ladder, it's face now totally consisting of a grey
crusty magma-like surface with leaking veins of
bright orange running lava. It had a face like parts of
the Big Island of Hawaii, and it was climbing toward
him with total commitment— "Gargalla Geeaagyah
GYAAAAHH!"

Zeke turned his attention back to the burners,
hoping a sudden lift and perhaps another body slam
twirl might help. But what he saw ahead gave him
little choice, for dead ahead was a rusty old farmer's
windmill turning and clanking in the breeze. A quick
blast and up he went, just missing the spinning blades,
although they bumped a short rat-a-tat on the basket
bottom. Then came a tug, a lurch and an ungodly
scream from down below. Coming to his feet, Zeke
saw the end of the rope ladder was caught in the mill
blades, and Sunglasses was none too happy. The
balloon tried to rise and the mill tried to pull down
with each gust of wind over the ridge from the Valley
of the Shenandoah, which was indeed picking up.

Over on the road a siren sounded, cars and bikes
were pulling up, even a news car from a local
Charlottesville network affiliate. They all piled out
trying to get the gate open to the field so they could
drive the still far distance across. Tommy jumped out
ahead on foot and climbed the fence, running fast
toward his endangered cousin. By then, the rope latter
was pulled around a full rotation and had slipped
down onto the mill's axel, now free of the windmill's

blades. This freed them up to the rushing wind and they turned much faster, thus wrapping and pulling the ladder down at a very rapid rate of speed. Zeke looked over in time to see an incredible sight. The strange and odd alien was being pulled downward, where it careened into the spinning blades and was immediately ground up into a spinning mass of smoke and burning chunks of lava-cat litter, or whatever the stuff was. Bits crumbled down all around the windmill, some thrown upward and even bouncing off the balloon, but soon there was nothing left!

The balloon had now been wrapped up tight against the mill where it bobbed harmlessly in the wind, allowing Zeke to climb down onto the platform and down the access latter to safety. Bits of hissing steaming particles were just burning away as Zeke slipped behind the mill's two out buildings. He then heard thumping footsteps behind him.

"Zeke! Zeke, it's Tommy! You gotta get outta here!"

"Don't I know it! Everything in the world is after me!" He eyed a smoldering piece of debris on the ground, "Make that the *Universe!*" A gun blast rang out as the sheriff shot the gate padlock. They ran across through some weeds to a nearby hedge and fence line, just as the cars and bikers were breaking onto the field. Running concealed behind trees and brush on the far side of the hedge, the two cousins came back to the road. While the crowd jabbered away beside the bobbing balloon atop the windmill, and the news team got some award-winning footage, Zeke and Tommy silently got into Jerry's car and were gone.

CHAPTER 31
Side Road Sanctification

They both stared silently dead ahead as Route 53 led them northward,their minds bulging with their recent incredible experiences. Although neither felt much like talking, Zeke ventured some conversation.

" I see Jerry's car looks good.."

" Yeah, I got it cleaned, it needed it..."

" That'll make him happy, he's pretty picky about it."

" Minnie called me last night.."

" Yeah, we're in good time to meet'em at Mitchie's...one of us will give you a ride back to your car in Scottsville.."

" OK..." They were closing in on Monticello now, and just down the hill from that was Mitchie's Tavern, a popular historic eatery still serving the same purpose as it did some 200 years before. Properly termed an "ordinary", it served the same bill of fare for each midday meal. Fried chicken, mashed potatoes, green beans, stewed tomatoes, with choices of pulled pork barbecue, black eyed peas, cole slaw, baby beets, corn bread and bisquits. Oddly enough that was the same stuff Zeke's Mom had raised him on (although he could do without the beets). These days they also had gluten free entrees. Discussion of all this had the boys' mouths watering and stomachs grumbling as they rounded a curve to go down the mountain. But there at the corner of a little side road before them was a small makeshift sign—

ALL BELIEVERS NOW
INTER-FAITH TABERNACLE

"*Stop!*" yelled Zeke.

"*Hey*, let's go *there!*" yelled Tommy, almost simultaneously. They looked at each other, and soon realized they'd both been on the same trail for sometime. Tommy revealed that he had been in touch with this group years ago soon after he'd seen his "demon saucer" east of Richmond, but try as he would, he could never find them again—until now. Zeke also enthusiastically explained the signs that he'd been receiving, and how this odd church must somehow hold the key to the mystery of the string of wild events he'd been privy too, for whatever reason.

They turned left down a narrow macadamized road through pleasing but somewhat bare and unkempt pasture land. At a crossroads, situated at an odd diagonal angle just back from the corner sat a compact little chapel built of corrugated aluminum and white clapboard, with the now familiar sign and blue praying hands beneath the all-seeing eye logo. A little gravel parking lot beckoned them onward, with more cars parked in the back. The two cousins gingerly approached the front door beneath it's miniature steeple.

Inside they could hear a preacher.

" Now Beloved, ye must know that ye are Sanctified!"

" Amen..Amen.." went voices from the congregation.

" *Sanctified* are ye, even before ye are *born!* Ye are
sanctified..while ye are in your mama's womb!.. You
are *sanctified*...even in the third trimester when your
mama was throw'n up, you were *Sanctified!* From the
beginning to the end, from Alpha unto Omega we are
Sanctified in the *Blood* of the *Lamb!*"

" Amen, Amen brother.."
Zeke wondered somewhat at the reverend's specific
choice of words but continued and grabbed the door
handle.

" Now will we all please stand as we sing?" At that
moment, the most extraordinarily fine hymn singing
came forth and filled the air as Zeke and Tommy
entered and stepped into the center aisle.

> "I've reached the land of corn and wine,
>   And all it's riches freely mine;
>   Here shines undimmed one blissful day,
>   For all my night has passed away."

The boys passed down a red plush carpet as the
people sang. It was that kind of carpet that made your
feet go several directions at once. An impressive
commercially produced shining wood-carved and
painted effigy of the praying hands hung on the far
wall, surrounded by a golden violet rainbow painted
with glitter and starlets from a discount store. Above it
also was painted a rather amateurish version of the

Masonic all-seeing eye of God. A wizened smiling preacher beamed at them as they walked to an empty pew space, indicating welcome as he kept time to the music with his fine big farmer's hands.

> "O Beulah Land, sweet Beulah Land,
> As on the highest mount I stand,
> I look away across the sea,
> Where mansions are prepared for me,
> And view the shining glory shore,
> My Heav'n, my home for evermore!"

The congregation, made up of a goodly mix of "po folk" black and white from the country around, turned warm loving faces to them as they took their place in the pew. Zeke was overcome with a great swooning power that zeroed in directly on his spirit, and gave him soaring uplift as the hymn went on;

> "My Savior comes and walks with me,
> And sweet communion here have we;
> He gently leads me by His hand,
> For this is Heaven's border land."

Zeke's eyes rounded wide. *Heaven's Border Land!* A clear voice in Zeke's head said to him, "Yes, that is what I've been seeking, and what I've been led to!" The hymn ended, still ringing in Zeke's ears and heart. The preacher rose up with shining countenance.

"BELOVED! We are blessed this fine day, let beauty and love shine among us, and let us greet with warmth and fellowship our newly arrived visitors! Amen, and may God's blessing be unto you!"

" *Amen!..Amen..*" The congregation nodded and smiled.

" And Sister Mary Elizabeth and the volunteers have blessed us with some fine fried chicken and potato salad and other fine fixin's in the kitchen, of which we may now also partake, *Praise* be to *God!*" People were talking, hands were shaking as they moved to the back parish hall and kitchen. Zeke looked and saw Tommy smiling broadly and engaged in laughing and happy communication with many of the members. He looked like he was at 'Old Home Week'. Zeke then looked about for a way that he too could somehow overcome his slight awkwardness at being in so evangelical a setting and join in. Clearly these people were of good and Godly spirit. And this was good thought Zeke. Here *too* must be some answers.

The solution itself seemed now to be coming his way, as the preacher had caught him in his smiling eye and was extending a firm handshake full of honest friendship.

" *Welcome Brother!* Welcome to 'All Believers Now Inter-Faith Tabernacle!' Where all true believers are welcome and given hope and rest on Life's path!"

" Thank you! I, I'm most happy to be here!" stammered Zeke, " It..it was by almost pure chance that we came here!"

" *Nothing* is left to chance in the eyes of God brother! Everything happens for a *reason!* A most blessed reason!"

" Yes..yes..I believe I see.."

" And do you *Believe?*" asked the preacher with strong piercing eyes.

" Yes! Of course! I have no choice! I have seen the *evidence* all around me!"

" Praise God brother! Praise God! I see you're a man of deep faith! It is *good* that you have come!" They were now moving into the back of the kitchen. The food looked inviting, Tommy was laughing out loud and telling jokes over in a corner. Then Zeke remembered Minnie and Jerry, and their proposed meeting down the road at Mitchie's Tavern, and all that had gone before these last few days. He decided there just wasn't much time so he asked the preacher straight out.

" So Reverend, do you know where the saucers..and the little men...come from? What do they want?" The reverend looked at him almost aghast.

" Where do they *come* from!?? Little *Men!!?*"

" Yes, and the wheel within a wheel..what's it all about?" The preacher began to bluster.

" They..they're from *HELL!*"

" But Reverend ..I'm Ezekiel! What am I..."

" *Ezekiel!* Then you're the one *foretold!* You must be cleansed! You must be *purified!* Come with me out back..." The big farm hands were reaching out to him.

" What? *Let go my arm!*" Zeke shook free, he didn't know what the reverend meant by 'purified' but he was sure he didn't want to find out. He worked on through the crowd, but felt the preacher's eyes upon him all the way. Coming close to Tommy he said it's time to leave.

" Oh go ahead man! I've already got a ride to Scottsville, here's Jerry's keys.. Hey, these people are *great!*" Well, 'like attracts like', 'birds of a feather' thought Zeke. He guessed everybody got to Heaven in their own way, but somehow this wasn't *his* way, he was sure of that. There was a convenient side door in the kitchen, so he slipped out into the parking lot, but the preacher's eyes were still on him, bold and intense. It seemed he'd experienced this feeling before. As he started up the Mini, the big farmer's head poked out the door as if he was coming after him.

BAROOOM! He spun out in the gravel, leaving the holy man standing spraddle legged behind him, hands outstretched. He prayed Tommy would be OK, but somehow felt he could take care of himself.

CHAPTER 32
Curiosity on the Mountain

With a feeling of great relief Zeke turned into the parking lot of familiar old Mitchie's Tavern, then pulling up next to his own car, and soon into the arms of Minnie.

" God I missed you! You can't *imagine*.."

" Even during your lighter than air experience? It's on the news and the internet!" She showed him video posts on her phone to Zeke's great interest, but there was no sign of the close-up terror he'd faced, only people chasing a run away balloon. Jerry was scrutinizing his car but quite happy to see it again. As they went inside and got a table, Zeke whispered his dangerous adventures both alien and ghostly,while surreptitiously scanning the crowded room for out of place characters, which only served to remind the trio of the incredible and strange forces out there, just beyond the pale of everyday life that exist and were for some reason still intruding upon their own lives.

And yet, as no threat was felt, (in fact just the opposite) and the day was so beautiful and the food smelled so good in these most pleasant of surroundings, Zeke easily put such thoughts aside and enjoyed a very satisfying meal with happy camaraderie. "Did you check out this Brunswick Stew? That's the *real deal!*

" It's the pulled chicken," said Minnie, "They originally used squirrel meat.."

" Mmm, sometimes I feel like one of those little corn kermals, spinning round and round, my destiny controled by the giant ladel, the soup expanding to infinity."

" There's something profound in that.."

" And tasty, but it needs a little pepper.."added Jerry.

" We're in the soup alright, but it's also depress-ing.." Minnie continued, "It's too vast and scary, I can deal with the carrots and butterbeans I'm bumping into right here, but not all that..I gotta just get back to me.."

" Me too.." Zeke agreed.

In the car Jerry was very cranked up at the close prox-imity of so many historical places and the anticipation of his first visit to Monticello, just up the hill. " Do you think it's got octagons? Octagons were very significant to the Masons and Illuminati.."

" It's got octagons.."said Zeke.

" I don't think Jefferson was a Mason.." added Minnie as they drove up the drive toward the moun-tain top.

" Yes, but he was a founding father...same thing, he rubbed shoulders with'em!"

" Now Washington," added Zeke, " *he* was a Ma-son, big time, wearing aprons and floating in the clouds and.."

" Whaat?" Minnie looked at him funny.

" Well, in those paintings an' all...always holding a trowel..."

" Jefferson was kinda ..you know, Unitarian..now *they're* strange!"said Jerry with assurance.

"No they're not," said Zeke, "they're very nice, I've been to their functions for the environment...very concerned and nice..maybe they could be a little more exciting..I mean you would'nt find comedian Sam Kinison going there..screaming to save the environment at the top of his lungs..'GLOBAL WARMING PEOPLE!! WE'RE GONNA *BURRRN*, LIKE YOUR FEET AT THE BEACH ON THE *SAAAND!!* An' your *FLIP FLOPS* AIN"T GONNA HELP EITHER, CUZ THEY'LL BE *MELTED!!!*' "

" That's pretty good..actually *that* might be a good idea.."said Minnie.

" Well he's dead anyway..maybe you could channel him for them.."

" I haven't got the vocal chords..."

" Hey, how 'bout snake handling evangelical environmentalists! Might work huh? Get something done?..think?"

They were now turning into a parking and administrative area known as the Jefferson Foundation. There they bought tickets and caught a shuttle bus up the mountain to the east front of the mansion. As the historic landscape rolled downward upon them from above, Jerry continued his yeasty Da Vinci codeish commentary, off on one of his conspiracy theory spoutings. When he was wound up this tight there was no stopping him,(nor making sense either).

"Yeah Jefferson was the most secretive of 'em all,

why I bet there's Knight's Templar treasure buried
around here, imbued with a special radiant power ya
know..where I grew up it's everywhere in the ground
ya see, and the Mafia tried to find it, up at this big
lake in Minnesota and..but Jefferson, now he.." Then
a stern looking man across the aisle from him turned
and stared.

" Thomas Jefferson was a Fascist!"

" No, he was..uh *what?*" Jerry was dumbfounded.

" You heard what I..." But before the man could
finish, the shuttle had stopped and everyone was
piling out. Jerry whispered to Zeke what had transpired, who looked around somewhat quizzically as if
to say he didn't quite follow, but at any rate the man
wasn't one of *them*, just a good ol' American nut case.

Soon they alighted from the bus at the front gate of
Monticello. Minnie seemed in some sort of ecstacy.

" Wow, what a vibration, can't you feel it? It radi-
ates from the hill top...all around.."

" Yes, I think I do," replied Zeke, holding her arm,
"The spirit of Jefferson?"

" Well maybe that too, but it's more..like he was
attracted to this place for the same reason.."

Zeke smiled, " I knew we should'nt have eaten so
soon before coming..come on, let's just enjoy it..."

They all strolled up the brick walkway to the portico, the imposing but friendly iconic architecture
rising before them. But Jerry was suddenly all nervous.

"Where's the dome? The eight sided dome, what'd
they do with it! *Conspiracy!* This isn't Monticello!"

" Don't worry, it's on the other side of the house,
it's how Jefferson designed it.." Zeke assured him.

"This house is full of little hidden wonders!"

" Hidden? Yeah, that's right, but *I'll* see right through the archaic symbolism, don't worry!" As the small crowd gathered, a docent/tour guide descended the steps. Jerry nudged Zeke again as the strange nut job guy from the bus drew near. He was staring hard at Jerry.

" Why don't you shut up your propaganda! I said he was a *Fascist!*"

Jerry turned on him, " Hey you can't talk like that!"

" You gonna take away my freedom of speech? Go ahead--*try it!*"

" No, I wouldn't do that....but he wasn't."

" *Was!*"

" *Wasn't!*"

" *Was!*"

Just then the docent stepped forward and began her talk.

" Welcome to Mr. Jefferson's curiosity!" she beamed, obviously in good humour and in love with her job. "And when I say that, it has a multiple meaning, as that was the term he often used to describe this, 'Monticello', his house on the mountain, Italian for 'Little Mountain', and curious because of his own great curiosity which kept him ever searching out new things, ideas, ways of doing things which included of course his house, his 'essay on architecture' which he kept experimenting on, pulling down and putting up, for 40 years in search of the ideal structure as he assimilated ideas from his travels and from books, indeed playing with the space and shapes which, as he said, was one of his greatest pleasures..."

Zeke smiled warmly to himself, knowing that the same attitude toward building had been passed down to the denizens of Albemarle County and beyond, including his own fine Virginyuh family, great gran Captain and granpa D. Early Gunderson and his noted architecture throughout the state.

"Communist!" blurted the nut case man suddenly, once again exercising his free speech, somewhat under his breath for no reason at all. Now Zeke looked hard at him too and leaned in on him. "Look, these people have the right to enjoy this afternoon and learn about Jefferson just as you.."

"Pervert!" shouted the man, "Jefferson was a pervert, and so are you!" The docent was now getting nervous, she looked around the area, and suddenly gave a little nod as she continued.

"And while it is as you see quite beautiful...it is also full of playful ideas as you shall see."

Jerry whispered to Zeke, "Ya think he's got a gun?"

"Oh no..we went through security before we got on the bus remember?" Suddenly from out of nowhere two large men in sleek business suits appeared on either side of the man saying, "Telephone for you sir!"

"Hey! Nobody knows me!"

"What's your name?"

"Smith!"

"That's right, come this way Mr.Smith, it's very urgent.." and he was as they say, whisked away down the hill. Zeke and Jerry stared along with Minnie and the others, but the docent smiled and continued her talk.

"He was indeed a most admirable but also a most

curious man! This way please..." They entered into
the fascinating entrance or 'Indian Hall', Jefferson's
'museum', full of scientific artifacts, art, maps, fossils
bones antlers etc., some from the Lewis and Clark
expedition, Native American objects presented by
visiting chiefs, as well inventive anomalies such as the
counterbalanced 'iron ball weight calender' which
vertically told the day of the week along the corner of
the wall, except for Saturday. For that the ball descended through a hole in the floor and to view it you
had to go to the basement,(apropos for a day full of
playfullness, when time is supposed to sort of go
away).

The group, made up of tourists from all over, and
still a bit keyed up from what had transpired outside,
carried on with various comments. "Maybe the Saturday room is where he had his Illuminati meetings!"
(this from Jerry), " Or where he kept his Men in
Black," "No, *they* were wearing gray suits!ha ha ha..."
"Or it's where he whipped Sally Hemings!" came
from somebody with a Bronx accent, " Or made her
get into leather!" Jerry was laughing a bit but Zeke
was boiling over.

" What the hell are you talking about! That's rude!
They really loved each other! She was his wife's half
sister! He wanted to abolish slavery but he couldn't,
trapped by the system, the others shouted him down!
Washington had *many* more slaves..Jefferson was a
good master, when he came home from France they
cheered and carried him up the hill!"

" *Oh,* looks like we have a Klan member in our
midst!" said the Bronx guy.

" No! But I'm not ashamed of my ancestors having

slaves, that's just the way it was! You Yankees de-
pended on it too! If you took the time to get your facts
straight you could--"

The docent interrupted, "Excuse me! Excuse me,
we are trying to conduct a tour here! We address all
these issues here at Monticello..in fact we have a
special slave tour, now if you'll just calm down we
can continue, otherwise you'll have to step outside!"
She was looking intently at Zeke. Minnie pulled up
close to him.

" You and your *rants!* Always getting us in
trouble!"

" Well, somebody's got to stand up for the truth!"
But they all soon simmered down and continued into
the parlor and the dining room. "I've always been
high strung since I was a kid.." he added, "I think
quick and react quick, I can't help it.." Minnie just
smirked and shook her head.

The beautiful full length windows provided a fine
view onto the west lawn. They listened pleasantly as
the docent spoke of soiree's with James and Dolly
Madison, among many other notables in this elegant
room. Jerry joked with Zeke that they must've served
plenty of Dolly Madison Cakes at the dinners, and
Minnie had to shush the boys up as usual. But now
Jerry was busy scanning the partial octagon shape of
the ceiling and pointing it out with enthusiasm. Soon
his eye came down the long window next to him and
fell on the outside view of the lawn.

Two men were energetically talking as they walked
swiftly across the lawn, not acting like tourists at all.
Also, they had a very middle eastern look. He quickly
tapped Zeke's shoulder to attention, who looked indif-

ferently and shrugged. Minnie was perturbed at their actions and thrust a Monticello historic brochure in their faces. They were sheepishly chastised for a moment, until Zeke also looked out the window. There was a man in plain black suit with black fedora and sunglasses walking straight after the other men who were now nearly off the lawn over by the woods.

"You think?" whispered Jerry.

"I've had a funny feeling all along.." answered Zeke. "Com'on , we better follow 'em." He made an excuse to Minnie about their needing a breath of fresh air.

" Well, *I'm* gonna stay here and *learn* something!" she scowled indignantly.

Out on the west portico the boys saw the sunglassed man ascend the side stairs of the mansion onto Jefferson's "North Terrace", a raised walkway set on top of a row of slave quarters or other service rooms, where you could walk and observe the views, whether earthly or celestial. It extended out from the side of the house north, turned at a right angle and west an equal distance, ending in a small two story house-like structure or pavilion, suitable for scientific pursuits in bad weather. It was from here that Jefferson famously had kept an eye through a tele-scope on the building of his beloved University of Virginia. Beyond this the forest began, descending down the mountain. Zeke and Jerry followed the route of the Middle Eastern looking men.

"You think they're *t-terrorists?*" stammered Jerry.

"Who knows, but they would'nt try anything-- too much security, besides, I'm more concerned about that *other* guy."

"Should'nt we leave this to the experts?"

"After what we've been through with *them*, we *are* the experts! Besides I just want to see what happens, not get involved...I've done enough of that!" They soon came to the pavilion at the far end of the terrace and stopped to go slow against the wall on the northern side. There was no sign of the Arabs or whoever they were. Coming up to the corner next to the terrace they stopped, peeking around. Up above on the terrace was the sunglassed man peering through binoculars.

"What's he doin'? Looking for the terrorists?" whispered Jerry with several nervous hand jestures, twitches and sniffs.

"I don't know.."

"Isn't he one of..you know..*them?*"

"I dunno..maybe he's CIA..I can't always tell. Too far away anyway.." Some kids with their parents were walking up along the terrace toward the man.

"Com'on let's see if we can see UVA!" said the boy.

"Yeah! That's where I'm gonna go to college!" said the girl pulling her Daddy's hand. Zeke and Jerry calmly walked along below, observing the doorways and early American tools on display. The sunglassed man paid little attention and moved off toward the mansion. Finally the family also left. With no one watching, Zeke suggested they take a look further down in the woods. They walked as quietly as they could through the leaves. Looking intently all around they didn't see anything, so they decided to start back.

All of a sudden there was a crashing and tromping through the trees. The two Arabs were running fast in their direction! Jerry quickly squatted down behind a clump of vines but Zeke wasn't so lucky, he had nowhere to hide except some very skinny trees. On came the Arabs, jumping and crashing. All Zeke could do was sort of turn away with his head down, like that shy girl named Ellen he remembered did when they played dodge ball in elementary school. She always was the first to get hit. The Arabs ran right by him, within a matter of inches! But as Jerry watched, there was more crashing. Out of nowhere came the sunglasses or CIA guy chasing fast. He stopped close by Zeke, pulled his gun and stared for half a minute, looking down the mountain.

Jerry stared nervously, trying very hard to hold still. He was about 10 feet away from the barrel of that gun, and one sudden move would be all that guy needed for his highly trained government reflexes to whip around and pop one off straight between Jerry's eyes. His inherent high strung nature could be held down only so long however, as his volcanic spinal column wanted to vibrate badly, and bubble up into some sort of allergic bodily reaction. Indeed he could see his right hand shaking. He slowly grabbed it with his left. But now his face was twitching, his left lower lip convulsing, his eye started blinking. The sunglassed man was turning slowly in his direction. He detected something, but didn't know what. Then the dam finally burst in Jerry's greatly suppressed system. *SNIFF!!*—went his madness of King George nose, and very loudly too. The man spun 180 degrees and back another 90 into a two armed kneeled firing position pointed straight at Jerry's head. Jerry shut his quivering eyes, he didn't want to look. Was his life going to flash before him he thought? No, he didn't have time.

Then came a loud BLISH!—over to his right. The man shifted his aim. Then *BLISH*—again. A squirrel was leisurely hopping among the leaves as squirrels do, hopping, then freezing, hopping then freezing and making a noise remarkably similar to one of Jerry's heroic nasal convulsions. In his case, a blish was as good as a sniff. The man put away his weapon and walked back to Monticello. Jerry melted. That squirrel might make a good under cover agent, but it had been the calvary to him. But soon he was also astounded, because he realized the man had been standing not 2 feet from Zeke and never noticed him! When all was quiet he ran up.

"Wow, was that that trick you were telling me about?" Zeke nodded. "Seems to me I've read about that among the Indians, they call it 'Fox Medicine' or something.."

"Sure comes in handy...if you know when it's working.." said Zeke, still breathless.

"Hey maybe you could teach me!"

"Yeah, I guess...let's get back to the house.." Thankfully they saw Jefferson's architecture through the trees again. They were passing a huge oak tree of immense age partially covered in ivy when a voice spoke in an Arabic accent.

"Ello..heckscuze a me!" A tall middle aged mustachioed man looked down at them from atop a large root of the tree. Somehow they must have doubled back and hid behind the giant tree trunk. The boys froze. From behind him peered a smaller younger man smiling broadly as if he were one of the local possum population. "We.. wan..to know someting.." the big one continued, and suddenly thrust out his hand, making Jerry and Zeke jump back from their tracks. In his hand he held a small brown object. An acorn.

"Could you tell what is dis? Dis a nut? What is?" Zeke was disarmed by the seemingly innocent interest in nature.

"That? It's an acorn.."

" Can you eat? Is good, no?"

" Uh no, not really. Animals eat it, squirrels, birds, pigs.."

" Ah!! *Peegs!?*" here he spoke rapid Arabic to his friend, then turned back. "But is big strong tree! What kind?"

" An oak. You know," He pointed to the tree they stood on, "From little acorns grow mighty oaks? It's the seed.."

" AAaah, an *oak!* Is so *big!*"
Jerry had been getting very agitated. "Yeah, and our generals have oak leaf clusters! So you better.." Zeke did an aside. "Quiet Jerry,besides I think that's a colonel.."

"What is?"

"Oak leafs.."
The big Arab continued enthusiastically. "So much life..the plants *everywhere!*" He thanked Zeke and they went away jabbering to each other.

"Ever notice how nice Arabs seem over here?" said Zeke as they watched, "But on TV they're always yelling? Jihad! Jihad! Allah kama lamma! And blowing up things..."

"Maybe it's cuz they don't have any trees..Think they're spies?"

"Spying on what, acorns?"

"I don't know *what's* going on around here.." said Jerry as they made their way along the terrace tool rooms back toward the east entrance. Ahead was the corner of the terrace structure. "I guess we'll have to join another tour to get back in.."

Just then the sunglassed CIA-ish man stepped out from the corner, looking. He then turned his head mechanically and stared straight at them. Zeke and Jerry nearly ran into each other, but managed to immediately start heading west, swiftly but not so swiftly as to arouse suspicion...hopefully.

CHAPTER 33
The Ecstacy of Octagons

Inside, Minnie had very much been enjoying the tour. They had viewed the dining room, the tea room, the north octagonal room and were moving toward the library. " Mr. Jefferson valued tranquillity above all things..", continued the docent. "He once told John Adams I believe, 'It is neither wealth nor splendor, but tranquility and occupation which give you happiness.' Which of course brings to mind his famous phrase; 'the pursuit of happiness' in the Declaration of Independence, as indeed was reflected in practise, for he was an ardent pursuer of happiness his whole life." Minnie smiled as the group moved on and she regarded the warmth and friendliness of his library.

A warming spirit enveloped her as she heard it mentioned that some had reported occasionally hearing the playing of TJ's violin wafting among these rooms. They moved on to his study, with it's reclining desk chair designed to get more blood to the head while reading, and the bed chamber. They were as ever intrigued by the alcove bed, situated in the wall space between the two rooms so he could get out of bed into one room on one side and the other room on the other side, a most original arrangement.

The bed chamber itself had a high ceiling reaching up two stories with a skylight which filled the room with a pleasing light. On the high wall above the bed were three strange but tastefully made oval holes in the wall. "Portholes" if you will. These were explained as ventilation openings for Jefferson's hidden clothes closet above his bed, reached by a steep closeted staircase in the corner. This oddness, coupled with the beauty and inventiveness of Monticello, this orderly labyrinth, of both confusion and balance, as if touring the ventricles of the human heart, naturally put Minnie into one of her moods of altered state. Part dreaming, part awakedness, this was the state that she used in much of her psychic work. Usually it took a special preparation to acquire this trance, familiar to most practitioners, but on occasion it could come on spontaneously, the same as when we are children and meet "secret imaginary" friends. She now was "in that place" and could "see".

The room was still there from her same point of view, but the tourists and tour guide were gone. It was evening by candle light at the turn of the nineteenth century. Thomas Jefferson, in a dark red robe had just finished writing a page on his unique "copy machine" which wrote on another sheet simultaneously as he wrote, and was retiring from his desk with book in hand, getting ready to go to bed. He turned suddenly to the hallway door, and put down the book on a side table. From The passage a beautiful woman of dark hair and eyes and tan complexion appeared in the candle light and came to his waiting arms. They caressed, moved from the study to the bed chamber, and tenderly sat on the bedside. As they did, they stopped their loving motions and turned toward Minnie, as if they saw her, smiling gently. Their faces were filled with warmth and happiness, and with a knowing, almost welcoming regard in her direction, looked exactly into her eyes.

But then their attention was quickly jerked away across the room as someone was knocking at the main bedroom door. Sally Hemings rushed deftly to the far corner door by the window, opening it with one hand while carrying a lighted candle holder. She ascended the steep inner stair and closed the door gently. Jefferson pulled on his robe and opened the main door which connected with the parlor. His daughter Martha stepped in to discuss some trifle about the next day's activities at Monticello, which as mistress of the house since her mother's death was her job. When his head turned away for a moment, Minnie noticed Martha glancing ever so quickly at the oval windows. She seemed to know. Then her father patted his daughter's hand to reassure her about something with a smile and off she went. Alone again, Jefferson looked up to the oval windows high over his bed. Sally came forward to the center one smiling, her face peering down at him amid the unique shadows of the flickering candlelight.

Before Minnie could fully feel the mysterious essence of her vision, a cold chill ran down her spine, her head shook and she was back in the present. The docent was commenting on the workmanship of the fireplace, but Minnie still stared at the oval windows.

Outside, Zeke and Jerry rounded the pavilion at the west end of the north terrace, looking around nervously. Before them was the classic shot of Monticello, the west portico and domed roof shining in the afternoon sun. They weren't sure whether to cross the lawn or not, but they had to get back to the tour. They saw their chance in a small group exiting the front door from the parlour to stroll the grounds. Rushing as fast as they could with out running, the boys looked somewhat like silent movie comedians. Zeke was focusing his site on the portico door, trying to make it in time to slip unobtrusively back inside without having to join another tour on the far side of the building. Halfway across the lawn a shadow passed over his head. Thinking it an airplane he took little notice until he saw the dark shape on the ground moving rapidly across to the northeast. It was perfectly round.

" Did you see that?" he called. Jerry responded yes. But on looking up it was already beyond the trees and gone from sight.

Reaching the door while the people were still there, they managed to sidle backwards, ending up back in the parlour, pretending they were greatly interested in the workmanship of the magnificent multi-panelled windows.

"Hmmm, cut glass..", said Zeke rubbing his chin.

"Well if they didn't cut it, it would'nt fit in the holes.." added Jerry,(looking positively professorial). Another tour was passing down the far hall on it's way toward the library, so the boys decided to meander over and join it at the end of the line.

At the other end of the house, Minnie, still enthralled with her vision, fell behind from her group which was returning to the parlour via the bedroom. She felt like returning to the study and library area to see what she could "see", again. She hoped the "book room" as they called it would be the perfect place to pick up the vibration of one who loved and valued learning, even though Jefferson's original books had long before gone to form the beginnings of the Library of Congress.

Down the hall, as Zeke and Jerry were waiting for the line of people to pass into the southern end of the building. Jerry was scrutinizing his Monticello brouchure he'd pulled from his pocket,which had a floor plan of the house.

" Hey Zeke! Let's go *this* way!"

" Huh?"

" Yeah, see here, 'The North Octagon Room', com'on!"

" Oh Jerry, you and your octa—" But before he could do anything his arm was pulled and they were gone. Inside the room Jerry was ecstatic. The room was a quite pleasing guest bedroom with fine views, but Jerry made a bit more of it.

" See? See? It's very symbolic, each corner means something! Why, this window probably lines up with the Louvre in France! Or maybe Roslyn Chapel!"

" Well..l don't know about tha..." Zeke had been looking out the front window as Jerry expounded, and now saw the man in sunglasses,(the CIA type/whoever), thrusting himself quickly up the hill. But then Jerry called over to him. Through the full length window on the north side, looking out on the walkway of the terrace and the side porch, were the two Arab men. Jerry had stepped back from the glass with a frozen face of fear. The Semitic men were jostling their positions, at a loss as to which way to go. Glancing around to the front, they quickly headed to the side door, which led to the hallway past the very room in which the boys stood. Then the two Arabic heads poked in the door of the octagon guestroom.

" Heckscuse please! Very Sorry!" Then popped back out. Zeke pointed and he and Jerry rushed out. But before they could exit, CIA Guy nearly crashed into them.

" Excuse me.." he touched his hat and moved on. The boys rushed into the hall. They heard doors opening and closing in the next room. There they found CIA Guy going through the closets.

" Security check.." he said and rushed off. They saw him disappear into the entrance hall and turn right into the parlour. Soon there was a scuffling of feet, and the two Arabs came through the entrance way from the dining room, and ran toward the end of the hall near the north terrace again, but turned at the hall corner left and disappeared. Jerry and Zeke decided to just stay put and watch the show.

CIA came along through the same entrance a moment later, looked around, then went around the same corner the Arabs did, but came back scratching his head. He then headed back outside onto the terrace. Jerry and Zeke went around the corner to have a look. They stood in a little alcove, between the outside wall and the serving hall for the dining room, not five feet square.

" I think I see what happened.." said Zeke. "This is T.J.'s famous revolving service door, see?" Zeke pushed the door and it revolved, revealing as it turned several shelves attached to it for serving dinner, which could be loaded and turned by the slave servants, so that guests could serve themselves as a buffet, which was to Jefferson's liking. "They crouched down here, and our Arab friends made their get away.."

" Fascinating!" said Jerry. "I wonder if there's ancient Egyptian symbolism in th—"

" Wait a minute," Zeke stopped him. "I thought I saw.." he pushed again the revolving door, revealing the buffet passageway. At the other end was a dumb waiter for bringing items up from the kitchen below. It consisted of a largish box on a pulley recessed in the wall. Such was fairly standard in old plantation houses, and Jefferson also had little ones hidden in the fireplace to carry wine bottles. But this was even more unusual, for in the box sat the Wise Alien.

Their eyes met for just half a moment, then the dumbwaiter quickly trundled upward, taking the alien with it.

"*Com'on!*" they said simultaneously, as the boys bolted out to the hall and to the small Jeffersonian staircase, which was made the size of a closet in Jefferson's mind, so as to minimize wasted space. But the narrow stairway was becoming suddenly full with another tour group coming down, and a docent discussing that very architectural theory. So Zeke and Jerry rushed across the entrance hall and down the other opposite corridor where Zeke knew they'd find another identical staircase. Here they saw Minnie down by the library and gestured wildly for her to follow them upstairs.

" But you can't!" hissed Minnie, "You have to have a special ticket for that!" The boys weren't to be stopped however so she ran up after them. Winding up the cozy claustrophobic space, they tumbled out onto the second floor corridor, the unique "hidden story" of Monticello, which is barely discernable outside.

Silence. Then, a far off trotting sound, and a quick "ga-flump".They explored down the other end where they rounded the half-octagon open balcony to the museum/artifact entrance hall where a new tour group was forming below. Jerry tried to wave but Zeke pulled him on.Now in the northern end, they looked but found the dumb waiter empty.

" Look!" said Jerry, "Another octagon roo—"

" Oh *come on!*" Zeke grabbed his arm. But Minnie kept looking in the room.

" There's somebody *in* there!" Zeke saw nothing as Minnie continued, "It's an old woman sitting in a rocking chair...I think with arthritis... Interesting, that must be Aunt Marks, Jefferson's sister.."

Zeke grabbed her arm. "But we've got somebody *else* to find!" He pulled her into the hall just as CIA Guy popped up the north stairs.

" Security check..." he tipped his hat and began searching rooms. The group continued down the hall a bit, but Zeke stopped, remembering his architectural studies. A quick look at the other bedrooms and back across the balcony, brought them back to the south stairs. Up they went. Now they were on the somewhat limited 3rd floor. A smaller hall way led to a few small rooms where children would've slept. Jerry immediately went on an energetic search for more angles and octagons. At the far Southern end, an Arabic head popped out in surprise and popped back. Then CIA arrived from the north stairs and began searching the third floor rooms.

While he was out of sight, the Arabs came out on tip toe,looking wide-eyed at Minnie and Zeke with fingers to their lips. They then stepped into a left door in the center of the hall. The friends began to follow, but before they could reach the door, CIA jumped from a door and across the hall, flinging himself inward.

" OK! Hands up!" He waved his gun decisively.

" No! NO! We done *nothing! No nothing! Please!*" The Arabs jabbered in speedy supplications.

" Oh yes you did! Com'on! Hand them over!" Zeke and Minnie had gathered behind him. They saw the men sheepishly hand the officer a small bunch of acorns.

" Let's go...we have some questions to ask.." CIA led them out while turning to Zeke and Minnie, " My apologies folks...please resume your tour with the compliments of Monticello, the President's home."

The two friends just stared at each other, until Jerry caught up from the rear, breathing and sniffing furiously. But then he suddenly was quiet, as he stepped zombie like, foot after foot into the room they were now in, blissfully breathing the surrounding air.

"Ambrosia..amazing...illumination of the Illuminati...oh Masonic holy of holies.." They realized now that they stood in the finely unique dome room of Monticello. A sublime simplicity of Virginian architectural elegance, it shaped around them on 8 perfect sides,with great circular windows of the colonial style, inspired from old Williamsburg's capitol building as well as T.J.'s visits to France and the Italian Renaissance work of Andrea Palladio.The light didn't exactly enter the room at angles, it was simply there, by virtue not only of the circle of circular windows, but because of a small circular skylight, known as an 'oculus' in the very top of the dome. The room nearly forced you to meditate, to fold up your legs and go "OOOhmmm". There were a few words like "whoa" and "wow", but mostly there was silence. Finally, Zeke made utterance. " I had hoped that...here would be an answer...maybe I've been hallucinating everything.."

"Hey, wait a minute, what about *me?*" said Minnie, "I've seen a helluva lot too!"

"And what am I, *chopped liver?*" chimed Jerry. Just then they heard a small a scratching. At the front of the octagon room, another door faced out toward the portico roof.

" Suppose it's a cat?" said Jerry.

" It's the 'Cuddy'..." said Zeke walking slowly over as the scratching continued.

" What, they gotta *cow* in there??"

" It's the little room over the west portico--storage space... Jefferson's grandaughters used to go there to write letters..."

" I still say it's a cat.."

Zeke reached for the knob, "Maybe." The door pushed open as he released the latch. Down low, below floor level in an tiny unfinished room with an arched window, stood the Wise Alien, smiling sheepishly.

" I..could not reach open device..." he extended his three fingered hand and they helped him up the rough steps, in wide-eyed disbelief. For several moments, no one knew what to say. Zeke made an attempt to break the interstellar ice.

"Uh..Who..wh...yyy..." The alien stopped him.

"I know, a million questions you want ask..and...I have no time to answer..." The friends were stymied, but then exploded verbally--

"What's been going on?--"Who are you? Where do you come from? "What about those other guys!? "

"What were you doing in our bedroom window!?"

"The World's in such a *mess!*"

"How does your *ship run?*"

"Hey Zeke!" said Jerry frantically, "You reckon this round room's gonna *take off?*" They jabbered all together.

"Global Warming!"-"Terrorists!"-"Environment!"-"Over population!"-"Health care!"-"Asteroids!"---"*Religion!*"

The Wise Alien blinked a soothing smile and held up his hand.

"Exactly!"

They were all dumbfounded again as he continued.

"The World..uh Earth, IS in a mess! That main reason we come..also.." The group was on verge of exploding once more but his hand again stopped them. "Those other..out worlders you mention..not so loving..caring or discrim..inating..

We can only interfere so much..they are..actually quite low creatures..lower than human..but have certain powers..They..climbed..uh, *hitched* a ride you say? On our ships..now they prey sometime on you and your planet..attracted to your lower animal fear thoughts..like you say..demon..ic, but you find new powers, new ways use your brain..evolve *too!*"

" But the dreams!" "The spirits!" "Why me!?" "Why us!?"

Again he stopped their jabbering. "There is an army..uh, expedition..helping you in your apocalyptic time..when your technology..how you say..Ezekiel.. tail wags the dog!"

"Yeah, that *is* what I say!" Zeke gloated a moment, then the hand went up.

"Spirit world, physical world..we work also...with both and with you..you Bov..niks.."

"Bovniks?" said Jerry, "Hey we're not Russians!"

"No, term like your concentration camp friend said.."

"*Lahmed Vavniks!!???*" Zeke was flabbergasted. "The 36 righteous people??"

"More than that..much more..you ones who complain, who see and talk and...rant! And *pray!* It's same thing. Yes Zeke, we *like* your rants!" Again Zeke sort of gloated around to his friends.

"Most of them.." the alien continued as Zeke quickly deflated.

"Careful of your health..relax and play! But pray! *Pray!*...be goofy, laugh, in between work..like Mister Jeff..here."

" Uh..Jerry.."

" Yes,..Others, you all..many many with seeing, thinking, *worry* talent..are our *eyes*..we monitor planet through you..animals too..thought waves..different infor...mation..we receive often..for example Ezekiel, as with others of your family..we have followed...you were an extremely sensitive child, I'm sorry for the allergies and over stimulations, caused by our probes..even *our* science is not exact, but we think it helped your talent.."

"The road.." murmured Zeke.

"That explains a lot.." murmered Minnie.
The alien's eyes suddenly brightened, " And your vision painting, of the rogue planet attack on Earth... very well done!"

" Thank you..what?" said Zeke in confusion, "rogue *what?*"

" So many dangers threaten, awareness of the people must rise and unify for planet welfare...already many souls have turned...but there must be more..we help where we can..." Zeke's right eyebrow raised knowingly, at least he thought so.

" So it was you...that vision..long ago.."

" Yes..we've been guiding you..recently..strange events..but now--"

"But what about our *old TV signals?*" piped up Jerry for some silly reason, "I Love Lucy!"

"Yes, that..'Ricky I go to the club..Fred Ethel..heh heh...these we know, watch in recreation room.." Seeing an alien laugh was an odd experience some how, but still pleasing.

"Well *there's* a whole new market for advertis-ing..", smirked Zeke.

"Oh, we delete those.."assured the alien innocently.

"But what of the wonderful New Age?"Minnie blurted anxiosly, "Aquarius? Peace love and under-standing— We've worked so *hard!*"

"These times..are the birth pangs of your so called New Age..over come effects of technology..souls must mature to a new level..World is a staging ground for soul development..incarnating in and out..but must maintain balance..health of planet as whole..Your dreams will come true, but will be different than you think..takes..time..*slow down* and tend garden Earth and yourselves..to be healthy. Keep up your good work Minnie...it is..valuable.."

" What about God?" asked Zeke suddenly. The Wise Alien smiled whimsically and looked up, then down and around.

" We are *all*...eyes of God..." By now, as he stood near the middle of the octagon, of what Jefferson called his 'sky room', the light and clouds were shifting. Through the oculus a shaft of sunlight appeared, which formed in essence a soft spot light onto the alien. His eyes narrowed, "But even now, they come...no more time.."

" But why-why—" They all shouted, question upon question, but one got through from Minnie. "Why *here?* Why did you come..here at this spot?" He shrugged another whimsical smile. "I was in the area..and..I always wanted to see Monticello.."

Just then there was a clumping and stomping out in the corridor. The friends turned and saw a new tour group expanding into the room. The docent, an older no nonsense woman was staring over her glasses with shock and outrage.

"*What!?* Who are..."
Zeke whipped his vision around to the alien, but he was gone. He rushed over to the cuddy and looked in. Nothing.

"Now just a minute!" The docent rushed up behind him. "You're not supposed to—" But Minnie intervened.

"We're very sorry, but we got separated from our group, my husband *does* get involved in architecture, he's doing his thesis on Monticello.."

"Well, that's alright, but you should have notified us down at the Foundation office before hand.."

"Yes, we certainly *do* apologize..." While Minnie ran interference, Zeke and Jerry happened to look back toward the hall door. It was silently closing all by itself. Zeke smiled. He knew.

"Come along dear," smiled Zeke, gently taking Minnie's arm, "We'll be late for the lecture at UVA..thank you all so much.." Jerry also smiled and nodded with hand on chin, in his best attempt to look professorial. Out in the corridor there was nothing to be seen, so they descended the stairs where Zeke turned on Jerry.

" *You* and your *'I Love Lucy'!* He was gettin' ready to say something *important!*"

" But *TV is* important!"

" Com'on you guys, lets relax and get some...you know, historic edification.."

After a long and leisurely stroll through Jefferson's gardens, enjoying the views but not talking much, and periodically glancing skyward, Minnie and Zeke found themselves down the hill standing by the car in the Jefferson Foundation parking lot. Jerry had gone in to use the facilities, but came out joyfully sniffing with a package he was destroying in his arms. From within the paper he held a jumble of wooden blocks of various shapes.

"Look! It's Monticello! Very accurate too, I can put it together, take it apart..look at all the octagons!!"

"Wow, that *is* neat!" enthused Zeke, when ya get it together let me know, I wanna play with it too!"

"Oh you guys with your toys..." said Minnie with a smirk, you sound like what Jefferson did with the real one!"

"EXACTLY!" the boys barked together.
"Hey whatta you call all that macrame you keep making?" asked Zeke, drawing her close enough to kiss.

" I call it *therapy!*"

" Well," laughed Jerry, "I guess sometimes all we've got to get us through life is our toys!"

" That reminds me," Zeke suddenly remembered, "I've got a comic to finish, that's *my* therapy!"

They dropped off Jerry at Mitchie's and he sputtered happily away in his orange and black Mini, while Zeke and Minnie settled back into Zeke's old Buick. A ride down the lush mountain as the autumn sun was starting to sink, brought a cozy vibration of calm to the couple. Already the day's events were seeming odd and distant, precisely because the present earthly existence was so warmly comfortable. They wouldn't forget, but somehow they were already. Their systems demanded a break, and all the other influences there are in life were now imposing themselves on them, just as children feel when returning from an exciting day at Grandma's. Besides, who could they talk to about it?

A bite to eat at a tasty boutique restaurant in Charlottesville soon saw them mounting the entrance ramp to I 64 and the trip home to Richmond. Zeke had felt restful and didn't say much, contemplating an urge to paint another picture, but Minnie had been regaling him with her psychic visions at the mansion, as well as others in her past, and her plans for more explorations in the future. Zeke listened dreamily as the darkness descended peacefully over the rolling hills, and weaving red tail lights appeared in the distance. It was always one of his favorite things. Then, two eager voices called out from the back seat.

"Are we there yet!?" "Are we *there* yet?"
He turned around to the bright eyed faces of Melvin the Gunk and Stupid the Cat, "Now you boys settle

down, we'll be home before you know it."

" Who in the *world* are you talking to?" asked
Minnie, interrupted from her enraptured monologue.

" Well," smiled Zeke, "you have your visions, and
I have mine..."

THE END

MELVIN THE GUNK & STUPID THE CAT

Zeke